Other books by A.L. Jambor

But the Children Survived
Kevin Chandler and The Case of the Missing Dogs
Divine Detective Agency Mystery Shorts:
The Body in the Bungalow
The Devious Dame
The Kid at the Candy Counter
The Room in Grandma's House
The House on the Shore
Where's Audrey
Libby the Psychic Dog in:
My First Christmas
Mystery in the Mansion
Where's Audrey?
The Tower in the Mist
Their Best Dreams

BUT THE

CHILDREN

SURVIVED

A.L. Jambor

Cover design by Amy Jambor
Photo Credits: © BigStockPhoto.com / digitalista

This book is dedicated to my Hansel.
He gave me wings and let me fly.

ACKNOWLEDGEMENT

I want to thank my good friend, Loraine O'Connell,
for all her help. She did the first edit on my manuscript.
Any mistakes in the text are mine and mine alone.
Loraine's input has been invaluable to me.
For over forty years she has been my best friend,
and I look forward to working on my next book with her.

Prologue

The Capital Beltway, Maryland

Jeff Greenway looked in the rearview mirror of the limousine. Horace Bagley was asleep. Jeff sighed. When he picked up the old man that morning, he had taken his wife's Infiniti because Horace Bagley had lost everything he owned, including his regular automobiles. The limo was the only vehicle he had left, and that was due to be picked up later that day. Horace had asked Jeff to drive him into Washington in the limo one last time. The request pissed him off, but Jeff had agreed out of respect for the old man.

His colleagues at the firm called it the "Pope Mobile" due to the safety features Horace had installed during the nuclear protests three years earlier. The glass was bulletproof and the interior was sealed from front to back to keep out smoke or gas. Horace hadn't taken any chances in those days. Since the government had shut down his power plants, the threats against Horace's life had dwindled. It didn't matter, anyway. They had taken everything from him, including the Pope Mobile.

Horace had owned 10 power plants that had supplied energy to most of the Eastern seaboard. He was a millionaire several times over, but when one of his older plants nearly melted down causing a chain reaction in several other plants, the country rallied to have them shut down. Horace had lobbied hard to keep his plants going, but in the end, the government chose to err on the side of caution. After all, it was an election year.

The government gave a generous tax break to those people willing to install alternate forms of power generation in their homes and businesses. The program proved so successful, that most of the citizens were able to sell back power to beleaguered energy companies nationwide. Everyone seemed to benefit from the program, everyone but Horace Bagley.

Following the shutdown of his power plants, the government audited poor Horace and found many questionable deductions on his tax returns. When all was said and done, everything he owned had to be sold.

His wife of ten years, Trixie, an exotic dancer 50 years his junior, left him a week before the government audit began, taking

1

her jewelry with her to Rio. She had also taken her Swedish masseuse, Sven.

Now Horace was on his way to Washington to beg the government for one last thing. He wanted to keep his house in Maine, the house he and his first wife Ginny had purchased when they got married. His children had been born there, and Ginny had died there. Surely they would understand how important the residence was to Horace, an old, broken man with nowhere to go, wouldn't they?

Jeff was sure the government would tell Horace to go pound salt, but when the old man called the day before asking Jeff for his assistance, he couldn't say no. It would have to be pro bono as Horace truly had no money left. Jeff had to put gas in the limo to get into town.

Horace had a one o'clock appointment with an old friend of his, Senator Crawley. It was just past noon, and they were making good time. As Jeff rounded the beltway, he could see traffic stopped ahead. He slowed the limo to a crawl before stopping completely.

The limo stopping hadn't disturbed Horace's nap. There were teenagers in the car ahead of them. They had gotten out of their car and were playing grab ass in the street. Jeff smiled, remembering what it was like to be seventeen and have your whole life ahead of you.

There was a young mother in the car next to him. She got out her car and put her young son on the hood, so he could see over the traffic ahead. She kept her arm around him. There was a biker on a Harley Davidson. He had tattoos covering his arms and neck. Jeff checked the locks on the limo to make sure they were down.

A half hour had passed and Jeff was getting anxious about the time. He took out his cell phone and called the Senator's office, advising them that Horace would be late. He explained the situation, and the secretary said she would speak to the Senator and call if they could see Horace at a later time.

Jeff began absent-mindedly tapping the steering wheel. He was looking at the teenage girl as she teased the boy mercilessly. She had a tee-shirt on that hugged her young, nubile breasts. Her jeans were tight, and Jeff began to fantasize about her cute, little butt.

The sun was hot, and even though the air conditioning was still running, Jeff thought about opening a window for some fresh air. It was the end of June, and Washington was hot. Jeff wished he had taken off his suit jacket before getting into the car.

He took off his seat belt. The radio announcer was talking about an early hurricane that should hit the west coast of Florida. It was a big one. Jeff made a mental note to call his parents in Tampa.

The young mother was holding her son in her arms. The teenagers were fighting verbally, and the biker was asleep in his saddle. Jeff was just about to take his arm out of the jacket sleeve when the mother and son fell to the ground.

What the hell, Jeff thought.

The teenagers were also down, and the biker had fallen off his bike. Jeff looked around and noticed anyone who'd been standing seconds ago was now lying on the pavement. His first reaction was to open the door to see if he could help and when he did, he died instantly, a small trickle of blood rolling out of his nose.

In the back seat, Horace Bagley never woke up but he, too, had a small trickle of blood rolling silently over his lips, down his chin, and onto his last crisp, white shirt.

But the Children Survived

PART ONE

MINDY LANE

But the Children Survived

Chapter 1

Largo, Florida

Mindy grabbed the little dog and ran to the back of the house. She ran into the master bedroom, where there was a small escape "door" in the side of the mobile home. She put Baby Girl down and slid the bolt over to open the door. The door hadn't been opened in many years, and she had to push it hard. It gave and opened. Mindy slipped onto the ground. She turned and looked at Baby Girl.

"Come on" she whispered impatiently. Baby Girl looked at her and then turned her head toward the inside of the house. Baby Girl knew she should not go out without her leash. "It's okay, you can come out." Still, Baby Girl just stared at her with her big bug eyes.

Then Baby Girl heard the people enter the house. She started to bark, and in a split second Mindy grabbed her mouth, put another arm around her body, and pulled her out. Mindy pushed the door closed with her rear end and went to the back of the mobile home. She crouched behind some bushes and held the dog tightly.

She could hear the people inside ransacking the house. She knew they wouldn't find anything. Grammy had seen to that. All the food that was left and the guns were well hidden. Mindy could feel the small pistol she had in her pocket. She knew that if they found her, she would shoot them all until all the bullets were gone. She wouldn't go down without a fight.

The people inside had slowed down. She could hear them talk to each other, but couldn't make out what they were saying. Baby Girl was being very good. She just sat next to Mindy awaiting her cues. Mindy stroked her and whispered, "Good girl."

Mindy heard the side door open. She heard the people going down the long metal ramp that led to the street from the house. She could hear them approaching the back of the house. They were going into the shed.

Mindy peeked around the corner so she could see the shed. The shed was dark and Mindy could see them turn on flashlights. There was nothing there but an old washing machine, dryer, and Opa's tools. The flashlights moved inside the shed.

"Empty, just like the house," a male voice said. "What the hell was Gerry talking about? There's no kid here."

Another male voice mumbled in response. Mindy heard them move down the driveway and turn onto the sidewalk. She heard them approaching her from the other side of the home. They were going into the mobile home next door.

Mindy lifted Baby Girl and moved to the other side of her house. She moved slowly in case anyone had stayed behind. There were no lights showing inside her home. She and Baby Girl crouched down under the metal ramp to wait it out a little longer.

There was a big, old dog bed under the ramp. Grammy had stored it there. Mindy and Baby Girl lay down on the bed and listened. She felt safe under the ramp. No one would see her there unless they really looked. Then Mindy heard voices.

"Gerry must have gotten the address wrong," the man said. "It's too dark now to find anything. I'm heading back."

"It's your call, Andrew," the other man responded.

She heard their footsteps walk down the street. She heard a door open on a vehicle. It then closed and the engine started up. It was a truck. The truck drove away, and it was so quiet that Mindy could hear its engine roaring for a long time as it went down the highway.

*****

Mindy didn't know how long she'd been under the ramp. She must have dozed off for a little while. Baby Girl was asleep next to her. Mindy felt the terrier's warm little body huddled next to her and felt sad. Baby Girl was the only one she'd hugged in a long time, and Baby Girl was getting older.

Mindy didn't want to think about the day Baby Girl wouldn't wake up next to her. Mindy stroked the little dog's head. She couldn't see Baby Girl's eyes in the dark, but she knew the little dog was looking at her. Baby Girl would be giving her a solemn stare, always looking to see what they would do next. It was all up to Mindy now.

Mindy longed for adult company. She wanted someone else to make the decisions, to take the weight off her shoulders. She missed her mom and dad. She knew they were on a trip. They should have been home by now.

Mindy had been crossing the days off Grammy's calendar to keep track of time. She knew her parents were supposed to be back in one week. It had been nine days since they left, and seven since

Grammy disappeared. They should have been back by now, but Grammy should have been back by now, too.

Grammy had gone to the store to buy supplies. A hurricane was coming and they would have to evacuate. Grammy was going to get food, and then take Mindy and Baby Girl to her parent's house where they would be safe. Everyone but the man across the street had left the park.

Grammy had asked Mindy if she wanted to come with her to the store, but Mindy wanted to watch TV. Grammy told her to keep the door locked and to take care of Baby Girl. Then she walked out the door.

The hurricane came and went, knocking out the power and the water. The old man across the street had sat on the porch throughout the entire storm and sat there still, his eyes staring into space. His skin looked really bad, too. Mindy waited for Grammy.

Mindy dozed off again. When she woke up, it was getting light. She sat up and yawned. She crawled out from under the ramp and stretched. Baby Girl stretched her doggie stretch and shook her whole body as if she had gotten wet.

"Let's go in and see what they did to our house."

Mindy and Baby Girl walked to the little door in the side of the house that she had escaped from the night before. Mindy pushed Baby Girl into the house and then she climbed in after her. The bedroom looked the same as it did when she ran through it the night before. Mindy closed and bolted the little door.

Baby Girl was sniffing around, smelling all the new smells of the strangers. Mindy went to the door of the bedroom and peeked into the hallway. She could see the inside of her bedroom. It was relatively untouched.

There wasn't much in there, and what was there was only worth something to a scared 9-year-old girl: pictures of her with her parents; a twin bed and some books; curtains on the windows and a chair. The closet door was open. She looked inside, but nothing had been taken.

She moved onto the kitchen. She looked in the cabinets. Everything looked the same. They had not been looking for food, but even if they had been, Grammy had a special place for the emergency food so Mindy would not go hungry. Grammy also had a special place for guns if necessary.

As she stood there, she suddenly felt all the energy drain from her body. She had been so scared last night, and every night since

9

Grammy left. She'd had to be strong and brave. An overwhelming sadness overtook her, and she just fell to the floor and cried.

Baby Girl came over and sat next to her. Mindy wanted to believe that Baby Girl was trying to comfort her, but she was probably only hungry. It was morning, and neither of them had eaten yet. Mindy couldn't stop crying. Her body heaved with the sobs. She wanted her mother so terribly much. She just didn't know if she could go on anymore.

But Baby Girl needed her, and she believed her parents would come to find her soon. Mindy tried to stop crying. Soon the sobs lightened and she got up off the floor. She looked in the cabinets for dog food and remembered she had given Baby Girl the last can yesterday.

"Come on, Baby," Mindy said. "Let's get some food."

Mindy quietly opened the front door. She couldn't see or hear anyone. She put Baby Girl's leash on and they left the house by the side door and walked onto the metal ramp. It was impossible to be quiet on the metal ramp, but it was the shortest way to the shed. Mindy jumped through the railings on the ramp and so did Baby Girl. They walked to the shed that was connected to the house.

Mindy opened the door and checked the floor. The men didn't see the door in the floor in the dark. Even in the daytime, it was hard to see that door. Grammy had done that. She had made it hard to see. Mindy closed the shed door. She lit the candle on the shelf. Then she opened the door in the floor.

Under the shed was a hole about six feet long and four feet wide. The door was made of plywood that fitted over the hole. Inside the hole were three plastic storage bins. One bin contained guns and ammunition and the other two canned food for people and dogs.

Mindy was careful how much food she took every day, but the stores were dwindling. She was not sure what she would do when it ran out, but she would cross that bridge when she came to it.

Mindy opened the food bin and took out a can of soup and one can of dog food. She replaced the storage bin lid and put the plywood door back in place. She shuffled some dirt over the top and slowly opened the shed door. She still didn't see or hear anyone.

She and Baby Girl left the shed and walked to the metal ramp. Mindy climbed up the side of the ramp. She put the cans down and reached for Baby Girl. Baby Girl jumped up on her hind legs and

Mindy grabbed her and pulled her up. She then picked up the cans and they re-entered the house.

Mindy took a can opener out of the silverware drawer and opened the cans. She filled Baby Girl's bowl. The refrigerator wasn't working, so Baby Girl had to eat the whole thing so it wouldn't go bad. Most times she did. Other times she would wait too long and vomit it up. Mindy just let Baby Girl decide what she wanted to do.

Mindy then opened her soup and put it in a bowl. It was chicken noodle, the condensed kind. Mindy didn't have water to add to it. She'd run out of bottled water two days ago. The soup wasn't too thick, but it was salty. It filled her stomach so she didn't mind too much. It was gone too soon. Now she would have to decide what to do the rest of the day.

Mindy put Baby Girl's leash on the little dog's collar. She got out the bicycle pump and went out the door. She thought about closing the windows, but decided it was just too hot. Besides, if someone wanted to get it, they'd just break down the door.

Mindy locked the door behind her. She and Baby Girl went down the ramp to the old three-wheel bicycle with the flat tires. It had been Opa's bike. The tires didn't hold air anymore, so when Mindy wanted to use it, she would pump up the tires. She kept a bicycle pump in the basket attached to the rear of the bike.

Mindy pumped the tires up. There was a small chain with a hook on it attached to the basket. Mindy hooked it onto Baby Girl's leash so she wouldn't jump out when they were moving. Mindy attached the chain to Baby Girl's collar and they rode out to the street. Grammy had adjusted the bicycle seat for Mindy so she could easily reach the pedals.

Mindy rode past house after house. She avoided looking at the house across the street. She was headed for the clubhouse. There was a pool table at the clubhouse. Miraculously, the hurricane hadn't damaged anything, and the pool table was still there and intact. Mindy liked to play with it during the day when there was enough light in the clubhouse.

There were also books and puzzles there. Mindy could while away a whole day reading. Baby Girl liked to roam around the rooms, delighting in seeing and smelling something new. Mindy pulled into the drive that led to the clubhouse. She opened the double doors, used a rock to hold each door open, and pulled the bike in behind her. No one had been in the clubhouse since her last visit.

Mindy detached Baby Girl and helped her out of the basket. Baby Girl trotted off towards the back of the clubhouse. Then she did something she'd never done before while visiting the clubhouse. She growled.

Chapter 2

Mindy stopped dead in her tracks. She couldn't see Baby Girl, but the terrier kept growling in a low, menacing tone. Mindy slowly walked toward the sound at the back of the clubhouse. She could see Baby Girl now. The little dog's hackles were raised and she stood very still. Mindy started walking again until she could see what had Baby Girl's attention.

It was a rat, a very big rat, about the size of a small cat. Mindy could see the rat was frightened and if Baby Girl didn't back down, the rat would bite her.

What is that called, the thing animals get that's really bad? Mindy thought. They get shots for it - what, what? Then she remembered - Rabies. What if the rat bit Baby Girl, or Mindy, and gave them rabies? Where would I take her for help?

As her mind worked, she felt the pistol in her pocket. Mindy pushed the thought away. What if she missed and hit Baby Girl?

Fear rose up Mindy's back. She couldn't move. Baby Girl was inching closer to the rat. The rat was hunched over and looked like it would go after Baby Girl. Mindy was afraid to speak. She didn't want to spook the rat further.

Mindy pulled the pistol out of her pocket just in case. The rat turned away from Baby Girl as if to walk away. Baby Girl started to move towards it.

"No!" yelled Mindy.

Baby Girl turned to look at Mindy, and the rat turned and started towards Baby Girl. Just as the rat rushed towards Baby Girl, Mindy fired. The rat dropped like a stone. Somehow, and she would never know how, she had shot the rat straight through its chest. Blood oozed on the floor. Mindy felt as if she might pass out. She had never liked the sight of blood - it made her feel woozy.

"Baby Girl, come here." The little terrier was going to the rat's body to sniff, but the sound of Mindy's voice stopped her and she trotted over to Mindy. Mindy picked her up, walked her over to the bike, and chained her to the basket.

Mindy knew there was a gardener's shed near the pool behind the clubhouse. She walked to the sliding glass doors that led to the pool area. As she stepped outside she saw the pool. It hadn't been cleaned for a while and the algae were growing thick. It didn't smell very good either. Mindy ran past it to the shed.

13

There were three shovels in the shed. One was large enough to carry the rat. The small one was like a spade. Mindy picked up the spade and opened the gate leading away from the pool to a field where there was grass. The mobile home park had held picnics there. Mindy found a nice shady spot and began to dig a hole. The rat wasn't very big, so she wouldn't have to dig very long.

The ground was harder than she thought it would be. She stabbed at it until she could move some of the dirt out of the way. The ground grew softer as she dug. It was just like with Grammy. Grammy had dug a hole for Snowball, her old cat. Mindy stopped digging. She didn't like to think about Grammy. She felt the tears coming again, but made herself stop.

"You can't do that all the time. You're not a baby," she told herself, and continued to dig the rat's grave.

Mindy walked past the pool and into the clubhouse. She had the big shovel with her this time. Baby Girl whined from the bike basket.

"Shush," said Mindy. "I have to take care of this and I don't need you running away."

Mindy gently picked up the rat with the shovel. The rat was still quite limp. It was a gray rat. It creeped Mindy out, and the blood bothered her.

Mindy carried the rat around the pool and out the gate to the hole she had dug. She shook the shovel until the rat fell into the hole. It fit. Mindy pushed the dirt over the body until it was completely covered. She picked up the shovel and walked back to the shed. She placed the shovel back where she had found it and went into the clubhouse.

As Mindy walked past the empty vending machine in the hallway leading to the main room, her foot knocked into it. She heard something shift inside the machine. Mindy started to feel excited. What if there was food in there? Potato chips, nacho chips, or better yet cookies. Mindy felt her stomach growl. She was very hungry, and the thought of all those carbohydrates was just too much for her.

Mindy ran back to the shed. She looked around, hoping to find a hammer. She spied a crowbar sitting on someone's small, castoff table at the end of the shed. She picked up the crowbar and ran back to the vending machine. She couldn't decide whether to break the glass or try to pry it open from the side. Mindy didn't want to be cut

14

by the glass. She reminded herself again that there was no way to get to a doctor, and set about prying the door open.

The crowbar was too thick to wedge between the door and the machine. She needed a screwdriver or a knife. Even scissors would have done the trick. Mindy walked to the front of the clubhouse. Baby Girl again protested at being left in such a humiliating state.

"Oh, shut up, Baby Girl!" she said. Baby Girl barked, just one bark.

Mindy looked around the room. She noticed for the first time a window and door that sat next to the entrance of the clubhouse. Mindy walked over to the door to inspect it.

The window had sliding glass, like in a doctor's office. Mindy stood on tiptoes and peeked inside. It looked like an office of some kind. There was a phone and computer. There was also a bulletin board. Inside the office, Mindy could see another door; another room she hadn't known was there. She walked to the door and tried the doorknob. It turned.

Mindy entered the office and looked around. In one corner was a dead plant. In another, on top of a filing cabinet, were checks that had never been deposited. Mindy crossed to the other door. It, too, was unlocked. Mindy opened the door and stood in wonder at the sight before her.

Chapter 3

Mindy entered the small room. It was lined with shelving from top to bottom, and on each shelf were supplies for the small office. There were other things there, too, marvelous things. Things Mindy had longed for and dreamt of. There were bags and bags of potato chips, nacho chips, peanut butter-filled cheese crackers, pretzels, and cookies. This must have been where they stored the vending machine refills. But that wasn't all. On the other side of the room the shelves held bottles and bottles of pure, clean water. There were hundreds of them.

Mindy grabbed a bottle and unscrewed the top. She gulped down the water so fast she vomited. When she stopped retching she started drinking again, only slower this time. That water felt so good. It was as if she could feel her cells filling up after months of being dry. Who would believe water could taste so good?

Mindy sat on the floor and finished the bottle of water. She then reached up and grabbed a bag of chips. As she opened the bag, the aroma of grease and potatoes filled her nostrils. Mindy sighed in ecstasy. She took a chip out, looked at it, and she shoved it into her mouth. The crunch felt so wonderful she swooned.

Mindy finished the bag of chips and started on another. Three bags later, Mindy felt overwhelmingly tired. She got up off the floor and took a bottle of water down off the shelf. She found a clean ashtray in the office and filled it with water. Baby Girl was sitting in the basket looking quite annoyed.

"I'm sorry I left you so long. But I have a treat for you." She unlatched Baby Girl and put the ashtray on the floor. Baby Girl pounced on the water just as Mindy had. She lapped and lapped until the water was gone. Then she too spit up half of what she drank.

"We really have to slow down, girl." Mindy smiled. She felt good. She felt full for the first time that she could remember, since before Grammy left. Mindy was tired and decided to take a nap.

There was a long credenza on the far side of the clubhouse, behind the pool table. It had a vent, and was deep enough for a girl and little dog to fit in. Mindy had taken the sofa cushions off the old sofa that sat in the "living room" of the clubhouse and laid them inside the credenza so she could sleep and not be seen. She suddenly felt the need to relieve herself.

"I bet you have to go, too," she said to Baby Girl. She put on the dog's leash and they walked out past the pool and the shed to the gate leading to the field. There were some bushes next to the clubhouse fence. Mindy squatted next to them. When she was done, she walked Baby Girl until she, too, squatted. They walked back to the clubhouse and got into her makeshift "bedroom." After she and Baby Girl were settled, Mindy closed the cabinet door making sure the latch was in place, stretched out, and instantly fell asleep.

Mindy dreamt of her mother. They were sitting in the kitchen of her old house and baking something. Her mother was telling her to wash her hands. Mindy couldn't so much see her mother as she could sense her. There was such sweetness to the dream, a feeling of home. Mindy was stirring something in a bowl. She looked at her mother. She wanted to tell her she loved her, but her mouth wouldn't work. No matter how hard she tried, she couldn't speak. Then her teeth began to loosen and fall out. Mindy woke up with a start.

Mindy's arm had fallen asleep. She shook it a little and then stopped to listen. Everything was quiet. She looked out the vent in the door and could see the bike where she had left it. Slowly she opened the door, and she and Baby Girl got out of the credenza.

"I think we should take some food home and have a party," Mindy said to Baby Girl.

Mindy walked to the office and opened the door. She picked out three bags of chips, three cheese and peanut butter crackers, three packs of cookies, and four bottles of water. There was a cloth bag on the floor by the computer. She emptied the contents, and put the food and water in the bag. Then she carried the bag to the bike.

She hung the bag on the handlebars, picked up Baby Girl and chained her to the basket. Mindy opened the double doors and pushed the bike outside. She then pushed the doors closed until they snapped. She got on the bike and pedaled towards home.

When they got there, Mindy unchained Baby Girl and kept her on her leash. She walked the little dog to the grass across the street. After Baby Girl had finished, Mindy walked back to the mobile home and lifted the bag handles off the handlebars. Holding the bag and Baby Girl's leash, she walked up the ramp to the front door. She checked the lock before entering the house. If someone were there, Baby Girl would let her know.

Mindy was excited. She had new food for dinner! She had water to drink! She decided it was a birthday party, and she and

17

Baby Girl would feast. Mindy took the last clean plate out of the cabinet. Without water, she hadn't been able to wash them so she just left them in the sink.

She opened a bag of chips and packets of crackers. She filled the plate with one bag of chips and one bag of crackers. She placed a sheet on the living room floor and put the plate in the middle. Mindy also brought over a bottle of water. Baby Girl trotted over to see what was happening.

"We're having a birthday party Baby Girl!"

Mindy was surprised to discover she felt happy. She started singing "Happy Birthday to You", and a vision of her mother singing came into her head.

"You look like a monkey, and you act like one too!" her mother had sung.

At that time, Mindy had giggled and her mother had grabbed her and tickled her. The memory brought tears to Mindy's eyes. Then she looked at Baby Girl. The dog was salivating, waiting for the chips to be passed out.

"I'm sorry, Baby Girl. Here you go."

The little dog grabbed the end of the chip and went under the old bed on the porch to eat it. Mindy tried to recall the happy feeling she had just a minute ago, but now she just felt lonely. After the food was gone, Mindy picked up the sheet and draped it over the sofa. She tried to wipe the plate off. She wouldn't use what little water she had to clean it.

Mindy felt so dirty. She really wanted to take a bath and wash her hair, but there wasn't enough water. She had brought home only four bottles. She drank one. Baby Girl would need some too. Maybe she could use one to wash. There wasn't much in one bottle, but if she was careful and used a washrag, maybe one would be enough. She just wouldn't use soap.

She took a bottle into the bathroom and put a stopper in the sink. She poured the water into the sink. First she took a rag and got it wet. The rag had soaked up most of the water, so Mindy rang it out. Then she took her toothbrush and brushed her teeth. After that, she took off her clothes and used the rag to clean herself.

Just that little bit of clean felt so good. She couldn't wait until she could fill a bathtub again. Her hair would have to wait - that would take too much water. She cleaned her face and ran the rag through her hair. Just getting her hair wet felt so good.

Now it was time for bed. She was tired again even though she'd slept most of the afternoon. She got into some clean clothes that she'd been saving, and decided that she and Baby Girl were going to sleep in Grammy's bed from now on. That was where the escape door was, and it just seemed right to be in there. Mindy moved her things into Grammy's room. Grammy wouldn't mind.

Mindy fell asleep full of food for the first time since Grammy disappeared. She thought about Grammy as she went to sleep. Where was Grammy? Why had her parents left her here so long? Where were they?

Baby Girl snuggled next to her. Mindy began to think it was time to start looking for them at her house. Maybe she and Baby Girl would have to ride to the big street outside the park. She would think about it and ask God what she should do. Then she closed her eyes and was asleep instantly.

Chapter 4

Mindy awoke up with a start. She heard someone in the house. Baby Girl was in the hallway barking. She could see the little dog's tail as it inched its way back into the room.

"Shhh," Mindy said quietly.

Mindy was on Grammy's bed. It was a very big bed, and the little fire door was on her right. The hallway door was on her left. Mindy remained as still as she could. She could hear the people coming closer to the room. She reached into her pocket for her little pistol, but it wasn't there. She'd left it in the bathroom last night.

Mindy kept watching the door. Baby Girl jumped up onto the bed and Mindy put her arm around her. Then she put her hand around the terrier's mouth. Baby Girl was using her paws to push her hand away. She wanted to bark and protect Mindy. Mindy looked at the little door. Maybe she could get to it. As Mindy was about to crawl across the bed, she saw a figure in the door.

He looked like a spaceman. His suit covered him from head to toe. It was bright yellow. Mindy knew that he had seen her. He walked into the room and came towards her. She let Baby Girl go, hoping she would scare him. Baby Girl barked and growled, but she wouldn't go near the stranger. The stranger came closer to Mindy.

"It's all right." It was a man's voice. "I'm not going to hurt you." He came closer, and Mindy turned and crawled to the little door. Baby Girl continued to bark.

Mindy grabbed the bolt on the door. The man reached over the bed and grabbed her as she struggled with the lock. Another figure appeared at the door.

As the first man held Mindy, the second man put something over her face. It smelled really bad and made her choke. Slowly, she fell asleep until everything was dark.

*****

Mindy slowly woke up. She felt very sleepy. She looked around the room. It looked like a hospital room. Mindy felt something stuck on her arm. She looked down and saw an IV drip. She put her hand by her side and felt Baby Girl next to her. She stroked the little dog's head. A pretty young woman came into the

20

room. She had long brown hair and brown eyes. She wore her hair in a ponytail.

"So, you're awake," she said. "How are you feeling?"

Mindy looked at the woman. She looked friendly, but Mindy didn't speak. She didn't like this place.

"Not talking to me, huh? Okay, I understand. You'll probably get hungry a little later on. Just press the button, and I'll bring you some breakfast." As the woman came closer, Mindy could smell her. She smelled like cherry blossom soap.

"See this button?" The woman held up a hand buzzer on a line attached to the bed rail. The woman smiled at Mindy. She had a kind face. "Just push it if you need anything," she said. "Oh, and my name is Christie." She turned away and walked out the door.

Mindy tried to sit up. She was dizzy and felt weak. The drug they had given her to keep her asleep was potent. She managed to rise up on her elbows and looked down at Baby Girl. The little dog was sleepy. Maybe they had given her something to make her sleep, too.

Mindy sat up a little more. Her head began to pound, so she lay back down and fell asleep. When Mindy woke again, she found Christie standing next to her checking the IV.

"I think we can take this out now," Christie said. She then removed the needle from Mindy's arm, and pushed the bottle stand to the side after placing a small bandage on her arm.

"How are you feeling?" she asked Mindy.

Mindy stared at Christie for a few seconds. She desperately wanted to know where she was and who Christie was, but her stubbornness kept her from speaking.

"At least tell me your name. Or even the dog's name. I just want to help you, sweetheart." Christie went to the cabinet next to Mindy's bed and took out a thermometer.

"Open up." Mindy obeyed her and allowed Christie to put the thermometer under her tongue.

"97.6, it's just a little low. But your color's a lot better, and I think it's time to bring you some food." Christie left the room, leaving Mindy and Baby Girl alone.

"How are ya doin', Baby?" Mindy stroked the dog's little head. "You look pretty good. Have they been nice to you?" Baby Girl nuzzled Mindy's hand. She climbed up near Mindy's face and licked her over and over again.

"Stop!" said Mindy, giggling, "too much!" But she loved the little dog's kisses. She hugged and hugged Baby Girl.

Christie was back with the food. It smelled wonderful, and Mindy could see steam rising off the tray. Hot food! How long had it been since she'd eaten hot food?

As Christie moved closer, Mindy could see pizza and ice cream. She felt her stomach rumble. As much as she wanted to hate Christie for kidnapping her, she couldn't refuse the food, and whoever had kidnapped her had brought Baby Girl with them too.

"What about my dog?" Mindy asked.

"She speaks!" Christie said. "Well, she's been sleeping the whole time with you, so she must be hungry too. What does she like to eat?"

"She likes dog food, the kind in a bag and the kind in a can." The pizza was cut in four slices, and Mindy picked one up. She bit into the warm slice and the flavors burst on her tongue. Seven days of eating condensed soup were quickly forgotten.

"I'll see what we have in the storeroom and be right back." Christie again left Mindy alone with Baby Girl.

Mindy broke off a small piece of crust and gave it to the dog. Baby Girl chomped the crust twice and swallowed. She sat staring at Mindy, waiting for the next piece.

Christie came back with a plate full of diced meat that looked like chicken. She had warmed it and when she put it down, Baby Girl immediately began to eat it. Christie also had Mindy's clothes in her hand. They had been cleaned and looked in good condition. Christie put them on the cabinet.

"When you're done, if you want to get dressed and maybe come outside, just let me know. I want to help you out of bed the first time. You were weak when they brought you in, so please wait for me to come. Just buzz for me with the button." And with that, Christie was gone again.

For the first time Mindy noticed how clean she felt. Her hair smelled good. She had been bathed while she was asleep.

After Mindy finished eating she rang for Christie, who came and helped Mindy out of bed by dropping the railing and putting an arm around her. Mindy's legs felt weak, but she stood up straight and didn't falter.

"I think you can come outside now."

"I can put on my clothes myself," Mindy said.

After she got dressed, she, Christie and Baby Girl walked into the corridor. Mindy could hear the low rumble of motors and fans. She'd never been in a place like this before.

The corridor was long, with doors on each side. Christie led Mindy and Baby Girl to the end of the corridor and through the double doors that led to the rest of the facility.

"My name is Mindy, and this is Baby Girl." Christie took Mindy's hand and shook it.

"Nice to meet you, Mindy and Baby Girl."

Chapter 5

As the trio passed through the door, Mindy looked over the railing and down into the center of the building. It looked like the center court of a shopping mall. There was a play area in the center and trees planted around to make it feel like Main Street, USA.

All along the street were old-fashioned street lights and benches. Mindy looked up and saw that the ceiling was blue with clouds floating by. It looked very real. The ceiling even had a sunroof and lighting designed to make it look as though sunlight was streaming through it. But as in a mall, the air just didn't smell fresh and Mindy knew that she was definitely indoors.

"What do you think of our little town?" Christie asked as they walked towards the elevator.

"It's okay." Mindy was still not sure how she felt about Christie. "Where are we?"

"The Wilmer Biosphere. I think you'll like your new home. We really tried to make everything as comfortable as possible."

"What's a biosphere?" Mindy noticed that there were kids all over the place. They all looked to be around her age.

"Well, a biosphere is a place that is usually built underground. Scientists use them to study different things like plants or animals. This one was built to protect people from the fallout from bombs and such."

When they reached the first floor, they stepped off the elevator and turned left. Mindy saw what looked like tiny houses, each with a window and front door. As they approached the first one, a girl came out and ran over to them. She stopped in front of Baby Girl.

"Oh, wow, a dog! Can I pet her?" The girl was smiling at Mindy with her hand hovering over Baby Girl.

"Yeah." Mindy was getting angry. Where had all these people been while she was alone and scared? She was feeling really mad now. She wanted to yell at Christie, but she didn't know what Christie would do so she kept quiet.

"Hi, little dog. What's her name?" The girl looked up at Mindy. She had brown eyes and long black hair, and she spoke with a slight Spanish accent.

"Her name is Baby Girl." The little dog was basking in the glow of all the attention she was receiving. She licked the girl's face, eliciting squeals of joy.

"Mindy, this is Maria Elena. She lives in this first house over here because she was the first child we rescued. Maria is 10 years old." Christie looked at Maria. Maria stood up and took Mindy's hand.

"How old are you?" Maria asked Mindy. Mindy let her hold her hand for a few seconds before pulling it away.

"I'm nine, but I'm going to be 10 soon." Mindy was studying Maria. A strange look passed over Maria's face when she heard how old Mindy was.

"I really like your dog. It's been a long time since I saw one. I left class to use the bathroom, and then I saw you," Maria Elena said. She was stroking Baby Girl. Christie said it was time to move on but that Maria Elena was welcome to come with them to Mindy's new home. Maria Elena tagged along behind Christie and Mindy, with Baby Girl close at her heels.

They passed several small houses until they came to number 199. It was a pink house with small purple shutters. Mindy loved pink and purple. They were her favorite colors. The door was painted lilac. Christie opened the door and beckoned the girls to come in.

There was one room that served as both a living room and a bedroom. There was a tiny kitchen and a bathroom in the back. The bathroom had a clothes closet and a linen closet. The rooms were all painted white. The walls were bare except for a TV mounted on one wall. In one corner was a small twin bed with a plain pink comforter. On the other side was a small kitchen table. The room also had a sofa with a small table next to it. Upon the table sat a piggy bank-shaped lamp.

"You can't cook in the kitchen, but you can have snacks and drinks in the fridge. You can clean your dishes in the sink. The bathroom has a full bathtub and shower. I think Maria Elena can take you to the commissary to get any toiletries you may need. Any questions?"

Mindy had a lot of questions, but she decided she would rather ask Maria Elena.

"No, I'm fine. Thanks," Mindy said.

Christie left the house and went back to wherever she spent her days at the facility. Mindy and Maria Elena stared at each other.

"Why don't I take you to the store?" Maria Elena headed for the door with Mindy and Baby Girl following behind.

25

"I have to get dog food. Do they have a store for that?" Mindy said.

Maria Elena looked thoughtful.

"I don't think so. But maybe they have some kind of meat in a can. You can also bring her scraps from dinner. They give us plenty of food to eat."

"Who are they anyway?" Mindy couldn't wait any longer to find out who her captors were.

"They're the people who take care of us."

"Yeah, but who are they? Haven't you ever asked them?"

Maria Elena looked down at the floor. She was obviously trying to think of an answer that would satisfy Mindy's curiosity. The truth was Maria Elena didn't know who they were and didn't really care. They fed her and clothed her, and they gave her a very nice house to live in.

"When I was alone, I prayed for someone to come and help me. They came and brought me here. That's all I know."

Mindy felt frustration rising up inside of her.

"But, what about your parents? What if they come looking for you? How will they find you?"

Maria Elena stopped walking and looked at Mindy.

"My parents are dead. All our parents are dead."

"All of your parents? What do you mean by 'all'?" Mindy asked.

"All of us came here because we were alone. All of our parents died of the poison." Maria Elena had a sad look on her face. She could see that Mindy was confused but couldn't understand why. Surely Mindy knew about the poison.

"I was with my Grammy for a while," Mindy said. "My parents were on a trip. My Grammy left to buy food because we had to evacuate and she never came back. My parents should have come back by now, but they haven't." Mindy walked away from Maria Elena, but Maria followed her.

"I'm sorry Mindy. I thought you knew. I thought Christie told you. It affected everyone, all the animals too. That's why I was so excited to see your dog. Please, Mindy, I'm sorry. I didn't mean to upset you."

They walked in silence down the long "street" until they reached a small storefront. Inside the store were all kinds of toiletries and snacks. There were also posters for decorating, some clothes, shoes, and backpacks. Mindy picked up a shopping basket and filled it with soap, shampoo, deodorant, chips, soda, and beef jerky for Baby Girl. Maria Elena explained that you didn't need money. You simply filled your basket. Then you bagged your items and took them home.

As they left the store, a group of boys and girls approached them from the "town square".

"The class must be over," Maria Elena said to Mindy. "I'm going to meet a friend. Dinner is at 5. I'll save a seat for you. Just follow the signs to Market Street." She pointed to a signpost next to the store. There was another one a few yards down the street. Mindy could see signposts running along the entire length of the street. Maria Elena ran to meet the group. Mindy and Baby Girl headed home.

Mindy put her groceries away. She looked at the bed and realized that she was still pretty tired. She lay down on the bed and fell asleep. She woke up an hour later. Baby Girl was nuzzling her hand. She was trying to get Mindy out of bed.

"Oh boy, you must have to go out!" Mindy said.

Mindy got out of bed and opened the front door. She looked around the house for somewhere Baby Girl could go. There was a small flower bed by the side of her house that would have to do for now. After Baby Girl did her business, they went back in the house.

Mindy put a bowl of water down for the little dog, which quickly lapped up every last drop. Mindy refilled the bowl. She took out the beef jerky, broke it into pieces, and put it on a plate. She put the plate next to the water bowl.

There was a clock on the wall, and Mindy noticed it read ten minutes to five.

"I have to go. I can't take you with me, but I'll come right back." Baby Girl whined a little as Mindy closed the door.

Mindy set off in the direction she and Maria Elena had gone earlier that day. When she got to the store she began reading the signposts until she came to Market Street. She could see the large, cafeteria-style dining room to her right. The tables were filled with children her age. She could see Maria Elena in the food line and moved towards her.

Mindy hadn't seen this much food in a very long time. There were vats of spaghetti, meat sauce, rice, diced chicken, canned corn, and glorious desserts. Mindy took a tray and a plate. She filled the plate to overflowing and grabbed a napkin and silverware at the end of the line. She followed Maria Elena to a table in the middle of the room. There were two other girls sitting there when she and Maria sat down.

"Mindy, this is Katie and Alyssa. Girls, this is Mindy. She's just arrived." Katie and Alyssa were identical twins. Mindy was fascinated watching the girls eat because they did so many things the same way. They lifted their forks the same way. They chewed their food the same way. Mindy couldn't take her eyes off them and found it hard to follow the conversation.

"Where were you, Mindy?" Alyssa was asking.

"Uh, oh I was in Largo." Mindy kept looking back and forth between the girls. They looked exactly alike! They had flaming red hair, freckles, green eyes, and dimples.

"We were in Gulfport. When our parents died, we were left alone for days. We had just run completely out of food when they came for us. I didn't like the bodies. I was glad when they found us," Katie said.

"I saw one body. There was a man across the street from Grammy's house. Everyone had left, the hurricane was coming, but he stayed. I thought he just died because he was old." Mindy stopped talking. She hated thinking about the old man's body. She changed the subject.

"Who are they?" Mindy asked, pointing at Christie and a large man in an apron. "They must have told you something?"

"Well, we don't know who actually picked us up." Katie said. "But Christie, Andrew and George take care of us."

"And nobody knows who they are, Christie, Andrew and George that is?" Mindy had a habit of half-squinting her eyes while pouting. She was doing that now.

"As long as we're cared for, does it matter?" Maria Elena was looking in earnest at Mindy as if to say "let it go". Mindy's face softened. She kind of liked Maria Elena and didn't want to hurt her feelings.

"Mindy has a dog." Maria Elena said. Katie and Alyssa looked up.

"How does she have a dog? Our dog died when our parents died, and our cat too. How do you have a dog?" Katie said it so loud that the kids at the tables around them stopped to listen. Alyssa elbowed her sister.

"I don't know why she's still alive. She belonged to my Grammy. She's just a little dog," Mindy said. She felt strange-as though she'd done something wrong. "I'm sorry your dog and cat died," she said to Katie and Alyssa.

"It's okay. It's not your fault." Alyssa looked at her sister and they nodded in agreement.

Mindy relaxed and started eating her dinner. She slipped several pieces of meat into a napkin for Baby Girl.

When they were done eating, they all got up from the table and took their trays to the garbage stand. They emptied the paper goods into the trash and put the trays in a dishwasher-like contraption. After they were done, they walked out into the town square.

The sky was getting darker. The angle of the lighting had changed to reflect the setting sun. The girls asked Mindy if she wanted to watch a movie. Mindy said she would love to, and they all went to Maria Elena's house. Mindy felt the glow of companionship for the first time since Grammy had left her. It felt good to hear human voices, female voices, and to sit with girls and laugh at nothing.

When Mindy went home to Baby Girl, she was greeted by a very annoyed little terrier. She immediately took Baby Girl outside. Before she went to bed, she put the meat she had saved for Baby Girl in the fridge for the dog's breakfast the next day.

When Mindy hit the pillow that night, she prayed to God that this place was okay. She wanted to feel safe. She was sick of being afraid, and as Baby Girl snuggled next to her, Mindy relaxed and drifted off to sleep.

Chapter 6

Christina Blair

Wilmer and March Pharmaceuticals recruited Christina Blair during her senior year at Princeton. Christie had created a fertilizer that not only produced hardy plants, but also repelled the pests that liked to destroy them.

When Christie graduated, Wilmer and March paid Princeton for the rights to Christie's discovery, gave Christie a research position in their Tampa, Florida research facility, and also took care of Christie's student loans as payment for her part in the creation of their newfound gold mine. At 22, Christie was on her way.

Christie bought a townhouse in Tampa's Carrollwood section. She also spoiled herself with a new car, a Lexus, and bought clothing she could only dream of as a student working at Starbucks. Now she had a six-figure salary with benefits and stock options.

Christie's parents were beaming as they told everyone they knew that it was their Christie who had created that wonderful fertilizer, the fertilizer that would change the world!

Wilmer and March had built a state-of-the-art laboratory on a piece of property they'd acquired in a rural area north of Tampa. The lab was like a playground to Christie. They had spared no expense, and Christie was free to experiment to her heart's content. She knew that eventually she would have to produce something viable, but for now she would continue to coast on the success of the creation that had given her this great life.

Christie met Neil Cramer at a New Year's Eve party thrown by one of her colleagues. He was tall, with great big blue eyes and brown hair. They fell in love quickly and married the following June.

Neil was a struggling criminal attorney in Tampa. He had a small office with two rooms, one for him and one for his legal assistant. He barely broke even as his clients more often than not were destitute, and his natural compassion led him to go above and beyond to help them. This left little time for developing a more stable client base. Christie's income allowed him to pursue his passion for the underdog.

Christie believed that someday Neil would tire of the ingratitude of the masses, and join a firm that would pay him a regular salary. Despite Neil's blind spot regarding drug addicts and alcoholics, Christie truly loved him. She could see herself with Neil forever. He truly was her soul mate.

The following June, Christie learned she was pregnant. As a scientist, the whole process of gestation was fascinating to her. Neil tried to share her enthusiasm, but the best he could do was rub her back and feet while pretending to listen.

Neil was prepping for a trial at the Hillsborough County Courthouse. The client was amazingly guilty, and just how Neil would keep this guy out of jail was occupying his mind as Christie talked about her pregnancy.

Their baby girl was born on Valentine's Day. She was a blonde, blue-eyed wonder they named Haley. Christie and Neil were both smitten with their little baby. After Christie went back to work six weeks later, Neil took charge of picking up little Haley from daycare.

When Haley was six months old, Neil picked her up from daycare during a terrible downpour. Neil was sideswiped by a drunk driver and forced off the road. He couldn't stop the car and couldn't see where he was going. The car went down an embankment and rolled over several times.

Haley's baby seat strap came loose, and the infant was slammed between the floor and the roof of the car over and over again. When the car landed upside down, Neil's head was crushed by the roof of the car. Haley died a short time later from extreme head trauma and internal injuries.

Christie thought it was the rain that was keeping Neil, so she didn't call 911 right away. She thought he might have pulled off the road until it let up, but when she tried to reach his cell, it went to voicemail. She tried to keep her thoughts positive. By eight o'clock that evening, she began to feel panic rising in her chest. She hadn't heard from Neil and she still couldn't raise him on the phone. She called 911.

The rain impeded the search for Neil and Haley. When the police came to the door four hours later, Christie knew the news was bad. The officer's grim expressions said it all. She maintained her composure until they asked her to come down to the hospital to identify the bodies. That was all Christie heard as she fell to the floor and passed out.

In the months after the funerals, Christie worked only sporadically. She had no interest in research and even less in money.

When they had married, she and Neil had purchased a life insurance policy worth $500,000. With the payout from the life insurance policy and the money from the equity in their home, Christie could live comfortably for a long time in less pricey digs.

She gave Wilmer and March her emailed resignation and drove to the Keys, where she bought a tiny cottage big enough for one. For weeks she spent her days in a folding lounge chair nursing a watered down margarita and avoiding eye contact with her neighbors.

Christie started to feel restless as time went by. She was a pragmatic soul - she was a scientist after all - and she knew that work, any type of work, would distract her from her misery. She applied at the local Starbucks and was hired immediately. She was working the bar one afternoon when Jacob Wilmer walked through the door and ordered a double espresso.

Christie recognized Jacob. Once a year he would appear at the company Christmas party. He was older, but it was definitely him. He looked at her and smiled.

Jacob told her he'd been looking for her. He said he had a special project that needed a scientist, especially a scientist with her background. Jacob wanted her to work the on project for him.

Christie eyed him suspiciously. She had to admit she was curious, but she didn't know if she was ready to go back to that kind of high-pressure environment. Jacob gave her his card and asked her to call him when she was ready to learn more.

Two weeks later, Christie found herself in Jacob's beach house Palm Beach.

"What I'm going to tell you must be held in strictest confidence." Jacob told her, as he handed her a confidentiality agreement. He made her sign it before he would disclose the details of his offer.

It seemed that Jacob Wilmer was a bit of an eccentric; an eccentric with unlimited funds. He had a large, extended family in New Jersey and New York. There were 200 members to be exact. He believed that a holocaust of some kind was on the horizon, and he was determined to protect his line.

Jacob owned a large piece of land in Palm Harbor. The property was a few miles south of Tampa. He told Christie that he was building an underground city, a place where his family could live in safety on that property. The city would have everything they needed.

The main floor of the facility would have small houses for each family member and a communal dining room. He would stock it with food and supplies, clothing, furniture, or anything else they might need for the immediate and distant future. There would be a farm with animals and large tract of land for farming. Christie couldn't fathom the size of this "city."

Jacob offered her the job of supervising the building of the vegetable farm. He said her expertise with fertilizer, coupled with the fact that she had no apparent family ties made the match ideal. When asked why he mentioned her family ties, Jacob said she would have to live in the city while she was working. She would be unable to communicate with anyone in her family while underground. Christie said she did have parents, and Jacob offered to compensate them if it would help her make a decision.

When Christie went home that day, she called her parents, Toni and Don. Her parents listened to Christie say that she had been offered a great opportunity to work in her field, but she wouldn't be able to communicate with them for a while. She lied and told them she would be entering a biosphere in Hawaii.

Toni and Don were thrilled for Christie. They hadn't heard their daughter sound so alive in months. They said they understood and gave her their blessing.

Three days later Christie met with an attorney to sign a will and durable power of attorney naming her parents as beneficiaries. She gave her attorney, Michael Crane, a key to her house and asked him to look after it for her.

As her legal counsel and so sworn to uphold confidentiality, she told him where she would be and whom she was working for. Michael cautioned her against doing it as it sounded a little too weird to him, but Christie was firm in her decision. She thanked him, handed him a $25,000 retainer, and left.

Chapter 7

Gerald Todd

Gerald Todd had been a researcher at Wilmer and March in New Jersey for 10 years. He was a tall, lean man with a receding hairline and horn-rimmed glasses. When they opened their new Tampa facility, he was invited to go to Florida.

Gerald had been hired as a research assistant when he graduated from Monmouth University. He had developed an interest in animal sciences while working for Wilmer and March Pharmaceuticals.

Gerald studied for his veterinary degree nights and worked days. He envisioned himself a warrior of science, eschewing sleep, driving himself to work harder and longer than anyone else in the lab. When he got his second degree, he approached his supervisor about consideration for a promotion. When a position opened up in the animal labs, Gerald received his promotion.

While working in the animal labs, Gerald established himself as an arrogant taskmaster, alienating his fellow researchers, and causing general disharmony within the lab. No one liked him. Even the animals seemed to back away when Gerald walked by their cages.

Gerald ate alone in the cafeteria, stood alone at company parties, and in general had no social interaction with anyone at Wilmer and March. Gerald Todd was a very lonely man.

One year the company held a party to celebrate the fiftieth anniversary of the company. Gerald arrived on time and took up his usual spot by the elevator door. He knew if things went the way they usually did, after an hour he could board the elevator and go home, having made the requisite appearance. Then he noticed a woman across the room – a beautiful blond talking animatedly to a man who seemed to hang on her every word.

The woman had a glass of wine in one hand and a cigarette in the other. Gerald screwed up the courage to go over to her. He awkwardly gained her attention by tapping her shoulder. She turned and smiled at him.

Her name was Arlene and she had a small sweet Southern accent. Gerald was hooked the minute she opened her mouth. Not having much experience with women, Gerald stammered on about

34

his work with animals and his research in general. When he noticed that Arlene's attention was flagging, he offered to take her to his lab. For reasons he couldn't fathom, she agreed to go with him, but first she would need a refill.

When Arlene, saw Gerald's lab she assumed he was the supervisor. She did the math in her head and decided he might be worth her time. He was cute in an ordinary way, and he obviously had a little money because he wore good shoes. Arlene flirted a little with Gerald. She could see him blush, which spurred her on. She touched his arm and she felt him shudder.

Arlene knew the effect she had on men, and she used it to her advantage regularly, but this guy was different. He was no kid, but he seemed totally inexperienced with women. She took Gerald's hands and placed them on her waist. She then put her arms around his neck and drew him to her. She kissed him lightly at first, then harder. Gerald wrapped his arms around her and held her tightly.

After a few minutes, Arlene pulled away and asked Gerald for a pen and his business card. She wrote her phone number on the back and left Gerald standing in the lab. He was hooked, and she knew it. In time he would call and she would answer.

Gerald had purchased a home in Oldsmar, Florida. The house was a one-story stucco ranch with a bedroom on each side of the house and two full bathrooms. It had a living room in the front and a kitchen in the back. Gerald lived a frugal life. His shoes and one good suit were his only indulgences. As such, he had made the final payment on his mortgage just before he met Arlene.

Gerald felt he was financially secure enough to marry. That, coupled with his feelings for Arlene sent him to the jeweler's the following day. It was the most impulsive thing he'd ever done, but he really liked Arlene and even though he had only known her for two months, he wanted to marry her. He wanted her to belong to him. He wanted someone for himself so that he wouldn't be alone anymore.

Gerald brought Arlene to his house a week later. He was ready to make a commitment. He'd arranged for dinner at Arlene's favorite restaurant. When he brought out the ring, Arlene feigned surprise and said yes. She hugged him close and played her part well. She drank a bit more than she usually did in front of Gerald, but this was a celebration, after all.

35

Arlene was a bank manager. She specialized in schmoozing customers over three-martini lunches. She convinced Gerald that she could handle their finances. Gerald had no reason to distrust her.

At first Gerald didn't check the bank statements. He took an allowance with each paycheck as he always had and believed that Arlene was paying the bills. With their combined incomes, they should have a nice nest egg put aside within a couple of years.

Gerald had been working for Wilmer and March for fifteen years. His last promotion was ten years before. He enjoyed his life and his position. No one was breathing down his neck or pushing him to produce. But Arlene kept "encouraging" him to ask for a raise, but Gerald knew that he hadn't produced anything relevant since he'd taken over the animal sciences lab and he didn't feel it would be prudent to ask for more money right now. When he mentioned this to Arlene, she would look away and head for the kitchen. He could hear the refrigerator door open and wine pouring into a glass.

On a Wednesday afternoon, Gerald knocked on his supervisor's door. He had finally given in to Arlene and was going to ask for a raise, if for no other reason than his 15 years of dedicated service. His boss Jake Rawlings, told him to come in. He was a short, angry looking man with bushy eyebrows and a five o'clock shadow.

Jake was sitting at his desk, looking at his computer. He spoke with a heavy North Jersey accent and liked to carry around little bottles of rum. He motioned for Gerald to sit.

Jake asked Gerald what he could do for him and Gerald said he would like a raise. He told Jake he'd been there for 15 years, how he always came in under budget, how clean his lab was, how well cared for his animals were. Jake studied Gerald for a moment before speaking.

He told Gerald that he was aware of Gerald's dedicated service. He had recently been going over Gerald's files. Jake told Gerald that his file had been pulled because they were looking to downsize the department and since Gerald hadn't produced one damn thing in the last 10 years, he was being considered for termination. The only thing that kept him on was his length of service.

Jake went on to say that they had wanted to give him a large severance pay and find a replacement willing to take Gerald's current salary, but it was proving problematic. It seemed the young people coming out of college expected quite a bit more than his current $80,000 salary. Young vets with college loans were looking to start at at least 100K. Jake suggested that Gerald go back to his lab and think over his request. Jake even suggested he take the afternoon off.

Gerald listened to Jake's suggestion and left the building. He went to Shorty's, a local tavern in his neighborhood, and drank five vodka martinis. Gerald wasn't used to drinking and didn't realize just how far along he was. All he wanted was to go home and be with Arlene, who should be home from work by now. He got up from the bar and took his keys out of his pocket.

Gerald dropped his keys twice while walking towards the door. The girl at the door asked if he wanted her to call a cab for him. Gerald politely declined. He got into his car and started the engine.

As he drove, his car seemed to be going to the left all the time. He would jerk the steering wheel to right it. About a mile from Shorty's, Gerald saw the cruiser lights in his rearview mirror. Gerald pulled to the right and stopped the car.

The officer came alongside and asked him for his license and insurance. He asked Gerald to get out of the car and to walk a straight line. The cop cuffed Gerald and booked him into the Hillsborough County Jail.

Gerald called Arlene to pick him up and he used his triple A card to post his $250 bail. Arlene sounded annoyed but she met him at the jail door and took him home. When they got into the house, Gerald noticed dishes in the sink and the house in disarray.

He asked Arlene what had happened and she told him she'd been off that day and hadn't had a chance to clean up before he got home. The booze was wearing off, and Gerald was feeling tired. It was just after two in the morning. He said they would discuss it in the morning.

Gerald woke up the next day with a splitting headache. He wanted to call out of work, but after yesterday he didn't dare. Arlene was still in bed.

He looked at the clock. It was well past 7:30. Gerald was usually in the lab by this time, so he didn't know when Arlene usually left the house. He assumed she had to be at work by 8 a.m. He shook her to wake her, and she pushed his hand away. He yelled her name and she told him to shut up. Gerald didn't know what to do. Arlene had never been this way before.

Finally, Gerald got out of bed. He had to steady himself from the throbbing in his head. He walked over to Arlene's side of the bed, shook her, and lifted her up into a sitting position. Arlene balled up her fist and punched Gerald in the eye.

Gerald was so shocked that he fell back into the closet and to the floor. His eye hurt and he couldn't open it. She really landed that punch. With his good eye, he looked up at Arlene. She was smiling and started to laugh.

"That's what you get for waking me up!" She got out of bed and headed for the bathroom.

Gerald sat on the floor for a long time. He had dozed off for a few minutes. He hadn't seen Arlene come back from the bathroom. Suddenly, he heard pounding on the front door and vaguely wondered who could be there at this hour. He thought it might be the mailman with a package. He heard Arlene open the door and say that Gerald was in the bedroom.

When he opened his eyes, Gerald saw two police officers standing over him. They asked him to get up and to explain the slowly swelling eye. He said his wife had punched him when he tried to wake her for work. One of the officers went to talk to Arlene.

The officers interviewed Gerald and Arlene for an hour and it was determined that Gerald had attacked his wife in a fit of rage. They concluded that he had attempted to drag her out of bed with the intention of raping her.

Gerald denied the allegations vehemently while one of the cops put Gerald's hands behind his back and cuffed him. The two officers helped Gerald put on his pants. They had to drag him out of the house and put him into the cruiser. As they passed Arlene, he could see tears on her cheeks and a cigarette in her hand. She also had a black eye.

While Gerald sat in jail, he tried to think of how Arlene had gotten a black eye. She had to have had it last night. It took a while for an eye to get that dark, at least hours. Had he hit her last night?

He was beginning to doubt his sanity. Twice in as many days he'd found himself behind bars. Gerald Todd had never gotten so much as a parking ticket. Now he had a DUI, a Domestic Battery, and an Attempted Rape charge. Gerald Todd was still a very lonely man.

After he was booked, Gerald had been given one free call. His bail totaled $26,000 and his triple A wouldn't cover that. He asked someone for the name of a bondsman and dialed the number.

The woman who answered the phone asked Gerald if he had a family member or friend who could help him arrange bail. Gerald said no, and the sound of that no shook him to his core. She said the next best thing would be to get an attorney. She offered him the names of three attorneys, but she said that Neil Cramer handled their legal needs.

Gerald dialed Neil's number and talked to his legal assistant. She took his name and date of birth, and told him to call back in ten minutes. When Gerald called again, Neil answered the phone. He asked Gerald if he could afford to post bail if Neil could arrange it. Gerald said yes, he had the money, but that Neil would have to talk to Arlene. Neil told Gerald not to be surprised if Arlene was uncooperative, but that he would do what he could to help Gerald.

Neil called Arlene and she answered the phone. It was obvious to Neil that she was either drunk or high. When he asked about the money, Arlene paused before answering. She said there was no money. She told Neil that she had been fired the month before and hadn't told Gerald. She then told Neil that she had been using the money in their joint account to drink at Shorty's and score Xanax from her dealer.

Then, since Neil seemed to really be listening to her, she told him that she had been hit in the eye by a guy she picked up and brought home the day before Gerald's DUI arrest. She had covered the reddened eye with makeup before she picked Gerald up at the jail. When he woke her the next morning, she was so annoyed she decided to call the cops on Gerald. The eye had turned a nice black and blue by then.

Neil asked if she was willing to sign a request not to prosecute and Arlene said yes. Neil drove to Gerald's house and had Arlene sign the paper. He then drove over to the courthouse in time for Gerald's advisory hearing. Neil immediately asked Gerald who owned their home.

By some miracle or act of God, Gerald had failed to put Arlene on the deed to his house. Therefore, Neil could use Gerald's home to secure his bail. Neil was also able to get Gerald's bail reduced to $6,000. For another $15,000, Neil would handle all Gerald's cases, and if necessary, his divorce.

Over the next month, while Gerald slept on a couch in Neil's office because he had to stay away from the "victim," and he was broke. Neil haggled with the State Attorney's Office and it was agreed that since there was no evidence of attempted rape, the State would drop that charge if Gerald agreed to plead guilty to the battery. Neil told Gerald it was a good deal because the battery was only a misdemeanor and that Gerald could still work as a vet. Neil also suggested he have Arlene removed from his house ASAP.

Within the next two months, Gerald was fired from his job for having a DUI, had his wife evicted from their home, and divorced her. Gerald also found out about Arlene's extracurricular activities, and the fact that she'd spent all his money on drugs and alcohol.

Neil Cramer handled his divorce from Arlene. Since they'd only been married a few months, the Judge denied Arlene's claim on Gerald's house.

Gerald sold his house in the middle of the housing boom and realized a cool $250,000. He converted half of it into gold and put the gold in a safe deposit box. He moved to a singlewide mobile home in a family park on the outskirts of Ocala.

Gerald used his veterinary skills at the local farms just to keep his hand in it. One day as he pulled into his driveway after spending most of the night birthing a breeched calf, he found Jacob Wilmer sitting on his front porch.

Chapter 8

The Wilmer Biosphere, Palm Harbor, Florida

Mindy woke up to Baby Girl's cold wet nose nudging her hand. It was breakfast time, and the little dog had become used to nice meaty tidbits. Mindy opened her eyes and noticed that the artificial sun was up.

"Give me a minute girl," she said to Baby Girl, but the little dog insisted.

"What is wrong with you?" Mindy said, as she put her legs over the side of the bed and stood up. She put her hands on her hips. "I could have slept another hour you know." She padded over to the bathroom. She took a shower and let then water run over her body. She hadn't realized how much she loved a shower until she couldn't have one.

After Mindy got dressed, she took Baby Girl outside. Christie had told her to take Baby Girl's poops and flush them in her toilet. Christie also told her she would get her some dog food. So far though, Baby Girl was sharing Mindy's dinner every day.

Mindy had been at the Wilmer Biosphere for a week. She knew most of the kids there, but sometimes she forgot their names. There were almost 200 of them. Her favorite was Maria Elena. Maria Elena was an eternal optimist, and her outlook was always positive despite their current situation. Mindy also liked the twins Katie and Alyssa.

They ate together at every meal, and now they were attending "classes" together. Mindy had made an uneasy truce with life in the bubble, but she still dreamed of getting out one day and finding her parents.

Mindy fed Baby Girl her morning scraps. She made sure Baby Girl had clean water, and spent some time rubbing her belly before heading to the cafeteria.

"I'll be back, I promise. You be good, and no barking," Mindy said.

Baby Girl sat and stared at Mindy with her little brown eyes. Then she turned, jumped up on the unmade bed and curled up in the sheets. Mindy closed the door walked to Market Street.

Maria Elena and the twins were already seated when she arrive. Mindy waved, and they waved back. She got her food, taking extra

41

pieces of meat, and joined the girls. The conversation was lively as they discussed a new boy who had just arrived the night before.

"I really hope he shows up this morning," Katie said. "I heard he was kicking Andrew, and Simon couldn't get him through the door. But I didn't see it so, well, you know."

"Coming through that door must be scary," Mindy said. "I woke up in the hospital."

"Well that's what I don't understand. Why was he even awake? I mean, I wanted to come and so did Alyssa, but when somebody fights, they usually put them to sleep." Katie's freckles were bright this morning. Alyssa seemed a little catatonic.

"You guys look tired," Mindy said, and motioned to Alyssa with her fork. Alyssa had her head on her hands. She had pushed her tray to the side.

"We woke up in the middle of the night. We saw the boy being walked to his house. He didn't seem too happy, but they managed to settle him in. He was kind of noisy." Katie yawned as she spoke.

"Does anybody know his name?" Mindy asked.

"No," Maria Elena said. "We'll have to ask Christie when we see her. Ah, there are the boys with the TV. We better get rid of these trays."

Mindy smiled. This "class" was held in the cafeteria, and consisted of watching old videos on a big screen TV brought in from the library on a rolling cart by the stronger boys. Jacob Wilmer had bought every episode he could find from the History Channel, National Geographic Channel, and some from the Learning Channel.

Every day the kids would watch one, and write something about what they had learned. Wilmer hadn't bet on having 200 10-year-old children to educate, and there was a heavy emphasis on World War II. No math, no science, no English or Spanish, or any other language for that matter - just history.

Everyone had emptied their trays and they all sat waiting for the show to begin. One of the TV boys popped a DVD into the player and another lowered the lights. The History Channel logo appeared followed by goose-stepping Nazis. Austin, a tall chubby boy with sandy blond curls and a low threshold for boredom, stood up and began to yell.

"Nazis – I can't stand Nazis. I hate World War II and I hate Douglas MacArthur. I hate Winston Churchill. I hate Franklin

Roosevelt. But most of all I hate Adolph Hitler because if it wasn't for that asshole, we wouldn't have to watch these damn Nazis!"

Mindy's eyebrows shot up. The girl's mouths fell open.

"Nazis, always Nazis. I can't stand to look at another Nazi!" Austin said, as he walked over to the DVD player and pushed the button.

The disc came out and Austin grabbed it. Grunting and groaning, he bent the disc in half until it broke into two pieces. He hurled the pieces across the room and headed out the door of the cafeteria.

Mindy looked at the girls and said, "Come on," and they all got up and followed Austin out the door.

The rest of the kids followed the girls. Austin was headed for the library. As the girls approached the library, they could hear Austin talking to himself.

"I can't believe that nutbag Wilmer. I HATE WORLD WAR II!" he said.

Austin was pushing on the walls of the library. Suddenly, one popped open.

"I knew it!" Austin cried. He then saw the sea of faces standing behind him.

"I had panels like these in my bedroom. My mom used to store stuff behind them. I've wanted to check behind them ever since I came here. Look – the mother lode!" Austin pulled box after box of DVDs out of the closet.

"Push on the other panels!" Austin shouted, and the kids started pushing on all the panels in the library.

It seemed as though every third panel was a door leading to another treasure of DVDs. There were movies, documentaries, and actual school lessons.

The kids began yelling titles at each other and dancing around the room chanting "NO MORE NAZIS! YAY!"

Austin ran around the room and any movie about WWII, no matter how good or bad it was, was broken in half.

Christie was on her way downstairs when she saw the wave of youngsters heading for the library. She followed the noise and heard the shouting. When she came to the library door, she saw the kids dancing around and throwing DVDs at one another. Chri stie
clapped her hands to try and get their attention. Then she shouted at the top of her lungs.

"HEY! What is going on in here?" she yelled. The kids stopped dancing and stood still. They all looked appropriately guilty. "Well?" she asked.

"Austin found more DVDs. We were all so excited not to have to watch Nazis anymore, I guess we got carried away," said a little girl named Jaclyn.

Christie walked over to Molly, a small girl with curly brown hair. She held out her hand and Molly gave her the DVD she'd been holding.

"Wow, an actual movie. Where did you find them?" Christie asked Molly. Molly pointed at Austin, who showed Christie how the panels opened and she frowned.

"No one told us about the secret panels." Christie said. "The box of WWII tapes and the box of Disney's were out when we came. We'd all been so busy; we never had time to look for any others. These look great. Well, guys, it looks like we're gonna have movie nights here."

All the kids cheered.

"And, no more Nazis," Austin said.

"I think we can burn the WWII collection," Christie said. The kids cheered again. "But I think we should organize these DVDs. Let's separate them alphabetically, and put them back in the boxes that way."

Christie saw the broken disc in Austin's hand. She put out her hand and Austin gave it to her.

"Oh Austin, not "Saving Private Ryan," she said. Christie looked genuinely upset. Austin looked down sheepishly. "Do not break another movie. Is that clear?" Austin nodded.

They spent the rest of the morning sorting DVDs and boxing them. Just watching how happy they were made Christie feel a little lighter. She'd had a bad row with Gerald that morning and she really needed this. The kids needed this too.

Christie left them to finish sorting while she went to check the crops she'd planted a few months before. Mindy watched her leave and followed her to the door.

Mindy peeked around the corner of the library to see where Christie was going. She then looked around and noticed all the kids were occupied with the DVDs, so she headed out the door to follow Christie.

Mindy inched her way down the street past the tiny houses until the signposts ended. She'd never been this far down the street.

When she saw Christie enter a door at the end of the street, Mindy crept up to the door and stood on tiptoes to see inside. She never noticed the boy following behind her.

Mindy couldn't see much through the window. She decided to take a chance, and opened the door slowly. There was a corridor behind the door. Mindy could see Christie going through another door to her right as she entered the corridor. She could see out over a railing opposite the door. What Mindy saw astounded her.

Chapter 9

Mindy walked over to the railing, she put her hands on it, and pulled herself up on a railing to get a better look. Laid out before her were rows and rows of plants in various stages of development. The field had to be at least a mile long and half long and a mile wide. Mindy had seen farms before, but never inside a building. Mindy saw a tall black man watering the crops. She saw him look over his left shoulder, and then she saw Christie approaching him.

They were talking, and the man pointed toward the field. Christie looked worried. She squatted down and was touching the plant in front of her. She then got up, touched the man's shoulder, said something, and then walked away. The man nodded and turned off the hose. He turned and carried the hose to the left side of the field where he rolled it up. Mindy could see Christie walking to the far end of the field.

Suddenly, Mindy felt someone standing beside her. When she looked up she saw a boy she'd never seen before. He was cute, with freckles on his nose, brown eyes, and straight dark, brown hair. He was wearing a tee-shirt with a peace sign on it. He looked at Mindy when she turned to see him.

"Who are you?" She whispered.

"My name is Mark," He said.

They stared at each other for a few seconds and then back at the farm.

"That thing is really big," Mindy said. "How did they ever make that?"

"They dug a big hole," Mark said, and then he turned and went out the door. Mindy followed him.

"My name is Mindy," She said as she ran after Mark.

"Good for you," Mark said. "Now please leave me alone."

"You bothered me," Mindy said, but Mark was already far ahead. She watched him going towards the library and followed him. She noticed him pass the library and keep going. She kept following him until she saw him go into the little store.

Mark was picking up some toothpaste and soap. Mindy noticed his feet. He was wearing children's Birkenstock sandals. His feet were very dirty. His jeans were torn at the knees. Mindy wasn't sure if he bought them that way, or if they were just old. She watched him pick up some paper and pencils.

46

"You didn't have to be so rude to me," Mindy said. Mark still wouldn't look at her.

"Fine. Be that way." She tossed her head and turned around. Mark looked up as she walked away.

*****

Women always seem to fall for the dark, dangerous rebel, and the girls of Wilmer Biosphere were no exception. Whenever Mark came into the cafeteria, all female eyes would follow him, Mindy's included. She was young, but she was starting to have feelings that she didn't necessarily understand. She'd had a crush once when she was five, but not since then. She'd been more interested in studying than in boys. And the boys here didn't interest her at all.

Not Austin, who always tried to make her laugh, not Tommy, who stuck straws up his nose, or the video boys who played video games six hours a day, until Christie pulled the plug on the TV. They were a boring lot, and Mindy would yawn when they spoke to her. But Mark, now there was an interesting boy.

"Why doesn't he eat in here?" Katie asked. "What's wrong with him?"

"Nothing," Alyssa said. "He's perfect."

"Oh, you always like the boys," Katie said as she sneered at Alyssa. It was true. Alyssa always liked the boys.

"Well, what's wrong with that? Why shouldn't I like the boys? Mark is super cute, and he's, ah, what's that word? You know, when you don't know what someone is thinking?" Alyssa said. She looked at Mindy.

"You mean mysterious?" Mindy asked.

"Yes, mysterious. He's mysterious," Alyssa said, and stuck her tongue out at Katie. Katie grabbed it and pulled.

"Owww," Alyssa screamed.

"Well, don't stick it out at me," Katie said. She got up from the table and took her tray to the garbage can.

"Sometimes I hate my sister," Alyssa said as she followed Katie to the tray station.

Mindy looked at Maria Elena. Maria Elena had been strangely quiet while the girls were discussing Mark.

"You okay?" Mindy asked her.

47

"Yes, I'm fine. I was just thinking that my birthday is next week. It'll be the first one I've had without my parents," Maria Elena said and she looked sad. Mindy sighed.

"How old will you be?" Mindy asked.

Maria Elena smiled. "I'll be 11. I think I'm the oldest one here." Mindy smiled too.

"Well, movie night is Friday. Maybe Christie would let us make a party," Mindy said, as she stood up and took her tray to the tray station. She looked up and saw Mark emptying his tray into the garbage. He'd eaten at his house and had brought the tray back to the cafeteria.

"Hi," she said. Mark nodded, and turned to leave.

"What did he say?" Maria Elena asked when she got near Mindy.

"Nothing. He's so snobby." Mindy was mad, but as usual, she didn't know what to do with her anger. "He thinks he's better than the rest of us."

"Maybe he's just shy," Maria Elena said.

"No, he's just plain mean."

Mindy grabbed Maria Elena's arm and pulled her out of the cafeteria just in time to see where Mark had gone.

"Looks like he is going to the library," Maria Elena said.

"I don't care where he goes," Mindy said. She strained to see if he did go into the library.

"Well, we can go there and look at the DVDs," Maria Elena said, and began to walk toward the library.

"Wait," Mindy said. "I, I'm not ready Maria Elena. Let's go to your house instead."

Maria Elena put her arm around Mindy and they walked to her house.

"Why don't you go get Baby Girl and bring her over?" Maria Elena said as she opened door to her house.

"Good idea. She's been stuck inside all morning."

So, as Mindy walked towards her little house, she noticed Mark walking on the other side of the street. He walked as far as she did, to house number 200. He lived just across the street from her. Mindy's heart gave a little tug as she opened the door and Baby Girl greeted her.

"Come on girl. We're going out to play."

Mindy and Baby Girl walked side by side to Maria Elena's house. From behind the window at number 200, a lonesome boy watched the bossy little blond girl walk with her little dog down the street, and he thought she could be the one who would help him get out of this place and go home.

Chapter 10

Christie entered the farm zone and went down the stairs. She walked towards Calvin, a tall middle-aged African-American man, who was watering the plants and she stopped to look over the crops.

"I finished the other end, and I'm almost finished with this side," Calvin said. "You don't look happy."

"I'm concerned. These plants should be growing faster," she said. Christie had developed a fertilizer that should have accelerated the growth of the plants so there would be less time between harvests. The plants were hardier, but the growth rate was not spectacular.

"I can just imagine if Wilmer were here." She squatted down and touched the leaves of the tomato plant in front of her. It was a beautiful shade of green, and the tomatoes had a nice shape. Christie stood up and looked at Calvin.

"You shouldn't still be watering that way. I'm going to talk to Simon and find out how much longer it'll be." Christie touched Calvin's shoulder and turned to head to the other side of the field. Calvin gathered up the hose and put it to the side. As he turned to follow Christie, he noticed two kids standing by the rail turn and walk out the door.

Calvin caught up with Christie halfway down the field.

"You know why Simon hasn't finished don't you?"

"Yeah, I know." Christie sighed in frustration. "And I know what he'll say if I ask him about it. And he'll be right. With moving cars and bodies out of the way so they can hunt for food, he doesn't have time to supervise the sprinkler system, especially when his only plumber is helping him out there." They continued to walk along the edge of the field.

"The kids found a ton of DVDs today in some secret panels in the library. I wonder what other Easter eggs Wilmer planted around here. If you have some spare time...," Christie said and looked at Calvin. Calvin raised an eyebrow.

"Okay, I know, but if you do, please look around and see if you can find anything we could use. You know, like food." Christie smiled at Calvin.

Calvin nodded. He was a good man and she didn't want to push him too hard, but he was the only one minding the store, so to speak, and she needed his help.

"Thank you, Calvin," she said.

"It's better than being outside, Christie. If I weren't in here, I'd be dead. So I'm glad to help you. It's also better than moving bodies."

When they reached the end of the field, Calvin turned back and Christie walked the length of the field until she reached the other side. She found these walks therapeutic. She needed the time alone to get her bearings. She had a job she couldn't quit. All her colleagues were men, so she had no female to talk to over the age of 11. And now she had a real problem.

She'd argued with Gerald that morning. She told Gerald that the food supplies were getting low and something had to be done. Gerald had proclaimed himself the leader of their group when the mass destruction happened. He was Senior Scientist, he said. Mr. Wilmer had put him in charge when he hired him, and there was no reason to change things now.

When the first child, Maria Elena, was found, Gerald was delighted. He saw it as a great opportunity to research the cause of the destruction, and to find out why it wasn't lethal to the little girl. Gerald was absolutely salivating at the thought of taking her blood and cell samples.

Christie stepped in to tell him that under no circumstances would his research hurt this little girl. He could take her blood and study her cells, but she drew the line at any kind of "harvesting." She feared the argument they had this morning was the first of many. Somehow she had to get the crew to move faster, to find more stores with canned foods and supplies.

When Christie came back to "base," a small office next to Gerald's where she coordinated the trips the crew made outside, she noticed that the hazmat suits were hanging on the hooks behind the door between the corridor and the "last room." She heard voices coming from Gerald's office. Christie stood outside the door and listened before entering the office.

"Gerry, if you find a kid and tell us where to go, we go and pick them up," Andrew said. "I can't waste time looking for an elusive child when I have 200 to feed right here. We didn't have a lot of luck today. We found a Granger's Supermarket that was pretty full, and we took what we could hold. If I could leave some of the guys here, we could get more in the truck."

"But that would impede your progress, Andrew. It takes all four of you to get the bodies out of the way," Gerald said.

Christie could tell by the sound of Gerald's voice that he was straining to be patient. His only goal was clearing the street so the crew could get farther down Highway 19. He was determined to find all the children who might be left, at the expense of losing the ones he had. Christie had been concerned for a while about the state of Gerald's mental health. He was so focused and single-minded that it was almost impossible to reason with him.

"Maybe you should focus on just moving the bodies for a while. Then, when the road is clear, you can fill the truck several times a day. Now, doesn't that sound better than the way you're doing it?" Gerald said.

Christie could hear Andrew sigh. She opened the door and walked in.

"I wasn't invited to the party," she said with a smile. "You guys got back early."

"Yeah, well, we worked as fast as we could, but Pat got sick again and we had to turn back. He's still out there washing out the inside of his suit." Andrew's mouth turned up just a little. "We did find some good stuff, lots of soup and veggies, tuna fish. The store still has plenty. I was telling our boy Gerald here that if I could leave Pat and George here next time, I could bring a lot more back."

"And I told them they should concentrate on moving bodies and clearing the road." Gerald was turning red trying not to lose his temper.

"And I told you this morning that we needed supplies and that food is a priority," Christie said, her eyes narrowing in anger. Gerald always backed down when she looked at him like that.

"Well, maybe for one day. Do it for one day and we'll see. But if one child dies because we didn't get to them, it will be on your head." Gerald walked over to his desk and sat down with his back to them.

"There's plenty of food out there," Andrew said. "Anybody living within a mile of a supermarket or big box store will be fine. And that's pretty near everybody. Simon and I will go out alone tomorrow."

Andrew left the office to check on Pat. Christie stuck her tongue out at Gerald's back and left the office too. She noticed Simon standing by the corridor door and went over to him.

"Simon, I know you've been busy, but is there any way you can get those sprinklers working? Calvin is watering, but the plants would grow so much better with sprinklers. If Pat stays behind tomorrow, could he work on them?"

She looked hopefully at Simon, an old-school plumber who had taken this job because work was scarce and at 50, he thought it might be an easy gig. Now he spent his days moving dead bodies and cars off the road, and loading supplies into an inadequate truck. And now Christie wanted him to leave Pat to work unsupervised. He loved Pat, but Pat never took anything very seriously, and he was a less than adequate plumber. But Christie's eyes were pleading with him.

"I'll see what I can do. Maybe I can supervise him nights." That was it. Simon had spoken.

Andrew and Pat came out of the last room and walked toward Christie. Andrew smiled when he saw her. Christie looked at that handsome face and felt her legs go a little weak.

Pat, on the other hand, reminded her of a puppy. He was short, cute, with black hair and black eyes, a Brooklyn-born Italian boy with a quick sense of humor and a light in his eyes. And every time he went out with the crew, he threw up in his suit.

"Miss Christie. How are you?" Andrew put his arms around her and Christie found herself in a big warm bear hug. "I can see good ole Gerry has taken his toll on you."

"He really is an idiot." Christie surprised herself by saying it out loud. "I mean, he just has his priorities screwed up."

"No, he's an idiot." Andrew smiled again and put his arm around Christie's shoulders.

He led her out of the corridor and into the city. They walked into the cafeteria and the kids yelled "Yay" when they saw Andrew. Andrew loved to get down on the ground and play with the kids. He let them ride his back, he wrestled with them, and he tossed them up in the air. The kids loved every minute of it, but Christie kept seeing broken bones.

Then the kids saw Pat and all hell broke loose. They came and stood around him while he told them jokes and stole their food off their plates. All in all, when the crew got back, it was a good day.

Andrew was sitting with Pat and Christie after the kids left the cafeteria. They were talking about the boy they had brought in a couple of days ago, Mark.

"That kid was just fine," Andrew said. Andrew was rocking back and forth. He did that when he was agitated, anxious, or thinking hard. "There was no reason to bring him here."

"But, he's only 10 years old," Christie said.

"You know, I've been wanting to ask you something," Pat said. "Why are they all 10 years old?"

"That is the million dollar question. We haven't determined the reason for that yet." Christie sounded genuinely discouraged.

"Well, it's weird." Pat added.

Andrew took Christie's hand. "You know, I really do believe you'll figure it out." He cupped her hand in his and looked at her. She found herself momentarily speechless.

"Shit," said Pat. "She's the only woman left on the planet and you score." He got up and took his tray to the tray station. Pat was still scowling as he passed them on the way out.

Andrew was suddenly serious. "I know that Gerald is not running on all cylinders. Is he dangerous?"

"I'm starting to wonder. I really don't know. He keeps talking about the kids, and he creeps me out. I wonder sometimes if he wants to cut them up to find out why they're still alive. Or use them to create some sort of antidote so he can leave the facility."

"Yeah, he does seem obsessed with finding them. Keep me posted. If he does anything off the charts, tell me immediately. Immediately, *capice?*" Andrew looked at her.

"You've been spending too much time with Pat." She smiled and took her hand away. "I need to check the kids. It's time for bed."

Christie got up and glanced at Andrew before leaving the cafeteria. Andrew went to the offices to check the computer servers before turning in for the night.

*****

The next morning, Patrick Luca was standing over a sprinkler. Simon was explaining how Pat should check each sprinkler before attempting to turn them on.

"It's like checking the bulbs on the strand of lights at Christmas. As long as they're tight, they should be fine. You have to check each one. Make sure they're tight on the bottom where the water enters the sprinkler." Simon was looking at Pat, who was looking at the railing above him.

"Are you listening to me?" Simon was losing his patience. "Listen, *goomba*, this is important." Pat turned to him.

54

"I know, I know. I promise, check them like light bulbs. Make sure they are tight before I turn on the water." Pat had been listening.

"Okay, then today that's your assignment. When I come back I better see half the field done." Simon walked away. Pat was watching the railing again. He could have sworn he saw a kid standing up there.

Chapter 11

Since Pat wasn't going out with the crew that day, he got to eat his breakfast with the kids. As the cafeteria emptied, he left his tray at the dishwasher and headed for the field. He just happened to notice a little girl following him. She was trying hard not to be noticed. He got to the door and went through. Then he waited on the other side.

When the little girl opened the door, she turned and found Pat looking down at her. The first thing he noticed about her was her long, thick, wavy blond hair. She had tried to pull it back in a ponytail, but it was so wild that it stuck out in different places all over her head.

"I saw you at the railing this morning." Pat tried to look mean.

She hesitated. Her mouth was twisting as she tried to come up with a plausible reason for her being here.

"I found this place one day and I just like to come in here because it feels like outside," she said. Pat smiled.

"Yeah, I think I see what you mean. But you know you're not supposed to come in here."

She looked at him with big blue-gray eyes.

"Why?" she asked.

Pat pondered her question. He didn't rightly know why. In fact, it had never been stated explicitly that the kids couldn't come in here. So, with that in mind, Pat asked her to help him check the hundreds of sprinklers in the field.

"What's your name?"

"Mindy."

"Well, Mindy, how would you like to spend the day in here checking these sprinklers with me?"

Mindy smiled. Thinking of a whole day in this place made her feel happy.

"I would. I would like to help you. Can I get my dog?" Pat stared at her.

"You're the one with the dog! I didn't recognize you all cleaned up. Well, you can't let him pee in here."

"It's a she, and I'll watch her." Mind thought for a few seconds. "Maybe I'll just bring her in after lunchtime for a little while."

"That sounds very reasonable."

Pat led her down to the end of the field. They met Calvin watering the rows of potatoes.

"Morning, lady and gentleman," Calvin said as he tipped his hat to them.

"Morning, Calvin. This here is Mindy. She's going to help me tighten the sprinklers."

"Now you know how I feel about slave labor, Patrick." Calvin had one eyebrow raised as he looked at Pat.

"Well, I ah, I thought maybe I could, well, we don't get paid! How am I going to pay her?" Pat looked genuinely perplexed. What could he give her in return for her work?

"I don't want anything," Mindy said. "I just want to be in here." Pat smiled at Calvin.

"Okay, Patrick, that's fine, but the rules are she gets a break every hour and you make sure she eats. And if she decides she's had enough, you let her go. Understood?"

"No problem. Now, Miss Mindy, let's get started."

They left Calvin to water and went into the back were they kept the tools. Mindy noticed that there was another set of doors here that must lead to the outside. She made a mental note of that and followed Pat back out to the field. Pat bent down and held a sprinkler.

"All you have to do is check the connection. See, this little nut down here. You have to make sure it's on good and tight so the water flies out the ends of the spokes. If there's any play in the nut, you take this wrench and tighten it like this." He placed the wrench over the nut and moved it to tighten the nut. "What do you think?" Pat was watching Mindy.

"I think I can do this."

She started down one row and Pat went down the next. While they worked Pat told Mindy his life story of growing up in Brooklyn and working in his mother's beauty shop from the time he was eleven until he turned eighteen. He would wash the ladies' hair, and they would pinch his cheek and give him a dollar. He loved working in the shop, especially watching his mother cut hair. She was a true artist.

When he turned eighteen, his dad told him it was time to join the Plumber's Union, and as soon as he graduated high school, he was apprenticed with his father's employer. He liked being a plumber. The money was good and he could work alone.

"How did you end up here?" Mindy asked.

"My dad died. I just kind of got sad, you know? My mom told me to take a vacation. I came down here and liked it. Then I saw an ad for plumbers at Wilmer and March, and I applied. They hired me." That was all he would say.

At noon, Mindy and Pat went to the cafeteria for lunch. The girls asked Mindy where she had been and she said she was helping Pat. Pat had joined them for lunch. They all stopped talking when Mark walked in and actually sat down to eat at a table - by himself of course.

"What's up?" asked Pat.

"That's Mark," Katie said. "He's a snob."

"He's mean," Mindy elaborated.

"He's just quiet," Maria Elena said.

Alyssa, as usual, said nothing, and just gazed dreamily in Mark's direction.

"So, we have a handsome, quiet snob with mean tendencies who has the power to stop a conversation in mid-sentence," said Pat. "He wasn't happy when we picked him up either."

"Where did you find him?" Mindy looked at Pat expectantly.

"Down by the beach near St. Pete. He had a really nice house. Ang, I mean Andrew, wanted to leave him there, but you never know. I mean, we really don't know how long you kids can survive out there all alone. So in the end, Andrew gave in and we took him. But the kid wasn't happy. He fought us all the way."

Mindy pondered what Pat had said. If she hadn't been knocked out, she would have fought too.

"Why didn't you just knock him out?" Mindy had a hard look on her face.

"We ran out of chloroform." Pat looked at his food and wouldn't look at Mindy. He remembered the day they picked her up and a wave of guilt washed over him. But it was his idea to take Baby Girl, so the guilt passed quickly.

When they finished, Pat and Mindy stopped by her house to get Baby Girl. After the little dog did her business by the side of the house and ate her jerky, they all headed for the field. Before they got there, Mindy looked up at Pat.

"I know how you can pay me," she said.

"Oh yeah, and how is that?"

"You can cut my hair."

Chapter 12

Andrew and Simon got into the truck. It would be strange leaving Pat and George, but there would be more room for supplies. They drove down the dirt road that led to Highway 19, turned left onto 19 and drove south towards St. Petersburg.

Along the way they passed the piles and piles of bodies that the crew had stacked in the weeks preceding this morning. The bodies were decaying fast in the Florida sun, leaving bones and rotting clothing. One good hurricane would finish the job by scattering the bones to the wind.

Andrew and Simon tried to keep their eyes ahead. They'd had their fill of death and decay. All they wanted to do today was fill the truck and get back to the biosphere. They knew they would have to do it several times, but at least it was clean work. Even Pat could do this without heaving up his guts.

They passed a shopping center where they had parked most of the abandoned cars found on 19. Some of the cars had bodies in them that had to be removed. Now the cars were neatly lined up in the mall parking lot. Andrew and Simon would stop there twice today to fill the truck with gas from their tanks.

They turned into a strip mall with two restaurants and a convenience store. There was also a bowling alley. The convenience store had canned goods and sodas, beer, etc. It also had candy, snacks, and cigarettes. The little girl with the dog had asked Andrew to get some dog food. He found ten cans and put them in a bag.

Old man Wilmer strictly forbade smoking in the facility and having a hazmat suit on made it impossible to smoke on the road. Residents of the Wilmer Biosphere who wanted to had to smoke behind the last door near the field. That way they could hide the smell as well as the actual smoke. So Simon filled a bag with cigarettes.

The bowling alley had snacks and canned drinks. The two restaurants, one Italian and one Chinese, had big cans of tomato sauce, sacks of flour, big cans of chicken broth, corn starch, and lots of packaged fried noodles. Simon also grabbed the little packets of duck sauce and soy sauce, anything to make the food more interesting. Everything else was rotted.

They went back to the facility to drop off their booty, and Christie beckoned Andrew to come to the window. She told him

59

that Pat had a request. She took out a slip of paper. He wanted them to go to a beauty store and pick up a pair of hair cutting scissors, a hair cutting razor, a skinny comb and good quality brush. He also wanted a hand-held mirror. As he heard each item read, Andrew's frown deepened.

"What the hell does he want that stuff for?"

Christie just shrugged and asked him to do his best. Andrew shook his head, ran his hand up and down his face, and shook his head again. Then he nodded at Christie and put his head gear back on.

Andrew and Simon had developed an easy friendship. Though they had little in common with regard to their work at the Facility – Andrew was a computer expert and Simon a plumber, they got along famously and would rather spend their time together talking football and women than anything else.

They worked well together too, with little friction. Simon didn't mind letting Andrew decide where they would go. Simon would close his eyes and put his head back while Andrew drove the gruesome miles to the next "shopping" location.

When Gerald gave them orders to pick up a child he had located, it was Andrew who took the lead. Children liked Andrew, and he was easy to trust. Lately though, especially with Mark, Andrew was becoming less inclined to do Gerald's bidding. The kids weren't in danger. There were no people that they knew of who would hurt them. Why not just leave them were they were and check up on them once a week, maybe put a few together in a house and see how they fared?

Kids should be outside, and these kids were special. If they hadn't died in the first wave, why did Gerald think they would die now? Andrew would rant on and on while Simon would grunt now and then in response. Their partnership worked well.

They were halfway on their run when Andrew saw a sign for Maureen's Beauty Barn. They pulled into the lot and got out of the truck. The store was locked, so they broke the window out and climbed in. There was no electricity, so no alarm sounded. Andrew turned on his flashlight. Fortunately, there were no bodies in the store. He found the scissors and combs, and those things girls liked to use to hold their hair back.

The razors were behind a locked glass door. He broke the door and grabbed three razors. Simon managed to find a mirror, and he also grabbed all the shampoo and conditioners he could bag. For

60

good measure, they threw in some tweezers, nail polish, and lipstick. They thought Christie might like that. There were also some plastic safety razors that they grabbed for the men.

When they left the store, Simon asked Andrew how he knew what scissors to take when there were so many different kinds. Andrew told him that when he was a kid, his mother had rehabilitated used Barbie dolls. She would fix their hair, give them a "boil perm," and cut the hair when necessary.

"And you used to watch this?" Simon said.

"Only the part where she would stick their heads in the boiling hot water."

"And why would she do that?" Simon asked.

"Because dolls' hair is plastic and the boiled water would curl it. It had to be put on a thing, you know, wrapped around this plastic and stuck in really hot water to bend the hair."

"Geez, who the hell thought of that?" Simon said just before he dozed off.

The rest of the afternoon went by quickly. They found a Granger's, which was full of food. They could come back tomorrow to fill up again. It was getting dark, and they didn't like being out in the dark. Dark these days meant pitch black dark, no street lights or lights from businesses. They felt very lonely out there in the dark.

When Pat saw all the goodies they had brought him, he almost wept. It reminded him of his mom's shop and the idea of his mom made Pat ache inside. The last time he had heard her voice was just before the biosphere sealed. He missed her so much.

That evening, after everyone had finished eating, Pat found a wooden box in the back room behind the field and put it in the cafeteria. He then placed a chair on the box. He told Mindy to go wash her hair at home and come back with it wrapped in a towel. When she arrived in the cafeteria dripping wet, he put her on the chair on the box and worked his magic on her unruly locks.

Pat had never actually cut anyone's hair, but he had watched his mother do it hundreds of times. So when he lifted the comb to Mindy's hair and started to carefully disentangle the waves, he felt a surge of energy rush through him. The scissors took on a life of their own as he cut strand after strand of hair.

Pat asked Mindy how short she wanted to go. She took her fingers and went from the back of her head around to the front pointing to just under her ears. So Pat followed the line her fingers

61

had drawn, and for good measure he thinned out the thick hair to a manageable fullness.

When he was done he backed away and looked at Mindy. During the process of cutting, the kids had started to come into the cafeteria to watch. Katie and Alyssa were standing in front of Mindy.

"Oooo, Mindy, it looks really good," Alyssa said.

"Yeah, it looks okay," Katie said.

"You look like a princess," said Maria Elena.

Pat held up the mirror for Mindy to see. She inspected the sides carefully. Pat handed her two barrettes and she put them on each side of her hair to hold it away from her face. Mindy thought she looked pretty. She smiled at Pat and when he took her off the box, she hugged him.

"Anybody else?" Pat asked the kids.

"Oh, me, please." Alyssa was holding up her hand.

"Why do you want to do that?" Katie was holding her sister back.

"Because he made her look soooo beautiful."

Pat told Alyssa to go wash her hair. He said he could do five more of them tonight. Three boys came forward and a girl. He told them all to go wash their hair and told the others to come by at breakfast and he would schedule "appointments" for the rest of the week. They would have to show up for their appointment with washed hair.

He asked one of the boys to run to the kitchen and find a broom and garbage bag. When the boy returned, Pat swept up Mindy's hair and put it in the bag.

Pat gave each of the boys Mohawks. Most of the girls got a trim, but Alyssa got the full treatment. She wanted her hair real short. She didn't like to mess with it, but it still had to be girlie. Pat managed to give her a sweet pixie cut. Katie was furious. They no longer looked exactly alike, and Katie didn't want a pixie cut. She left the cafeteria in a huff.

When all the kids' hair had been cut, Pat took the box and put it near the side wall for the next time. He felt really good and really tired at the same time. He had worked all day long and it was time for bed.

Simon caught him as he was leaving the cafeteria and asked him how things went with the sprinklers. He told Simon that he had finished the whole field. He left out the part about Mindy helping him. Simon seemed impressed.

"Then we'll give it a dry run tomorrow before we leave."

"Do I have to go tomorrow?" Pat was hoping for one more day off.

"Yeah, Gerald wants us finish clearing 19. We have to leave after breakfast."

Pat's heart fell. He just hated moving bodies. It always made him hurl. And then he had to wear the vomit in his suit until they got back to base.

But Pat couldn't say no because the other guys had to go too. The only one who got a pass was Calvin. Before the destruction, Calvin's job had been truck mechanic, but now it was tending the field, and he was too valuable to send outside.

So Pat the plumber was picked as part of the crew sent out daily to clear the roads and collect supplies, and he really hated it.

Chapter 13

Mindy felt light and airy. Her neck felt liberated. She opened the door to her house and Baby Girl greeted her suspiciously.

"It's me, Baby Girl! I got a haircut! And, I've got some dog food for you."

Baby Girl rolled over on her back and Mindy rubbed her belly. The little dog loved it and kept rolling over begging Mindy to rub and rub. Mindy got on the floor, hugged the little dog and the Baby Girl licked her face over and over. Mindy felt so happy for the first time in a long time. She was rolling around with Baby Girl when she heard a knock on her door.

Mindy thought it might be Maria Elena come to visit. She didn't look out the window to see who it was, she just opened the door. Mark was on the other side. He had a look of surprise when he saw Mindy.

"Who butchered you?" he asked.

"What do you want?" Mindy couldn't help her sarcastic tone. He was just so rude.

"Can I come in?"

Mindy thought for one second of saying NO and slamming the door, but she was dying to know why he had come over to her house, so she let him in. Mark came and looked around at her house. He seemed unimpressed by what he saw.

"All these places look alike. No imagination." He sat down on the one guest chair she had and waited for her to speak.

"What do you want, Mark? Why did you come over here?" Mindy was getting impatient.

"I saw you go to that place today with the skinny guy. I just wondered what you were doing there, that's all."

"Well, maybe it's none of your business." Mindy had her arms folded over her chest and she was looking down at Mark. "You are the meanest boy I've ever known!" Mindy began flailing her arms around while she yelled at Mark. "Why don't you just go away?"

Mark sat back in the chair and sighed. "I just wanted to know what you were doing with him down there. I watched you for about an hour."

This made Mindy even more furious. She balled up her hands and yelled "grrrrr" at him. Mark started to laugh at the sight of Mindy. She looked so angry and red in the face.

64

"Stop! Stop laughing at me!"

Mindy started punching Mark with both her fists. Mark put his hands up to protect his face. He managed to get up out of the chair and go to the other side of the room. She went for him again, and he pushed her on the ground and sat on top of her.

"You have to calm down. You're really acting silly." Mark just sat there while Mindy kicked her legs up and down and punched him with her fist. After a while, she got tired and stopped.

"Got that out of your system?" Mark got up off Mindy.

Mindy stayed on the floor, humiliated by her behavior and Mark's indifference. She was glad she hadn't cried. Mark sat back in the chair.

"Now, can we talk?" Mark sat there looking at Mindy. He was like some mini-man, not a child at all. Mindy was confused by him. Maybe he was a little person disguised as a child.

"How come you talk like that?" Mindy asked him.

"Like what? I just talk." He was looking at Baby Girl. The whole time he was sitting on Mindy, Baby Girl had been pulling at the hem of his pants. Now she was sitting by Mindy growling at Mark in a low tone.

"Nice dog. I like her. What's her name?"

"Baby Girl. She belongs to my Grammy." Mindy sat up and got on her sofa bed. She felt drained of all her energy. She wished Mark would leave.

"Why don't you just go home," she said in a tired voice.

"I really want to know about that place. You spent a lot of time down there. Please tell me what it was like." Mark looked so cute. Mindy hated herself for thinking about his looks.

"It's a big farm. We were making sure all the sprinklers were working so they could turn them on and Calvin wouldn't have to water anymore."

"Who's Calvin?" Mark asked.

"He's a black man who lives by the field. He takes care of it. He's very nice and he wanted Pat to make sure I had breaks and ate." Mindy was looking at the ceiling, trying to avoid Mark's eyes.

"What do you mean he lives down there?"

"I don't know. I guess he does. I've never seen him up here. I think I saw him go into a door in the side wall. Maybe he has a room there."

Mark was thinking hard. "What else did you see there?"

"Just a room in the back where they keep tools and stuff. It has a door in back like the ones in the front where you come in."

"Doors like the ones up front, with three or four compartments?" Mark sounded excited.

"Yeah." Mindy began to see where Mark was going. "You want to leave. You're trying to find a way out."

"I can't stand it here. I was fine where I was. I had a house, I had electricity. I had food. They could have left me there and I would've been fine." Mark was angry now.

Mindy felt a pang in her heart for Mark. She knew how it felt to be ripped from your home against your will and taken to a strange place. She knew how it felt to lose all your people. She also knew how lonely it could be out there all alone.

"I know what that feels like." Mindy was watching Mark. "I was alone a long time. I didn't want to leave my house either. But the one thing I have here that I didn't have there is friends. If you leave here, you'll be all alone again. Do you really want to be alone?" Mindy stopped talking. The silence hung in the air. Mindy could see Mark's hard facade crumbling.

"I buried my parents. When they died I wrapped them in tarpaulins we had in our shed and took them out to our boat. I put them in the boat, started the motor, and when I got a little ways out I dropped them in the ocean. I asked God to keep them. But I don't know if I believe in God anymore"

Mark slowly began to cry. First the tears rolled quietly. Then the sobs began full on as he cried harder and harder. All the months of holding it in came upon him all at once. He turned his face into the chair.

He cried for a long time before Mindy got off her bed and walked over to him. She knelt down next to him and put her hand on his hand. He turned and looked at her and put his arms around her neck still crying. Mindy put her arms around him and cried too.

When they had finished crying, Mindy went to the kitchen. She found two bars of chocolate and brought one to Mark. They sat eating their chocolate in silence. Then they looked at each other. Mark spoke first.

"I want you to come with me."

"Why? You don't even like me." Mindy was squinting at him.

"Because you're smart. You wanted to know about this place too. And you're right. I don't want to be alone. I also like your dog."

"Do you have a plan?" she asked. Mark tightened his mouth and pressed his lips together.

"I want to make my way back to my house. We would have everything we need. My parents believed in all that ecology stuff. They had solar panels and well water with a filter system in the whole house. We were by the ocean and the wind blew the smells away from the house.

"They had a great garden in the back, and we grew food. It's probably all dead now, thanks to those morons. But we could get it going again. It's a big house. There's plenty of room for us and Baby Girl."

This was the most animated Mindy had ever seen Mark. His excitement was rubbing off on her.

"It really sounds nice. But I would want to find my parents first. I would want to go to my old house and see them first."

"But you do know that they're dead. Are you sure you want to see that? Believe me, it sucks." Mark was hoping Mindy would change her mind.

"I just don't feel that they're dead. Why does everyone keep saying that?"

"Because they all saw their parents die, and there's not another living soul out there except for us kids. Even the animals are dead. I don't get Baby Girl, but I'm glad she survived."

Mindy was all cried out so she couldn't muster any tears.

"Can we at least go by and see?"

Mark nodded his head. "Yeah, we can go by your old house."

"Then I'll help you. When do you want to go?"

"We'll start to make a plan tomorrow. I'll come over and we can work it out. We'll make a list of what we'll need. Are you helping Pat again tomorrow?"

"No, we finished the whole field."

Mark looked down. "Is that guy, Calvin, always in the back?"

"He lives there, so I guess so." Mindy was wondering what Mark had planned.

"Maybe I can sneak in there and get a look at those doors. I want to see how many there are. I know I came through a hatchway when they brought me in at the front. But I have never seen the back of this place. We could get lost. Maybe there's some way to find a map of this place."

"We should look in the library. Meet me there tomorrow after class." Mindy said.

Mindy got up, indicating that it was time for Mark to go. Mark got up and went to the door.

"I don't have to tell you not to talk to anybody about this, do I?" Mark asked. Mindy rolled her eyes.

"What do you think?" She opened the door. Mark smiled and left.

"Baby Girl, what have we gotten ourselves into?" Baby Girl stood at the door as if to say "Take me out mom." Mindy opened the door again and walked with Baby Girl to the side yard. As Baby Girl did her business, Mindy saw the light go on at Mark's house. She thought about walking all the way back to St. Petersburg. How would they ever do it?

Going home! Mindy was happier than she'd been in a long time. Tomorrow, she and Mark would plan a course for home. Before Mindy took Baby Girl into the house, she looked up into the electric sky.

"Thank you," she said.

Chapter 14

George Ranier

Los Arma, New Mexico

George Ranier got up from his breakfast table. He put his dishes in the sink and then slowly made his way to the living room. As he moved, he barely lifted his cane and feet off the floor so there were long scratches in the linoleum. George made it to his recliner and turned to face the TV. He knew it would hurt going down, so he had to prepare himself. After pondering it for a minute, George lowered himself into the recliner.

"Ooo." His hips and knees hurt so bad. His great-granddaughter Becky had offered to buy him one of those lifting chairs. George felt funny having her buy him something, so he declined. Besides, it only hurt for a few minutes, so what the heck.

George shifted a little until the pain became bearable, and reached for the remote control. Damn! He had knocked it to the floor when he got up for lunch and forgot. Now he would have to get up, bend over, pick it up, and lower himself back into the seat. It almost didn't seem worth it. But Judge Judy was on the other channel, and he didn't like any of the doctor shows. If he didn't change the channel, he would have to watch a doctor show.

George rocked the recliner back and forth to get the right leverage. On the third rock forward, he propelled himself up out of the chair, put his arms out to his sides to balance himself, and turned towards the chair. He put his left hand on the arm of the recliner while reaching for the remote with his right hand. He was able to grab it on the first try. Then George once again prepared himself to go down into his chair. George was 91 years old today.

Becky was supposed to stop by for a visit this evening. George looked forward to her visits. It was nice to see young people, but especially Becky. She reminded George of his wife Alice. She even talked like Alice. This brought a great deal of comfort to George. He hadn't been a very good husband to Alice, and he felt he could make it up to her by being kind to Becky.

Earlier that afternoon before his shows came on, he made sure that the tea cups were clean and the silverware had no spots. Becky would bring a small cake and they would celebrate.

George had wiped the lunch crumbs off the table and tried to catch them in his hand. The rest would have to be swept up when Becky came. He decided the house looked presentable and went back to his bedroom to put on his good shirt. Might as well make an effort on your birthday.

Becky arrived right on time with the small cake. She asked George if he had eaten anything for dinner and he waved his hand.

"Pop Pop, if you don't start eating I'll make you come and live with me." Becky always threatened George with forcing him to leave his home of sixty years to live with her in the city. "I will, I will force you to come with me. Then you'll have to watch PBS, no more Judge Judy. Do you hear me, Pop Pop?"

George just waved his hand again. Becky came over to the recliner and kissed him on the cheek.

"I don't want to lose you, Pop Pop. You have to take care of yourself. Please, for me." Becky smiled and kissed George's cheek once more, and went to the kitchen to set up the cake. George got up off the recliner, steadied himself, and followed her.

They sat down together after Becky lit the 9 +1 candles and sang "Happy Birthday" to George. He mustered up all his breath and blew out the candles. Becky clapped and cheered. Then they each had a slice of cake, and Becky told George about her day.

Around 9 p.m., Becky cleared the plates and cups and told George she had to go. He said he would get the dishes done, just leave them. She did. Then she kissed George on the cheek again and said good night. She told him she would come by over the weekend. George followed her to the door and made sure the locks were all in order. Then he turned off the lights and went to bed.

*****

George had been a military hero during World War II. When his plane crashed two miles from the British coast after a routine photographing mission over Germany, George carried what was left of the flight crew on his back as he paddled his way to the shore. George received the Medal of Honor for saving Matthew Wilmer's life. In return, Matthew Wilmer had offered George the opportunity of a lifetime. He told George to look him up when he got out of the Army.

Matthew Wilmer's father had a small manufacturing plant in Freehold, New Jersey. During the war, he'd won a government contract to produce artillery for the armed services. The old man made a mint during the war. When his son came home, he went to work for his father. He came into the plant with a host of new ideas.

The younger Wilmer believed that biological weapons were the wave of the future, and he tried to persuade his old man to convert the plant into a chemical laboratory where they wouldn't just research weapons, but also pharmaceuticals. This was a fairly big gamble.

The old man argued that it was too risky an investment, but Matthew Wilmer was determined. If his father wasn't interested, he would take his share of the business in cash and go out on his own. Try as he might, the elder Wilmer just couldn't bring himself to take on the risk. So, with his 20 percent share of the business, $20,000, Matthew Wilmer left New Jersey and headed for New Mexico.

When George Ranier was discharged from the Army in 1947, he headed for Freehold. He was disappointed when he found that Matthew had already gone to New Mexico. He took his last dollar and bought a train ticket to Albuquerque. Matthew's father gave him a heads-up that George was on his way, and Matthew met George at the train when he arrived.

Matthew drove George to a small piece of land Matthew had acquired to build his laboratory on. He had named his little town, his small piece of land, Los Arma, or the weapon.

Matthew had dreams of big government contracts, and he was determined to be one of the first to hit the big one, the chemical weapon to beat all chemical weapons. And to this end, he asked George to begin his career with Wilmer by going to night school on the G.I. Bill.

To his amazement, George found he had an aptitude for chemistry. He was fascinated by the table of elements and the reactions he got from combinations of different chemicals. He was adventurous and loved to experiment, even though his ideas often resulted in a small explosion.

Matthew was as excited as George and promised George his own lab when he graduated from college. Right now though, George would have to be satisfied assisting a man named Helmut March in the Wilmer lab.

George was not fond of Helmut March. He was suspicious of Germans, as many Americans were at that time, but Helmut was particularly annoying. He was fastidious and haughty. Helmut believed his word was law and anyone disagreeing with him was dismissed from his lab. He had no time for slackers and detested competition. Worse than that, he was brilliant. Helmut was God in his laboratory, and George one of his minions.

George finished college in the spring of 1952. True to his word, Matthew gave George his own lab on the other side of the small building in Los Arma. Matthew also gave George the task of developing a biological weapon so great that the government would be knocking down the doors of Wilmer Chemicals. George was happy to oblige Matthew as it meant he would be kept on a loose leash.

This didn't sit well with Helmut, who felt he had earned the right to work on the Holy Grail of weapons. But Matthew reminded Helmut that the American people weren't ready to have a German creating the ultimate weapon right in their own backyard and convinced him to be patient. Helmut was, after all, the head of the pharmaceutical division, and right now the pharmaceutical division was the only division bringing in any money. So Helmut resigned himself to heading the drug division as they called it in the hallways.

George's curiosity led him to investigate all the latest trends in biochemistry. He found an obscure article in Life magazine about a young woman named DeMorte who had discovered a plant in the Brazilian rainforest that seemed to have medicinal as well as poisonous properties. This ying-yang quality fascinated George. Wilmer's could greatly benefit from both properties of this marvelous Mortevida plant, as it was now being called. George quietly began attempting to contact Miss DeMorte to see if she would be willing to give him one of her fabulous plants.

Margaret DeMorte was having the time of her life. She had discovered a previously unknown species of plant, a botanist's dream. The natives had shown her that it could be used as a friend or foe.

Margaret wasn't eager to share her discovery until she had a firm plan in hand for how she wanted to use it. The idea of biological weapons was abhorrent to her, but the medicinal qualities of this plant were remarkable - particularly for women.

The plant had been used by the natives for years to prevent miscarriages. The success rate of the Mortevida bringing a woman to term was remarkable. This was what Margaret DeMorte wanted to produce, a medicine that could help women with a history of miscarriage maintain a pregnancy to term.

When George Ranier contacted Margaret in the spring of 1953, she wrote and told him he should come down to the rainforest. She wanted to introduce George to the Mortevida in its native environment. So George requested a short leave from Matthew, who granted it.

George had to travel first to California to board a ship headed for Brazil. The trip took him several days. Fortunately, Margaret had arranged to have him escorted to her camp deep in the rainforest.

When he arrived at her camp, George immediately asked to see the Mortevida. He watched Margaret as they walked to her lab which was housed in a Quonset hut. She asked George to call her Maggie. She was tall and thin, with short brown hair that she covered with a strange short-brimmed hat. George found her somewhat attractive, but not as attractive as Alice, the waitress George was dating back in Los Arma.

Maggie showed George the Mortevida plants. She had been quite successfully growing the plants, which were proving to be particularly hardy. She told George only to touch the outer purple line that went along the edge of each leaf. That was the medicinal part of the plant and wouldn't harm him.

The green part, however, was dangerous. That part of the plant bore a lethal poison that could kill on contact. George felt the edge of the leaf and noted its texture. He also noted that purple edge had a spore-like quality, enabling it to rub off on his fingers.

Later that day, Maggie showed him where the Mortevida grew and she introduced him to the local people who were helping with her research. Over dinner that evening, they discussed the future of the Mortevida and Maggie's hopes for the plants.

George's heart fell when she said she was vehemently opposed to using the poison of the Mortevida. Her main interest was fostering the medicinal qualities of the plant, perhaps even propagating the plants to produce a larger purple edge while diminishing the poisonous green center. George politely agreed that that was the "right" thing to do, for the good of mankind and all that.

"What happens to the leaves after you remove the spores?" George asked Maggie.

"They wither and die. The cells turn into tiny little balls. After that they're harmless," she replied.

George tried to figure out how he could get her to part with the plants so he could use them in the creation of his ultimate weapon. He would have to lie and lie well. She was hundreds of miles away from civilization. She would never know how he had used her Mortevida plant. George had to win her confidence and trust. And he had to do it in five days.

For the next few days, George wooed Maggie. He complimented her for the least little thing she did. At dinner each evening, he would crank up the old Victrola she had in her hut and dance with her. Maggie wasn't used to so much male attention. In fact, she had always been shy around boys, and now even more so around men. George was very attractive, and Maggie was falling for him.

By the end of the week, Maggie believed George had feelings for her, too. She asked if he would return someday, and while George wouldn't commit to coming back to the rainforest, he never said he wouldn't. Maggie heard what she wanted to hear, and George took advantage of her.

George headed home with five Mortevida plants and instructions for their care. Maggie had agreed to give them to George in exchange for a steady stream of supplies to be sent to her on a monthly basis.

Maggie also extracted a promise in blood, literally, that George would use the plant only for the good of mankind. She had punctured his left pinkie and collected three drops of blood that she mixed with hers in a Petri dish. Maggie told him that this was his sacred promise and she would keep it with her. If he ever betrayed her, she would give it to the natives, who would put a curse on it that would destroy George.

As a scientist, George was amused. In fact, he was surprised that Maggie would believe such hogwash. But he solemnly shook her hand, and she gave him the plants. Maggie then hugged George and kissed him on the cheek.

"I look forward to seeing you again soon, George." She smiled up at him. He'd made promises to Maggie in the acquisition of the plants, and now he felt a brief pang of guilt. Maggie was a lovely woman, but George kept his focus and gently removed her arms from around his neck.

"I'll do my best. I'll miss you, Maggie." George boarded the small boat that would take him back upriver. Maggie waited on the landing, watching George until he was out of sight.

George babied the plants all the way home. When he got to the lab, he had an area sequestered on the side wall to create a harmonious "garden" for his babies. He placed prominent signs reading "Do Not Touch!." He then set about studying the mystical properties of the Mortevida plant. He gave the purple edges to Helmut who sniffed a little and walked away with a dish of purple spores.

In a room specifically created for testing biological weapons and wearing a hazmat suit, George tested and tweaked the green centers of the leaves. Every time he cut the leaves from the mother plant, the cells would die and the poison would be rendered harmless. George had to find a way to keep those cells alive.

Finally, after years of experimentation, he believed he'd found a way. By distilling the leaves and extracting the oils, George was able to create a base capable of nurturing the cells.

The resultant poison was capable of replicating itself a million times over. George believed that once the poison was released into the air, it could travel thousands of miles. He also discovered that the poison would live for several days after being released, and then began to die off. The residue left behind was harmless, like the dead cells of the Mortevida leaves after they'd been cut from the host plant.

When one trial revealed that the structure of the poison broke down when exposed to saltwater thereby losing its toxicity, George concluded that the only deterrent to the poisons survival was saltwater. In a worst case scenario, a whole continent of human beings and animals could be wiped out within a matter of days, but once the poison hit the ocean, it would simply die.

When George reported his findings to Matthew Wilmer, Matthew was elated. George told him that he'd been working alone on the project. He hadn't trusted anyone else to handle the test tubes as it took only one broken test tube to wipe out the whole country.

Matthew decided that the 6 test tubes that had been created so far would have to be frozen and placed in the vault at once. He told George to keep the plants in the vault as well, and to lock up his research records.

The promises made to Maggie were forgotten, save for a standing order to send supplies to the rainforest once every month. He was so enthralled by his creation that he completely disregarded her threat of a curse. George would be famous, if only among ammunition manufacturers, but famous nonetheless.

George wanted to share his news with someone, but he was a single man and lived alone. He had no one to tell, so he put on his coat and drove to the little diner he ate in every night to see pretty, sweet Alice, who would smile at him and pour his coffee. Alice, with her auburn hair and bright green eyes, would bring him his apple pie. Alice would let him tell her his news.

Chapter 15

George and Alice had been married for 10 years. They had three kids, a boy and two girls. They lived in one of the small stucco houses Wilmer Chemicals had built for its employees in Los Arma, and there they raised their small family. George continued to work for Wilmer, which had recently changed its name to Wilmer and March Pharmaceuticals. George wasn't happy with the change, but he'd been given a raise and was still able to research to his heart's content.

Alice began feeling ill. She went to see Dr. Eisner and he found a serious mass on her left lung. She chose not to tell George right away. She felt it was nothing and would go away on its own, despite the doctor's admonition that it most definitely would not. But Alice didn't want to upset George, and she couldn't imagine dying with three small children to raise.

When Alice became unable to get out of bed in the morning, George contacted Dr. Eisner, demanding to know why he'd not been able to diagnose his wife's malady. Dr. Eisner told George that Alice had been told months ago about the mass but had chosen not to enter into treatment. George was angry at both of them.

Alice was sweet and pretty, but she didn't have a brain in her head. What had attracted George to her had lately begun to irritate the hell out of him. And now she was going to die and leave him with three small children to raise!

Try as he might, George found it very hard not to go into the bedroom and give her a piece of his mind. Instead, he went to the local bar where he had a few drinks and calmed down. After that day, George would stop there for a few drinks every day before coming home.

He arranged for a nurse to stay with Alice and to help with the children. When Alice died, George was having a drink with a young lady he'd met the week before at that very same bar.

When he got home that evening and the nurse gave him the news, George wrote her a check and thanked her for her service. He then called his sister in Toms River, New Jersey, and arranged for his children to live with his sister and her husband while he "sorted out some things." After the funeral, he and the children boarded a train to Atlantic City.

*****

1985 was not a good year for George Ranier. He was 65 years old, and he was being asked to start thinking about retirement. Helmut March had died 5 years before and his son had assumed the position as head of the chemical discoveries division. This gave him authority over George.

Matthew Wilmer had also died recently, and his son Jacob, who had been running the Wilmer and March operations in New Jersey, didn't have the same respect for George's value that his father had. Yes, Jacob knew that George had saved his father's life, but that didn't amount to dollars and cents, and that was what the company was about now.

George Ranier had outlived his usefulness to Wilmer and March, and his ultimate weapon lay frozen in the freezer vault, never to be used by any government. George's weapon had proved to be too powerful. The government officials who researched his findings decided that the weapon was uncontrollable and had the potential to wipe out the entire United States within a matter of days.

The officials advised Wilmer and March to destroy it, safely, and never produce it again. If it landed in the hands of enemies, it could prove disastrous. So Wilmer and March did the only thing it could do; the company placed the test tubes in the freezer vault and forgot about them. The research had cost them a pretty penny, and they weren't about to destroy years and years of work.

For thirteen years, the tubes languished at the back of the freezer, but they remained front and center in George's memories. Those test tubes were his babies. If George had to go, then his babies would go with him.

George prepared a place in his home freezer for the test tubes. He took his lunch box to work the next morning. George was friendly with the security guards who watched the video screens overlooking the vault. When he came to work that morning, he casually asked who would be working that night, just in case George had to work late. The guard at the desk looked up the schedule and told him Jerry would be working the late shift. George had cut a break. Jerry would be easy to distract with a Playboy and a beer.

As a senior staff member, George had the code for the vault. He also knew that security rarely checked the items that had been frozen over five years, and would have no reason to check on his babies. George was confident he could get into the vault and take his babies home without anyone ever knowing.

He left at his usual time of 5 p.m. He saluted the guards and walked to his car. He had left his lunch box in his office. He ate dinner at local Mexican restaurant and then went to a movie. By the time the show let out, it was close to 11.

George went into a small local drug store and bought a Playboy magazine. The store didn't have beer, so he settled on a bottle of Coke, anything to get Jerry into the bathroom. George then headed back to Wilmer and March.

Jerry was sitting at the security desk when George arrived. They exchanged pleasantries and then George offered Jerry the Playboy saying he had finished it and also gave him the coke. Then George headed for his lab.

Since the lab guys were always going in and out at odd hours, Jerry didn't think anything of George's being there. Also, as a senior staff member, George didn't have to clock in to show he'd been in the building. So, with Jerry happily gulping down the Coke, George waited. About an hour later, Jerry got up from his post, took the Playboy, and headed for the bathroom.

George quickly grabbed his lunch box, went to the vault, punched in the code, and opened the door. He went to the back of the vault to the freezer. He opened the freezer and moved the front items out of the way. There in the back, covered with layers of ice, were George's babies.

George noticed that the ice was stuck to the back of the freezer. He went back to the lab and got some warm water. He then went back to the freezer and used the water to melt the ice until he could gently pry the tubes away from the wall without breaking them.

George carefully placed the tubes in his insulated lunch box, secured the latch on the lunch box and placed it outside the vault. He then closed the freezer and the vault and headed back to his lab.

He collected his coat and left the lab, lunch box in hand. He passed the security desk and noticed that Jerry was still absent. He left the facility and took his babies home.

When George got home, he placed the tubes in his freezer in the specially prepared spot. He checked the seal on the freezer and decided he would have to get a generator that would kick off in the event of a blackout. He then turned off the lights and went to bed.

George had never stopped to think about what he had done. He only thought about his life's work being shut up in a vault, unappreciated and unloved. He never realized that he was also thinking about George Ranier.

George retired shortly after the daring rescue of his babies. Wilmer and March closed the Los Arma facility and left New Mexico. For a time, George worried that someone would notice his babies were missing from their inventory. He spent many a sleepless night during the facility's shut down, sure that someone would find the tubes listed somewhere. Everyone George had worked with on the project was dead, so when the final truck pulled out of Los Arma without so much as a knock on his door, George relaxed.

George had bought the house he'd been living in from Wilmer and March when they closed the Los Arma lab. He met a nice woman named Sylvia, whom he married in 1990. With his pension from Wilmer and March, George had a comfortable retirement. He had invested well and was careful with his money.

Sylvia was also well off, and they kept their finances separate. She would often ask George why he was so picky about the freezer shutting off. By now, George had graduated to a stand-alone freezer with a generator attached that would switch on if the power went out. George would simply say it was a quirk of his, but he wouldn't allow her to put anything in that freezer.

The freezer had a lock on it, and the key was in a safe deposit box. It had a special custom made seal to keep anything outside out and anything inside in. George was taking no chances of his babies escaping their frozen home.

Sylvia tried to get George to move away from Los Arma. Sylvia wanted to move to Albuquerque. She pushed and prodded George until he finally put his foot down. He told her that they would never move to Albuquerque. Sylvia had had enough. She didn't want to live in the sticks with an unreasonable man. She left George a year after they married and never saw him again.

George's children rarely spoke to him. Since he had deposited them on his sister's doorstep, they'd found they didn't need the company of their father, preferring that of their aunt and uncle. One of his children had died, but the others did send him cards for birthdays and Christmas. Other than that, there was little contact. His grandchildren followed suit.

His great-grandchildren, however, were a little more interested in their great-grandfather, especially with the advent of

Ancestry.com. His granddaughter Becky came out to New Mexico to meet her great-grandfather, whom she insisted upon calling Pop Pop. It was to differentiate him from her other grandfathers.

She and George got on famously, not only because of her resemblance to Alice, but also because she was charming. One day, Becky decided to move to New Mexico to keep Pop Pop company.

*****

The day after his birthday, George flipped through the channels. He stopped on the news and heard that the last of the nation's nuclear power plants had been shut down as the new amendment banning nuclear energy went into effect. He watched the smiling anchors talking about an accident on I-25. Suddenly he saw a picture of the Wilmer and March laboratory. The old building was being razed to build a highway that would run past George's house.

George had been feeling more useless than usual. The news about Wilmer and March and the impending highway didn't make him feel any better. He was 91, he had no friends, could no longer drive, was taking medication to allow him to do the most personal things, and the only contact he had with the outside world was with his doctor and his great-granddaughter.

George would never hurt Becky for the world, but he was tired. He had lived long enough. He decided to stop taking his medications. George knew that if he stopped taking them, he would eventually die. So, after hearing the news, he stopped taking his pills.

A few days went by and George didn't feel any different. He began to think that maybe he could just go on and on, that the medication hadn't been necessary after all.

A week went by before George began to feel a little funny. He was growing weaker. His head pounded from his blood pressure soaring. Without his diuretic, his feet were swelling.

George was just sitting down in his chair to take a nap when the thought struck him that if he died, his babies wouldn't be safe, nor would anyone else in the world. George had to get rid of his babies.

He decided to dig a hole, a deep hole in the back yard, away from the house. It had to be very deep. Oh, if only he could drive. He could go miles into the desert. But he was stuck here on the outskirts of Albuquerque, and he couldn't tell a soul what he had done.

George slowly made his way to the shed. He put down his cane and picked up a shovel. The dust was thick on the old shovel. George used it like a cane to walk out a ways from the house. He stamped the dirt to find a soft spot. He then began very slowly to dig small shovelfuls of dirt.

The sun was hot and George was feeling the heat. He had actually been able to dig down quite a ways. The hole had to be deep, not wide, so it wasn't as bad as he thought it would be, but he realized he'd better get out of the sun before he passed out.

George stayed in the house for a little while, cooling off. He was feeling a bit dizzy from the digging. He wanted to get his babies into the ground before dark, or he wouldn't be able to find the hole.

George went into the attached garage where he kept the freezer. A couple of weeks ago, he'd been in town with Becky and without her knowledge, had retrieved the key from the safe deposit box. He also took out his will and some jewelry he'd kept there. Then he closed the account for the box.

Now as he stood in front of the freezer, he wondered at the divine providence that had made him get that key. He hadn't been thinking about doing this at the time. It must be fate.

At that moment, George remembered the curse Margaret DeMorte had talked about. He thought about Alice, about his children, and about his lonely life and wondered if Margaret had found out what he was doing with her Mortevida plants. Maybe she had a native fulfill her promise of a curse. Maybe that's why George was so miserable and why he'd been such a terrible husband and father.

George opened the latch on the freezer and saw the insulated lunch bag. The bag was stuck to the ice. George opened it and removed his babies. They were frozen solid. They had been in that bag for 22 years. He shuffled to his kitchen table and placed them in the center. He put the napkin holder on one side and the salt and pepper shakers on the other so that if they tilted they wouldn't fall down.

George felt dizzy and weak and tried to sit down. He didn't make it to the chair. He collapsed onto his knees and then fell over.

Becky found him in that position when she came by that weekend. George had had a massive stroke that killed him instantly.

As she was rolling him over, his body pushed the table, knocking the babies over, causing them to roll to the floor where they broke into a million pieces. Becky fell like a stone as the poison entered her brain through her nose, killing her instantly.

*****

Within days the population of New Mexico was decimated, with other states going down fast. One by one, state after state fell in the wake of George's babies. There was no panic because people died so suddenly. Relatives separated by miles didn't know anything had happened to their loved ones as they too succumbed to the aggressive poison. No news anchors were left to report about it. People would be out shopping and drop where they stood. Bodies littered the streets and shopping areas. Office buildings were full of rotting corpses.

Soon, there was no one left in the continental United States. Within days of removing them from their safe hold, George's babies had ended all life in North America save for group people in a Florida biosphere, a bug-eyed terrier, and several very special children.

Chapter 16

The Wilmer Biosphere, Palm Harbor, Florida

Mindy ran through the "city" looking for Mark. She hadn't seen him at breakfast or in the library. She had looked in the store and had even gone to the field. Now she was headed for his house. She stopped for Baby Girl to give the dog some exercise.

As they approached Mark's house, Mindy looked around to see if anybody was watching. The girls didn't know about her relationship with Mark and she didn't want them to tease her. When she was sure no one was around, she went to his door and knocked. There was no answer. She turned the knob. The door opened, and she and Baby Girl went inside.

Mark wasn't there, but his bed was messed up. Mindy looked in the bathroom and found towels all over the floor.

"Slob," said Mindy out loud. Baby Girl wagged her tail in agreement. But it did look like he'd taken a shower that morning.

Mindy walked to the kitchen. There were no dishes in the sink, just lots of snack wrappers in the trash bin. Wherever Mark had gone, he was full and clean.

"Well, Baby Girl, I think I have to do this by myself. I think we should go find a grown-up."

Mindy and Baby Girl left Mark's house and walked toward the cafeteria. She saw Andrew sitting on a chair in the cafeteria drinking coffee and reading a magazine he had picked up on one of his runs. All items brought back had to go through the decontamination chamber, so the magazine was all wrinkled. Mindy slowed down as she approached him.

She had never talked to Andrew before, but Mindy knew he'd been one of the men who found her. She knew she shouldn't like him for that reason alone, but Andrew was always playing with the kids and he seemed really nice. She just couldn't bring herself to dislike him.

"Andrew," said Mindy. Andrew looked up from his magazine and smiled.

"Hi," he said.

His smile seemed to light up his whole face. "You're the little girl with the dog. What can I do for ya?"

"I was wondering." Mindy held her hands behind her back and looked upward. She bit her lower lip, rolled her eyes, and then looked at Andrew. "I wanted to know, well, do you think you could show me the outside?"

Andrew frowned. He wasn't sure what she was asking.

"The outside of what? You mean the outside of this facility?" Mindy nodded her head. Her short waves bounced up and down.

"I can't take you outside, sweetie. They'd never allow it. And besides, you'd have to go through decontamination, and that sucks."

"But I *really* want to go outside," Mindy said, just short of whining. She put her hand on Andrew's arm to show how sincerely she wanted to go outside.

Andrew stifled a grin. He made his most serious face.

"There's no way we're going outside."

Mindy lowered her forehead and squinted her eyes to show her disapproval. She made her deepest frown.

"But I really miss being out there. Please, please take me outside." She was whining now and getting on Andrew's nerves.

"Look, what if I show you around the whole facility, all the places in the biosphere? In the animal room there's a screen that shows you what the pasture looks like. It's just like being outside. What do you say I take you there?"

Mindy thought for a minute. If he took her to every room, she could imagine what it must look like from the outside. She could ask a lot of questions and figure out the lay of the land that way.

"Okay," she said, nodding her head.

Andrew got up from the table and put his coffee cup in the trash. He folded up his wrinkled magazine and put it in the long leg pocket in his jumpsuit. Then they headed back toward the field with Baby Girl in tow.

*****

Mark had gotten up early that morning. He was excited about the prospect of leaving this place and he wanted to get a jump on the research necessary to do it. He showered and stuffed a couple of bags of chips in his mouth, downed a can of soda, and left his house. He headed for the field but at the last minute changed his mind. It was very early, no later than 6 a.m., so no one was around. He turned instead towards the stairs leading up to the labs on the top floor.

He climbed the stairs quietly. He decided that if anyone found him going up the stairs he would just say he was trying to get some exercise. He got to the top and walked toward the metal doors leading to the labs. He quietly opened the doors and listened. When he didn't hear anything, he entered the hallway and gently closed the door behind him.

He tiptoed down the hallway. He noticed the labs were empty, so he kept walking until he got to the first chamber. The double doors were sealed shut. Mark knew the button on the right side wall would open those doors, but he didn't know if it would sound some sort of alarm. He couldn't remember from when they'd brought him in here because he'd been too pissed off and fighting instead of looking around. Now he wished he'd paid more attention.

Finally, he decided to take a chance and hit the button. The doors slid open. No alarm sounded, so Mark entered the first chamber and hit the button on that side of the wall. When that door closed tightly, he went to the next set of doors and repeated the process.

Finally, at the last chamber, he was standing underneath the hatchway to the outside. He knew that if he went outside, he would have to undergo decontamination, at least if he wanted to come back in for Mindy. He would have to decide what he wanted to do once he got out.

Mark climbed up the ladder until he could touch the hatchway cover. There was a button to his left that opened the hatchway. Mark pushed it. The hatch lifted slowly until it was standing straight up.

Mark stuck his head out the hatchway hole and looked around. It was a beautiful summer day. The sun was shining, and it must have rained because the grass glistened and the ground was moist. Mark continued to climb out of the hatch.

As he stood on the ground surrounded by nothing but air, Mark felt exhilarated. He looked to his right and saw the trucks the crew used to bring supplies to the facility. He turned around and saw that there was nothing in the back except a long empty field and woods. The woods surrounded the property.

There was only one road going in and out. The road ran through the woods. Mark headed for the road. He wanted to see how long it was and where he would come out at the end of it. He got to the road and walked away from the trucks toward the woods.

Mark walked for about a mile before the end of the road. He kept going for about another half mile. When he emerged from woods he found himself standing on an access road leading to U.S. 19 North. There was a sign reading "Palm Harbor 2." Mark had to make a decision. Would he just start walking, or would he go back and get Mindy and Baby Girl?

It would be so much easier to just go. The responsibility of a girl and dog seemed overwhelming to the 10-year-old boy. But he did like the idea of company, and Mindy was different from any other girl he'd ever known. But then again, Mark hadn't known any other girls. He hesitated for several minutes before deciding to turn around and head back to the facility.

Before heading into the biosphere, Mark walked toward the end of the facility. He walked quite a ways before he found the other hatchway door.

To his right was a large fenced-in pasture where the skeletal remains of animals lay roasting in the Florida sun. Mark wondered how they got there. There were big ones and small ones. There was a huge panel built into the ground that must have opened up to let them out. It was sealed tightly, but there were cameras mounted next to the panel, so whoever was inside could keep an eye on the pasture.

Mark also wandered toward the woods. He broke off branches of bushes and trees as he entered the woods so he could find his way back out. He was not more than a quarter mile in when he saw a clearing ahead.

In the clearing he saw several wind towers, their blades mounted high above the top of the woods. There were also solar panels mounted on tall towers.

"So this is how they get their power," Mark said out loud. He turned to the right and saw another clearing not far into the woods. Mark walked towards it. When he reached the edge of that clearing, he saw mounted in the middle, the biggest satellite dish he'd ever seen.

"So that's how they found us."

Mark couldn't wait to tell Mindy what he'd found.

*****

Mindy and Andrew entered the door leading to the field.

"The door to the animal room is this way." Andrew turned to the right and Mindy followed. When they went through the door, the smell almost knocked Mindy over.

87

"Ugh, what is that?" she said, holding her nose.

"We still have chickens here, and we never finished the filtering system so we can't open the vents just yet. But since the chickens are the only ones in here, it's not too bad."

Andrew went down the stairs that led into the animal room. Mindy reluctantly followed. She wanted to see as much of it as she could, especially the screen that showed the outside. They came to the bottom of the stairs and Mindy noticed a row of empty pens.

"There used to be cows and sheep in there," Andrew was saying.

"What happened to them?" Mindy asked.

"Gerald left them outside and they all died. Dumbass."

Mindy's eyebrows shot up. Andrew looked at her face.

"Sorry, sometimes I forget about kids' delicate ears."

He walked over to the chicken coops and said hi to the chickens. The chickens were clucking happily and scratching the ground. Their pens were wide open affairs built with plenty of room for each hen. They had access to grass in the front and a trough of water to the right. There were 20 hens and three roosters. Andrew was leaning over the fence and poking a rooster.

"Lucky dogs." He said with a smile. "I wish I had those odds."

"Odds for what?" Mindy was looking up at Andrew.

"The odds of having a date with 6 different women every week." Andrew smiled. He pointed to the roosters. "That's Sakima, Buster, and Jackson."

They walked over to the wall, where a panel had been built leading outside. There was about a half mile between the chicken coops and the outside wall. That would have allowed plenty of room for the cows and sheep to wander.

When they got to the wall Andrew pointed out the screen. Mindy had already seen it. She looked at the trees blowing in the soft breeze and could also see the corpses of the animals.

"Why didn't anybody bury them?" Mindy looked sad.

"Because we couldn't see any point in it. The sun is doing a good job of returning them to the earth. Besides, we were so messed up that first week, we never thought of it. Then Gerry found Maria Elena and that gave us something else to do."

Mindy didn't like to look at the animals. She and Baby Girl headed back towards the chickens.

"What's out there?" Mindy pointed to the back of the animal room.

"That's where Calvin lives."

"Where else can we go?" She was looking up again at Andrew.

"You know, there is a place we can go. And there is something there that you'll really like. Do you want to invite some friends to come too?"

Mindy thought for a minute.

"Yeah, I'll have to go find them."

They walked up the stairs and out of the farm area back into the city to find Maria Elena, Katie, and Alyssa. If they saw Mark along the way, they would bring him too.

*****

Mark looked at the satellite dish. It was huge and had U.S.A. written all over it. As he looked up, he noticed that it, too, was high above the woods. From what Mark could decipher from this vantage point, the wind machines and satellite dish were viewable only from an airplane. They would have been totally invisible from the road. If Wilmer had owned this land too, then he *could* have kept this all a secret.

Mark turned around and headed back to the facility. Out of the corner of his eye, he saw a body lying just to the right of the Satellite dish. He walked over to it. The body had on shorts and a polo shirt.

The polo shirt had a logo on it that said "Wilmer Biosphere" and the name "Jasper" written underneath it. The guy must have been out here working on the lines when the poison hit him. Mark backed away and again headed toward the facility.

He followed his broken twig trail until he was out of the woods. When he reached the front hatchway, he pushed the button and the lid slowly rose. As Mark climbed back in, he took one more look around the compound. Then he lowered himself in and pushed the button to close the lid.

When he got to the bottom of the stairs, he noticed Gerald going into his lab. He ducked to the side hoping to remain hidden. He waited but didn't hear the doors sliding open. No one would want to touch him anyway, not without the decontamination shower. He peeked around the wall and didn't see Gerald. Then he pushed the button to open the doors. This chamber was the decontamination chamber.

Mark turned on the showers. He figured he would have to go in clothes and all, so he plunged into the stream. He knew they were on a timer so he just stood there until the shower turned off automatically. He peaked out the door and still saw no one.

The doors were timed to open after so many minutes of the shower turning off, so Mark had to stand there and drip dry. When the doors opened, he slowly entered the next chamber and waited for the doors behind him to close. Then he pushed the button for the next set of doors. He was about to go through when he looked up and saw Gerald glaring down at him.

"Don't you dare move," said Gerald. "SIMON!"

Gerald was yelling for Simon to come and help "handle" this boy. In the meantime, Mark and Gerald stood watching each other. Mark figured he could outrun this old man, but if Gerald caught him he wasn't so sure he could win the fight. So he stood and waited for Simon.

Simon came down the hallway from one of the labs. He didn't seem to be in any hurry.

"What's up Gerry?" He asked.

"I found this boy coming out of the decon chamber. He's soaking wet."

"You been outside, kid?" Simon asked Mark.

"Yeah. That's why I took a shower, moron." Simon suppressed a smile because when Mark said 'moron' he was looking at Gerald.

"See Gerry, he took a shower. Everything is fine. Now, can I go back to my game?" Simon was addicted to the computer's solitaire game and could play only when he had a day off. Gerald was wasting precious playing time with this bullshit.

"Simon, we can't have these kids coming and going as they please. He has to be punished. We have to make an example of him." Gerald was a nice shade of red by this time.

"Look Gerry, I ain't their father so I don't have to punish them. I'm their indulgent uncle who visits on weekends and takes them to the boardwalk. If the kid took a shower, then there's no harm done. You want to keep them in, install a lock. Now, don't bother me with this shit again." Simon headed back to his game.

At that moment Christie entered the hallway from the city.

"What's going on here?" she asked.

"This boy went outside." Gerald was trying hard not to smack Mark's face.

"Well, it looks like he took a shower, so what's the harm?"

"What is wrong with you people? What if they all want to go cavorting outside, bringing their germs and contaminants back inside? Don't any of you have a brain in your heads?"

"Oh Gerald, shut up. Mark is the first one to even try to go outside. We'll just have to activate the lock on the doors to this hallway and that should solve the problem. The locks are there, I just have to have Andrew create the security codes. Come on, Mark, let's get you into some dry clothes."

"He doesn't leave this hallway. Do you hear me?" Gerald moved to the hallway doors. Christie stood and thought for a moment. She then turned to the right and entered Gerald's lab. Gerald looked anxiously at the door of his lab. When Christie emerged, she had a headshot of a Guernsey cow in her hand.

"You put that back this instant!" Gerald screamed at her.

"I will hand it to you as we walk out that door."

Christie put her arm around Mark and headed toward Gerald. She could see his eyes going from side to side. His anxiety was peaking. When they reached the door, Gerald grabbed the picture out of her hand and headed for his lab. Christie smiled at Mark, and they both walked out of the hallway onto the porch overlooking the city.

"Was that a picture of a cow?" Mark asked.

"Yup," said Christie. "That was Martha."

They walked down the stairs and into the city. Mark had missed breakfast, and as Mindy was meeting the chickens in the animal room, Mark and Christie were eating a late brunch and discussing the glories of the outside world.

Chapter 17

When Jacob Wilmer hired Martin Prevost to design his biosphere, he told him he had to have an area for himself and his wife that would replicate their Rumson, New Jersey, home. Their Dutch colonial house sat on a small incline, with a large sloping yard on the right and absolutely flat land on the left. The house had been built into the incline, creating this odd effect.

Over the years, rooms had been haphazardly added to the house making it hard for the uninitiated to navigate the huge residence, so Martin Prevost spent many days in the Wilmer home sketching rooms and furniture. With his sketchbook filled, he believed he had all he needed to reconstruct the Wilmer residence.

Preovst received fabric swatches and carpet samples from the home of the original designer. The designer had kept them "just in case." This is the type of service Jacob and Emily Wilmer were used to receiving when they were footing the bill.

Jacob accompanied Martin to Palm Harbor, Florida, to show him the land he'd purchased to create his underground city. The land he had acquired was huge, several hundred acres of flat land with good drainage and acres of woodland.

Together they plotted the position of the underground areas that were to be built – three laboratories, four hospital rooms, a "city" with a main street, cafeteria, library, and store, a mile long and mile wide growing field, a mile long and one half mile wide animal room, housing for the scientists and other experts, and 200 tiny houses, one for each member of his extended family. There would also be the aforementioned living quarters for Jacob and Emily. Jacob reiterated the importance of the residence replicating his home. Emily had insisted upon this.

When Jacob first mentioned his dream of living underground to avoid nuclear fallout, Emily thought he was joking. Their life in New Jersey was everything an elderly matron could hope for. She was a member of several committees; she belonged to a garden club and attended several charity balls a year.

Emily had no desire to leave her comfortable home and her beautiful sloping gardens to take up residence in a hole in the ground in Florida. It took many months and a promise of the replication of her home to get Emily to agree to Jacob's folly.

So as he and Martin walked the grounds of the Wilmer 21st Century Biosphere, he chose the section just left of the "field" to build his home. He told Martin that he would need a special room for Emily, a room where she could go and feel as though she were outside surrounded by nature and her garden. He just didn't know how he could do this if the whole residence was underground. Did Martin have any ideas?

"Well, we could build a virtual reality room." And so, Jacob Wilmer's underground home had a room with a view of his New Jersey garden, or rather, a room that was his New Jersey garden, where his Emily could sit and enjoy a simulated breeze while watering some beautiful hot house plants.

*****

Andrew took Mindy and the girls to the back of the building. Mindy thought they were going to the field, but Andrew turned right and led them to a door Mindy hadn't noticed before. It was hidden behind some potted plants.

Andrew had to get the key for this door from the labs. He turned around and asked the girls if they were ready to enter this amazing room. The girls all jumped up and down and yelled "YES!" He unlocked the door and bade them enter with his hand outstretched toward the room.

The girls were not impressed. What they walked into was an ordinary looking living room. The furniture was nice, but not what they had expected. Andrew could see their disappointment.

"Ladies, do not look so forlorn. This is but the beginning of our journey. Follow me and you will not be disappointed."

The little band headed for the next room on Andrew's agenda. They walked to a small hallway with a door on the right and a door on the left. Andrew stopped at the door on the right. He opened it and the girls filed in.

They were at the top of what looked like a large movie theater, seating for 225. The girls ooed and ahhed as they gazed at the elaborately appointed theater. It was a mini movie palace with a working organ in the corner and curtains that opened and closed. It had a stage for putting on plays. Jacob had thought of everything.

"Ladies, we must press on. The best is yet to come."

The girls followed Andrew to the room on the right. This door led to the special room that Jacob had created for Emily. There was

93

a switch outside the door that Andrew flicked on. Then he opened the door and the girls entered.

The virtual reality room was amazing. When inside the room, you had the feeling that you were standing outside in a garden. There was no smell, of course, as they hadn't brought in any real flowers yet. There were no simulated bug or bird sounds yet either. But the flowers looked real, as did the sky. It surrounded the girls, and Maria Elena began to cry.

"What's wrong?" Mindy asked.

"I miss my family. I miss the outdoors. I want to go home."

Maria Elena tried to find the door, but it was camouflaged. Andrew helped her and got the door open. She ran from the room and Mindy followed her. They ended up in the living room, where Maria Elena fell onto the large over-stuffed sofa with Mindy right behind her.

Mindy put her arms around Maria Elena and let her cry on her shoulder. Andrew came in and saw the girls together. He quietly went back to the virtual room to check on Katie and Alyssa.

Andrew told the girls to follow him and they left the virtual room and flicked off the switch. Andrew led them to the kitchen, where they marveled at the huge double ovens and refrigerator. Alyssa noticed a big panel on the floor of the kitchen and asked Andrew what it was.

"It's the basement. I haven't been down there in ages. Let's take a look."

Andrew pulled the panel up from the floor and laid it against the wall. He flicked on the light switch and descended the stairs. The girls were watching him go. When Andrew got to the bottom of the stairs, he looked around. He then looked up at the two little heads staring down at him and waved for them to follow.

When the girls got to the bottom of the stairs, they saw row upon row of supermarket-sized freezer units. They heard Andrew say, "That son of a bitch" under his breath.

Andrew then asked the girls to each take a side and count the units as they walked down the aisles. Katie went right and Alyssa went left. When they got to the ends, Andrew asked them, "How many?"

"I counted 10," Alyssa said.

"I counted 10," Katie said.

Andrew called the girls back.

"You've gotta see it, Andrew. The food is unbelievable. There's one with nothing but cakes!" The usually reserved Katie was overwhelmed by the sight of all that real food.

Andrew walked by the first two units. The first rows were different kinds of meats including beef, pork and fowl. The chickens in the chicken coops must have just been for laying eggs. There were bags and bags of frozen vegetables to have until the fields were producing regularly. There were birthday cakes frozen in anticipation of family celebrations. It was the birthday cakes that made Alyssa break down. She began to cry.

"I don't even know what day it is. I missed my birthday."

"It was my birthday, too, Lyssie," said Katie as tears rolled down her face.

"I'm sorry girls. If I'd known it would upset you, I wouldn't have brought you here."

Like most men who don't know what to do when a girl cries, Andrew did what most men do to relieve the tension in the air. He started tickling the girl's sides. The girls started to giggle between the tears.

"Come on, I think we better go see how the other girls are doing."

Andrew let the girls go up the stairs first. When they got to the living room, Mindy still had one arm around Maria Elena.

"We found a whole basement full of real food!" Alyssa yelled.

"Yeah, it looks really good. There are birthday cakes too," Katie said as she walked over to Maria Elena's other side. She sat down and put her arm around her too.

"Girls, it's time to leave. Everybody up." Andrew opened the door and let the girls leave before following them. He closed the door and made sure it was locked.

"Sorry, I thought it would be more fun." Andrew looked down at the girls.

"No, it was fun. I loved that room. And it was different. Thanks for letting us come." As usual, Katie took the lead. She and Alyssa turned and ran toward the center of the city.

"She's right, Andrew. It was fun because it wasn't the same old thing." Mindy smiled at Andrew. She motioned him to bend over and when he did she hugged him. Maria Elena also hugged him. Then the girls ran toward Mindy's house, leaving Andrew far behind.

*****

Andrew walked to the cafeteria. He went into the kitchen area where George was putting what they laughingly called lunch together. He was opening can after can of prepared spaghetti. He threw the contents of the cans into a big pot to heat up on the stove. He looked up when Andrew walked in.

George was a short, plump middle-aged man. What little hair he had was tousled wildly about his head. George didn't get much company when working in the kitchen and he welcomed Andrew heartily.

"Andrew my boy, what brings you to my humble establishment?"

"George, why do you do the cooking?"

"Why, it's my passion, my boy. Always has been. My medical degree was my parents' dream."

George had been hired as the biosphere physician, but no one ever got sick so he asked if he could prepare the meals. His only regret was that most of the food the crew found on their excursions was already prepared.

"What if I told you there was real food to cook located in a basement under Wilmer's residence?" Andrew waited for George's reaction.

George looked skeptically at Andrew. He knew Andrew liked to joke.

"You wouldn't joke with me about this, Andrew. This is too serious to me to joke about." George was frowning at Andrew.

"I'm not joking, George. Meat, vegetables, sugar, flour, you name it. I'd like to punch Wilmer in his fat, ugly face right now. How many weeks have we been eating that dreck?"

Andrew pointed to the big pot simmering on the stove.

"I was down there the first week I came here, but the basement was empty. It must've been that special crew he sent down from Jersey. They must've set it up. The son of a bitch never told *us* about it." Andrew was fuming.

George's face lit up. He rubbed his hands together and smiled.

"My boy," he said to Andrew, "Stop frowning. Tonight we dine al fresco!" He then asked Andrew to lead the way to the land of milk and honey.

Chapter 18

Mindy and the girls ate their lunch of spaghetti. They talked about the virtual room and the kitchen. They also talked about the basement full of food.

"I bet we eat better tonight," Katie said. "I hope we have a birthday cake."

Alyssa was staring dreamily into space. "I wanted to grab some of that cheese. I really miss cheese."

Mindy felt good today. Surrounded by her friends and knowing that future meals would be made with real food, food she could share with Baby Girl, made Mindy's heart warm. Then she remembered that Mark was still missing.

She also remembered that he wanted to leave the biosphere and she wasn't sure that she wanted to go anymore. These girls had become her sisters.

Mindy said she had to leave and she dumped what was left of her lunch in the trash. She put her tray on the stand. She waved at the girls as she ran out the cafeteria doors.

Mindy stopped for Baby Girl and then headed over to Mark's house. This time when she knocked, and Mark told her to come in.

"You're not going to believe what I found out there. I've been trying to make a map."

Mindy looked confused. "What are you talking about?"

"Oh yeah, I went outside this morning. I just thought of it and did it." Mark grinned at Mindy. "I couldn't sleep, and it was really early. I would've taken you but you were asleep."

"Did you even try to wake me up?" Mindy had her hands on her hips and her "Mindy" frown on her face.

"Well no, but Mindy, it was so interesting. Out that back door is the way to the woods. In the woods is this huge satellite dish that they must have used to find us." Mark was breathless as he spoke. He was so excited.

"And there are wind towers and solar panels for the energy. That Wilmer guy thought of everything. Oh, and there was a body of some guy who worked here too."

Mindy made a face and sat down on the floor next to Mark. She looked at his map.

"That's the pasture," she said, pointing at the area next to Mark's drawing of the fence with the dead animals in it.

"How do you know that?" Mark asked.

"I asked Andrew to take me outside. He said he couldn't, but he showed me all around. He showed me a place where Wilmer would have lived. It has a virtual room and movie theater in it. And underneath it is all this food in freezers." Now Mindy was breathless talking about her morning adventures. But there was no stopping Mark.

"I went up the road to the highway. It's a pretty long walk if we go at night. It might be too dark out there. We should go during the day, and we'll have to go soon because they're going to set locks on the hatchways." Mark waited for Mindy's reaction. When she didn't react, he looked over at Baby Girl.

"How much does she weigh?"

"I don't know." Mindy looked at Baby Girl too trying to figure out how much she weighed.

"There's a ladder to the hatchway. What if we can't get her up there?" Mark was petting the little dog.

"Well, I'm not going to leave her here!" Mindy stood up. She again had her hands on her hips.

"We're going to have to figure out how to lift her up. Maybe we can tie a rope around her middle." Mark put his hands around the little dog's belly. He tried to lift her that way and she yelped.

"Well, that won't work." Mark set Baby Girl down. The little dog's bug eyes looked at him and Mark could swear she had the same look on her face as Mindy. "Maybe we could put her in a back-pack and pull that up with a rope or something."

"I didn't see any rope around the field. Where would we get rope?" Mindy was feeling frustrated. This undertaking might be more than she and Mark could handle.

"Mindy, I don't give up easy, and now that I've been outside, I can't stay in here. You promised you would go with me. Don't give up on me."

Mark looked so cute. His eyes were so dreamy. Mindy knew she couldn't say no to him.

"I think we should take a walk around the animal field today. You have to see it. We can sneak in. There may be rope there. Let's put Baby Girl back inside and go there."

After they put Baby Girl in Mindy's house, Mark and Mindy went to the field. When they got in the door, Mindy took Mark's arm and turned right. They walked through the animal room door and down the stairs. Mindy showed Mark the chickens and the screen showing the pasture.

While they walked by the large animal pens, Mark spied a piece of rope tied to one of the walls in a pen. It was just long enough to hoist a little dog in a backpack up a ladder. While he was wrapping the rope around his hand, Mark looked up and saw Calvin watching them. He came down the stairs and walked over to Mindy.

"So, who invited you in here?" Calvin looked mad. Mindy wasn't sure if he was kidding or not.

"Andrew showed me this room today. I just wanted to show Mark." Mindy smiled her sweetest smile.

"That sugar don't work on me, little lady. And I see you're stealin' my rope." Calvin was glaring at Mark. "Now, just what do you need rope for?"

"To pull a little dog up a ladder." Mark was mad now himself.

"What's your name, boy?" Calvin walked closer to Mark.

"Mark. Mark Bennett."

"So that makes you Mark and Mindy, eh?" With that Calvin burst into a big smile. "Mark and Mindy, that's really funny." Mark and Mindy looked at each other and then at Calvin.

"You don't get it, Mark and Mindy. Well, I guess you're too young for that one. Anyway, Mark, what are you planning to do with my rope again?"

"I told you. We want to pull Baby Girl up the hatchway ladder." Mindy was frowning again. Why had he told Calvin that?

"And just why would that little dog need to go up there?"

"We want to go home." Mark looked genuinely sad. Calvin pursed his lips and looked at the floor.

"Son, we all want to go home." Calvin walked over and squatted down to look Mark in the eye. "We're all tired of living in this place."

"But we *can* live out there. I had everything I needed. I can live out there." Mark felt tears of anger welling in his eyes. He didn't want to cry in front of Calvin.

"Well, you kids did survive a long time out there." Calvin thought for a minute. "Where are you plannin' to go?"

"My house is near St. Petersburg. I live by the beach. Mindy's parents live there too."

Calvin's eyebrows rose when he heard that. He stood up and turned to Mindy.

"Little lady, you do know your parents couldn't have survived."

Mindy balled her fist and punched Calvin in the stomach.

"STOP SAYING THAT! THEY COULD BE ALIVE! THEY COULD BE!" Mindy's face was on fire. She was so red she looked like she would burst.

"Calm down, calm down, okay, it's alright." Calvin leaned against the pen wall. He looked like he was in pain. "When are you plannin' to leave?"

"They're going to set the locks soon, so I guess we have to go tonight." Mark stood up holding the tightly wound rope.

"Not a good plan. It's too dark out there at night. You wouldn't find your way to the highway, and even if you did, it's pitch black. Better to travel during the day." Calvin paused again. "What if I were to take you by car?"

Mindy and Mark looked at each other. They felt a spark of excitement.

"You would do that?" Mindy said.

"If you're determined to leave, I would. My conscience would never stand it if you got lost in the woods. At least this way you'd be safe, the dog would be safe, and I would know where to find you."

Mark wasn't sure he wanted Calvin to know where they were going. But he could always have him drop them off a few blocks away.

"I like the idea. What do you think, Mindy?" Mark asked.

Mindy thought for a moment. "I like it, too."

The three shook hands on their alliance. Calvin told them to meet him at the back room behind the field tomorrow morning at 6 a.m. He told them to bring some food and water in their backpacks, and any clothes they could fit in there.

Mark and Mindy went up the stairs and out the field door. They walked to Mark's house where Mindy said goodbye. She wanted to spend this last night with her friends. They shook, hands and Mindy walked to the cafeteria to look for Maria Elena, Katie and Alyssa.

Chapter 19

The next morning, Mark knocked on Mindy's door. She was awake and dressed, and she had grabbed an extra backpack at the store the night before for Baby Girl. Mindy opened the door and let Mark in.

"We've gotta get going," he said urgently.

"I know. I just have to make sure I have enough food for Baby Girl."

Mindy looked in the backpack for the umpteenth time. She had put several sticks of beef jerky in there along with all her clothes, cans of dog food, shampoo, and soap. Her pack was heavy.

"Will you hurry up?!" Mark was trying to control his temper. "Calvin told us to be there at 6."

"Do you think he'll go without us?" Mindy was looking down her nose at Mark.

Mindy took one more look around the room. She had no more excuses to stay. She had packed everything she needed.

"Okay, I'm ready."

She made a kissing sound to alert Baby Girl to follow her. When Mark and Baby Girl were out the door, Mindy followed, closing the door tightly behind her.

The trio walked to the back of the building to the door leading to the field. Mark opened the door and hurried inside, followed by Baby Girl. Mindy hung back, taking a look at the city she was leaving behind, along with her three best friends. Mark grabbed her arm and pulled her in.

"What's the matter with you today?"

"I just wanted to say good-bye. I'm going to miss my friends."

"That's why I didn't make any," Mark said as he turned left and went down the stairs to the field.

Mindy and Baby Girl descended the stairs slowly. As soon as their feet hit the floor, they began to walk faster to catch up to Mark, who was sprinting to the back room. So far they hadn't seen anyone who might ask where they were going. When Mindy reached the back room, she could see Mark talking to Calvin, who was getting one last cigarette in before donning his hazmat suit.

"Hey, little lady, glad to see you could make it." Calvin smiled wide when he saw Mindy. "You ready?" he asked as he put out his cigarette. "Last night before it got too dark, I took the truck to one of the parking lots and picked up a nice Mercedes to take us to St. Pete. Has a full tank and everything. I'm hopin' I get back before anyone notices the truck is missing."

Calvin opened the first set of double doors and they all walked through. Then he closed them and opened the next set. When they were all in the last chamber, Calvin secured his hazmat suit by lifting the headpiece over his head and closing all the zippers and Velcro closures. Then he climbed the ladder to the top and pushed the button that opened the hatchway.

The hatchway flew up and Calvin climbed out. Next Mark went up the ladder. He had the piece of rope in his hand. He climbed out of the hatchway and turned around to face Mindy. He lowered the rope.

Mindy put Baby Girl in the extra back-pack and tied the rope around the straps. Mark hoisted Baby Girl up the ladder and pulled her out, handing her to Calvin.

Then Mindy climbed the ladder and, with the aid of Mark's hand, got out of the hatchway opening and onto the ground. It felt damp. It made her knees wet. She stood up and Calvin closed the hatchway door. They all headed towards the road where the car was parked.

Calvin opened the back door of the car and Mindy, Mark, and Baby Girl all climbed aboard. The interior was leather and smelled musty. It also held faint traces of the scent of human decay. Mindy put on her seatbelt, but Mark refused. Baby Girl got on Mindy's lap and stood on her hind legs to look out the window.

Calvin got into the driver's seat. He had brought a flashlight with him that he put on the seat next to him.

"Hang on everybody, here we go."

Mindy rolled the window down so Baby Girl could stick her head out. Her little ears flapped in the breeze as the car picked up speed. When they finally got on the highway and Calvin pushed the car to 55, Baby Girl backed off. The air conditioner was on so Mindy closed the window.

"Wish there was radio," Calvin said. "I used to love cruisin' the highway with my music on. Just me and Miles Davis."

"Who's Miles Davis?" Mindy asked.

"Child, who raised you? They certainly left out a big part of your education. Miles Davis was just the greatest jazz trumpeter that ever lived!"

"Oh, I don't know what jazz sounds like. I do like Justin Bieber though." Mindy was watching Calvin for a reaction, but his head was completely obscured by the hazmat suit.

"Shit, Justin Bieber! That boy was the most overrated, why my daughter used to …" Calvin stopped talking.

"Used to what?" Mindy asked. Calvin was silent. After a few minutes he started talking again.

"Nothing, just nothing. Hey, Mark, Mindy, I want you to look at each other, and I don't want you to look out the window until I say so."

"Why?" asked Mindy.

"Just do it."

Mindy looked at Mark and he looked at her. They both started to giggle.

"We can't do this," Mindy said.

They turned away from each other and saw the bodies piled high on both sides of the road. They quickly looked back at each other.

"That's what he didn't want us to see," Mark said. "I saw that at my house, at least at first." They both looked down at Baby Girl asleep between them. They each started petting her. They rode in silence for a long time, then Calvin began to speak.

"Mark, we're going through Largo now. We should be in St. Pete soon. What street am I lookin' for?" Calvin asked.

"Pasadena Avenue. It's between Treasure Island and St. Pete Beach." Mark was getting excited. He would be home soon. Mindy was stroking Baby Girl.

"Is there going to be enough food there, Mark?" Mindy asked.

"Kinda late to be thinking about that." Calvin was looking in the rear-view mirror. Mindy could just see his eyes.

"There's plenty of food. I still had some and there's a Granger's not far from me." Mark was worried that Mindy might change her mind and go back with Calvin. "We have to get you a bike. Calvin, if you see a store that might have bikes, can you stop?"

Calvin looked at him in the mirror.

"I really have to get back, kid." He looked at Mark's face in the rearview mirror. "Yeah, if I see anything I'll stop."

A few miles from St. Petersburg, Mark spotted a Big Mart store.

"Calvin, over there, turn left."

103

Calvin saw the store too and pulled to the left. He didn't want the kids to go inside. The parking lot was full of cars. There were bodies everywhere.

"I'll go in and see what I can find." Calvin parked the car and got out.

"Keep the windows closed. I'll be right back."

Calvin grabbed the flashlight. He closed the door and the kids watched him pick his way through the bodies while he walked towards the Big Mart. Then they turned back to watching Baby Girl sleep.

About fifteen minutes later, they saw Calvin emerge from the store with a pink two-wheeled bicycle with a basket on the front and streamers on the handlebars. He opened the trunk of the car and put the bike inside. Mindy was glowing.

"Thank you, Calvin!" She was now as excited as Mark was. "Do you think Baby Girl will fit in the basket?"

"Might be a little snug, but I think she'll be okay." Calvin's eyes smiled at her.

They got back on the road going south. Calvin turned off the road at 18th Avenue South and headed towards the beach. Mark was grinning from ear to ear.

"It's really happening Mindy, I'm going home."

And then Mindy remembered her home.

"Calvin, can we go by my house?"

Calvin was silent. He knew what that child wanted to do and he didn't like it. He couldn't stand the thought of her hurt face, her crying, when she realized her people were long dead.

"Calvin?" Mindy was waiting for him to answer.

"I don't know where you live." Calvin was driving faster.

"I lived on 22nd Avenue. Can we please go by there?"

"Calvin, we gotta show her." Mark put his hands on the backrest of the front seats. "It's the only way she'll get it, Calvin."

Reluctantly, Calvin found himself turning off 18th Avenue South and heading towards 22nd Avenue. He tried to hold back his feelings for the sake of his little lady.

They reached 22nd Avenue and Mindy was earnestly watching as each house went by. She believed they were going in the right direction, but 22nd Avenue was long and they might have entered it at the wrong spot. Then she saw her school and knew she was getting nearer.

"There's my school!" Mindy shouted.

"How much farther?" Calvin asked.

"I guess, I don't know....maybe a couple of blocks?" Mindy grew anxious. She was so worried and so excited at the same time. Then she saw her little white house with the green shutters.

"STOP! It's right there."

Mindy stood up and put her finger in front of Calvin's facemask pointing left. He slowed down and stopped. He then reversed the car until they were parked in front of Mindy's house.

It was daylight but the house was dark inside. Like a lot of homes in Florida, the windows were covered to keep the intense heat out. The covers also kept out the light. They all exited the car and slowly walked towards Mindy's house.

Mindy stood at the front door. She turned the knob but it was locked. She turned and looked at Calvin. Calvin tried the door and then kicked it with his foot. It didn't open. Afraid to tear his suit, he looked around for something heavy. He found a rock and threw it into the front picture window, breaking the safety glass into a million pieces.

Mindy and Mark took rocks to break off the little pieces left in the window frame. They then climbed into the house. When they got in, they opened the door for Calvin to enter.

The house was very quiet. It had a musty, shut-up smell. Mindy walked from room to room but couldn't find her parents. Their bodies weren't there.

"Maybe they went to a neighbor's?" Calvin suggested.

"I don't understand this." Mindy was crying quietly. "I don't know where they could be. They should've come home by now."

Calvin walked to the back of the house and looked in the yard. There was a pool full of leaves and debris, but no bodies. The yard was clear.

"Well, do you want to check your neighbor's?" Calvin wanted to get moving.

"Yes, just the ones next door."

The little band, dog in tow, walked to the house on the right of her house and checked there. That door was open and the neighbors were sitting on the floor decomposing. They all left in a hurry and went to the house on the left of Mindy's house.

There the house was also open, and the little family of four was also dead. Mindy had known the children living there. She had played with them often. The sight of them lying on the floor that way made Mindy break down. She ran out of the house and into the car with Baby Girl close behind. Mark and Calvin closed the door of the house and walked to the car. Mindy burst out of the car yelling.

"I have to check something!"

She ran into the house. She was searching frantically for something her parents had given her before they left. She had forgotten to take it to Grammy's. Mindy found it in her bedroom on her dresser. It was a brochure from a hotel casino in Las Vegas.

Her parents had gone there and had given Mindy the brochure with the phone number in case she wanted to call them. She folded the brochure and put it in her pocket. She also took a picture of her with her parents and went back to the car.

"I really wish we had found her folks," Calvin said. "Where the hell are they?" Mark raised his shoulders up and down.

"It's really weird," Mark said as he got into the car and Calvin into the driver's seat.

Mindy soon joined them. After she buckled her seat belt, they headed back to 18th Avenue South and Mark's beachfront paradise.

Chapter 20

Mark's house was on a road right near the beachfront. You had to walk a few feet to the left to see the beach, but it was close enough. His parents had been trust fund babies who decided to live off the land, as long as the land was on St. Pete Beach.

They used their considerable fortunes to create a small haven for themselves and their son. Mark's father was Jeffrey Bennett, who'd had a brief career as a rock singer in the 1990s. He had one hit song, which he sold to a company that had used it in its commercials for five years.

His wife, Penny, was the daughter of a real estate king who developed most of the land on St. Pete Beach in the 1960s. She had inherited the bulk of his fortune.

Penny and Jeff insisted on installing solar panels in their home and encouraged their neighbors to do likewise. They dug a well and installed a reverse osmosis filtering system throughout the house. They built a garden where a pool had been, and they grew most of their food organically. On weekends they traveled to farms outside the area to pick up raw dairy products. They did not eat meat.

Mark was their pride and joy. Besides inheriting his father's musical talent, he also liked to work in his mother's garden. Penny home-schooled Mark, but even when she tried to get him to participate in home-schooling activities designed to give the kids social interaction with kids their own age, Mark preferred staying home. He just didn't like other kids.

Most of the kids he'd met during those outings just weren't interested in what he was interested in, and it was torture spending an afternoon with them hearing about television wrestling and TV shows about pawn shops. Mark would rather stay home and read a good book.

When he watched his parents die, he had tried to revive them. He had pounded on his mother's chest and begged his father to wake up. When that didn't work, he tried 911, but there was no answer.

Mark didn't know what to do with his parents. When their bodies began to smell bad, he went to the shed and found two tarpaulins his dad had used to paint the shutters last year. There was a rope on each end of the tarpaulins, so Mark rolled his mother into one and his father into the other. He pulled the ropes tight and tied them. He then rolled his parents' bodies one at a time out the front door towards the beach.

When he got them there, he put rocks in each tarpaulin, put them in a neighbor's motorboat and took them out to the ocean. He rolled them over the side of the boat, and as he watched them go down, he sobbed uncontrollably.

For the first two weeks, Mark was afraid to leave his house. He had enough food and the freezer was working. He had his video games and DVD's as well as all of his books to keep him company. He was afraid to go outside and find bodies. He'd seen some when he was taking his parents to the dock, and he didn't want to see any more.

The smell of rotting corpses grew stronger every day, but the wind blew strong there so it wasn't too bad. The sun was doing its job along with the humidity. The flesh was being eaten by insects, the only survivors of this catastrophe. By the end of the second week, the bodies had decomposed to bone.

When Mark decided to leave his house to search for food, he cautiously opened the door. The smell was much better, and he walked out into the sunshine. He looked around and noticed that not one body remained on the street. No bones, no clothing, just grass, street, and beach. He walked to the beach and looked north and south. He turned and walked north.

About halfway up the beach from his house, he found piles of clothing and bones. He turned around and walked south. Again, halfway from his house, he found clothing and bones littering the beach. The one mile stretch of beach near his house was completely void of debris. It was as if God, or aliens, or angels had reached down and swept them all away.

Mark walked back to the street and up the block. He didn't see one body, human or animal. The street had been cleared. Now he was starting to freak out a little. Was there someone else around here? He hadn't seen or heard a living soul for two weeks. Who could have done this?

Mark walked the three blocks to Granger's and saw that there were bodies left a few blocks away. The doors of Granger's were propped open so he walked inside. He took a shopping cart and started to walk up and down the aisles.

Mark's parents had shopped in health food stores so he was unfamiliar with the brands he saw. His parents didn't subscribe to cable so he hadn't seen commercials, except those his father's song appeared in. But those were for some computer, so no food brands there.

He looked at the labels on the boxes. They might as well have been written in Japanese. Finally, he just started filling his cart with whatever looked okay. Towards the back of the store the smell was overwhelming.

The fruits, vegetables, and meats that had been there were gone. But the smell of their decomposition lingered on. Again, who had cleaned them out? Mark contemplated this as he walked out of the store with the shopping cart.

If there was someone else there, he would have to keep his door locked. He would also have to find a store that sold guns so he would have some protection.

For the first time, Mark wished he'd gone to the home schooling parties and met some of the kids. He wished he had made a friend, someone whose voice didn't sound like his mother's or father's; someone who may have survived and could be with him now.

Mark's loneliness overwhelmed him. He was really all alone, except for some neat freak living within a mile of his house. He pushed his cart fast up the road and pushed it right into the house. He locked the door behind him and ran to the kitchen to lock that door too.

After he emptied the cart, he put it out on the porch and found a stick to put in the bottom of the sliding glass door to keep it from being opened. He checked every window to make sure it was closed tight and locked. After he had finished, he sat in the corner of the living room, and listened to see if he could hear anyone moving outside.

*****

A week went by without Mark seeing anyone, and then another week went by. He worked outside on his garden and kept close to the house. His vegetables would be ready soon, maybe another two weeks. His mom would have been so proud.

The next morning he woke up and heard something outside. He ran to the window. He could see a truck stopping in front of his house. He saw four hazmat-clad figures exit the truck.

"Geez, looks like somebody's been busy here," one of them said. "No bodies."

They were walking towards Mark's house. Mark panicked. He ran upstairs and closed the bedroom door. He locked it and put a chair in front of it. He forgot the connecting door in his parents' room.

He heard them talking in the living room. How had they opened the door so fast? Then Mark remembered he had walked outside last night to look at the moon. He must have forgotten to lock it. Mark backed away from the door. He tried to be really quiet.

"But Gerry said there was a kid here. We have to look or he'll be impossible," one of them said.

There were footsteps on the stairs. He heard them go into his parents' room. Mark looked at the connecting door. It was unlocked. He heard the knob being turned. His feet were frozen to the floor. He couldn't move. A man entered his room.

"Hey, there you are." The voice sounded friendly. But Mark was freaked out, and he made a run for it. The man grabbed him.

"Hey, it's all right. We're here to help you. We want to take you where there are other people so you're not alone. We won't hurt you."

Mark was kicking and punching, trying to get away. One of the other men grabbed his arms while the other tied a rope around his hands and feet.

"Sorry kid, if you calm down we'll take them off."

Mark kept moving, trying to get the rope off his hands. One of the men picked up his feet and the other his arms, and carried him downstairs and out to the truck. The other two men were waiting by the truck.

One opened the door of the truck while the other slid inside. The two men carrying Mark gently placed him in the truck while the third slid in beside him and closed the door.

"My vegetables are gonna die, you morons." Mark stared at them furiously.

The one on his right just looked at him and his eyes smiled.

"What a shame to lose fresh vegetables, but they were probably contaminated so it was for the best," he said.

The one on his right kept telling him jokes to try and get him to laugh. All the way back to Wilmer's, Mark refused to talk.

When he got to Wilmer's, Christie greeted him by squatting down and looking him in the eye. She asked him his name. He wouldn't talk. She stood up and held out her hand. He wouldn't take it. She asked him to follow her and he did, anything to get away from the hazmat idiots who put him through a decontamination shower without a change of clothes.

Christie led him past one tiny house after another. He saw a lot of kids walking around and talking. At the very last house, Christie said, "We're here," and opened the door to Number 200. Mark wasn't impressed.

Christie told him she would get him some things from the store and that dinner was in a couple of hours. She said there was food at the store if he was hungry now, but he would have to get that himself.

After she left, Mark took off his wet clothes and sat naked on the bed. He then fell into a sleep so deep that he never heard Christie come back with a change of clothes and soap.

When he woke up, he changed into the new clothes and walked outside. He saw Christie walking his way. He didn't think she saw him, so he went back inside and closed the door. He watched out his window until she had passed. He was going to open his door when he noticed someone following Christie. It was a girl with wavy blond hair.

She was cute for a girl, and she piqued Mark's interest. After she had passed his house, he cracked the door open and looked outside. He saw her going into a door at the end of the building. She was obviously sneaking into that room.

When she shut the door, Mark walked outside and ran to the door. He opened it and saw her hanging on the railing overlooking something. He quietly walked over to the railing and stood next to her. She was looking at a big field full of vegetables.

She turned suddenly when she felt him near her. He looked into her blue-gray eyes and thought she was an angel. He couldn't let her know that he liked her.

"Who are you?" She whispered.

"My name is Mark," he said.

They stared at each other for a few seconds and then back at the farm.

"That thing is really big," Mindy said. "How did they ever make that?"

"They dug a big hole," Mark said, and then he turned and went out the door. Mindy followed him.

"My name is Mindy," She said as she ran after Mark.

"Good for you," Mark said. "Now please leave me alone."

111

*****

Calvin noticed the lack of bodies littering the street where Mark lived. He mentioned it to Mark.

"Yeah, the beach is clean too, but just around here."

They all got out of the car and walked toward the beach. Baby Girl ran ahead with her ears flapping in the wind. When they got to the beach, Calvin surveyed the area. It really was strange that the beach was so clean.

"See, down there," Mark said. "You can still see stuff on the beach. And look down there."

Calvin agreed it was weird. He wished he could strip off this suit and smell the salt air and feel the wind on his face.

"I gotta get back, kids." And with that he walked back to the car. The kids followed behind him.

When they got to the car, Calvin turned to look at them.

"I wish I could hug you, but I'm afraid to rip your suit," Mindy said.

"That's okay, little lady. I can imagine it. Now, you hear me, big man, you take care of this woman, you hear?"

Mark nodded.

"I'll come back in a couple of weeks to check on you."

Calvin climbed into the driver's seat. He looked at the kids and waved. He then started the car and drove away. Mark and Mindy with Baby Girl at her feet, walked up to the house.

"Wait till you see my vegetables," Mark said as he let her inside the house.

PART TWO

ANTONIO RUSSO

But the Children Survived

Chapter 21

Florence, Italy

Antonio Russo was a good boy. His mama always told him so. He was a kind, loving boy with a keen interest in science. Even at the age of 6, he was already astounding his teachers with his keen observations. This made his papa very proud.

Antonio was devoted to his mama. He would follow her around the house and when someone asked him a question, he would whisper the answer in his mama's ear so that she could relay his response. He would often stand behind her when he was with strangers. Even though his mama scolded him for being too shy, secretly she enjoyed his dependence. It made her feel needed.

Antonio was born with a gift for persuasion. He could talk his papa into anything, but his mama not so much. When his papa asked Antonio why he always came to him with his requests, Antonio would reply, "Because mama always says no." Then his papa would look into Antonio's big brown eyes and give in.

As he grew older, he was able to talk most people into doing what he wanted them to do, and they wouldn't know how he had done it. He was charming and attractive, and he frequently used his powers of persuasion on the ladies, young and old.

When Antonio was 8 years old, his mama suffered a miscarriage. This was the latest of several she'd experienced over the last 8 years since Antonio was born. The doctor had warned her against having another pregnancy, but Ramona Russo was a devout Catholic who loved her husband very much, so another pregnancy was inevitable.

This was her fourth miscarriage. She was making lunch for little Antonio when she felt a sharp pain in her abdomen. Ramona was familiar with the pain and she cried out for Antonio to call the ambulance. She fell to the floor and passed out while little Antonio ran for the lady who lived next door. She ran to Antonio's apartment, shielding him from the sight of Ramona bleeding out on the kitchen floor.

The men from the ambulance tried to revive Ramona without success. Antonio grabbed her hand and held on tight as they removed her body to the ambulance. That night, and for many nights thereafter, Antonio cried himself to sleep grieving for his mama.

Antonio's papa owned a small bakery in Florence. His shop was near the university and, between the students and the tourists, Guido Russo was kept quite busy. When Ramona died, Guido began spending more time at the bakery and less at home with little Antonio.

He gave some money to the neighbor, Signora Calabrese to care for Antonio. Signora Calabrese was a widowed grandmother who indulged Antonio as if he were her own child. She encouraged his interest in science, and when he said he wished he could have saved his mama, she told him to learn his lessons well so he could find a cure for the loss of babies. With Signora Calabrese, or Nona as he called her, Antonio had been able to overcome his feelings of loss and was able to remember his mama with love and peace.

Antonio excelled in school, and at sixteen he entered the University of Florence to study biochemistry. His professors were impressed at the speed with which Antonio learned and were forever challenging him. Antonio would make a fine doctor one day they would tell him. But Antonio didn't want to become a doctor. He wanted to find a cure for the condition that caused his mother's continued spontaneous abortions. He decided to visit his mother's doctor, Dr. Fabiano, and ask him what he believed had caused his mother's miscarriages.

In the waiting room of Dr. Dominic Fabiano, Antonia was surrounded by pregnant woman. The women were all smiling at Antonio and occasionally would talk to each other and giggle. When he was called into the Dr.'s office, Antonio turned and bowed to the ladies.

Dr. Fabiano was a large, handsome man with a huge mane of gray hair. His eyebrows were bushy and his face was quite red. He stood when Antonio entered and told Antonio to sit down. Dr. Fabiano had delivered Antonio 18 years before and was delighted to see what a fine young man he had become.

"Ah, your mama would be so proud of you. You are so tall and handsome." He beamed at Antonio.

"Thank you, doctor. I came today to ask you something about my mother. I am studying biochemistry at the University and I wanted to know the cause of my mother's miscarriages."

Antonio watched Dr. Fabiano. He could see a cloud come over the doctor's face.

"Well, you know, Antonio, that is private information. I don't know if I should share that with you." Dr. Fabiano put on his most serious face.

"But surely when someone has passed away, it's okay to discuss these things with their families." Antonio flashed a smile at Dr. Fabiano. "My mama had a dream, Dr. Fabiano. Her dream was to help other woman to have children. I was with her when she died, Dr. Fabiano. With her last breath she said, 'Antonio, you must help the ladies' and then she died in my arms. I couldn't promise my Mama to her face, so I promised her in my prayers. Please, Dr. Fabiano, you must tell me."

Dr. Fabiano was truly moved by Antonio's plea, however fabricated it may have been. He could see no harm in sharing a dead woman's medical history with her adult son. He had followed protocol at all turns, even advising Ramona to use precautions to avoid pregnancy.

"You have argued well, young Antonio. Let me ask my nurse where your mama's file would be."

Dr. Fabiano slowly rose from the desk and walked to the office door. He opened the door and called to his nurse. He spoke to her in low tones and then turned around and closed the door.

After he sat back down, he told Antonio that he would have to order her file and would have it for him in a couple of days. He stood again and put out his hand, indicating to Antonio that the interview was over.

Two days later, Dr. Fabiano's nurse called Antonio to tell him the file was ready. He picked it up after school and read it on the bus home. His mother had a condition called cervical insufficiency. Her cervix would begin to dilate too early in the pregnancy. Her miscarriages would occur while she was well into her second trimester.

With Antonio, she had been ordered to bed. With her other pregnancies, she had been caring for Antonio and would not stay in bed long enough. In order to help women like his mother, Antonio would have to discover something that would help strengthen the cervix to keep it strong until the infant had reached maturity.

Antonio now had a plan to follow. He would study cervical insufficiency and find a chemical formula that would end this type of miscarriage forever.

*****

117

In the spring of 1987, Antonio was sitting in the university library. He had recently graduated with a master's degree in biochemistry and was working on his doctorate. Antonio was closing a book when he was approached by an older professor named Dr. James Wilmer.

Dr. Wilmer was the son of the pharmaceutical magnet Matthew Wilmer of Wilmer and March Pharmaceuticals. Dr. Wilmer had chosen a life in academia rather than join his father's research labs in New Jersey. His reason for approaching Antonio was to ask him about his research into human conception.

"I was told you are determined to end the spontaneous loss of pregnancy. Have you made any headway?"

Antonio noticed that Dr. Wilmer, while semi-fluent in Italian, would perhaps be more comfortable speaking English. Antonio, like many of his European brothers and sisters, had been taught English throughout his years in primary school and was fluent. He also believed that his American accent was superb.

"Dr. Wilmer, we may speak in English. I've been having little success in this particular field."

"I'm sorry to hear that." Dr. Wilmer sat down on the opposite side of the table. He had a file in his hand and he slid it towards Antonio. When Antonio opened the file, he found a Life magazine dated April, 1953.

"A magazine. A very *old* magazine. Thank you, Dr. Wilmer."

"Open it, Antonio. I've marked the page," Dr. Wilmer said. "I am trying to help you."

Antonio opened to the marked page. There was a picture of a young woman dressed in a khaki tailored shirt with buttoned pockets. She had short brown hair over which she wore a short-brimmed hat. She had expressive brown eyes. Behind her was a primitive looking village with grass huts and small, brown-skinned natives. The young woman was holding a strange looking plant with a dark green center edged in purple. The caption read "The Miscarriage Miracle in the Rainforest."

"Why have you shared this with me, Dr. Wilmer? You don't even know me."

Dr. Wilmer sat and thought for a minute.

"I heard you were a great student. I also heard you were a decent man. I don't know for sure, but I believe my father had some dealing with Miss DeMorte sometime in the 50's. My father

118

believed that all his kids should work a real job so we could all appreciate the value of a dollar.

"I worked in the warehouse for three years while going to high school. I used to pack up and ship out medical supplies to a woman in Brazil named Margaret DeMorte. One day I asked the foreman who she was and he said he had no idea, but the order came from the New Mexico labs. This has to be the same woman."

Antonio was looking through the article.

"It says this plant has been taken by the natives for hundreds of years to prevent miscarriage. Why would your father be sending her medical supplies?"

"I think he was trying to use her plants to create some sort of anti-miscarriage drug. That means he has research somewhere at Wilmer-March. But who knows? Maybe he just had a thing for her, or it was a tax write-off. I wasn't privy to that kind of information, and he never talked about it and other than the stuff I sent her. I never saw her name or the name of her plant anywhere else. If he had worked on a drug, it never passed trials or we would have heard about it. I just thought it might help you to see if this woman is still alive."

Antonio's eyes lit up. "Yes, I could ask her about this. It's a place to start. I was getting very discouraged. What a wonderful idea, Dr. Wilmer."

Dr. Wilmer smiled a weary smile. He remembered being that enthusiastic until time and disappointment had taken their toll.

"I would need to go to Brazil. I could take a sabbatical from my studies to go there. I'll have to ask my father to help me."

Dr. Wilmer looked at Antonio. He reached into his pocket and pulled out his checkbook. He wrote a check for $5,000 American dollars and gave it to Antonio. Antonio blushed and shook his head.

"Listen, kid, I've got more money than I know what to do with. Besides, if you can kick my brother in the ass with this money, that would make my day."

James Wilmer got up and reached across the table. Antonio took his hand and shook it.

"Let me know what happens, kid."

Dr. Wilmer turned and walked out of the library, leaving a very excited Antonio shaking from head to foot.

*****

119

Antonio arranged his leave from the university. When he told his nona, she cried and told him she would die while he was in the jungle. Antonio hugged the old woman, trying to reassure her that he would come back and she would see him again. He kissed her goodbye and, taking his suitcase in his hand, left the old apartment and headed to his papa's bakery.

Papa was pounding dough when Antonio arrived at the bakery. His papa was covered with sweat and flour. The older man looked at his son and tears filled his eyes. He knew his Antonio was on his way to a new life, even if Antonio didn't know it yet.

Guido walked him to the sidewalk outside the bakery and lit a cigarette. They stood there a few moments contemplating what to say to each other. They hadn't had much contact over the years, but they still loved each other. They just didn't have much in common anymore. After a few minutes of silence, Guido looked into his son's eyes, took his face between his hands, and kissed him on each cheek.

"I'm sorry I left you so long, Antonio. I missed your mama so much. Please don't forget your papa. You come back soon, you hear?"

"I will, papa, I have to finish my studies at the university. I will not leave you, Papa."

Guido cried and hugged his son. Antonio held his papa tightly. When they parted, Guido went back into the bakery and Antonio, brushing bits of flour off his jacket, walked to the train station to catch a train to Roma and the airport.

Chapter 22

Brazil

Antonio landed in Manaus, Brazil and headed for the Porto Flutuante, where he bought a ticket on a boat heading up the river. He hadn't been able to contact Margaret Demorte; however, he had found someone at the Italian Consulate in Rio de Janeiro who had heard of her and knew where he needed to go to find her.

The gentleman had also arranged for a guide to take him there. All he had to do was get to Itacoatiara, where the guide would meet him and take him the rest of the way. Antonio was thrilled when he reached Itacoatiara and he saw the guide standing by the dock with a sign that read "Russo."

They paddled up the river for several miles. Just before nightfall, the guide docked the boat at what appeared to be a dirt path leading into a dense forest. Antonio felt apprehensive, but he had no choice but to follow the small man, who seemed to be in an awful hurry.

They walked through the darkening jungle until they saw lights ahead. Antonio was swatting insects and trying to keep up while hauling a large duffle bag. Finally, they emerged into a clearing where several huts lined one side, with two larger huts on the other side. There was a really old Quonset hut at the end of the row of smaller huts.

The guide walked over to the first large hut and climbed the steps to the door. He knocked and entered the door and Antonio, who was waiting at the foot of the stairs, could hear him talking to the hut's resident in Portuguese. Then the little man turned to Antonio and waved at him.

Antonio left his duffle and went up the stairs. As he entered the door, he was greeted by a larger man. The guide indicated the big man could help him. The guide made a small bow and left Antonio with the large gentleman.

"You want to see Maggie. Why do you want to see her?"

The man looked to be in his late 60's, early 70's. He looked like one of the villagers Antonio had seen in the Life photo, but much larger. Antonio was glad to hear him speak English.

"I'm a student from the University of Florence. I read an article in Life magazine about Miss DeMorte. I wanted to meet her." Antonio was noticeably nervous.

"Life magazine, when the hell was that?" The man had a big face with small, oval brown eyes that were looking Antonio up and down.

"I believe it was dated 1953." Antonio waited for the man's reaction.

"1953! Are you crazy? What makes you think she's even here after all that time?"

Antonio sighed. He looked at the man and indicated with his hand that he would like to sit down. The man nodded.

"I'm here to ask her about her Mortevida plant. The article said she had found a miracle plant that helped women hold a pregnancy. I'm working on the same thing. I really need to talk to her. Please, is she still here?"

"There's a cot over there. You sleep there tonight. We'll talk about this in the morning."

The man turned back to the desk he'd been working at and finished his paperwork. Antonio went outside and got his duffle bag and brought it inside the hut. He placed it beside the cot, and the man got up to leave.

"Goodnight," he said and closed the hut door behind him. Alone for the first time, Antonio could hear the sounds of the jungle surrounding him. It felt like the loneliest place on earth.

In the morning, the scent of coffee wafted through the windows of the hut. Antonio sat up and threw his legs over the side of the cot. Then he saw the tall, thin, elderly woman sitting at the desk. She was looking at him.

"I spent many a night on that cot waiting for a mother to give birth," she said.

Antonio looked around and noticed the table in the corner with stirrups. This was a makeshift hospital room.

"Are you Miss DeMorte?" he asked.

"I am indeed. And who might you be?" Her hair was white now, but the hat shown on the cover of Life still sat on her head and her brown eyes sparkled mischievously.

"I am Antonio Russo of Florence, Italy. I read an article in Life magazine about your amazing plant and I came to ask you about it."

Antonio was looking at the floor the whole time he was speaking. Maggie was watching him with a benign little smile on her face.

"Why, that was a very long time ago. Where on earth did you find that magazine?"

"A professor at my university knew of my work and he gave it to me." Antonio looked up at Maggie.

"You have very nice eyes, Mr. Russo. Why don't you come outside and have some breakfast with me?"

Maggie got up and left Antonio alone to collect himself. He got off the cot and looked into an old mirror on the wall above the desk. He took a brush out of his duffle and worked it through his thick black hair. He looked around and was grateful to see a small bathroom with a door in the corner of the room. When he was done, he walked outside and down the stairs.

He could see Maggie and the big man from the night before sitting at a picnic table near one of the huts on the other side of the clearing. They were talking when Antonio walked up to them. Maggie indicated the spot next to her and Antonio sat down. A young girl brought him a plate of food and left.

"Do you need some coffee Mr. Russo?" Maggie asked.

"Yes, please," he replied.

Maggie called the girl and asked her to bring some coffee. Then she turned to Antonio. "What makes you think I'd give you my plants?"

Antonio was surprised by Maggie's candidness. He hadn't told the big man that he wanted to take her plants. He was going to work up to that. Antonio knew he had to be as persuasive as possible. He wanted her to believe his sincerity regarding his mission.

"My mother died on the floor in front of me when I was 8 years old. She bled to death waiting for an ambulance. It was her fourth miscarriage. I have all my life wanted to help women so this would not happen again." Antonio managed a very sincere expression on his face.

"That's a very tragic story, Mr. Russo. I genuinely feel for you. However, I trusted someone with my plants many years ago, and I will not do so again. I'm sorry you came all this way. You're welcome to stay for a few days if you like." Maggie had finished eating and she got up to leave the table.

"This is my friend, Mateo. If you need anything, he can assist you. Goodbye, Mr. Russo."

123

"Please, Miss DeMorte, please wait." Antonio followed her while Mateo jumped up and blocked his way. "I want to work with you. I want to learn from you."

Mateo was looking down at Antonio. Maggie kept walking away. Antonio went back to the table and sat down.

"Why won't she listen to me?"

"She didn't invite you here," Mateo said and walked in the direction Maggie had gone. Antonio sat dejected at the table. The girl came out and gestured towards his breakfast. He gave her the plate but kept his coffee.

That day Antonio watched for any opportunity to talk to Maggie. He saw her occasionally through the window of the other large hut, but she didn't come out again. He was very disappointed by her lack of understanding of his plight. He also couldn't understand why she hadn't taken to him the way other women had.

Antonio saw Mateo walking towards the jungle. He followed him and caught up with him just inches from the foliage. He grabbed Mateo's arm to get his attention.

"Please, sir, please, I just want to talk to her."

"You heard her. She doesn't trust you."

"But she doesn't know me!"

Antonio had a low threshold when it came to frustration. He was using all his strength to remain calm. His sad face must have had some effect on Mateo for he suddenly said, "Come with me." Antonio followed Mateo into the jungle.

"We don't get many visitors here. Maggie isn't used to talking about herself anymore. No one has found her interesting enough to visit in over 30 years." Mateo was cutting some of the leaves out of their way with a machete.

"I'm going to show you something," Mateo said.

They went a little deeper into the jungle. The insects were really doing a job on Antonio.

"We have to get you something for that," Mateo said when he noticed Antonio's discomfort.

Soon they stopped before a large tree. There were small purple particles around the base of the tree.

"Look behind the tree, but don't touch it."

Antonio walked over to the tree and looked around. There, at the back of the tree was the Mortevida plant in all its glory. It was magnificent to Antonio.

124

"That's the plant!" he said, smiling at Mateo.

"Yes, that's the plant. But don't touch it. The center will kill you in a heartbeat."

Mateo turned to walk back to the village. Antonio stood transfixed by the Mortevida. If the plant was so deadly, how did Maggie manage to cultivate them? Antonio had so many questions. Maybe she would relent if he pretended not to care about it anymore. Maybe she would just talk to him out of friendship. That's what Antonio would try.

That evening at dinner, Antonio asked if he could join Maggie and Mateo for dinner. Maggie said yes, if he would refrain from asking her about her plant.

"I'm sorry I offended you Miss DeMorte. I will only ask you questions about your life here. I'm amazed that you could live out here so long. Don't you miss the United States?"

"Well, when I first came here I did. But I have no family in the States so after a time I became used to it here. It's so peaceful here. The people accepted me and educated me. I in turn gave them what I had to give. We all got along swimmingly. Until lately, when for the first time this beautiful jungle is in peril." Maggie was referring to the daily encroachment upon the jungles of the rainforest.

"And now this is your home." Antonio was trying to make a connection with Maggie.

"Oh, yes. This is my home. I will die here."

Maggie looked wistfully at the little village. She had had such hopes that this place would be the cradle of discovery she had so longed to find. What she had discovered instead was that no one seemed interested in this part of the world, that they were more interested in toxic chemicals than natural substances that could save millions.

"Will you share with me some of the things you've learned here, the discoveries you've made besides the Mortevida?" Antonio's face was an open book. While he believed his face was pure innocence, Maggie could read him like a book.

"You're not going to go away, are you, Mr. Russo?"

"Please call me Antonio. I just want to learn." He could see Maggie's hard outer shell crumbling.

"Oh, very well. But I warn you, I'm old and when I'm done I'm done." Antonio quickly nodded. "Meet me by the infirmary tomorrow morning after breakfast. Good evening Antonio."

Maggie got up from the table and walked inside the hut. Mateo, who had been listening without speaking, looked at Antonio with hard appraisal.

"She's a good woman. She will help you because she wants to. But if you turn out to be a little snake, I will crush you. Do you understand me?"

Antonio nodded. He understood completely.

Chapter 23

Antonio stayed with Maggie for three months. During that time, she showed him all the plants she'd cultivated with the help of the indigenous people. After the first month, when it was clear Antonio was not leaving, Maggie decided to show him her Mortevida. She didn't make this decision lightly.

In 1953, after George Ranier had so thoughtlessly used her, she'd made a decision never to allow anyone near her miracle plant again. Maggie had been attracted to George the moment she saw him. He was a striking man, tall and muscular, and Maggie thought he looked like Cary Grant. She remained aloof for fear of appearing too interested.

However, by the end of the week, she had agreed to his request for her Mortevida because she felt George had intentions of returning to see her again. George had never said this to her, but Maggie still believed it in her heart. She was lonely and George had paid her so much attention that she naturally felt he was interested in her as well.

When the supplies began arriving, it confirmed her belief in George. She didn't know that George lived in dire fear of her showing up at the lab in New Mexico, demanding to see what he'd done with her plants. That fear had kept George Ranier authorizing supply shipments for 30 years.

But George himself never materialized, and after two years of pining for him, Maggie finally understood that George had only been interested in her plants. She was heartbroken and threw herself into her work, and she never forgave George, nor had she forgotten what he did to her.

Now, she had this cute little Italian panting after her day after day. Not bad for a 72-year-old woman! Besides, she liked to make Mateo jealous once in a while. It kept things fresh. She liked Antonio. He was such a flirt and she knew he was full of baloney, but she still found him so enjoyable that she could overlook his blarney.

"If you were Irish, I would have bet your mama'd hung you over the Blarney Stone straight out of the womb, Antonio," she would say. Antonio had no idea what that meant, but he would smile just as though he did.

He liked Maggie as well. For an old bird, she had it all going on upstairs. She never missed a beat. One day they were walking through the jungle and Maggie began telling Antonio how she happened to learn about the Mortevida.

"I'd been here a few months. The woman who acted as midwife came to get me one afternoon. She wanted to show me what they did for a woman who had suffered a previous miscarriage.

"The woman was in a hut and when we entered it I saw a cup filled with a purple liquid. The midwife gave it to the woman to drink. When the woman drank the liquid, her face glowed with a mild purple sheen. It was the damnedest thing I'd ever seen.

"The midwife explained that this is how they stopped the loss of the baby. Somehow this liquid tightened the cervix, allowing the woman to carry the baby to term. After a minute her face normalized, but I never forgot that glow. I asked the midwife where I could find the plant and she told me I couldn't touch it or I would die. Only what I now call a Mortevida baby could touch the plant. Subsequently, I discovered that if you hold only the outside edge, anyone could touch the plant.

"I started working with the midwife to see how she prepared the purple liquid. I thought this was a marvelous discovery that would benefit so many women. Back then there was a baby boom and pregnant women were everywhere. The midwife showed me how she would scrape the spores off the edge of the plant. She would then mix them with water until the mixture thickened slightly. Too much and the mother would gag, she said. That was all. It had been working for hundreds of years.

"She told me the babies born with the Mortevida spores never got sick and lived a very long life. She also told me one more thing. She said that Mortevida babies were immune from the poison of the plant.

"I asked her how they disposed of the poison center. She told me that once they are separated from the plant, the leaves will wither in a few days and lose their power. The cells that produce the poison dry up. I studied them myself because I didn't believe it could be that easy. But it was. The leaves wither and the cells dry up into tiny hard balls. They die and are rendered harmless. Then you can burn them for fuel or let them decompose naturally. It always amazes me how nature takes care of itself."

By the time they had finished walking, Antonio glowed with excitement. He could see himself creating a living elixir out of the

Mortevida that would save all women with cervical insufficiency from ever suffering another miscarriage.

Antonio also began to wonder if the Mortevida could help people already born. Could its amazing properties cure sickness and the ravages of old age? At dinner that evening he brought this up to Maggie.

"I've thought of that many times. In fact, Antonio, I was thinking of offering myself up as a sort of guinea pig for the sake of science," she said.

Antonio's eyes widened.

"I have a little secret that I've not shared even with Mateo. If he were here tonight, I wouldn't be talking about it. I believe I have cancer. I've been having a bad pain in my right side for some time. Nothing I take seems to stop it. Sometimes it gets so bad I long to touch the center of the Mortevida leaf. It would be quick and painless. But then I think that the spores might have some sort of effect on the cancer, maybe even shrink it."

"Have you tested your blood, anything to be sure you have cancer?"

"I'm relatively sure, and our local Shaman has confirmed it. Oh, look at your face. That man has powers, believe me. I've seen things in this jungle you can only imagine."

Antonio thought for a minute. "What do you want me to do?"

"I want you to bear witness, to record the experiment. If this trial is a success, then you would be famous as the man who found a cure for cancer!"

After pondering her request, he agreed to witness Maggie's experiment with the Mortevida plant. They agreed to meet in the infirmary the next day so he could watch Maggie prepare the liquid Mortevida elixir.

In the morning, Antonio had breakfast with Maggie and Mateo. Maggie explained that she had told Mateo what they planned to do and why. She told him about the cancer. Mateo slowly got up from the table and walked away.

"He has to be alone for a while," Maggie said to Antonio. "He'll come to terms with it in his own time."

When they finished eating, they walked to the infirmary. Maggie had already cut the leaves she planned to use and had them laid out on the lab bench. She put on gloves and picked up a small knife to scrape the purple spores into the mortar. She placed some on a glass slide and put it under the microscope.

129

She motioned for Antonio to come to the microscope. Under the microscope, the Mortevida spores looked like mildew spores with a brilliant purple color.

"Take a look," she said to Antonio.

Maggie then took her pestle and ground the powdery spores to better enable them to disperse in water. She gently poured water into the mortar until there was about a half cup of water mixed with the spores. The elixir was not too thick or too thin.

Maggie poured the elixir into a cup and handed it to Antonio while she got into the infirmary hospital bed. She then reached for the cup.

Maggie slowly drank the elixir, pausing only once to take a breath. When she was done, she handed the cup to Antonio. Antonio put the cup down on the lab bench and when he turned back to look at Maggie, he watched in amazement as Maggie's face glowed with a slight purple sheen.

The glow lasted only a minute, but the thrill it gave him lasted the rest of the day. That evening, they enjoyed a special dinner with a homegrown beverage that sent warm shivers down Antonio's spine. Maggie was having a good time with Mateo, teasing him about marrying her and making an honest woman of her. For the first time in three months, Antonio saw Mateo smile.

For the next two months Antonio monitored Maggie's vital signs. She seemed to be growing younger every day. Mateo noticed the changes too. Maggie reported that her pain had decreased considerably and that she was hopeful that the healing properties of the Mortevida were at work reducing her tumors and perhaps even destroying them. Whatever the outcome, she was glad she had participated in the experiment because she felt so damn good! Just like a teenager. When she said this, she would wink at Mateo.

As much as Antonio loved being with Maggie, he was longing for home. He missed his papa and his nona, and wanted to finish his doctorate. His time in the rainforest had been better than any classes he might have taken at the university. He'd learned so much from Maggie, and he truly believed he could never repay her for all her kindness. When he told Maggie that he would be leaving, she smiled and told him she understood. He was young and there was a whole world to conquer.

On the morning he was set to leave, Maggie accompanied him to the landing spot on the riverbank. She had a boy follow her with four Mortevida plants specially wrapped to protect Antonio from accidentally touching the leaves.

"You will take care of these plants, won't you, Antonio?"

Antonio nodded his head and grabbed Maggie in a big bear hug.

"I will protect them with my life," he cried.

When he let her go, she looked him in the eye and said, "Antonio, use them for good. Please use them for good, even if you have to do it on your own. The women need them. Don't let the greedy bastards keep this miracle away from the women who need it."

"I promise you, I will do this even if I have to do it in my basement."

They both smiled and hugged again. Maggie kissed him on the cheek and he kissed her on both cheeks. Antonio then handed her a slip of paper.

"You will write to me, yes?" He looked at Maggie with big puppy dog eyes.

"I promise to let you know how things progress. Goodbye, my Antonio. Go in peace."

Antonio got into the small boat with a boy from the village who paddled him upriver to Itacoatiara where he could get a boat to Manaus and an airplane home. He turned to wave to Maggie but she had already left the landing.

Six months after returning home, he received a letter from Mateo saying he had found Maggie's body lying in the jungle beside a group of her beloved Mortevida plants. She had stopped taking the Mortevida elixir because she thought it had cured her. Mateo said her pain returned and was growing worse every day. After much soul searching, Maggie had placed her thumb in the middle of a leaf. She had chosen to leave the world on her own terms, just as she had lived her life. Antonio wept as he remembered Maggie, and he vowed to use her discovery in a way that would make her proud.

Chapter 24

Colts Neck, New Jersey

Antonio sat at the kitchen table trying to read the morning paper and eat his breakfast. He was examining the little dog seated opposite him on the kitchen chair. His wife Teresa treated the dog like a favorite child, but Antonio drew the line at having a dog at the table when he ate his breakfast.

"Teresa! Chloe is in the chair again," he said. He stared at Chloe. "Get down." The little dog just stared back at him with her little brown bug-eyes.

Teresa came out of the bedroom and saw Chloe sitting opposite Antonio. The sight tickled her so much she broke into giggles.

"This is not funny, Teresa." Antonio didn't understand his wife's strange American sense of humor. "A dog is not to be at the table while I eat."

"Oh, Antonio, stop being so stuffy. She's so cute!" Teresa loved to tease Antonio. She sometimes purposely did things to see him get all ruffled. "Okay, I'll get her down."

Teresa walked over to the dog on the chair and shooed her off. Chloe obeyed Teresa by jumping down and walking to her bed. She sat down and continued to stare at Antonio from the floor. Antonio turned to see her staring.

"Make her stop," he said.

"What can I say? She adores you. Besides, all terriers stare." Teresa got a piece of toast and a cup of coffee and sat in Chloe's chair.

"I much prefer seeing your beautiful face to that of the dog." Antonio flashed his brilliant smile, and Teresa remembered why she had fallen in love with this serious scientist.

"I have something to tell you, Antonio." Antonio looked up from his paper. He lifted his eyebrows expecting to hear her tell him he would be a father. "Oh, no, not that," she said. "I'm thinking of breeding Chloe." She waited for his reaction. "No, no, no. I say no. I don't want any more dogs around here. I don't mind her so much because you love her, but no more dogs, please."

"Antonio, you don't keep the puppies, you sell the puppies. And Chloe is so cute. I was in the library and found out that people

132

are breeding Jack Russell Terriers with Rat Terriers. I could find a male just like her, and we could sell them."

"Aren't there enough dogs in the world without homes?" Antonio could see her closing in for the kill.

"I know Antonio, but it would be so much fun, and I would make sure each puppy got a good home. Please agree to let me do this. I won't ask you for anything. I'll do it all myself."

Antonio always had a hard time saying no to Teresa. She was the love of his life and he wanted her to be happy no matter what. But a house full of puppies!

"I don't want to agree to this." Antonio was trying to look stern. She smiled at him and teasingly batted her eyes.

"What can I do? You win. You always win." Antonio gave Teresa a stern look.

Teresa jumped out of her chair and hugged Antonio.

"I promise you'll never notice they're here." Antonio shrugged and smiled. He knew she meant it when she said it, but things rarely worked out the way she planned.

Antonio had fallen in love with Teresa from the moment he saw her walking across the University of Florence campus three months after he returned from Brazil. He followed her and asked her to have coffee with him. She looked at the handsome Italian and agreed.

Over coffee, she decided she would date this man if he asked her. He did, and over dinner the following evening she decided she would marry him if he asked her. He did, and three months later they were on their honeymoon in Roma.

Antonio received his doctorate in biochemistry at the end of the semester and Teresa was set to return to the States that spring. They packed up everything they had and moved to America to begin a new life together. They were confident that Antonio would have no trouble finding employment with his background and a Ph.D. If nothing else, he could teach.

Teresa would continue working on her degree in art and taking care of Antonio. For a while, they lived with her parents, Ed and Dorothy Schuyler, in Marlboro, New Jersey.

Antonio had brought his Mortevida plants with him from Italy safely wrapped and stored them in his father-in-law's basement with a sign that read "DO NOT TOUCH." He checked on them every other day to ensure they were alive and well. The plants were remarkably hardy and showed no signs of withering.

Teresa's father had a friend who worked for Wilmer and March Pharmaceuticals, and he managed to get Antonio an interview with the human resources director. Antonio knew the name Wilmer very well. James Wilmer, Matthew's youngest son, had given Antonio the money to travel to Brazil to meet Margaret DeMorte. The HR Director looked over Antonio's impeccable resume and called him back for a second interview.

Wilmer and March hired Antonio to head a lab in the new Cranberry facility researching new drugs in competition with Eli Lilly and Pfizer in the fall of 1988. Jacob Wilmer had moved his base of operations out of Freehold and into a sparkling new building in Cranberry two years before, shortly after closing the New Mexico laboratory.

As Antonio found his way around Wilmer and March, he often inquired as to how he could have a word with the man himself, Jacob Wilmer. He was told that he would need an appointment as Mr. Wilmer rarely spoke with the researchers.

Antonio spoke to the head of his department to see if there was any chance he may be able to do some research on his own time. The head of his department, Jake Rawlings, told Antonio that personal research was strictly off-limits. Jacob Wilmer always made the final decision on what would be researched in his labs and Antonio should forget about using the labs for any unauthorized experimentation. Antonio said he understood and went back to his lab.

His first assignment had been to create a new drug to combat migraine headaches. Antonio decided to take the opportunity to learn all he could at Wilmer's. He delegated tasks to his research team and worked tirelessly to fulfill Mr. Wilmer's orders.

He searched through the company's brand new computer databases to see if there was any mention of the Mortevida. If he was going to create something out of the Mortevida, then he didn't want to fight for the rights to it with a company like Wilmer and March. It had to belong to him and him alone. He owed it to Maggie to do the right thing with her miracle plant.

Antonio was able to supervise the lab and still research the computer with ease. He had good team members and he cultivated their loyalty by engendering a spirit of camaraderie. His assistants respected Antonio as someone who would do the grunge work right alongside them. They worked hard for Antonio, and he, in return, treated them with respect and an occasional night on the town. So when Dr. Russo was out of sight for a while, his assistants gladly covered for him.

One night just before falling asleep, Antonio remembered the conversation he'd had with James Wilmer regarding the summers he had worked in his father's warehouse. James had shipped supplies to Margaret DeMorte. Antonio wondered if he could find any of those old orders to determine who had been authorizing them.

The next morning, after handing out the assignments in his lab, Antonio headed for the computer room. He'd been running searches on the Mortevida plant, purple spores, etc. Now, he ran a search for Margaret DeMorte. He came up with nothing.

Antonio got up from the computer desk and walked to the elevator. He took the elevator to the main lobby. There was an old security guard sitting behind the reception desk, and Antonio casually approached him.

"Excuse me, sir, but how long have you worked for Wilmer and March?"

The old guard looked Antonio up and down. He checked the security badge attached to Antonio's lab coat carefully and then answered him.

"I've been with the company since 1948." He sounded tired and it was only 10:30 a.m.

"I'm new here. I was wondering, where was Wilmer and March before it moved here?"

Antonio was sounding more Italian by the minute. Maybe the old guy would take pity on the poor foreigner and help him out.

"We were in Freehold, right by the railroad tracks." Then the old guy sighed.

"Thank you, sir. Thank you very much." Antonio turned to walk away and then a thought struck him. "Sorry, but are any of the men from the warehouse still here? The men from Freehold?"

The old guy thought for a minute.

"There might be someone. Yeah, a guy named Charlie has been here a long time. He must have been there too. Just go to the warehouse and ask for old Charlie."

"Thank you, thank you, sir," Antonio said with a small bow.

He started running to the warehouse with the old guy shouting at him to slow down. Antonio got to the warehouse and stood in front of the door. He pushed the buzzer. This area was heavily guarded as the drugs were stored here until they were shipped. A disembodied voice began to speak.

"Who is it?" the voice asked.

"I'm Antonio Russo. I'm the supervisor of pharmaceutical research. I want to see old Charlie."

"Charlie S. or Charlie R.?"

Antonio was stumped.

"They just told me to ask for old Charlie."

"Old Charlie? Oh man, you must mean Charlie Weise."

The door opened and a man in a company jumpsuit came out and stood before Antonio. He was tall with a full head of brown hair and brown eyes. He wore glasses and a Yankees baseball cap.

"Charlie Weise retired last year. I can give you his phone number, but that's about it."

Antonio thought a minute.

"Can you tell me anything about Freehold?"

The man looked to be in his forties. He may have worked with James Wilmer.

"I started in Freehold out of high school, 1965. What'd you want to know?" The man's security badge read Paul Christopher.

"I have some questions about shipments from the warehouse in the 60s."

"This official?" Paul was watching Antonio.

"Well, ah, no. I have a personal reason for asking."

"You got some time?" Paul turned to walk back into the warehouse. He turned at the door and held out his hand. Antonio stood watching Paul, not knowing what to do next.

"Your coat, give it to me."

"Why, I just asked a question." Antonio pulled his coat around him.

"No, no, I want to put your coat in the office until we come back."

"Come back? Where are we going?" Antonio took his coat off while he walked towards Paul.

"It's time for my break. Let's go into town and get some coffee. I'll drive."

Chapter 25

Paul and Antonio walked over to a small Mercedes Benz delivery truck. Paul unlocked the door and Antonio got in. They drove to Route 33 and headed towards Freehold. Paul turned onto Route 9. When they got to Freehold, Paul turned into the parking lot of the Jersey Freeze. They parked the truck in front and walked inside. Paul told Antonio to take a seat while he ordered.

"This is the Jersey Freeze, Antonio, the best ice cream store in Freehold. You want anything?" Paul asked.

"Just coffee, please."

Antonio found a seat by the window and slid into the booth. Shortly thereafter, Paul walked over to the table with two coffees. He put them on the table and went back to the counter. He returned with the biggest sundae Antonio had ever seen.

Paul put the sundae down and slid into the other side of the booth. He put the plastic spoon into the mountain of orange sherbet with marshmallow sauce and whipped cream, scooped out a huge spoonful and shoved it into his mouth.

"Man, that's the best. Better than drugs, sex, booze – anything. I come here for lunch every day and I have one of these. I don't give a shit what my doctor says. Let every artery clog. I just love this."

He scooped up another spoonful and gulped it down. Antonio stared in wonder at Paul's total ecstasy over the frozen mound of sugar and fat. The idea of diabetes kept popping into his mind.

"Don't let them fool you, Antonio. This is unbelievably wonderful."

"It looks nice," was all Antonio could think to say. He sipped his coffee and waited for Paul to speak. When Paul finished his sundae, he sat back and rubbed his stomach.

"Sorry man, I just love that shit. I know it's bad for me. But it gets me through my day, if you know what I mean." Antonio just nodded politely. "So, you had some questions about the old Freehold facility. You know, they still own it. That's where they house the old files."

Antonio felt the hairs on the back of his neck pop up.

"The old files, like from the sixties?"

"Yeah, and older than that. Wilmer's grandfather started there building guns and shit, and his dad started the lab. The place is filled with files." Paul took a swig of coffee. "What are you lookin' for?"

137

"I met James Wilmer in Florence when I was in school. He told me he sent medical supplies to Brazil. I wanted to see who authorized them." Antonio waited for Paul to answer.

"I worked with Jimmy in the warehouse. His dad was a ball buster. He made his kids do the grunt work. Said it built character. Well, Jimmy was a character all right."

Paul slapped the table and laughed at his joke. Antonio stared at him.

"Not funny, huh? Well, anyway, Jimmy and I would pack those boxes once a month. I remember they sent different stuff every month, kind of rotated it. This month thermometers, this month antibiotics. Always the same different stuff if you know what I mean. Never varied. No new medicines, etc. Nothing invented after 1955, it seemed. Like they were emptying out the warehouse and sending it to the rainforest. I used to imagine all these little brown kids with thermometers hanging out of their mouths. They are brown right?"

"Yes, they are brown, I was there." Antonio had finished his coffee. "Is there a chance we can go there, to the warehouse here?"

Paul thought for a minute.

"Let me make a call." Paul got out of the booth and dropped the paper items into the trash. He went outside to the pay phone. Antonio saw him speaking to someone. Paul hung up the phone and motioned for Antonio to come outside.

When Antonio got outside, Paul was getting into the truck. Antonio got into the truck and Paul started the engine.

"I called in to tell them I would be checking out the warehouse here." Paul said as he pulled out of the Jersey Freeze onto Route 9.

They headed towards Main Street and crossed over the railroad tracks. At the first right, they turned and parked in front of an old factory building. Paul got out and walked to the padlocked door. Antonio followed him inside once Paul got the door open.

The whole factory floor was covered with shelving units filled with banker's boxes. Antonio could see signs taped to the top of each row with a year written on it.

"Up here we've got the thirties and forties. Next section should be the fifties and sixties."

Paul headed towards the next section by walking towards the back of the building. Antonio once again followed him.

When they got to the middle of the building, Paul stopped and pointed to his left.

"Fifties that side," he then pointed to his right, "and sixties that side. What year you want to search?"

"The year you worked here with Jimmy."

"1965 it is."

Paul turned right and walked down the aisle. He got about halfway through and stopped. He waved Antonio over.

"This is the row for 1965. Up and down."

He pulled a box off the top shelf. He placed it on the floor between him and Antonio. Paul pulled the lid off. He moved his fingers along the file tabs so he could read them. He found one from January that said "Medical Requisitions," pulled it out of the box and handed it to Antonio.

Antonio eagerly looked through the file. There was one page listing a shipment to Margaret DeMorte. It listed what supplies had been sent and where they were going. Under authorized it said M. Wilmer.

"Who is M. Wilmer?" Antonio asked.

"That would have to be Jacob's dad. It might have been a standing order, you know, the same over and over. It wouldn't require real signature. They would just kind of rubber stamp it."

Antonio felt so disappointed. He knew that any file they found here would be the same.

"How do we find out who started it?" Antonio asked.

"Geez, I have no idea. This was going on for a long time before I worked here. And according to this," Paul took the paper from Antonio's hand, "it didn't originate here. The original order came from New Mexico, see?"

Antonio looked at the paper. On the bottom of the paper under location were the initials NM.

"New Mexico! Wilmer's has a lab in New Mexico?"

"Not exactly, and I'm not supposed to know this, but in the forties or fifties daddy Matthew left his old man to build a lab in New Mexico. He was really building a lab to create biological weapons. Now you didn't hear that from me. It's all very hush-hush now that they've gone all respectable, but that's where old Matthew started.

"I think the name of the place was Los Arms or something like that. Jimmy told me about it. I do know they abandoned the place some time ago and shipped all the shit from there here. We were told they were consolidating and it was more 'cost effective' to ship from the east coast. My ass. Since when is it more cost effective to ship anything from New Jersey?"

"And the weapons?"

"I don't think they ever created any. They did come up with some great over-the-counter stuff, but the lab was really small. Jimmy went there once. He said it was divided into two sides. That's how he found out about the weapons. He snooped around and got the old guy in charge of that side talking. Scientists like credit for their work and this guy was no exception. Jimmy said the old guy almost spilled all the beans and caught himself."

Paul looked thoughtful. "Geez, I can't believe I remember that. Anyway, the old guy must have been sitting on something big because he really had to hold back. Weird nothing came of it. All we were ever told was that it was an old lab due for retirement. The weapons side was never mentioned."

They were both sitting on the floor now, resting against the shelves. Antonio was thinking about Maggie and the man she'd given the plants to. He had promised to use the plants for good. Was he the old guy creating weapons?

"What happened to the employees there?" Antonio asked.

"Don't know. Maybe some transferred here, but I don't work in the labs at all so I don't know. I do know Betsy in HR though. She could tell you if any of them transferred here."

"She's been with Wilmer's a long time."

"Oh, yeah. She's the one that got me the company. She's my mom."

After Paul put the box back on the shelf, they walked out the door and he put the padlock back in place. Before going back to Cranberry, Paul stopped at the Jersey Freeze and picked up another sundae to go.

Paul talked all the way back about Freehold in the sixties, about going to high school and realizing years later that the skinny sophomore he picked on during his senior year was Bruce Springsteen. He talked about how much Freehold had changed and how sad it was. Antonio talked about Florence and his dream of creating a drug to save babies.

When they got back to Cranberry, Paul took him up to HR and introduced him to Betsy. He handed her the bag with the sundae in it and shook Antonio's hand.

"Drop by anytime, Antonio," Paul said as he walked away.

Betsy was a nice-looking, chubby blond woman in her early sixties. Antonio asked her if anyone had been transferred to Freehold from New Mexico three years ago. She nodded her head.

"Oh yeah, we got plenty of them. I had to process them all in. What you asking for?"

"I need to talk to someone about the lab. I have a question to ask them."

Betsy looked skeptical. She wasn't sure if this was an appropriate thing to do. She had little knowledge of the New Mexico lab, but she did remember things that had been whispered about when she came to work at Wilmer's as a young girl out of secretarial school. Someone snooping around asking questions about that might cause her no end of trouble. She was too near retirement and her pension to mess around with that.

"I'm sorry, but without their permission, I can't tell you."

"I understand, Betsy. A beautiful woman like you with an important job like this, you must do the right thing."

"Son, you're full of it." She looked at Antonio and sighed. Paul had introduced him to her, so maybe he was okay. "What kind of stuff are you trying to find out?"

"Years ago someone was sending medical supplies to a woman in Brazil. I just want to know who was authorizing those shipments."

"Your English gets better and better, doesn't it?" Betsy sat down by her computer. She had glasses around her neck on a jeweled string, and she placed them on her nose.

"I'll see if I can find out who had the authority to do something like that." She started typing and then stopped. A screen came up that said "org chart". She looked at the names and titles of each individual listed.

"Looks like John Wilmer, Helmut March, and a man named George Ranier were the only ones with that kind of authority in New Mexico. It was a small lab. Looks like Helmut ran one side and George the other. That's all I can give you. I hope it helps." She turned and looked at Antonio.

"*Grazie mille!*" Antonio took Betsy's hand and kissed it.

"Yeah, whatever." She took her hand back, waved Antonio away, and turned back to her computer.

*****

141

Antonio went to the public library that evening. He asked the librarian if there were any books on Wilmer and March Pharmaceuticals. She looked in the card catalog and pulled out a title in the reference section.

"'Wilmer and March: The Founding of a Dynasty.' You'll find it in the reference section under R806.7. There's another librarian up there if you can't find it."

Antonio made his way to reference and, with the help of the other librarian, was able to find the book. It detailed the founding of Wilmer and March as a small lab in Los Arma, New Mexico. There was no mention of weaponry whatsoever.

The book discussed Helmut March's contribution to the founding of Wilmer and March, but George Ranier figured in only one paragraph, where he was given credit for discovering a prophylactic lubricant that would not cause irritation. Antonio was becoming very frustrated.

When he got home that evening, he told Teresa what he had been up to. He explained that unless he could guarantee full ownership of the purple spores, Wilmer and March could swoop down and take all his research away, claiming any miracle drug for themselves. Or even worse, keep it from being used at all.

"Why don't you take a little vacation in New Mexico?" Teresa offered.

"You wouldn't mind?"

"Of course not, besides, I'll be busy finding Chloe a mate."

Chapter 26

1988 Los Arma, New Mexico

Los Arma hadn't changed much since George Ranier traveled there in 1947. It consisted of a large, two-sided empty laboratory, several small houses, most of which were empty, and a convenience store with a gas pump.

Antonio rented a car in Albuquerque and asked for a map showing the route to Los Arma. The woman behind the counter had a hard time finding it on the map until a co-worker gave Antonio directions.

When he drove into Los Arma, Antonio felt as though time had stood still. The houses were all from the late 1940's, built by Wilmer to house his employees. The one car he saw was at least ten years old, and the convenience store was made of wood.

Antonio parked his car in front of the store, walked up the two wooden steps, and entered. There was a counter on one side where an older man was drinking coffee. Behind the counter was a short, round Mexican man. Antonio approached the counter.

"Excuse me, please. My name is Antonio Russo. I am looking for someone." Antonio put out his hand and the man shook it.

"I am Javier. This is a very small place. Who are you looking for?"

"A man named George Ranier. I believe he used to work here for Wilmer."

At the sound of the name Wilmer, Javier spat on the floor and muttered a Spanish curse.

"May he rot in hell," said Javier.

"Yes, I agree. He's a bad man. But, can you help me? Do you know where Mr. Ranier is?"

Javier began wiping the counter with a rag. He shook his head.

"No, I don't know this man. I have been here for a short time. Sorry."

The man drinking coffee got up, put a dollar down on the counter and left the store. Antonio thanked Javier and ran after him. He saw the man walking down the street and ran to catch up to him.

"Excuse me, sir," he called. "Please, sir, I just want to talk to you."

The man stopped and turned around. Antonio guessed he was in his late 60s. He was very tall, and his form suggested he may have once been well muscled. He stood looking at Antonio.

"Well, what do you want?" the man asked impatiently.

"Excuse me, please. I wanted to ask you if you knew Mr. Ranier. He was a scientist with Wilmer and March, and I believe he still lives here. Can you help me?"

"Well, the first thing I would ask is why you want to see Mr. Ranier. Do you have some sort of prize to convey upon him?"

Antonio thought for a minute. He suspected this was George Ranier, but wasn't completely sure.

"I have to ask him a question only he can answer."

"Really?" The man paused. "Well, you might as well come in."

The man turned towards a small run down house with a picket fence. He opened the gate and Antonio followed him to the front door, leaving the gate open.

"You mind closing the gate there fella?" Antonio rushed back and closed the gate.

Once inside, it was hard to see. There were heavy curtains on the windows, and the man hadn't left any lights on. The sun was blazing outside. It took a few minutes for Antonio's eyes to adjust.

"Sit down, Mr. Russo was it?" Antonio took a seat next to the window. The man plopped down on his recliner.

"Yes, my name is Russo. You can call me Antonio."

"And you can call me George. Now what in the blazes brings you out here?"

"Mr. Ranier, ah George, I need to ask you a very important question. Do you remember going to the rainforest in 1953?" Maggie had told Antonio that this was when George had visited.

"God, what makes you ask that?"

"I went there myself to find Margaret DeMorte. She said you had been there also."

Antonio watched George's face for any sign that he knew what Antonio was going to ask. George hid his feelings well.

"Well, I guess I did then. That woman would never lie. She was a handsome woman. Smart too." George had a funny little smile on his face, and then a shadow crossed over it, making him look a little gray. "What made you go there?"

"I read about her marvelous plant in a magazine. I have a desire to help women who miscarry. I want to make a drug out of her plant."

144

"That wouldn't be an article out of Life magazine would it?"

"Yes!" Antonio beamed. "I went there to see her plant because of that article."

"How is Maggie?" he asked.

"She passed away," Antonio said quietly.

George sat back and looked at the ceiling. "She was a good woman," he said. Antonio nodded in agreement.

"I read the article, too. I saw an opportunity for the lab. Matthew Wilmer didn't agree, but I went anyway. She gave me some of her plants in exchange for medical supplies."

"So you were the one who sent them."

George nodded. "So, is that what you wanted to ask me?"

Antonio squirmed in his seat. He wasn't quite sure how to phrase his question. What if George himself had a patent on the purple spores?

"Is Wilmer still studying the Mortevida plant?"

"Wilmer never studied the Mortevida plant. I studied it." George could feel his blood pressure rising.

"Then they have no interest in the plants, or patents on them?"

George could see where the little *goomba* was heading. He could put him out of his misery and admit there were no patents, or he could play with him a little while longer to see what the kid was up to.

Rising from his chair, Ranier said, "Look Russo, I'm a tired old man who was 'retired,' let loose from a job I loved, to sit in the desert and rot. Jacob Wilmer never gave a damn about me or my research. I made the best damn..."

George stopped himself from saying more. He was standing over Antonio and his face was very red. He stood there trying to compose himself before he gave away his secret. He didn't want to endanger his "babies" safely hidden in the garage freezer.

"Best damn what, sir?" Antonio had been hanging on his every word.

"Nothing. Best nothing. That's what it was. The answer to your question is no, no patents. Nobody showed any interest in using the plants. Truth is no drug company is interested in curing or saving anything. That would put them out of business. So, whatever you want to do with the Mortevida, go and do. No one at Wilmer's gives a damn." George walked back to the recliner. He sat down and sighed deeply.

"What about you, George? Would you allow me to have the Mortevida spores free and clear? How do I know you won't sue me for them later on?"

"Anything I did was under Wilmer's banner. I can't lay claim to the research. It all belonged to them." There was bitterness in George's voice.

"I'm sorry they treated you with such disrespect, George. You seem like a nice man." Antonio paused and looked around the sad, dreary living room. "Well, thank you, George. I am most appreciative of your help."

Antonio rose from his seat. He walked over to George and put out his hand. "I wish you well, Mr. Ranier."

George took his hand and shook it. He even managed a small smile for Antonio.

"Son, you make your drug, but you protect it. They'll eat you alive if they find out you've got something they want. I don't think Jacob Wilmer remembers anything about that plant, but that doesn't mean anything. His father knew everything that went on in that lab. He knew I brought those plants back and kept them in my lab.

"Don't be surprised if some lawyer digs up some dummied-up file saying they own the Mortevida, some lawyer that will falsify patents. Change the name of it if you have to. I don't believe Maggie would mind you covering your ass. She was all about helping people. If that's the only way you can get your drug out there, then lie and keep on lying for the rest of your life."

George was holding tight to Antonio's hand. Antonio pulled it away.

"I won't say a word, son. I don't want anything from this but your word that you will give those bastards a black eye."

Antonio nodded his head. He asked George for his telephone number in case he had any more questions and George gave it to him.

Antonio walked to the front door, bowed, and walked out the door leaving George with memories of the rainforest and a pretty woman who had made him think, if only for a minute, of staying in the jungle forever.

Chapter 27

All the way back to New Jersey, Antonio thought about what George Ranier had said. He hadn't thought about Matthew Wilmer. He hadn't thought about written research from the New Mexico labs. He had searched the computer for any mention of the Mortevida spores and found nothing. What if there were files from the fifties mentioning George's research locked up in Freehold?

Antonio was going to have to ask Paul Christopher if he could get him into the warehouse on a weekend so he could search those files to see if there was any mention of the Mortevida spores or the research regarding them. Only when he had checked those files would he truly feel free to begin his work on a miscarriage drug.

He also thought about George's suggestion of changing the plant's name. Had Maggie ever filed for the patent on her discovery? Antonio didn't know how to find out this information. He was growing tired of all the loose ends he had to deal with in order to create his miracle drug. He was a scientist, a researcher; why did he have to deal with all this? It was time to find someone to help him, someone professional who could give him advice.

When Antonio returned home, Teresa greeted him at the door with a big smile on her face.

"I found him! I found him Antonio and he's perfect!"

Antonio was looking at her as though she had gone mad.

"The father for Chloe's puppies!"

"Ah, the dog daddy. Yes, I remember. Where did you find him?"

"The vet said she knew someone with a combo like Chloe and she contacted them. They told her about Rocky, the daddy dog. She gave me Rocky's parent's phone number and I called them. They agreed to have the dogs meet. I'm going there this weekend. Would you like to come?"

"Not this weekend. I have to work to make up the time I missed. It breaks my heart to miss it, but what can I do?"

Teresa rolled her eyes at Antonio.

"You could be a little more convincing, you know. But I understand that work comes first. I just finished my finals and I'm off until September. That gives me the summer to have the puppies and raise them until they can be sold. How was your trip? Did you find what you were looking for?"

147

Antonio told her about George and what he said about ownership of the spores. She agreed that Antonio needed an attorney. She told Antonio she would talk to her father in the morning and see if he knew anyone.

"No, Teresa, don't ask your papa."

"But why?" Teresa looked perplexed.

"Your papa has ties to Wilmer and March. If they ever find out what I'm up to, they'll ask him. It's not for lack of trust, Teresa, but to protect him. It's better if he truly knows nothing."

Teresa could see the logic in Antonio's words. It would be better if her father could be truthful if asked about Antonio's research. Antonio was glad she didn't press further because, in truth, he didn't trust her father and his connection to Wilmer and March.

Antonio tried to think of someone he could trust to ask for the name of an attorney. Everyone he knew in the States worked for Wilmer and March. When he came up with no one, he reached for the Yellow Pages.

He flipped through the splashy ads and looked instead for the small ads featuring a name and phone number. There were hundreds of them and Antonio finally closed his eyes and just pushed his finger down on the page. When he opened his eyes he looked at the name his finger landed on. It was Stephen McKenzie, Esq. He wrote the name and number in a notebook he had purchased on the way home. He was going to document everything he did from now on.

The next morning Antonio called Mr. McKenzie before he left for work. The secretary who answered said that Mr. McKenzie could see him on Friday afternoon at 3 p.m. Antonio jotted the time and date in his notebook and went to work.

It was very hard to concentrate on the migraine research he had to review. He was anxious about all he was planning to do. Could he pull this off? Could he make a drug that would save millions of babies?

During his break, he went to see Paul in the warehouse. He asked if Paul could get him into the Freehold warehouse over the weekend.

"Geez, Antonio, I don't know. The Yankees have a home game this weekend. My friend's got tickets." Paul shrugged his shoulders.

"Could you just let me in? You can go to the game and come back for me later."

Paul laughed. "The game's in New York, Antonio. I won't be back till late at night." Besides, Paul thought, if the little guy

148

screwed something up then it would be Paul's ass on the line. He seemed okay, but you never knew.

"I don't think so, Antonio. I like you and all, but it's my job, you see?"

"What if you made me a key? How would they know?"

Paul thought about this. There were three keys, and generally they weren't locked up because they were in the office and the office was pretty secure. Anybody could take one.

Paul put his finger up and left Antonio standing in the parking lot. He went inside the warehouse and came back out a few minutes later. He walked over to Antonio and put his out his hand. Antonio shook it and Paul put the key in his hand.

"There's this idiot working here, his name is Ben. If they notice the key gone I'll blame it on him. The guys will back me up because he's a real moron. Just give it back to me on Monday. Just remember, Antonio, leave it like you found it, understand?"

"*Capice.*"

Antonio smiled from ear to ear. Paul waved and went back into the warehouse.

That evening Antonio told Teresa he was going to the attorney's office on Friday. He left her to think he was working on Saturday. He told her he would be in the vault and she wouldn't be able to communicate with him, but he would be home early, around 3 p.m. She was so excited about meeting Rocky that she just kissed his cheek and didn't question him further.

"I'll try to take a picture of him. I just can't wait to see them together," she said.

Teresa was cooking dinner. She looked so happy. Antonio couldn't understand how this whole process of creating puppies could bring such joy to Teresa. He liked animals well enough, but she seemed a little too obsessed with Chloe, a dog with little personality.

Antonio looked at the dog sleeping in her little bed. She had a long body, not like a dachshund but more like a small barrel, and her legs were not that long either. Her head was small with a short snout, a button nose, eyes that bulged a little like a frog, and a tail that curled slightly at an upward angle. When Chloe was happy, she would shake her head from side to side and go around in a circle as if she had worms.

Antonio shook his head. He just couldn't appreciate Chloe's inner beauty. For Teresa's sake, he hoped that Rocky could.

149

The week went by so slowly that Antonio's patience was sorely tried. He was short with his assistants. He was short with Chloe and yelled at Teresa frequently. So much was riding on his meeting with the attorney, a man he didn't know at all. He could be a complete charlatan, for all Antonio knew. He might take Antonio's money and rat him out to Jacob Wilmer.

All week long, Antonio's stomach churned. Finally, Friday arrived. He went to work early so he could leave at 2:30. The attorney's office was in Freehold, so Antonio gave himself plenty of time to get there.

The office was in an old Victorian home on Main Street. Antonio took the stairs to the second floor and was greeted by an older woman who had a sweet expression and asked Antonio to take a seat.

"Mr. McKenzie will be with you shortly. Can I get you anything?"

Antonio shook his head and thanked her. He sat down and she resumed her position behind an old oak desk. There was an electric typewriter off to one side and a large file cabinet farther over. The woman began typing.

Antonio looked at the magazines on the table next to him. Forbes, Newsweek, Time, and Sports Illustrated. He picked up the Time magazine.

Just as he was about to read, Mr. McKenzie came out of his office and greeted Antonio. He was an older man, maybe in his fifties. He had silver white hair, horn-rimmed glasses, an expensive suit and tie, and wingtip shoes. He introduced himself and asked Antonio to come into his office.

Antonio was surprised by Mr. McKenzie's office. It was a very plain affair, a modest desk, a file cabinet, family pictures on the walls, and a dog sleeping in the corner.

"That's Chester. He's a German Shorthaired Pointer. Had him since he was a pup. Now he's 10 and lazy. Hope you don't mind him."

Antonio said no and they sat down, Mr. McKenzie behind the desk and Antonio opposite him in a comfortable wingback chair.

"So, Mr. Russo, my secretary said you didn't give her any specifics with regard to this visit. How can I help you?"

Mr. McKenzie had a very calm air about him. His manner put Antonio at ease. The office surroundings suggested a man who wasn't interested in showing off his wealth, but rather someone who had a desire to genuinely help his clients, no matter how much money they did or did not have.

"I have to make sure about confidentiality."

"Confidentiality between an attorney and his client is sacrosanct. If I were to violate it, I would lose my license."

Antonio believed him. He began to recount all that he had been through, about Maggie, about his trip to New Mexico, and about his plan to search the files on Saturday. Mr. McKenzie listened attentively. He took notes on a yellow legal pad and when Antonio finished his story, Mr. McKenzie spoke.

"You were very wise to seek counsel, Mr. Russo. I've done some work for the Wilmer's in the past, and they aren't the most pleasant people. They also have a gaggle of lawyers hired just to watch out for people like you. You say this Mr. Ranier told you that there are no patents on the purple spores."

"That's what he said, yes."

"And you're not sure if Miss DeMorte had a patent on her plant?"

"No, I never thought to ask her when she was alive."

"If you retain me, I'll do some research through the patent office to see if any patents were ever filed for or granted. I'll also look into Mr. Ranier's background. Tell me, Mr. Russo, have you any idea why James Wilmer gave you the $5,000?"

"No, sir, he just said, ah, he said that he wanted to, ah..."

"What, son? What did he want to do?"

Antonio blushed slightly. "He said he wanted me to kick his brother in the ass."

Mr. McKenzie laughed out loud.

"Son, if you knew the things I've heard in my life. It's refreshing to see someone can still blush." He laughed some more and then he looked seriously at Antonio.

"Mr. Russo, this is a very serious undertaking you have planned. Do you believe you have the guts to go all the way with it? The Wilmers are mean bastards. They'll kill you if they think you are taking something from them.

"We have to cross our T's and dot our I's. Mr. Ranier's suggestion of a new name isn't a bad idea at all. After I check for patents, we'll discuss a new name for your plant, because it's now going to be your plant.

"I also have to find out how Brazil feels about this, quietly of course. I don't want to wake a sleeping giant now, do I?"

151

He smiled at Antonio, who felt so relieved to have someone to help him at last. He had no trouble trusting Mr. McKenzie.

Mr. McKenzie told Antonio that he wouldn't be noting Antonio's foray into the Freehold warehouse.

"I would have to disavow knowledge of your search, Mr. Russo. I cannot be a part of it. Do you understand?"

"But what if I find out they have research there? Won't I have to tell you?"

"Mr. Russo, if they have research there, then we are at an end. They'll have the right to stop you if they figure out that they own research that supersedes your investigation, especially if you create something that could hurt them financially. On the other hand, if there are no patents and we can find no ownership of the plants, then you can give them a new name and we can go forward applying for a patent for you."

Antonio again felt overwhelmed.

"All I want to do is save women and babies."

"I understand that, Mr. Russo, and I'll do everything I can within the law to help you create your drug. We will enter into an agreement by which you will pay me a flat fee of $1,000. If I find that the investigation requires more work than anticipated, I'll prepare an addendum to our original agreement for another $1,000. I'll send you a report of my findings as soon as I'm able to acquire more information."

Mr. McKenzie pulled a Fee Agreement out of his drawer and handed it to Antonio. Antonio read it and signed it at the bottom.

Mr. McKenzie rose from his chair, indicating that the meeting was over. He came around the desk and opened the door. Antonio got up and followed him.

"This is my secretary, Grace. If you need to call, you'll most likely be speaking to her. Talking to her is like talking to me. You can trust her. You can leave a check with her. It was very nice meeting you, Mr. Russo. I'll be in touch."

Mr. McKenzie disappeared into his office. Grace smiled at Antonio. He pulled out his checkbook and wrote a check, which he handed to Grace. She in turn wrote him a receipt and gave him Mr. McKenzie's business card.

"Call us if you have any questions Mr. Russo." He nodded and left the office.

All the way home he thought about what Mr. McKenzie had said about Wilmer being capable of killing him. He knew the

Wilmers were tough, but he hadn't thought he was putting his life in danger.

And what about Teresa? The more he pondered his plan, the more his fear grew. Tomorrow he would carefully check the files. He would make sure there was no research there. He had to find out, but he also had to protect his family. For the first time in his life, Antonio was not sure of the path he was following.

Chapter 28

Saturday morning Teresa rose early. She loved the springtime. She and Antonio had bought a house in Colts Neck after they drove down Route 537 and fell in love with the area. Teresa's parents gave them the down payment as a wedding present.

Teresa loved that she could pass horses grazing on her way to school. Today the daffodils were in full bloom and she looked outside at the riot of yellow that covered her front lawn. She was waiting for her friend Lorraine to come so they could take Chloe to meet Rocky. Antonio had left early that morning, and she and Chloe were all alone.

Chloe was acting funny. She kept hanging around Teresa's feet. Teresa looked at her and tried to see if there was something wrong. The little dog was lying on her side. Teresa noticed tiny drops of something red on the floor. She took a paper napkin and wiped Chloe's nether regions.

The napkin revealed tiny spots of blood. Teresa rolled her on her back and looked at her tiny vagina. It was swollen. She would have to cancel their meeting with Rocky today.

From what Teresa read, they would have to be brought together 10 days from now if she wanted to get Chloe pregnant. She called Rocky's parents, the Sheridans, and made arrangements to bring her over in 10 days. Then she called Lorraine to say they didn't have to go to May's Landing today.

"Yeah, Chloe's in heat. She's miserable. I may have to get her some diapers or something. Antonio is going to love this."

"Oh, he'll survive." Lorraine said.

"Yeah, but he hates the idea of me breeding her as it is. If he finds little drops of blood all over, it won't be pleasant."

They made arrangements to get together in 10 days to take Chloe south. After Teresa got off the phone, she put Chloe on a towel on her lap and they sat together while Teresa brushed her. Every time Teresa stopped brushing, Chloe would let out a little whine meaning, "Keep brushing." Teresa happily obliged.

"I wish someone would do this for me when I have the curse," she said to the little terrier.

*****

Antonio had sifted through five years of files, covering 1950 – 1955. He found several references to George Ranier, but no mention of the Mortevida plants. He was growing hopeful that George's plants were so unimpressive that they didn't even deserve a mention in the records. He was on the third manila folder in the 1956 box when something caught his eye.

There was a reference to a formula that George had produced in his lab. The report mentioned a strange poison of unknown origin that George was trying to cultivate as a bug repellent. Antonio thought this might be the center of the leaf of the Mortevida plant.

He went through file after file, but didn't see this poison mentioned again. He went through the rest of the 1950s and took a break. He wished he'd asked George how long he'd worked with the plant. Antonio decided to go to the Jersey Freeze and try to call George on the store's pay phone. He could also have something to eat while he was there.

As luck would have it, he beat the lunch crowd and ate in relative peace. Then he went to the pay phone. He took out his wallet and found the small piece of paper he'd written George's number on. He dialed the operator and asked her to put the call on his home telephone number. Pretty soon he was talking to George and asking him how long he had worked with the Mortevida.

George told him he'd worked with it until 1969. He'd extracted the parts he wanted to work with and had them frozen. The full plants had been kept in the vault, but had died due to lack of care.

"So you stopped working with them altogether in 1969?" Antonio was taking notes as George spoke.

"Yeah, we had what we needed by then." George paused. "Why don't you look under 1979? There may be something there. Good luck, kid."

George hung up before Antonio could say good-bye.

Antonio went back to the warehouse. He pulled the files for 1979 from the bottom of the shelving unit. He looked through the manila folder tabs and saw one marked "George Ranier." He extracted the file and spread it open in front of him.

The file began with a statement regarding a certain plant that George had brought back from the rainforest in the fifties. He had extracted the poison from the leaf of the plant and created the perfect base for a biological weapon. It was stable and remained effective after freezing and defrosting. Several lab rats could attest to that.

155

George was attempting to create a method that would drop the poison over a controlled area. That was in 1969. Matthew Wilmer was still hoping to produce a bomb that would send countries scurrying to New Mexico. He was hoping for a bidding war. George was on the precipice of producing just such a weapon.

Then came 1972 and the Biological and Toxin Convention. The Convention extended the 1925 ban to almost all production, storage and transport of biological weapons. This effectively killed Matthew Wilmer's dream. He put George's research on hold and put the poison in deep frozen storage. Antonio read the rest of the file and could find no mention of the name of the plant. Still, he decided to go a little further.

After 1985, there was no mention of George. His poison was never mentioned again either. That was just 4 years ago. Antonio went through the late sixties and seventies. He was exhausted and it was beginning to get dark. He had promised Teresa he would be home by 3 p.m.

He put the file boxes back in their places, leaving the George Ranier file out. He put it under his arm, left the warehouse and replaced the padlock. He stopped at Jersey Freeze and called Teresa. He apologized for being late, saying he'd had a flat tire. He bought her a sundae and drove home.

*****

Whatever George Ranier had been working on, it hadn't involved the purple spores. Antonio believed he'd found what he needed. He began to draw up plans for his home laboratory. He met with an architect who designed a basic research lab that met Antonio's needs. He contracted plumbers and electricians, and installed freezers. Finally, he installed a sterilizer.

When it was done, the lab provided Antonio with the means to create a miracle from his purple spores. He had chosen a new name for the plant – Dono di Russo – and contacted Mr. McKenzie to ask if he'd learned anything during his investigation.

Stephen McKenzie was in the process of dictating a report to Antonio Russo when Antonio telephoned his office.

"Hello, Mr. Russo. I've finished my investigation. Do you have time to come to my office?"

Antonio agreed and arrived at Mr. McKenzie's office 20 minutes later. Grace escorted him into Mr. McKenzie's office. He

156

sat down in the same comfortable wingback chair he had sat in during his first appointment.

"I have good news for you, Mr. Russo. I was unable to find any patents filed by either Wilmer and March Pharmaceuticals or Miss Margaret DeMorte. Now, that doesn't mean that Wilmer will have total amnesia regarding the Mortevida, especially if old Matthew Wilmer told Jacob anything about Ranier's research."

"I have to tell you something. It's about some information I've acquired." Antonio waited for Mr. McKenzie to respond.

"I am not going to ask where you acquired your information, Antonio."

"George never used the purple spores. He used only the poison. The name Mortevida is never mentioned in any report I could find."

"Interesting. Well, have you thought of a name for your discovery, Mr. Russo?"

"I thought Dono di Russo sounded nice. It means Russo's gift."

"Umm, that does sound nice. D O N O D I R U S S O. Yes, that should work out very nicely. I'll get the patent application ready. I'll need some input from you regarding species, genus, etc. My understanding of botany is extremely limited.

"I'll get the standard form ready, leaving blank spaces for you to fill in. When you send it back, I'll have Grace finalize it and you can come in and sign it. Any questions Mr. Russo?"

"No, not right now. I'm so excited!" Antonio was bursting. He was closer than ever to his dream.

"As far as Brazil is concerned, we have to get permission from the indigenous people from wherever you harvested the plant. Once we reach an agreement with them, we can get a patent. I have a friend who's worked with patents for years and he's going to assist me with this aspect of the process. Any questions relating to the patents?"

"Can we trust him?"

"He's bound by confidentiality just as I am. Now, I've had no luck in finding any information regarding George Ranier."

"I'm satisfied he will be no trouble."

"Well, that's good then." Mr. McKenzie stood up and walked around the desk. He shook Antonio's hand and said he would be in touch.

Chapter 29

When Antonio got home, Teresa was nowhere to be found. He saw a note left on the kitchen table. It said that she and Lorraine had taken Chloe to visit Rocky in May's Landing and she would be home later that evening. Antonio grabbed a sandwich and headed to his lab.

Antonio was eager to start working on his new drug. He walked over to his plants and said "Hello, Dono di Russo." He then donned gloves and cut a leaf off the plant. He placed it in a dish and gently scraped the spores off the leaf. Then Antonio set the center of the leaf on a paper towel to dry out. When it was sufficiently withered, he would throw it away.

Antonio used his pestle to disperse the spores. Tiny purple filaments flew around the dish. He added a little water to the spores. He stirred them some more. The formula took on a pasty texture. He added a little more water until it flowed when he lifted the pestle. Now he was ready to put them in the freezer. He would wait a week and take them out of the freezer to see if they retained this elastic consistency.

When Teresa got home she announced that the mating had been a glorious success. She expected Chloe to be pregnant very soon. She would take her to the vet in two weeks to have her examined. Teresa took Chloe off leash and put her arms around Antonio.

"I'm in a mood to celebrate, Mr. Russo. We are about to become parents."

She gently kissed Antonio, who responded in kind. He put his arms around her and passionately kissed her and held her tight.

"I have such good news too," he said when they separated. "The lawyer says we can apply for the patent. We're calling the plant the Dono di Russo."

"Russo's gift. I like it. Wow, this is big news. Now we really have to celebrate." Teresa got on the phone, called the local pizza place, and ordered pizza with extra cheese.

*****

Chloe started acting different within a few days of her "tryst" with Rocky. She was moody and kept throwing up. By the second week, she was scratching her bed trying to make a nest. Teresa just knew she was pregnant.

Every day she would greet Chloe with "Hi, Mommy" and give her special treats, which she sometimes threw up right away, or sometimes threw up later. By the third week, Chloe was looking a little rounder around the middle. Teresa felt her tummy but could not make out the puppies yet. She took her to Dr. Kemp to have her examined.

"She seems just fine. She's pregnant and all signs seem normal. Is she getting exercise?" Dr. Kemp was feeling around her belly.

"I walk her every day. I make sure she's getting enough water too." Teresa looked anxiously at Dr. Kemp.

"I have some vitamins for you to give her. Also, no pesticides right now. Use something natural like a shampoo with citrus oil until she delivers."

Dr. Kemp left Teresa with the technician, who gave Teresa Chloe's vitamins. She took Chloe home and the little dog quickly went to her bed. She was tired from all the day's excitement. She slept most of the day, with Teresa peeking at her at regular intervals. If all went well, the puppies should be born in six more weeks. Teresa didn't know how she would wait that long.

*****

Teresa was awakened at 3 a.m. by the sound of Chloe crying. She got out of bed, careful not to wake Antonio, and went down the stairs to the kitchen. The little dog was lying on her side whimpering. She was bleeding from her vagina.

Teresa ran over to her and stroked her head. Chloe looked at Teresa and Teresa could see the pain and fear in her eyes. Teresa didn't know what to do. She called the vet's service and they told her they would try to contact Dr. Kemp. Chloe was five weeks along. Suddenly, a puppy fell out of Chloe's vagina.

It was so tiny and lifeless that Teresa began to cry. She tried to help Chloe by taking the puppy away, but soon another puppy emerged from her. There were three altogether. When it was over, Chloe began to settle down. Thankfully, there was no excessive bleeding following the miscarriage.

Teresa put the puppies in a plastic bag and into the trash. She didn't know what else to do and she wanted to get them away from Chloe. She went back to Chloe and sat down next to her. The little dog was sleeping now. Dr. Kemp called within half an hour, but it was already over by then.

When the sun came up, Teresa took a shower and got dressed. She was going to take Chloe to Dr. Kemp's at 8 a.m. She couldn't eat. She was crying when Antonio came downstairs for breakfast.

Teresa told him what had happened, and he genuinely felt sorry for the little dog. He put his arms around Teresa, who buried her face in his arm and cried uncontrollably. He offered to help her take Chloe to the doctor, but she said she would be okay.

Dr. Kemp examined Chloe and said she would be fine. She said this sometimes happened if the dog wasn't mature. If Teresa waited another year, she should be ready to carry to full term. Teresa thanked the doctor, but said she didn't think she could put Chloe through this again.

She took her baby home and together they sat on the recliner while Teresa brushed her and softly hummed a lullaby. She promised Chloe she wouldn't put her through this again. The little dog raised her head to look at Teresa and seemed to smile with her eyes. Teresa hugged her close and wept into her fur.

*****

Antonio took the test tubes out of the freezer. He allowed them to defrost and checked the consistency. The purple goo looked good. He was satisfied that it had passed the first test. Now he would let it sit at room temperature to see how it fared after several days. He repeated the freezing and defrosting experiment for several weeks. He wanted to see how well the spores would adapt to different environments.

After several months of experimentation, he was satisfied that the Dono di Russo spores were everything he had hoped. He believed he was ready to use them on a living subject, but wasn't sure where to start. He was on the verge of getting two white rats when Teresa announced that she was going to try to mate Chloe again.

"I thought you were totally against that!" Antonio was saying. "You promised the dog you wouldn't put her through that again."

"I know, but Dr. Kemp said she should be fine, and I really want to have puppies. I don't know why. I just love the idea of seeing them born and raising them."

160

"This is a very selfish idea. It's wrong to put that little dog through this again. I won't let you."

"Since when do you care so much about Chloe? I think you're just jealous because when she was pregnant she was the center of attention." Teresa's voice softened. "Please, Antonio, let me do this. I'll take very good care of her. You'll see. I'll keep her close to Dr. Kemp."

Then the thought struck Antonio. He needed a living subject. Chloe, who had suffered from cervical insufficiency, would be the perfect candidate. He would have to keep it secret from Teresa or she would accuse him of using Chloe as a guinea pig, which of course he was. Accordingly, he relented.

"Well, if it means that much to you, I'll suffer through it." Teresa hugged Antonio tightly and then ran to Chloe. She picked her up and cradled her like a baby. Antonio rolled his eyes and walked over to kiss his wife good-bye.

"Thank you, Antonio. I love you, you know." She kissed him and then put Chloe down.

She walked Antonio to the door and waved him goodbye. Then she called Lauren Sheridan to tell her Chloe would be calling on Rocky again.

Chapter 30

Chloe became pregnant as easily as she had the first time. She had a better appetite this time also. As a matter of fact, she ate all the time. Teresa was a little worried she might get too fat. She was a little dog, and this would be a big problem.

Antonio kept telling her to calm down and enjoy the experience. Meanwhile, he tried to determine the best time to give Chloe the drug which he was now calling "Fetura," the Latin noun for "bringing forth." His drug would allow women to bring forth a child they would otherwise lose. He decided to treat her later this evening, when Teresa went out with Lorraine for their weekly girl's night out.

"I don't know if I should leave her," Teresa said to Antonio at dinner. Antonio had to play this just right.

"Do you think I'm not capable of caring for her?" He hoped he would sound indignant enough.

"Oh, no, of course not, it's just that she's at that critical time. She wouldn't understand if I wasn't here."

Antonio took her hand.

"Bella mia, you go. Enjoy yourself with Lorraine. You need to talk and talk. I will watch her."

"You're right about that. I do need to talk. Okay, but I won't be late. Maybe just a couple of hours."

Lorraine was honking outside and Teresa kissed Antonio on the cheek as she ran out the door. He waited until he heard them drive away. Then he ran down to the lab and grabbed the test tube he had prepared for Chloe.

Antonio wasn't sure how much to give a little terrier, but he made the same amount that Maggie had made and figured a portion based on Chloe's weight. He ran upstairs with the test tube in hand.

Chloe was watching him from her little bed. He approached her slowly so she wouldn't try to run under his bed.

"*Piccola*, how are you tonight?"

Antonio put Chloe's bowl in front of her. He wasn't sure how the mixture tasted or if Chloe would even try it. The mixture smelled like wet plants. He poured it into her bowl and sat down next to her. Her big frog eyes looked at him suspiciously. She sniffed the air to see what was in the bowl. Antonio kept smiling at her, trying to remain calm.

"*Cara mia*, please try it. It will not harm you."

162

Antonio actually reached out his hand and stroked the dog's head. She pulled back, but then relented. She liked the feel of a human hand on her head. She crawled closer to the bowl. She then got up and came to the bowl. She sniffed. Then she licked. Then she lapped. She even licked the bowl until it was clean. She then looked up at Antonio hoping for more.

"*Ti amo, piccola mia,* there is no more!"

Antonio scooped up the little dog, and as he did he saw her pink belly glow purple for a moment, and then fade back to pink. Antonio put her down and looked into her eyes. They were bright and healthy looking. She showed no ill effects of the drug. Antonio got up and found her treats. He gave her one and she wagged her tail.

"We are friends now, right?" She walked over and he bent down to stroke her head. "But we will not tell Mama. This is our secret."

The rest of the evening Antonio watched Chloe. She was full of vim and vigor and she ran back and forth to Antonio with her toys. He would throw them and she would chase them down and bring them back. She seemed tireless. Antonio prayed that she would stay this way.

"Please let these puppies be born."

Seven weeks later, on July 24, 1990, Chloe gave birth to two beautiful puppies, a male and a female. She went into labor in the afternoon and gave birth just before dinner. Teresa was in attendance the whole time.

When Antonio came home from work, Chloe was in the last stages of labor with the first puppy. The humans sat side by side and watched as the little dog pushed the puppy out. Teresa got a strange look on her face when she saw the afterbirth.

"Antonio, is that placenta purple?" She asked.

"Well, it could just be that it's wet."

He was just as surprised as she was. Maggie had never mentioned this when discussing the women who gave birth to Mortevida babies.

"No, I don't think so. It's definitely purple."

Chloe was licking the puppy and ate the placenta. She licked and licked, getting the puppy's system circulating. The puppy began to squirm. Then Chloe went into labor again. Teresa gently moved the puppy away so Chloe had room. As she moved it, Teresa noticed its belly was a light shade of purple.

"Oh my God, his belly is purple too!" She looked at Antonio. She thought a minute and then her eyes went wide. "You didn't. You didn't make Chloe your guinea pig." She knew he'd been searching for one and she knew the drug was purple.

"Cara, what does it matter? She had her puppies without a problem."

"But they're purple Antonio. How can I sell purple puppies?"

Antonio didn't remember seeing any purple people in the jungle.

"The effect will wear off. I promise. Look, the second one is out."

The little female had been born. She, too, had a purple placenta and belly.

"I hope for your sake it does wear off. How could you do this without telling me?"

"Because you never would have allowed it, and I knew she would be safe. I couldn't let her lose these puppies when I knew I could help her."

He looked so earnest that Teresa forgave him. He was right. The puppies had made it and Chloe was a mama. Lauren Sheridan had asked for the pick of the litter and Teresa had agreed. Teresa had hoped for more puppies, but a deal was a deal.

"I'll let her know in a few days. I have to be sure the purple goes away first. Otherwise I have to lie to her. I can't give her a purple puppy."

Teresa got up from the floor and got some water for Chloe. Chloe was exhausted, and she put her head down. The puppies were already rooting around for a nipple. Antonio stroked Chloe's head.

"Thank you, my *piccola*. Thank you."

*****

Three days later the purple color faded from the puppies' bellies. They were very healthy puppies and they nursed vigorously. Chloe was a good mama. She groomed the puppies and took very good care of them. Teresa was entranced by the way they looked.

"They are the sweetest things I've ever seen," she kept saying. "I want to keep the male. I just love the coloring of his face. But I don't like Rocky. I think I'll name him Ricky. I had a friend named Ricky when I was in elementary school. What do you think of Ricky, Antonio?"

164

Antonio was reading the paper. Teresa knew he wasn't listening, which is why she asked him. She snuck over to his side of the table and peeked over the top of the paper.

"I said, what do you think of the name Ricky?" Antonio jumped a little.

"Why do you always do that? What do I think of what?"

"The name Ricky, for the puppy?" Teresa sat back down on her chair.

"It's okay. It's for you to name him. Ricky sounds okay."

Antonio had just about had it with puppyland. Yes, they were very cute, but the sooner they sent one of them away the better. When Teresa insisted on keeping one, Antonio extracted a promise in blood that there would be no more.

"No, I promise. Chloe is going to be spayed when she's ready." Teresa was cuddling the puppy while Chloe whined in the birthing box.

"I guess I have to call Lauren and let her know the puppies were born." Teresa sighed as she held the puppy to her face and nuzzled it.

"Yes, call her please. TODAY!"

Antonio got up from the table and kissed Teresa on the forehead. She lifted Ricky up for a kiss too, but Antonio shook his head and muttered something in Italian. He then left for work.

Teresa called Lauren Sheridan and arranged to bring the female to her in 10 weeks. Lauren was happy all had gone well and said she looked forward to meeting her new baby girl.

Chapter 31

Teresa and Lorraine drove to May's Landing with the little female between them. The puppy climbed onto Teresa's lap and put her front paws on the door so she could look out the window. After a time, she settled on Teresa's lap and slept the rest of the way.

It was a two-hour trip to May's Landing, and the women decided to stop in Atlantic City to have lunch and play the slots after they dropped off the little girl.

Lauren Sheridan's house was located on a little side street off Cologne Avenue. It was a cute yellow semi-Cape Cod with a large front yard and a stream flowing by in the back. Teresa and Lorraine parked in the driveway behind Lauren's minivan. Teresa carried the little dog to the front door and rang the bell.

Lauren answered the door with two kids standing behind her. The kids were pushing each other to get closer to the door.

"STOP! Go get dressed," Lauren yelled. The kids ran to the living room and jumped on the couch. "Hi, come on in."

Teresa and Lorraine entered the house. The first thing they noticed was that Lauren's daughter Sue was sitting on the couch completely naked. She looked to be around 4 years old.

The next thing they noticed was the noise. Sue and her brother Micky were screaming in unison that they didn't want to get dressed.

"You will get dressed or I will spank your bare bottoms!" Lauren seemed to be at her wits' end. "My husband worked last night so I haven't had much sleep. Sorry."

Sue noticed the puppy in Teresa's hand.

"WEEEE! Is that my puppy?" The little girl seemed unable to speak below a bellow. "Let me have him, let me have him." She put her hands up and was pulling at the puppy's legs.

Lauren grabbed her arm and turned her around. "I said go and get dressed!" The little girl frowned and went to her bedroom.

"I'm really sorry. Oh, she's so cute." Lauren held out her hand and Teresa reluctantly gave her the puppy. "Oh, my, what a face! She looks just like Rocky. He's out in the yard. Let's go out there and introduce them."

Lauren led the way to the back yard through the kitchen. There were plates on the table, and the sink was full of dishes.

"Please excuse the mess. I worked yesterday and was exhausted when I came home." She opened the sliding glass door and led Teresa and Lorraine to the wooden deck on the back of the house. Rocky was chasing birds off the lawn.

"Hey, Rocky, come here!" Lauren called. He stopped what he was doing and just stared at her. "Oh, come on, Rocky. Don't be so stubborn."

Rocky slowly made his way over to Lauren. Lorraine asked if she could pet him and Lauren nodded her head. When Lorraine bent down to stroke his head, Rocky jerked his head to the side and closed his eyes as if she were about to strike him. Lorraine backed off, not wanting to cause him anymore distress.

"Are you sure you can handle another pet right now?" Teresa asked.

"Oh, sure, I have plenty of room and I promised Sue she could have the puppy. I can't go back on that promise."

Teresa was very unsure of what to do. Lauren obviously couldn't handle another pet. But she had promised her the pick of the litter and she wasn't sure what would happen if she reneged. Lauren might sue her for the puppy anyway and win. She looked at Lorraine and knew she was thinking the same thing.

Sue came running out fully dressed. She smiled and ran over to her mom. Lauren handed her the puppy and she ran into the middle of the yard clutching the puppy close to her. She sat down on the ground and put the puppy down in front of her.

The puppy tried to run back to Teresa, but Sue grabbed her and clutched her close to keep her there. Rocky ran over to Sue to inspect this new interloper. He growled and barked at Sue.

"Rocky!" Lauren yelled, "Back off!"

Rocky backed off and ran to the other side of the yard with a scared look in his eyes. He looked at Lauren and then at the puppy.

"I'll keep them apart until she's big enough to handle him."

Lauren seemed satisfied with this arrangement, but Teresa was still feeling guilty about leaving the puppy in this madhouse. She looked at Lorraine who shrugged her shoulders.

"Well then, I guess we should go."

Since this was a combo breed not yet recognized by the AKC, Teresa didn't have papers for the dog. She had only a record of her shots. She handed that to Lauren.

"Thanks for bringing her down. Call anytime and I'll tell you how she's doing."

Lauren led them to the front door and waved goodbye. She walked back to the yard to check on Sue and the puppy. As she approached the sliding glass door, she heard Sue yell for her. She ran out onto the deck and saw Rocky with his mouth securely wrapped around the little puppy's neck, shaking her from side to side. The little female was whimpering.

Lauren ran over to them and got the puppy away from Rocky. The puppy wriggled out of Lauren's hand and ran to the edge of the fence trying desperately to get away. Sue went over and picked her up.

"It's okay, Baby Girl," she said. "That's her name Mommy, Baby Girl."

She clutched the little dog to her chest and ran into the house. She spent the rest of the afternoon keeping the puppy in her room, dressing her in doll clothes.

*****

Two weeks later Lauren Sheridan sat crying at her kitchen table. She couldn't stand the noise in the house anymore. Her mom had told her to bring the kids over so Lauren could have some peace.

Lauren had dropped them off at her mother's house and come home to find that Rocky had bitten Baby Girl again. This arrangement was just not working out and Lauren didn't know what to do. Her Aunt Mimi was visiting Lauren's mom and came back to the house with Lauren. She saw Baby Girl and picked her up.

"It's not too bad. It doesn't look like he wanted to really hurt her, just warned her. Look, he hardly broke the skin."

She showed Lauren the tiny mark on Baby Girl's neck.

"There's no blood, Lauren, so I don't think she needs to go to the vet. I'll wash it off and put some antibiotic cream on it."

Aunt Mimi held the puppy to her face and kissed it. She took her over to the sink and gently washed her neck. She then wrapped her in a towel and held her like a baby.

"I just love this dog. I think she's the cutest thing I've ever seen. Yes, you are the cutest thing I've ever seen." Aunt Mimi was nuzzling the puppy.

"You want her?" Lauren asked.

Aunt Mimi's old dog, Benny, had passed away six weeks earlier. Her husband, Fritz, was devastated by the loss. He sat in a chair and stared into space most days. But that dog had been big and Aunt Mimi, who would take in any dog, was not sure how Fritzy would take to a little dog like this, a puppy no less.

Aunt Mimi missed having a dog so much. Any animal they had owned had been her choice. She was always bringing home strays. She decided right there and then to take the puppy home.

"Are you serious, Lauren? Won't Sue be upset?"

"She's bored with her already. She has no interest in her and rarely thinks to feed her or care for her. It's my decision and I want you to have her if you want her."

"Oh, I want her all right. I love her already."

And so it was that Baby Girl came to live with Aunt Mimi and Uncle Fritz Lane, otherwise known as Grammy and Opa to Mindy Lane of St. Petersburg, Florida.

Chapter 32

Colts Neck, New Jersey

Teresa had been sad about the puppy for a month now. She just kept hoping the little female would be alright. Antonio told her to call Lauren and ask her how the puppy was doing. She didn't know what she would do if Lauren answered the phone with screaming dogs and children in the background, but she mustered her courage and dialed the number. Lauren was home alone when Teresa called.

Lauren told Teresa that her aunt, an elderly lady from Tuckerton, had taken Baby Girl and the puppy was very happy there. Teresa sighed with relief. She thanked Lauren and hung up. Then her stomach turned over and she ran to the bathroom and threw up.

Teresa had been feeling tired lately. She had missed her period and now was throwing up almost daily. She knew she was pregnant, but hadn't gone to the drug store yet to purchase a test. She was almost finished with her master's and she didn't really want a baby just yet. She hadn't told Antonio what she suspected and wouldn't until it was confirmed.

She went to Lincroft Pharmacy and purchased a pregnancy test. The next morning, she took the test and it came up positive. Now she would have to make an appointment with Dr. Tangen.

Donald S. Tangen had been Teresa's gynecologist since she was in high school. He was an avid Yankees fan and his office was covered with sports memorabilia. Dr. Tangen had contemplated going into sports medicine, but gynecology was much more lucrative. It was the end of the summer and Dr. Tangen was brown as a berry. He coached a Little League team and had spent most of the summer in the sun, bronzing his olive skin. His brown eyes twinkled when he told Teresa she was indeed pregnant and the baby should be born sometime in May. He prescribed prenatal vitamins and told her to eat well and get plenty of exercise.

When Teresa got home, Antonio was sitting with his paper at the kitchen table. She walked over to him and put her arms around his neck. She hesitated for a moment, thinking about college. She might make it through the whole term if she doubled up on some of her classes. But she was so tired already that she didn't think that would work. What choice did she have? She could never terminate

170

the pregnancy. But would Antonio let her continue college? His fear of miscarriage was so intense he might insist she sit on her butt for nine months.

Teresa sat down in her chair. She looked at Antonio, who had put the paper aside.

"I have some news. I'm pregnant."

"*Cara mia*, my beautiful girl."

Antonio got up and walked over to Teresa. She got out of her chair and they hugged each other tightly.

"I'm so happy. You've made me so happy." Antonio was beaming.

"You're not afraid?" Teresa was searching his eyes for a telltale sign of fear.

"Afraid? No, you're healthy. You'll be fine. And I've never noticed anything wrong with your cervix." He winked at her.

"Then you won't mind me finishing college?"

"Why should I? You worked hard. You must finish. If you feel tired, you take a rest. If you don't finish, you finish after the baby is born. We can work it out."

Teresa hugged him even tighter. She was so relieved he wouldn't fight her on this.

"Well, we must go out and celebrate," Antonio said.

Teresa nodded and kissed Antonio passionately.

*****

Teresa was in her second trimester when Dr. Tangen noticed a thinning in her cervix. The baby was sitting low and Teresa appeared to be slightly dilated. He insisted she go to bed and stay there until the baby was born.

"But I have classes. I can't be homebound. And you can't tell Antonio."

"I won't tell your husband without your permission, but you have to stay off your feet or you'll lose this baby. You're dilated already and you have four months to go. Teresa, there will be time later to finish your degree. There may not be another baby. You never know. You have to go to bed and stay there. I will arrange for home visits so you have someone to help you in and out of bed for bathroom breaks. Get a good long book and stay in bed!"

Teresa could have punched him at that moment. Men thought it was so easy for a woman to just drop everything. But Teresa knew

171

once the baby was born it would be a lot harder to finish school. It wouldn't be impossible, but much harder. She slid off the examining table and checked out of the office.

On the drive home she began to cry. She remembered Chloe's miscarriage and the pain it had caused. She couldn't imagine what it would be like to lose this baby. She would have to tell Antonio. She had no choice.

That evening at dinner she told Antonio what Dr. Tangen had said. Antonio raised his eyebrows and smiled.

"I can give you the drug. It will stop this." He had the biggest smile on his face. He could help her, and it made him feel so good. "You can finish school."

As much as she trusted Antonio, she wouldn't drink that purple stuff. She absolutely refused.

"No, I will not have a purple baby. No. I will do what Dr. Tangen says."

"But Teresa, it will work. And the baby will only be purple for a little while."

"Are you listening to yourself? No, no purple babies. I'll stay in bed until he or she is born."

Teresa got up from the table and put the dishes in the sink. She started putting water in the sink when Antonio came over and told her to go to bed, that he would finish the dishes. Teresa kissed his cheek and went to their bedroom. She put on her softest nightgown and got into bed.

Two weeks later, despite doctor-ordered bed rest, Teresa miscarried her little baby girl. When Antonio brought her home from the hospital, Teresa went straight to bed and refused to get out for three weeks. Her mother came to the house and stayed with her while Antonio went to work.

Antonio was careful not to mention the drug that would have saved her from this pain. Dr. Tangen had told Antonio that if they tried to have another baby, Teresa might have to be in bed for the whole term of her pregnancy, but there was every reason to believe she could have a baby. Antonio knew that if she ever got pregnant again, he would give her the purple spores even if he had to do it intravenously.

*****

In the spring of 1993, Wilmer and March opened their new Tampa, Florida facility. Jake Rawlings approached Antonio to ask him how he felt about moving to Florida. The company wanted Antonio to run their Tampa research labs.

This was a wonderful opportunity for Antonio, but he wasn't sure how Teresa would handle it. She loved living near her parents. They had a wonderful life here. He told Jake he would have to think about it.

"Don't think too long, Antonio. They have some guy named Todd in animal research jockeying for the position. I know for a fact that they would rather have you. I vouched for your abilities. You're the best in this lab."

This was a shock to Antonio. In all the time he had worked with Jake, he'd never heard him say one thing about his performance. Even during his reviews, Jake would say "Keep it up" without specifying what "it" was. Antonio knew he was up to the task and he hoped Teresa would be willing to support him. She would graduate in a few weeks and was firming up her resume. She could easily transfer those skills to Florida.

That evening Antonio brought home flowers. He came through the back door into the kitchen. Teresa looked up from her cooking and saw the flowers. She frowned as he gave them to her.

"Who died?" She said.

"No one died. What a thing to say," Antonio said.

"Well, you never bring me flowers unless you have bad news."

Antonio thought about this and realized it was true.

"I hadn't realized I did that. No, this is good news, maybe," Antonio said.

Teresa was still frowning. She took the flowers out of the wrapper and cut the ends off before putting them in water.

"So, you might as well spill it," she said. Antonio gave her a strange look. "The news, spill the news, tell me."

"Oh, well, I've been offered a big promotion."

"But..." Teresa instinctively knew that there was some big catch.

"They want me to go to Florida."

Teresa sat down at the table. Antonio took his seat there too. She looked at him for a long time before speaking.

"This is very important to you, your career, isn't it?"

"Yes, it is. I would be given a lot more responsibility, more assistants, and more important assignments. It would be very good for me."

Antonio could see the wheels spinning behind Teresa's eyes. He knew what she was thinking.

"It's far away, Antonio. Florida is too far to drive. My parents are getting older and I would feel very guilty leaving them alone here. You have to let me think about this. When do they need to know?"

"Jake says soon. Some other guy is being considered, but they really want me. It's a brand new facility in Tampa."

Teresa could see the excitement behind Antonio's grim facade. He was trying to look as though this would be hardship for him too, but he wasn't fooling her. He was chomping at the bit.

Teresa thought about how he'd always gone along with everything she wanted to do, how he had encouraged her. He'd never held her back except where more puppies were concerned. He even left his country and his family to be with her. And he'd never asked her for anything like this before.

"I want to call my mother," she said and headed for the bedroom.

When she came out, she was smiling. Her mother told her that they would be fine, and that they had even been considering relocating to Florida themselves. The Jersey winters were getting to be too much for them. She encouraged Teresa to go and support her husband. Teresa didn't know that she was pregnant.

Chapter 33

They drove to Tampa with Chloe between them and Ricky on Teresa's lap looking out the window. Every so often he would bark at a passing car. They followed the moving van to the house they had rented sight unseen in Brandon.

They had sold their house in Colts Neck for a huge profit and Teresa was learning how to invest it. In the meantime, they would stay in the rental house. Teresa suggested they put most of their stuff in storage until they knew where they were going to live and Antonio agreed.

The house was a small stucco affair with two bedrooms and one and a half baths. There was a pool in the back yard and an attached garage. The moving men emptied the van quickly and left Teresa and Antonio to sort through the mess.

Teresa had been feeling really tired and was concerned she might be pregnant again. She remembered Dr. Tangen telling her she would have to be on constant bed rest if she ever got pregnant again.

Teresa took Chloe and Ricky to the vet to get them squared away for their new licenses. She told the vet's technician that she was new in the area and was looking for an OBGYN. She told the tech that she had lost a baby and needed someone who specialized in that area. The young woman thought a minute and then asked her colleague if she knew anyone.

"Yeah, I know somebody. Let me make a quick phone call."

Five minutes later the woman came back and gave Teresa the number of a Dr. Michael Tomlinson in St. Petersburg.

"Isn't there anyone closer?" Teresa asked. St. Petersburg was miles away.

"I talked to my sister. She had the same problem and he was real good. I don't know anybody local."

So Teresa thanked the young woman and left the office. Not being familiar with the area or having any friends to ask, Teresa decided to give Dr. Tomlinson a call.

When she called, the receptionist said the doctor was booked for the next two months. Teresa made an appointment anyway and asked the receptionist to call if he had a cancellation. Then she waited for Antonio to come home so he could make her a batch of the nasty looking purple drug.

*****

Antonio had transported his lab to Florida, but right now it was sitting in storage. When Teresa asked him to prepare her some of the drug, a look of dismay crossed his face.

"But you have the plants here," she said.

"I know, but it is not that easy. I have to have the right equipment."

Antonio thought of Maggie scraping the spores into a bowl and adding some water. He felt uncomfortable giving his wife and child a dose he hadn't properly prepared in a lab. But he also knew that the women of the rainforest had been giving birth this way for hundreds of years, maybe thousands, and he really needn't worry about Teresa or the baby.

"Please, Antonio, I can't get in to see the doctor for two months. What if something happens before then?" Teresa was on the verge of tears.

"When I offered it to you the first time, you said you didn't want a purple baby."

"Better a purple baby than no baby at all. Antonio, I trust you. Look at Ricky. He's so healthy. Please help me."

She was pleading with Antonio and he could see how important this was to her. He sat for a minute thinking of the consequences should something go wrong. The placenta would be purple. How could that be hidden from the doctor who delivered her baby? How would he explain a baby with a light purple sheen to its skin?

"It would work. I know it would. But how do we hide the purple placenta?" he asked.

"We could get a midwife to deliver me at home."

"No, not after what happened before. You have to be in a hospital," said Antonio.

They sat together for a long time thinking about what to do. In the end, all Antonio cared about was saving his wife and baby. So that evening, he brought a plant into the house from the garage and cut one of the leaves off it.

He scraped the spores into a paper bowl and pounded it into a paste. He added a little more water, and when he thought it was ready presented it to Teresa in a paper cup.

"God, that looks nasty. It doesn't smell good either."

176

"Chloe liked it." Antonio was smiling at her.

"Well, here goes," Teresa said as she sipped the drink.

She raised her eyebrows signifying it did not taste that bad. Then she drank the rest down quickly. She put the cup down on the table. Very shortly thereafter, her face glowed in a light purple sheen for a few seconds and then returned to normal. That always amazed Antonio, and it let him know the spores were going to work.

"Do you feel anything?" he asked Teresa.

"I feel good, like I could run a marathon." Teresa was smiling a big smile. "I think I need to put some of this stuff away."

There were still boxes to unpack and Teresa attacked them with a fervor seldom seen in womankind. She cleaned the house once over and then started to clean it again. When she slept, she entered into a deep sleep. When she woke up, she jumped out of bed ready to conquer the world. She felt she could do almost anything.

When she went to see Dr. Tomlinson, she noted that he looked like Santa Claus. He had long white hair and a short white beard. He wore small round metal rimmed glasses. He also had a big belly.

"Yes, I know," he remarked, "I'm a jolly old elf."

Teresa laughed with him because it really was true. Dr. Tomlinson was a genial soul. He examined her and told her that she was fine, that her cervix was doing nicely and there was no sign of dilation.

Dr. Tomlinson told her that she was four months along and if she remained this well he could see no reason for concern. She left his office feeling as though Santa had come early, which of course he had.

Antonio was thrilled with his wife's progress. She glowed, thankfully not purple, and she said she hadn't felt this good, pregnant or not, since she was a teenager. With each passing month, she and Antonio relaxed. They knew this baby would be fine and that she would carry it full term.

When she began to approach her final weeks, Dr. Tomlinson suggested she stay in St. Petersburg until the baby was born. He didn't want her going into labor so far away. Antonio worked with a man whose parents owned a waterfront home on St. Pete Beach that they used only in the winter. Antonio asked if Teresa and her dogs could live there for a month until she delivered. The man's parents agreed and Teresa moved in with Chloe and Ricky. Antonio would come down on weekends.

Lorraine said she could fly down the last week to stay with Teresa when Teresa told her it was time. Teresa's parents would come a week later to give Teresa time to settle in.

Lorraine was reading a book she'd bought at the airport. She and Teresa were sitting on the beach in lounge chairs. Teresa felt a pang. She wasn't sure what it was until it happened again and her eyes bugged out of her head. Lorraine, who had never given birth, got up and ran to phone the doctor, leaving Teresa splayed out on the beach in her chair.

When she came back, Lorraine helped Teresa up as best she could. Teresa first had to roll over with Lorraine watching helplessly by her side. Finally, she was able to get herself up on her knees and Lorraine was able to help her balance so she could get up.

By the time they got off the beach, the ambulance was there to take Teresa to the hospital. Lorraine called Antonio, who said he'd meet her at the hospital as soon as he could get there.

Lorraine was in the room with Teresa when Antonio arrived. She took Antonio aside.

"She was in bed when her water broke." Lorraine was looking rather grim. "Antonio, she asked me what color it was. I didn't want to look, but she kept insisting. I wanted to get the nurse. But I did look. Antonio, it was purple. The most beautiful shade of purple I've ever seen. Is that normal? I mean, is that the color of the stuff around the baby?"

Antonio suppressed a smile. Lorraine was so earnest he dare not laugh.

"Umm, well, sometimes. It depends on what the mother eats. I know that Teresa was very fond of eggplant during this pregnancy. She also ate a lot of grapes and plums. So maybe it affected her amniotic fluids."

"I can see that," Lorraine said. "It's all over the sheets."

Antonio peeked under Teresa's covers. Indeed the sheets were damp and purple. Antonio asked Lorraine to ask the nurse for a new sheet and padding. When Lorraine brought them back, Teresa got out of the bed and Antonio changed the sheets before anyone could see them.

"Shouldn't the nurses do that?" Lorraine said.

"Ah, they are very busy tonight, full moon and all. I try to help when I can."

"Damn, Antonio." Lorraine was smiling at him. "No wonder she puts up with you."

178

Antonio asked Lorraine to get him some coffee because he wanted to be alone with Teresa. Lorraine took the hint and left the room. When they were alone, Antonio closed the door and sat next to Teresa on the bed.

"How are you feeling, Cara?" He put his arm around her.

"I'm not in hard labor yet, so it's not too bad. But it's bad enough. I can't believe the color of those sheets. How are we going to hide the placenta?"

"We may have to bring Dr. Tomlinson into our confidence. I don't know what else to do," Antonio said.

"I think we can trust him. How can he argue with the results of us using that drug? I am nine months pregnant without a hitch."

Teresa grabbed Antonio's arm and her monitor went off the charts. The pain ripped through her like a hot poker on her back. Antonio called the nurse, who came in to check her vitals. She also checked Teresa's dilation.

"It should be pretty soon, now. I'm going to get the doctor," the nurse said.

The nurse didn't mention anything unusual about Teresa's nether regions. When Dr. Tomlinson came in, he examined Teresa and told the nurse to move her to the OR. Teresa was wheeled into the OR while Antonio dressed in scrubs and a mask. The actual birth took very little time.

"It's a boy!" cried Dr. Tomlinson with a big grin.

Then all noise in the OR stopped. They were all looking at the baby. He was a very pretty shade of purple, not too light, not too dark. Dr. Tomlinson was taken aback. He had never seen this before.

Teresa and Antonio just looked at each other and back at the baby. The doctor handed the baby to the nurse so she could clean him. Soon after, Teresa pushed out the placenta. Dr. Tomlinson looked at the placenta and then at Teresa.

"This is the damnedest thing I've ever seen." He called Antonio over to look at it. Antonio saw a perfect placenta marbled with red, pink, and purple. "It's beautiful," was all he could say.

When they laid the little boy on Teresa's chest, she looked at the little purple face. She could see he had his Daddy's chin. She prayed he would lose his purple hue sooner than later. But she loved him with all her heart.

"What's his name?" the doctor asked.

"Jason. Jason Antonio Russo."

Chapter 34

St. Pete Beach, Florida, 2001

"Jason. JASON!" Teresa was yelling for her son to come in from outside. It was getting dark. Jason and Ricky were out on the beach in front of their house.

"Okay Ma. Come on, Ricky."

Jason was seven years old. He would be eight in a couple of weeks. This year he'd asked to go to one of the giant theme parks in Orlando. Teresa and Antonio agreed it was an appropriate request for an 8-year-old, and made arrangements to stay there for a week before school started. Jason and Ricky were full of sand and dragged it into the kitchen.

"Ugh – gritty floor. Go back outside and take your shoes off, Jason."

Jason turned around and went back outside to take his shoes off. Ricky whined for food and Teresa put his plate on the floor. When Jason came back in, she told him to get ready for his bath.

Jason ran into his room and took off his clothes. He heard his mom running his bath. He ran into the bathroom where Teresa waited for him. He shook his butt and made her laugh. Then he climbed into the tub.

Teresa sat on the toilet watching Jason play in the tub, making sure he cleaned himself at the same time. When the water got cold, she said it was time to get out and she held up a towel. She wrapped the towel around him and dried him.

Teresa helped Jason to put on his PJ's, and then followed him into his room to tuck him into bed. Jason's eyes were heavy as she kissed him goodnight. Ricky had his own bed, but he preferred Jason's. He was snuggled up next to Jason. She patted his head before turning off the light.

"Will Daddy be here in the morning?" Jason asked Teresa.

"Yes, he will. It's Saturday. Goodnight fellas."

Teresa left the door open and walked into the kitchen, where she had a small computer. Chloe was sitting in Antonio's chair at the table. She smiled and stroked the dog's head. Chloe's snout was covered with gray hair.

Teresa had learned how to trade stocks online and she was very good at it. She was so good, in fact, that she didn't have another job.

180

She worked online for four to six hours each day when Jason was at school.

Teresa shut down the computer and put Antonio's dinner in the microwave until he came home. She shooed Chloe off the chair when she heard the garage door opening.

Antonio had been promoted to Senior Research Analyst six months before. He worked longer hours, but he was able to negotiate his Fridays off. This was the last Friday he would have to work before his new contract took effect.

Antonio came home and he was exhausted. He kissed Teresa on the cheek and looked in on Jason, who was fast asleep. Antonio hadn't been looking good lately, and Teresa had resolved to ask him what was going on. She warmed his dinner and put it on the table. Then she sat down in her chair to keep him company while he ate his food.

Teresa kept the conversation light until he was done eating. Then she put his dish in the dishwasher and poured some wine. She suggested they go out on the deck and Antonio agreed.

Antonio sat quietly contemplating whether to tell Teresa all that was weighing on his heart. He had something he'd kept from her, and he didn't think he was ready to tell her. Antonio had made a pact with the devil, and now he was afraid he wouldn't be able to shake the devil loose.

*****

When Jason was born eight years earlier, Dr. Tomlinson had bided his time. He saw Teresa on and off for several years. He never mentioned Jason's unusual color. He was the same kind, genial soul he'd always been.

Then one day, about a year ago, he called Antonio at his office and asked him if he would come in to see him. Antonio agreed thinking there might be something wrong with Teresa. They set an appointment for the following Tuesday.

Antonio arrived at the doctor's office at the appointed time. He walked in and noticed that there was no receptionist at the desk. He was the only one in the waiting room. Dr. Tomlinson came out to greet him with his coat on and suggested they go to lunch. Now Antonio was really concerned. Just what was going on?

Dr. Tomlinson took him to the yacht club and was greeted by name by the maître'd. They were shown to a secluded table by the window, and the waiter took their drink orders. When the waiter left, Dr. Tomlinson turned his attention to Antonio.

"Well, Dr. Russo, I hear you're doing very well at Wilmer and March."

Antonio thought, Ah, he wants to form a relationship with the company and thinks I can give him some kind of discount.

"Yes, I am doing very well. My research team is the best in the country and we have several new drugs that are due to be introduced in the next year." Antonio began to feel uncomfortable.

"That's fine, just fine. Dr. Russo, I've been meaning to ask you something for a long time." Dr. Tomlinson paused for effect.

"Yes?" Antonio was trying to read the jolly old elf's face, but the glasses and beard made it difficult.

"I've never forgotten the color of your son's placenta, not to mention your son himself. Unusual that your wife was able to carry him so well wasn't it, considering her medical history. I've never seen a woman with cervical insufficiency turn around like that."

Antonio was trying to remain casual. "Yes, it was a miracle."

"I don't think it was a miracle, Dr. Russo. I think your wife had help, very specific help, perhaps in the form of some kind of experimental drug?"

Antonio began to squirm. Even though he'd received a patent on his Dono di Russo plant four years ago, he had been unable to fund the research of the purple spores that was necessary just to submit an application to the FDA.

He'd consulted lawyers who were willing to help him, but money was always an issue. He didn't have the deep pockets of a Wilmer and March.

Antonio had thought about bringing his findings to Wilmer and March, but the fear that they would remember George Ranier had permanently blocked that option. He was also afraid that any other big drug company would question why he hadn't taken it to Wilmer and March and do their own investigation.

With that in mind, Antonio had decided he would have to do it on his own. Now, six years after his successful use of the Dono di Russo on his own wife, he was still waiting to give his Dono di Russo to the world.

"I don't know what you mean, Doctor. Her placenta was an unusual color, of course, but her pregnancy was completely normal in every way."

"Every way, Russo? You had a purple baby!" Tomlinson was struggling to keep his voice down. Old St. Nick was beginning to show his true colors. "Listen, we both know her delivery was anything but normal. She had an extremely short labor. When she did deliver, her placenta *and* her baby were purple. I want you to tell me why." Dr. Tomlinson paused and looked at Antonio, waiting for him to say something. Antonio remained silent, so the good doctor continued.

"I believe we can help each other. I have dozens of women who are desperate to have a baby and the only thing keeping them from having one is a worthless cervix. Whatever you gave your wife, and I am convinced it was you, it worked. I want to use it on my patients."

Antonio shifted in his seat. Dr. Tomlinson had played the right card.

"I do have something that would help," Antonio said. Dr. Tomlinson's eyes lit up. "But I don't have enough money to fund the application to the FDA. How could we do this without that approval?"

Antonio was eager to hear what Tomlinson had in mind.

"In the United States, supplements don't need FDA approval. As long as you list that it hasn't been approved by the FDA, anything goes. We both know this stuff is safe. Why not manufacture it as a supplement and distribute it through my office? We would be heroes! We'd save thousands of women from losing their babies." Tomlinson was leaning forward as he spoke. Antonio could see the excitement in the doctor's eyes.

"I must think about this. We'd have to make a plan."

"Of course, Russo, whatever you want, but please remember one thing." Tomlinson's eyes narrowed, "I know you haven't applied for citizenship. When you gave that drug to your wife, you endangered her and your unborn son. The authorities frown on that kind of thing in this country. It could interfere with your visa. You think about what we discussed, but I expect to hear from you in the next 48 hours. Now, what would you like to have for lunch?"

Dr. Tomlinson picked up his menu. Antonio finished his drink and excused himself. He left the restaurant and got into his car.

Antonio sat a long time watching Tomlinson through the restaurant window. The more he thought about Tomlinson's threat, the more he came to hate the man. Antonio knew that the doctor had him. He couldn't refuse to share his Dono di Russo with Tomlinson.

Antonio had thought about becoming a citizen, but he loved his country, and his marriage to Teresa enabled him to stay in this country on a special visa. Tomlinson was right. He had to keep his nose clean, and using an untested drug on a pregnant woman, even with her consent, would be frowned upon by the government. Several minutes passed while he thought about the consequences of *not* doing business with Dr. Tomlinson.

Finally, he decided he would agree to go into business with Tomlinson, but he'd never give Tomlinson the formula. He would never give him access to the plants themselves either, or show him how to extract the spores. If Tomlinson found out just how easy it was, he could cut Antonio out by paying him a fee for use of the Dono di Russo, thereby allowing Tomlinson to make the drug himself. Antonio would lose all control of his beloved Dono di Russo.

He would tell Tomlinson that he'd manufacture the supplement and bring it to Tomlinson for distribution. The doctor would pay Antonio a fee for his drug and the doctor could then charge anything he wanted for "treatment" with the supplement. Desperate women seldom asked what they were being given. If it cost a lot, it must be good. Tomlinson stood to make a fortune, even with Antonio's cut.

Antonio saw the doctor leaving the yacht club. He got out of his car and approached him. Antonio told Tomlinson that if he was willing to buy the manufactured supplement from Antonio, he'd agree to go into business with Dr. Tomlinson.

"Look at this as research trials, Russo. When would you ever get a chance like this? I'll get the women to sign a waiver allowing me to use their medical histories for research. You'll see, it will benefit everyone equally." Antonio reluctantly shook the doctor's hand. Then a thought struck Antonio.

"If this is going to be a research trial, we should limit it to 100 women until we know what we're dealing with. I think I must insist on this."

Tomlinson looked annoyed. He'd almost had him. Well, give the little guy what he wants and then renegotiate.

"Fine, agreed. Let me know when the first batch is ready. Stay in touch."

Tomlinson got into his Mercedes and drove away, leaving Antonio in the parking lot. Antonio slowly walked back to his car. He decided to keep his association with Dr. Tomlinson a secret from Teresa, at least until he knew the results of the "trials."

184

Antonio hated keeping it from her, but it would only cause her unnecessary anxiety. He had a small room off the kitchen he used as a lab. He'd tell Teresa he was experimenting with something new, which would explain his long evenings in the lab. He'd rent a post office box to receive bottles for his supplements and to send orders to Tomlinson.

Antonio called his secretary and told her he wouldn't be returning to the lab that day. He got into his car and drove home.

Chapter 35

There was a breeze blowing off the ocean, and the moon was full. Teresa looked at her husband. She asked him if he needed to talk, and Antonio just shook his head. He said work had been hard lately, a lot of deadlines.

What he wasn't telling her was that he'd found out two days before that Dr. Tomlinson had treated well over 300 women. The good doctor had divided the bottle Antonio sent him into four doses each. Antonio told him he would no longer supply Dr. Tomlinson with any more supplements.

Antonio was concerned about treating so many women without careful scrutiny. What if something went wrong? How would they ever explain the treatment of so many women?

Antonio had almost punched Tomlinson. Tomlinson told him he'd been selling the supplement as FDA approved. They'd fought in the doctor's office so loudly, that one of his medical assistants came to ask if the doctor needed help. Antonio was now waiting for the FBI to show up at his door and haul him back to Italy, or worse, prison.

After they went to bed, Antonio had been unable to sleep. He got out of bed and went to the first floor. He looked at the plants being grown in the lab.

Antonio had converted part of the lab into a mini-greenhouse with natural and artificial light. He sat down at this desk and wrote out a plan of things he'd need to do in the next few days. He also wrote a letter to Teresa.

Antonio went to the office on the second floor of his house and opened the safe. He removed his notebook. He opened the desk drawer and removed a bunch of business cards held together by a rubber band. He looked through them until he found the one he wanted.

It was almost 6:30 a.m. Antonio went back to the first floor. He carefully wrapped his plants and placed them in boxes. He took them out to his SUV and put them in the back. He looked around to see if anyone was watching him. Antonio knew he was being paranoid, but he wouldn't be surprised if Tomlinson tried to steal the Dono di Russo plants.

Antonio took a shower and got dressed. It was Saturday morning so he didn't have to go to work. He made coffee and had something to eat. Then he went up to their bedroom to see if Teresa was awake. She was, and he told her he had some errands to run and should be back later this afternoon.

"I told Jason you'd be home today," Teresa said.

"I won't be long. I'll be back by as soon as I can." He kissed her on the forehead and left.

Antonio backed out of his driveway and looked both ways. He didn't see another car on the street. As he made his way to the highway, he kept looking in his rearview mirror to see if anyone was following him. So far he hadn't seen another car.

It was still early in the morning. Antonio picked up Alternate 19 in Largo and headed north. When he got to Dunedin, he turned onto a dirt road leading to a nursery with a large greenhouse. He could see someone working in the greenhouse. He pulled into the parking lot and got out of the SUV. He wanted to talk to the man, the father of a colleague, about his plants before bringing them into the greenhouse.

The door to the greenhouse was open and Antonio walked in. The elderly man was watering plants and he turned around. He smiled at Antonio and asked if he could help him.

"I worked with your son Jake in New Jersey," Antonio told him. "I wanted to ask you a favor."

Antonio walked over to shake hands with Mr. Rawlings. "I have some very special plants I'd like you to care for. I'll pay you, of course. These plants are not for sale."

Mr. Rawlings gestured towards the door at the rear of the greenhouse. They walked through the greenhouse and entered a small, cramped office. Mr. Rawlings asked Antonio if he would like some coffee and Antonio declined. They sat down opposite each other in matching lawn chairs.

"I brought these plants here from Brazil many years ago. I have a patent on them. I plan to study them and make a medicine out of them. But I have a problem, and I must hide them." Antonio looked at Mr. Rawlings to see his reaction.

"You need to hide them. That must mean you're afraid they'll be found. The question is by whom."

"Yes, they're precious to me and I must keep them safe. And yes, there's someone I need to hide them from."

"So, my ass may be on the line if I agree to keep your plants."

Antonio thought before he spoke. He hadn't been followed here, of that he was sure. Tomlinson had no way of knowing any of

Antonio's colleagues at Wilmer and March, and Jake Rawlings was still working in New Jersey. It seemed a safe bet that Mr. Rawlings was in no danger, save from the plants themselves.

"I've been very careful. No one saw me coming here. If you have any doubt, please tell me. Perhaps you know someone else who can help me," Antonio said.

Mr. Rawlings sat thinking. He reminded Antonio of his Papa back in Italy. He was short, round, and grizzled. He sported a gray bristly beard, and the bags under his eyes were deep. He looked nothing like his son Jake.

"Listen, what's your first name?"

"Antonio."

"Listen, Antonio, I know you're not bein' straight with me, so why don't you cut the bullshit?"

Rawlings was watching Antonio intently. He noted Antonio's drawn face and the dark circles under his eyes. Vinnie Rawlings had seen that look on every face that answered his knock on collection day. The mothers with kids hanging off their skirts, digging into their empty purses for change had that look. This guy, this Antonio was in trouble, the kind of trouble Vinnie was very familiar with.

Antonio took a deep breath in and let it out. His shoulders seemed to visibly shrink inside his shirt. He looked like he was about to cry.

"Kid, get up. We're goin' to get something to eat." The old man led the way out to his old battered truck. As he was about to put the key in the ignition, his cell phone rang.

"I really hate these mother..., sorry." Vinnie answered the phone. He was speaking in Italian to someone on the other end. He seemed to forget Antonio was Italian.

"Yeah, tell him I got the drops ready. Yeah, two hours. I'll be there." Vinnie hung up the phone and looked at Antonio. "Shit, you could understand that, couldn't you? Well, you got something on me, I got something on you, keeps it nice and friendly."

The old man turned the truck around and drove down the dirt road to Alternate 19. He drove Antonio to Tarpon Springs to a Greek restaurant that served a huge breakfast. Antonio ordered his usual coffee. The old man ordered the works and a bear claw for Antonio.

"You're too skinny. Your mama would kick your ass. Where is your mama Antonio?"

"She died when I was six."

188

Vinnie looked up from his eggs. "Santa Madre, no one should lose their mama that young." Vinnie made the sign of the cross when he said this.

"That's why the plants are so important. They can cure what happened to my mother."

"I like you, Antonio. You've got guts. Like me when I was a kid, if you know what I mean. Started working for Louie Marcos when I was 15. He was a good guy, Louie, and I really liked him. I used to go to different apartments delivering bags of money. It was easy, and I made good money. But my dad wasn't Italian, so they kept me doing jobs like that, kept me out of the big stuff, if you know what I mean.

"Anyway, one day Louie gets the idea that he wants to have some kind of operation in Florida. Just trafficking, nothing too big, so no one would notice, if you know what I mean. Exchanging money, that's all. I says why not me? My wife's dead, my kids are grown, why not send me? I always liked growing plants, if you know what I mean, so I set up the greenhouse.

"Every so often I get a call. Sometimes they leave money, sometimes they pick it up. At the end of the month there's a little something left for me. It works out." Vinnie paused to swallow. "Now, you know my story, what's yours?"

Antonio told Vinnie his story. He told him about finding his mama on the floor, about the Dono di Russo, about his wife's miscarriage, and about Tomlinson's threats of deportation. Vinnie listened carefully to Antonio.

"Tomlinson was the name of our old Sheriff. He wouldn't be related to that scumbag, would he?" Vinnie was putting way too much sugar in his coffee.

"I think he's the son." Antonio's shoulders seemed to be drooping even further down. He was so tired he could have fallen asleep right there.

"I'll tell you what. I'll keep your plants. I promise not to touch the leaves, or tamper with them in any way. I'll just water 'em. When you want 'em back, you come and get 'em. You need anything, you call me."

"But I want to pay you. I wouldn't feel right. Jake was always fair with me. I couldn't take advantage of his father."

"Yeah well, that rat bastard son of mine, he forgets he has a father."

189

"No, no, he is very proud of you. He showed me your card. He's the one that gave it to me."

Vinnie looked skeptical. "No matter. I meant what I said. I like you, kid. I believe you, too. Don't you worry about your plants."

Antonio reached for his wallet and the old man put his hand on Antonio's hand.

"Your money's no good here. Put that away." Then he threw a $20 bill on the table and got up.

Vinnie was stiff from sitting so long and kind of limped to the door. Antonio opened the door for him and offered his arm.

"I'm fine, just a little stiff. Getting old really sucks the big one, if you know what I mean, kid."

Antonio just nodded. When they got back to the greenhouse, Antonio brought the plants in and showed them to Vinnie. He made sure the old man understood that he should never touch the inside of the plant.

"Have you ever seen anybody do that, kid?"

"No, I just heard it happens really fast." Antonio had to get on with the rest of his errands. Vinnie put his hands on the younger man's face and kissed his cheeks.

"For your mama," Vinnie said. The old man actually brushed a tear away. "Nobody should lose their mama that young kid, if you know what I mean."

$$*****$$

Antonio entered the bank lobby an hour before closing at noon. He sat and waited for someone to assist him. Finally, a woman came over and escorted him into her cubicle. He said he needed to rent a safe deposit box. She asked him what size and he said not too big.

She pulled some papers out of her drawer and had Antonio fill them out. He designated Teresa his beneficiary so she would have no trouble getting into the box if something should happen to him.

The woman took Antonio to the vault where they kept the boxes and showed him how he would need two keys to open it, one he'd keep and the other the bank would keep. She opened the little door marked "27" with hers and then indicated that Antonio should use his key. Antonio noticed that the key had the same number stamped on it.

The door swung open and she pulled out the inner box. She placed it on the table in the middle of the vault and left Antonio alone.

Antonio pulled the notebook out of his pocket and placed it inside, along with the letter he had written to Teresa. When he was done, he closed the lid and placed the box back in its slot. He used his key to lock it and called the woman back so she could re-lock the bank's tumbler. Antonio thanked her while he folded the bank papers and slipped them into his pocket.

Antonio now felt he had done everything he could to protect the Dono di Russo plant and his formula for the drug. Even if Tomlinson hurt him, he'd find nothing. The only thing Antonio wanted to do was fortify his home to make it more secure for Teresa and Jason. He'd do that when they came back from Orlando.

*****

A week before they were set to leave for Orlando, Teresa had her yearly visit with Dr. Tomlinson. The doctor told her she was doing well and asked about Jason. She said for his eighth birthday they were taking him to Orlando and would be staying at the La Palma resort near Universal. She told him how excited Jason was, and the good doctor told her he hoped they had a splendid time.

While Teresa was packing for the trip, Antonio came to the door of the bedroom and asked her if she could stop for a minute. He took her outside on the deck so Jason couldn't hear. He sat down on one of the lounge chairs and she sat on the other.

He told her about his deal with Tomlinson, how they were going to treat 100 women as a sort of "trial" for his drug. He told her Tomlinson's idea of selling it as a supplement so they wouldn't need FDA approval. He then told her about his last visit with Tomlinson, when he'd told Antonio he'd used the drug on over 300 women and had told those women the drug was approved by the FDA.

"Then I told him I wouldn't give him any more drugs. He threatened me, Teresa. He said he'd tell the FBI and they would have me deported."

"I don't think they can do that. You've been here for years and we're legally married. Your visa has never been questioned. What makes you think Tomlinson would do that when he'd be implicating himself?"

191

"Because his father was the sheriff! He has pictures all over his office of him with policemen getting all kinds of awards. He'd tell them I lied, and he'd make it out like I fooled him. Who am I, Teresa? Why would they believe me over him?"

"Listen, Antonio, we can get you a good lawyer. We have enough money. Tomlinson is full of wind. He's just as culpable as you are. He gave these women something no one has ever heard of. It's not like a Chinese herb or chamomile. What he did is worse than anything you did, and I would bet the old son of a bitch charged those women through the nose.

"When we get back from Orlando, we'll go see Evelyn Moore. She's an attorney in Tampa my father used for the closing on his house. If nothing else, she may be able to point us in the right direction. Now, calm down and let's finish packing. We have a very excited 8-year-old waiting to go to Disney World."

"I know, I know, but first I have to give you this." Antonio pulled a small box out of his pocket. In it was a 24 inch solid gold chain with a small key hanging from it.

"Keep this on all the time. Don't let it out of your sight. It's for a safe deposit box in the bank. It's very important that you don't lose it."

Antonio put the chain around Teresa's neck. She promised him she'd never take it off.

*****

On the third day of their trip to Orlando, the Russos visited a water park complete with slides and swimming pools. Antonio accompanied Jason on every slide.

Father and son were bonding well. Antonio was feeling closer to his son than ever before. After they emerged from the 10th slide down the Mammoth Slope, Teresa asked Antonio if he would go to the locker and get her sunblock. He put his arms around her neck and kissed her, saying, "Cara, of course, anything for my princess." She smacked his butt playfully as he turned around. Jason yelled for Daddy to watch him and Antonio did.

Antonio walked through the park to the hallway that housed the lockers. He opened the locker. As Antonio reached into the locker, a man passed behind him, grabbed him, and pushed a knife up through his ribs and into his heart. The man then walked away without anyone noticing what he'd done.

192

Antonio fell to his knees. His heart was slowly bleeding out. As he lost consciousness, he thought of his son yelling for Daddy to watch him, and the smile on Jason's face when he did. It was the last thought Antonio Russo had before he died.

Chapter 36

Teresa Russo sat with her friend Lorraine in the office of the funeral director. He was explaining the different types of services they could have to celebrate the life of Antonio Russo. Teresa was still numb from shock. Lorraine had taken on the responsibility of deciding what they should do during the funeral, and Teresa had allowed her to.

All of his colleagues at the pharmaceutical company and most of their neighbors would attend the service. Teresa's parents, Ed and Dorothy, would also be there. The Bennetts would be there for sure.

The Bennetts were their neighbors. Jessica Bennett had confided in Teresa regarding her miscarriage history. Teresa could kick herself for recommending Dr. Tomlinson to Jessica, but she was six months pregnant now and hadn't miscarried. So, whether Teresa liked it or not, Jessica had needed the Fetura treatment.

The service was held in the big chapel of the funeral home. Teresa asked for a closed casket. She wanted Antonio for herself and Jason alone. Antonio's father was unable to fly due to illness, but Teresa's parents were doing all they could to comfort Teresa and Jason. When the service was over, Teresa's mom asked if she should take Jason home with her, and Teresa said no. She was still numb when the service ended.

Teresa took Jason by the hand and they walked up to the casket. She asked him if he wanted to see his Daddy one last time. Jason solemnly nodded his head. Teresa asked the director to open the casket so they could see Antonio. He looked so peaceful lying there. There was no sign of the agony he must have experienced. Jason looked upon his father's calm countenance and began to cry. Teresa knelt down and took him in her arms.

They held each other and sobbed, overcome by the pain of loss. Teresa stood up and took one last look at her beloved Antonio. She lightly touched his arm. Then she took her little boy's hand and left the funeral home.

Teresa was staying with her parents. She hadn't been home since they'd left for Orlando. She and Jason would head back to her house after the interment to pick up some fresh clothes and check on the house.

Some of the mourners had traveled to the cemetery. Teresa and Jason sat in front of the casket with her mother next to her and her father next to Jason. After they lowered the casket into the ground, she and Jason left for home.

When they arrived home, Teresa pushed the button on the garage door opener. She pulled in and parked the car. Jason got out of the car, and as she was getting the bags out of the trunk, she noticed him walk into the house. She put down the bags and followed him. That door should have been locked.

When she got inside, Teresa found Jason standing in the kitchen looking at a mess on the floor. Everything in her kitchen had been emptied. Her computer was still there. She ran to the living room. The pillows and sofa cushions were cut open. Drawers were pulled out and emptied. Teresa ran to the phone and called 911.

The police took a report and asked Teresa if there was anything missing. Her TV and stereo equipment were still there, and her computer and other kitchen appliances hadn't been touched. It didn't look like anything had been stolen. The officers asked her what the thieves could have been looking for. She said she had no idea.

Teresa had Jason pick out some toys to take with him. She took the dogs' bowls and their beds. After she packed some clothes, they headed for Ed and Dorothy's.

Ricky greeted them at the door. Lorraine, who was leaving for home the next day, hugged her. Chloe was sitting on Dorothy's lap and wagged her tail when she saw Teresa. She then jumped down and went to the door, looking for Antonio.

"He's not coming, girl," Jason said as he stroked her head. Teresa felt tears welling in her eyes. She put her arm around Jason and brought him into the living room. Jason sat on Ed's lap and Teresa sat down next to her mom.

She told her parents about the break-in. She told them she was going to stay in a hotel for a few days so she could sort some things out. She asked them if they could watch Jason and the dogs. They agreed, and Teresa made a reservation at the Marriott.

After dropping Lorraine off at the airport, she checked into the hotel and called attorney Evelyn Moore. Evelyn's secretary made an appointment for the next day. In the meantime, Teresa bought a diary and started writing down everything she could remember about her life with Antonio. She wrote through the night because she couldn't sleep. In the morning, she took a shower and headed for Evelyn Moore's office.

Evelyn Moore was a short, round woman with gray hair and glasses. She was pretty and smiled in a way that put Teresa at ease right away. She led Teresa to a conference room she used for interviews. There were several leather chairs with high backs around a long table. Teresa chose one on the side while Evelyn sat at the head of the table.

Teresa explained her situation, how Antonio had been murdered, how she believed Dr. Tomlinson was involved, the ransacking of her home, her fear that someone might try to hurt Jason, and Antonio's involvement in Tomlinson's scheme.

Evelyn listened intently until Teresa was done. She asked about Teresa's financial situation. Teresa told her about her online trading and the money she had in the bank. That combined with the insurance policy from Antonio's job would leave her somewhere in the neighborhood of $2,000,000.

"In that case, Mrs. Russo, I would suggest you hire someone to fortify your home, new locks, security windows and shutters, alarm systems, etc. You should consider putting your son in a private school with good security. You also may want to install security cameras. Where is the safe deposit key?"

Teresa pulled on the chain around her neck and revealed the key.

"Did Antonio have a will?"

"Yes, I have a copy."

"Good. I'll need that to file probate. Where are the plants now? Were they in the house?"

"I don't know," Teresa said. She hadn't checked the greenhouse the night she called the police.

"Go check out the safe deposit box and bring in the will. Let me know what you find."

When Teresa left Evelyn's office, she felt better. At least she had a plan. She'd been unable to think these last few days, let alone plan. She needed to see Jason so she drove over to her parents' house and visited him.

Teresa told her parents she had a plan and as soon as her house was ready, she would bring Jason home. In the meantime, he would stay with them. Jason wasn't happy to see his mother leave again and let her know it.

"Look, kiddo, I have to make the house safe for us. You be a brave boy and let Mommy do this, okay?" Jason nodded his head but still cried when she left.

The next day Teresa went to Farlands Bank. She spoke with the manager regarding the safe deposit box. He took her into his office and they sat down. He checked the account and noted that Teresa was Antonio's beneficiary. He had her sign some paperwork and then led her to the vault. There he used their keys to remove the box. He placed it on the table and left Teresa alone.

Teresa opened the box. Antonio had been the last person to touch this box. She felt the tears welling in her eyes as she touched the sides of the box, trying to feel his fingers. She saw the notebook along with what looked like a letter.

She flipped through the notebook and decided to leave it in the box. She opened the letter and read it. It contained information outlining what Antonio had done and where his plants had been taken. It was a confession of sorts. He was clearing his conscience. Teresa kissed his signature. She then folded the letter and put it in her purse.

A few weeks after Antonio's death, Teresa received a large check from the insurance company. She wept bitterly at the sight of the check. It was all she had left of her husband.

Teresa kept herself busy fortifying the house. When she was done, no one would enter her house again without her knowledge. She picked up Jason from her parents' house and brought him home. She showed him the security screens and told him not to open the door without checking them first, or calling Mommy. She showed him how the shutters closed at night, or during a hurricane.

That night when she tucked him in, Jason asked her to stay while he fell asleep. Teresa gently lay down next to him and held him. He fell asleep in her arms.

*****

Teresa now turned her thoughts to Dr. Tomlinson. She talked to Evelyn about how she could bring him down. Evelyn said it would be hard without implicating Antonio. If Teresa chose to sue, any petition she filed would contain information regarding the Dono di Russo. It would also be a public record, available to anyone, including the lawyers at Wilmer and March. As soon as they found out where Antonio discovered his Dono di Russo, Jacob Wilmer might put two and two together and sue. Also, Tomlinson's father had deep ties to law enforcement, which made him almost invincible.

197

This was a bitter pill for Teresa to swallow. She could stand to lose everything, putting her and Jason's future at risk. Evelyn told her to think long and hard about doing anything concerning Dr. Tomlinson.

In the end, Teresa had to let it go. At least the old bastard would never treat another woman with Fetura. Antonio had seen to that.

The next day Teresa drove up Alternate 19 until she reached a dirt road. She made a right, and drove to end of the driveway where she saw a greenhouse. She parked the SUV and walked to the greenhouse door. She knocked and then opened it. She saw a short, round older man watering plants. He turned and smiled. He asked if he could help her.

"My name is Teresa Russo. My husband told me you were holding our plants for him."

Vinnie Rawlings waved for her to follow him. She walked to the back of the greenhouse and followed Vinnie into the office. He sat down on a lawn chair and indicated she do the same. He offered her some coffee, and as her husband had done three weeks before, she declined.

"So, where is the little *goomba*? I expected him back before this." Vinnie was smiling at Teresa.

"I, uh...I'm afraid he was...murdered." Teresa was trying very hard not to cry. Vinnie's eyes darkened.

"When? When did they get him?" His voice sounded flat and menacing.

"Two weeks ago while we were in Orlando. He was....was by the lockers...and...he was stabbed. From behind. He never saw them." The tears were now rolling slowly down her face.

Vinnie hated shit like this, shit where somebody good, somebody genuinely good was hurt.

"He was good, your Antonio. He was a good person. What my old friend Saul would call a mensch. He didn't deserve this." Already the wheels in Vinnie's head were turning. "Look, Teresa, I have Antonio's plants. They're safe here. I won't let anybody near them. Anybody shows up here and I'll cut their throat. *Capice?*"

Despite what the old man had said, Teresa found that she liked him, maybe even trusted him. She had no idea what to do with the poisonous plants. She knew Antonio's will bequeathed them to her, and Evelyn would have the patents transferred. But what would she do then?

"You really don't mind?" she asked.

"You just leave them here and when you know what you want to do with them, you let me know. Don't you worry about a thing. I'll take care of everything."

There was something about the way he said "everything" that made Teresa cringe. She convinced herself it was just her imagination, but still he did remind her of an actor on The Sopranos. She thanked Vinnie and gave him her phone number. She said to call if he needed anything. Then she drove back to St. Petersburg to pick up Jason from school.

Chapter 37

When Teresa left the greenhouse, Vinnie called the kid who did the pickups and asked him to come over. When the kid arrived, Vinnie asked him if he knew a girl who could make a phone call for him. Somebody with a sweet, convincing voice. The kid, a Hispanic boy who called himself Cash, said he thought his new girlfriend, a 17-year-old named Trixie, would fit the bill.

Trixie had just arrived from the Panhandle, straight from the sticks. She had liked the taste of blow he'd given her a week before and was itching for more. She would do it for a hit, Cash said, and her sweet Southern accent was perfect. Vinnie asked him to bring Trixie by in the morning around 9:30.

Trixie looked like a 17-year-old trying to look like a 21-year-old. Her clothes were way too tight and her makeup bordered on clownish. Vinnie brought her back to the office while Cash wandered around the greenhouse. Cash knew better than to mess with the purple-edged plants. Vinnie told him if he did, his balls would fall off.

Vinnie gave Trixie the telephone number for Dr. Tomlinson's office. He wanted her to call and make an appointment with the good doctor. If she did a good job, he said, she could have a hit on him. Trixie smiled and picked up the phone.

When the receptionist answered, she made an appointment for three weeks later. The woman told her it would be $120 for the visit if she didn't have insurance. Vinnie signaled her to say fine and to hang up. He then passed a small packet of coke to her.

On the morning of Trixie's appointment, Vinnie told Cash to bring her into the office again. He told Cash to have Trixie fill out the paperwork at the doctor's office with false information.

"Just tell them anything. Make sure it's all bogus." He handed Cash $120. Then Vinnie turned to Trixie.

"When you get the doctor alone, I want you to tell him that Antonio sent you. You got that? Antonio."

"Antonio sent me," Trixie repeated.

"Right. When he asks you 'who,' you say 'I have the plants.' That's all. Then give him this number." Vinnie gave Trixie a slip of paper with a number from a throw-away phone he'd purchased just for this occasion. "Then get the hell out of there. Don't stop for nothin'. They won't have anything on you anyway."

When Cash and Trixie got to Tomlinson's office, she filled out the paperwork as instructed. Cash paid for the visit and they waited their turn. When she was called, Trixie was led to an examining room.

She was asked to take off her clothes and put on a gown. Trixie had no intention of staying, so she put the gown on over her tube top and mini-skirt. It looked like she was naked underneath. When the doctor walked in, her first thought was of course, Santa Claus.

"Good afternoon, Mary is it?" He walked over and shook her hand.

"Antonio sent me." Trixie had wasted no time. "He said to give you this."

She handed him the slip of paper with the phone number on it, ripped off the gown and ran out of the room.

She and Cash high tailed it out of there and into the parking lot. Cash put the key in the ignition and the pedal to the floor. When Dr. Tomlinson came out to find them, they were too far away for him to read their tag.

Vinnie asked Cash to bring Trixie to the office to wait for Tomlinson's call. She told Vinnie she forgot to tell him about the plants. Vinnie wasn't worried. He said just the name Antonio should do the trick.

Around 6 that evening, the throw-away rang. Trixie picked it up and said "Hello." Tomlinson demanded to know what she was talking about. Vinnie had instructed her to say she had his plants. When she did, there was silence on the other end. She asked if he was still there and he said yes. Finally, Tomlinson asked what she wanted.

"I want to give you the plants. I'm sure you'd be willing to give me some kind of reward."

"What kind of reward?" Tomlinson didn't sound happy.

"$50,000 should be okay." Vinnie gave Trixie the thumbs-up. There was another long pause.

"Fine. Where should I bring it?"

Trixie gave Tomlinson an address in Tarpon Springs by the docks. There was an old warehouse there that belonged to a friend of Vinnie's. She told him to meet her there in two hours at nine o'clock.

"And Doc, no cops. If I see cops, I burn the plants, *capice?*" Vinnie cringed at the way she said "*capice*." The Southern accent killed it.

"I'll be there, you little slut."

Trixie frowned. Vinnie told her to hang up. Vinnie told Cash to go to the warehouse and wait until he saw the good doctor arrive alone. If he wasn't alone, Cash was to call Vinnie immediately. Vinnie was counting on the doctor's greed. He believed Tomlinson would show up alone.

Two hours later Cash called. He said the doctor was there alone. Vinnie was sitting just down the road with a plant. He drove to the warehouse and parked next to the doctor's car. The doctor was sitting in it waiting for Trixie.

"You must be the good Dr. Tomlinson. Antonio told me so much about you." Vinnie was smiling at the doctor. He was holding the plant.

"Where's the girl?" he asked Vinnie.

"Oh, it was past her bedtime. She asked me to take care of you for her. Won't you come in?"

Vinnie walked over to the warehouse and opened the door. The doctor got out of his car and reluctantly followed. The warehouse was brightly lit, which helped assuage the doctor's growing anxiety. He now wished he'd called his brother the police captain to come with him, but he hadn't wanted to jeopardize this exchange. Only someone with the plants would know about him and Antonio.

Vinnie placed the plant on a table by the warehouse office.

"I thought there were more," Tomlinson said.

"Well, there are, of course. This is kind of a teaser, if you will. Have you ever seen one of these beauties?"

"No, there was no need. Mr. Russo made the drug. He duped me into believing he had FDA approval."

"Yeah, that's our Antonio. A real lowlife." Vinnie pulled the cord on the overhead light. "So, whadda ya think?"

The plant Vinnie chose was in full bloom. The leaves were big and the purple edges sublime. The doctor sucked in his breath when he saw it under the light.

"It's quite breathtaking isn't it?" He came closer to the plant.

"Yeah, and you should smell it. Like a rose."

"Really? The purple solution smelled like wet plants." Dr. Tomlinson leaned closer.

"You gotta get right on top of it, Doc. Put your nose right to it."

Tomlinson put his nose closer. He was less than an inch from the large green center of the leaf.

"I don't smell anything," Tomlinson said.

202

"You actually have to touch the plant, Doc. Rub your nose to release the oils."

Antonio had never mentioned the plant's poisonous centers to Tomlinson. He put his nose to the leaf and rubbed it. He fell over so fast it surprised Vinnie. There was blood dripping from his nose.

Vinnie picked up the plant and put it back in his car. He called Cash to come in and remove the body. Cash came in and dragged Tomlinson's body to the back of the warehouse. There was a dock outside where the river ran. Cash hoisted Tomlinson's body over the edge of the dock, sending him into the river after carefully placing some nice smooth rocks in his pockets. Vinnie spit into the water.

"That's for Antonio you son of a bitch." He then paid Cash and waked back toward his car.

He opened Dr. Tomlinson's car door and found a bag containing $50,000. Vinnie was surprised the good doctor was ready to pay. He took the money and put it in his trunk.

"Hey, Cash, wipe for prints and make sure there's no blood on the floor, will ya?"

"Okay, boss."

Cash walked through the warehouse, washing up the drops of blood leading to the dock. He checked the floor and the dock for traces of blood and wiped the door and table for prints before locking up and going home.

When Teresa read about Dr. Tomlinson's disappearance in the St. Petersburg Times, her first thought was Vinnie. When his body washed up on the shores of the Anclote River, she knew it was Vinnie. He had avenged her Antonio, and even though she found what he'd done morally repugnant, she secretly cheered him. He had done what she couldn't do. He had protected her Antonio's memory.

*****

Jason was thirteen years old when Teresa decided to send him to a good prep school in Connecticut. Lorraine had investigated it for her and said it was one of the best on the East Coast. Jason was adamant that he wouldn't go, but in the end Teresa won out and he left for New England. Teresa missed him terribly, but she felt he needed to be around boys his own age and men other than her father.

Teresa had always felt inadequate when it came to Jason's needs. She had been an only child and a girl at that. She hoped he wouldn't blame her one day for his abandonment issues, and that he would understand why she had sent him so far away. Jason would come home during breaks and summer vacation, and each time he'd grown an inch.

By the summer of his seventeenth year, he was a strapping six feet tall. He looked like Antonio with her father's build. He had brown hair with a slight wave to it and brown eyes. He was a good-looking boy who turned heads at the mall when Teresa took him shopping for school clothes. Antonio would have been proud.

One day shortly after Jason had returned home for summer break, while Teresa was cooking Jason some eggs, she fell to the floor with blood running from her nose and was dead before she hit the ground.

PART THREE

JASON RUSSO

But the Children Survived

Chapter 38

St. Pete Beach, Florida

When Jason Russo woke up, he could see Ricky sleeping in his bed next to the wall. Ricky was snoring. He was eighteen years old, but he hadn't changed much since Jason's eighth birthday. He had no gray on his snout or his body. His belly skin looked fresh and pink, not mottled and dark like some older dogs. Jason was happy Ricky hadn't aged because that meant he might be around for a little while longer.

Ricky was the only living, breathing being he'd seen in weeks. Ricky's mother, Chloe, had died when Jason was eleven, leaving the little dog in a state of grief for several weeks after. Jason and Ricky had always been close, even though Jason had been gone for months at a time. Now they depended totally on each other for survival.

Jason got out of bed and stretched his six-foot frame until his hand touched the ceiling. He walked over to the sliding glass door that looked out onto the beach and slid it open.

He stepped onto the porch and felt the sun on his face. He had cleared the beach the first week. Then he'd tackled the street in front of his house and in the surrounding area for about a mile around so he could travel without encountering death at each turn.

Jason took a few deep breaths. The smell of rotting flesh was still faintly wafting through the air. Jason had done a good job. With the beach and streets clear, he could begin using the table on the deck to eat his meals. He liked the fresh air, and now that the air was clear, Ricky would join him. For the first week Ricky had refused to come outside except to relieve himself. Now he stayed outside a little longer.

Jason went back inside and closed the sliding glass door. Ricky was still asleep. Jason walked to the stairs going down to the lower level of the house, passing his mother's room. He kept the door closed as the smell of her perfume always made him tear up and he refused to give in to that weakness. He'd shed enough tears. With the door closed, the smell in the hallway had dissipated. He took the stairs two at a time until he reached the bottom three at which time he jumped, landing in a squat and giving himself a perfect 10.

Jason walked to the kitchen and opened the fridge. He was happy the electricity was still on. As most of the neighborhood had, his mother installed solar panels when the Bennetts had petitioned them to. It was a good investment. They had been able to sell some of the power back to the electric company.

This had been a very hot summer so far, but Jason's frozen food supply was safe. He had emptied Granger's freezers a few days after the disaster, so he had plenty of frozen waffles and concentrated orange juice. He also was able to salvage eggs.

His mother had shown him how to freeze raw eggs by adding a little salt or sugar to them before freezing them. He'd spent a good part of that day preparing the eggs. He had grabbed some ice cube trays at the store and used them to freeze the eggs. Now he just popped one or two "cubes" out a day and had eggs every morning. He was running out, though. Soon he'd have to change his breakfast menu.

The first day had been almost unbearable for Jason. His mother died right before his eyes while he was on the phone with his friend Justin. As Teresa fell, he heard a thump on the other end of the phone and then nothing. He knew the phone was still on because he could hear the sound of the ocean in the background. But Justin wouldn't answer.

He dropped the phone and ran to Teresa. He started CPR but he could hear no heartbeat. He tried to dial 911, but no one answered the call.

Jason looked at Ricky, who was whimpering over Teresa's body. He sat down on the floor near his mother with his back up against the kitchen island and for a long time, he just stared at her. He was tired from the night before. He had gotten home late from Justin's house. He closed his eyes for just a minute and soon fell asleep.

When he woke up a few hours later, Ricky was licking his hand and trying to get his attention. Teresa was still lying where she had fallen. He looked at Ricky and the little dog jumped up on his shoulders and licked his face. He had to go out.

Jason hauled himself off the floor and walked over to the sliding glass door leading to the first floor deck. He opened the door without looking up. Ricky hesitated as he sniffed the air. Jason gave him a little shove with his foot, and then looked up.

He saw bodies littering the beach. The shock made him step back. There had to be at least 50 people on the stretch of beach behind his house. He could see them for at least half a mile each way.

Ricky ran to the side of the house where there was grass. Jason couldn't move. He just looked at the beach. Ricky ran back to the deck and barked at Jason. He was hungry. He broke Jason's concentration and snapped him back to reality. He barked again.

"Okay boy, okay." They both walked back into the house.

The dog food was in a cabinet next to Teresa's body. Jason went to the refrigerator and pulled out some cold cuts. He ripped them into little pieces and put them in Ricky's bowl. He set the bowl down on the other side of the kitchen near Ricky's bowl of water. The little dog sniffed it and gobbled it up voraciously. Then Jason turned his attention once more to his mother's body.

She would begin to stiffen up soon. He would have to make a decision. Once again, he picked up his phone and dialed 911. Again, no one answered. That's when the tears began to roll down Jason's face.

Jason felt embarrassed to be crying. He would be eighteen in two weeks and to be crying at his age was just humiliating. He hated feeling so weak. Then he thought of Justin. Maybe he could find someone over there to help him.

Jason, with Ricky at his heels walked over to Justin's house. It was one house over near the convenience store. As Jason passed the house next door, he saw the lady who lived there lying on the front porch with a newspaper in her hand as if she had just picked it up when she fell over.

He jogged past while Ricky trotted. Before he got to Justin's house, he could see Justin's little sister Caitlyn lying in the driveway. He walked over to her and could see the blood coming from her nose. He saw the family dog, Nora, lying in the grass. He looked at Nora and she, too, had blood coming from her nose.

"What the hell happened, Ricky?" Jason said.

He walked to the front door, and it was open. He entered the house and saw Justin's mother, Janice, dead on the sofa with the TV still running. He walked into the kitchen and there was Justin's father, David, with his face in a plate of eggs. Justin was on the floor with the phone in his hand. Jason turned and ran out of the house.

He threw up on the lawn, just missing Nora's body. He fell onto his knees and threw up again. His body was shaking all over and he couldn't stop it. What the hell was he going to do now? And why were he and Ricky still alive when everyone else had died?

Jason walked back to his house. He had to take care of his mother. He went to the shed and looked around to see if he could find something waterproof to wrap her in. He found an old tarpaulin from when the house had been painted. He picked up the tarpaulin and then looked around for something to tie it with.

He found an old dog tie-out they had kept Ricky on until it became apparent that this dog would never run away. He took that in his other hand and went back into the house.

Jason laid the tarpaulin out in the living room. He then gently lifted Teresa's body up and carried her to the living room. He laid her on the tarpaulin and then stood back. He knelt down next to her and took her hand. She looked like she was asleep. The blood under her nose had dried and darkened. He broke down again and sobbed uncontrollably.

Jason willed himself to stop crying. He pulled the tarpaulin around Teresa's body. He thought about putting something inside the wrapping to help it sink to the bottom of the ocean. He walked outside and found some decorative rocks Teresa had put there a few years ago. They were heavy enough to do the job.

Jason continued to wrap Teresa in the tarpaulin. There were rivets on the sides of the tarpaulin and Jason wove the dog tie through the holes. Just before he finished weaving, he slipped the rocks into the tarpaulin. He took the dog tie and wrapped part of it around the bottom by her feet to close it. Then he turned to do the same to the other end.

He looked at Teresa's face. It would be the last time he ever looked upon his mother's beautiful face. He had to close his eyes as he wrapped the ends of the tarpaulin around her head and then wrapped the rest of the dog tie around it, pulling it closed. He made sure the knots were secure before he tried to move her.

The rocks made her body heavier so he had to drag her to the deck. He was going to use David's 20 foot sailboat to take her out to sea. Jason and Justin had taken the boat out alone several times, and Jason felt well able to handle it.

He pulled Teresa's body out to the deck. He was careful when he got to the lip of the sliding glass doors to lift her head over the bump. He did the same when he got her to the end of the dock.

The sand was soft and it took him a while to get her to the Carsons' dock. When he got there, Jason had to lift Teresa's body up to the dock, about four feet off the ground. He was able to sit her up, grab her arms through the tarpaulin and hoist her up onto the dock. The rocks were all at her feet.

Jason then dragged her to the boat, which was docked on the right hand side of the dock. Again he had to lift and hoist to get her onto the boat. Once she was aboard, Jason cast off the lines and unfurled one of the sails. The wind was picking up and the boat easily sailed away from the dock. Jason tried not to think of what he had to do next.

When he was out about a mile, he lowered the sail and waited until the boat slowed down. He threw the small anchor over the side to stop the boat.

Jason tried to remember something from the Sunday school classes his mother had taken him to before his father died. After Antonio died, Teresa had lost her faith and stopped going to church. Jason wasn't sure what to do when suddenly he remembered an old song they had taught him. He hummed it quietly and then sang the first line. "Jesus loves me this I know, for the Bible tells me so." He couldn't remember anymore, so he just started to talk to his mother.

"I'm sorry, Mom. I'm so sorry I couldn't save you. I know I didn't tell you enough but I love you. I will always remember you and ..." He started to cry. Then he started to shout. "What the hell, God? What were you thinking? WHAT AM I SUPPOSED TO DO NOW?!"

He sat down on the deck of the boat and felt the waves gently rock him, like a mother rocking her baby. He looked at his mother wrapped for burial. He knew he couldn't stay here forever and that sooner or later he would have to go back to the shore. He couldn't leave Ricky alone.

Jason put his arms around Teresa and held her, clinging to these last few seconds with his very life. He cried so hard his stomach began to hurt.

"I can't." He whispered. "I can't do this." Jason shook his head.

Teresa's body felt hard, not like his mother at all. He sat up and let go of her. His shoulders went up and down.

"But I have to because there isn't anybody else, is there?"

His grief had suddenly turned to something deeper, a depression that would enable him to do what he had to and not feel. He put his hand out and touched Teresa. "Bye, mom."

He got up off the deck and lifted Teresa up. He put her over the side and after one second of hesitation, he let her go. Jason watched as she disappeared feet first into the ocean. The rocks would ground her to the bottom so she wouldn't wash up on the beach.

Jason didn't want to linger. He pulled up the anchor and unfurled the sail. He took hold of the wheel and turned the boat around, careful not to get hit by the boom. He steered the boat towards Justin's dock and just before he reached it, he lowered the sail and gently guided the boat next to the dock. He was glad Justin had taught him to sail. He would use those skills many times over in the next three weeks.

Chapter 39

Jason heard Ricky's nails on the stairs. He must have smelled food cooking.

"Hey, buddy, you woke up."

Jason smiled at Ricky. He had put some pet stairs by one of the kitchen chairs so Ricky could climb up and sit while Jason ate. Sometimes Jason would give him some of his food one piece at a time.

Ricky had a sweet little face that Jason found comical. When he opened his mouth to pant he looked like he was smiling. His bug eyes made him look skeptical, especially when he was looking up at Jason from the floor.

"Guess what, Rick, we can go shopping today. I cleaned the streets off and now we can walk the neighborhood without looking at zombies all day. Right, fella?"

Jason reached over and ruffled Ricky's head. He had filled his cabinets with paper plates so he wouldn't have to do dishes. He did have to wash any pans he used, and silverware, but that wasn't so bad. Anytime he could get away with just using a paper plate and the microwave, he did.

He put the plate in the garbage bag he had by the sliding glass door and then went upstairs to shower and get dressed. When he came back down, he gave Ricky a small can of dog food. While the dog ate, he went back upstairs to do his daily check of the neighborhood with Justin's binoculars.

He grabbed the binoculars and went up one more flight of stairs to the roof. There was a modern version of a widow's walk up there and he perched himself on it while he used the binoculars to scan the area.

Where he stood, he could see them but they couldn't see him, so to speak. As usual, there were no living people in sight. A week or so ago he had thought he heard a truck drive past his house, but he was just waking up and decided it was his imagination.

He went downstairs three at a time this time and told Ricky to get a move on. He opened the door and he and Ricky walked the two blocks into the shopping center of town. They walked past the stores that Jason had cleared of bodies and rotting food.

"Buddy, I think I need some new shoes. Let's hit the shoe store."

213

Jason opened the door of a small surf shop and held the door for Ricky. There was plenty of light from the sun today so he was able to see the racks of clothes and shoes. He picked out a pair of Converse Pro Leather Sneakers, cargo shorts, and some graphic tees.

Jason looked at the underwear and grabbed those too. Most of his clothes were getting too small. Dragging and lifting bodies for two weeks had pumped him up and he continued to lift weights over at Justin's. His chest was getting bigger, as were his arms and thighs.

"You see anything you like, Ricky?" Ricky made a sound that greatly resembled a harrumph. "Guess not." Jason threw the clothes in a bag, left the store and headed home.

When he got back to the house he was hungry again. He popped a frozen pizza into the oven and set the timer so he wouldn't forget. He had 15 minutes to kill and now that he had finished cleaning up the neighborhood, he was finding it hard to fill time.

Last week he had entered his mother's office. He had been avoiding that room for fear it, too, might smell like her. But while he was throwing bones into the sea the day before, he had the strangest memory. It hit him out of the blue.

He was listening to his mother talking to her friend a few days after his father died. Her friend made a strange remark about how his father and Teresa had created a purple baby and how it was too bad Antonio had never been able to make that drug. Teresa had nodded her head. When Jason asked what they meant by a purple baby, Teresa told him they had been talking about a movie.

Jason had forgotten all about it until that moment. He knew his father had been a biochemist who grew these weird plants in the basement. He knew that his dad had given them to an old man named Vinnie.

Jason and his mother used to visit Vinnie until the old man died. Jason had been about 12 years old then. He remembered seeing the plants at Vinnie's greenhouse. He knew they were poisonous. Then he remembered they were also very purple.

When he got back home from clearing the bodies that day, he stripped off his clothes before entering the house. He went inside and looked around the greenhouse to see if any remnants of his father's lab still remained. There was nothing left. Teresa must have had it all removed at some time.

He then went upstairs and took a shower. After he ate, he reluctantly went into Teresa's office. The scent was different in

214

there. There was an old air freshener on the table by the air conditioner vent. There was an ebony desk with very little on top. Teresa had been neat. There was a small safe in one corner and a file cabinet next to the desk. Teresa's laptop sat on the file cabinet.

Jason sat on the chair behind the desk. He tried the drawers and they all opened. Inside he found the usual office stuff, paper clips, etc. He opened the file cabinet and flipped through the files. Here again were the usual things like utility bills and bank statements. In the second file drawer he found a filed marked "Jason." He pulled out the file and opened it on the desk.

The file contained his birth certificate. He had been born in St. Petersburg General Hospital. There were no pictures in this file. He had been delivered by a Dr. Michael Tomlinson. Jason looked at the rest of the file but found nothing else about his birth. His mother had photo albums in her bedroom. He might *have* to look in there someday.

Jason then turned to look at the safe. It was a small boxy thing with a combination lock. Not the most secure thing in the world. Jason bet he could figure out the combination. He tried all the birthdays he knew and they didn't work. He then tried names. Finally, he tried his mother's cell phone number. It worked, and the safe door swung open.

Inside the safe was a small box. Inside the box was a gold chain with a key. The key had the number "27" on it. It looked like a post office box key. Or maybe a safe deposit box? Jason went back to the file cabinet and opened the top drawer.

He looked at the bank statements until he found one from Farlands bank, which had debited the rent on a safe deposit box every month. Jason looked at the key. Now that he knew what it was for, he had to figure out how to get into the box. When he finished moving bodies, then he would work on cracking the bank vault. He put the chain around his neck and closed the safe.

*****

Jason's pizza was ready. He ate fast and decided to go to the bank to see just how hard it would be to get into the vault. If he succeeded at all, he would have to be careful about getting locked in there.

"Ricky, I have to leave you home for now. Don't whine - I'll be back."

He filled the dog's bowl with kibble and refilled his water. He left a window open with just a screen in case the dog had to get out of the house if something happened to Jason. Jason believed Ricky could break through that screen if he got desperate. He grabbed his backpack and left the house.

His friend Justin's father had been an apocalyptic nut who believed the Mayans had it right and the end of the world was approaching fast. He had fortified his home and collected relics of the two world wars. He found the perfect gas mask in a survivalist magazine and purchased enough for the whole family.

Jason was grateful for David's fantasies as it gave him the perfect weapon against the smell of rotting flesh as he removed bodies for three weeks. Jason thought about riding through Zombie Town, the areas that still had bodies littering the streets, and decided to get a mask from Justin's house.

Jason had taken care of Justin and his family the day after he buried his mom. He also gave Nora a burial at sea. The house that had been so full of life lay quiet and empty when Jason came over to get the mask.

He remembered Justin showing him a satellite dish his father had installed. It was anchored by huge beams drilled right through the house. Justin's mother hadn't been amused by that at all. But Justin loved the thing, and he and Jason spent hours using it to pan over Europe and South America. Jason hadn't thought about the satellite dish in ages. After he checked out Farlands, he was going to spend some time on that dish.

He got onto Justin's scooter and headed for Farlands. He passed the point of his body-clearing efforts and came upon Zombie Town. After four weeks, there were nothing but bones and clothing left. The smell wasn't too bad either, as the sea breezes blew constantly.

The streets were filled with parked cars, still occupied, still waiting for the light to turn green. He weaved his way around them. He found the Farlands Bank and parked in the parking lot. He put the mask on and entered the bank.

The hurricane that hit Pinellas County just days after everyone died had knocked out the power. For some reason, it had never been restored. This place could have had a generator, but if so, it had stopped working. The building was extremely hot.

There was a guard by the door with keys in his hand. There was a man behind a desk in one corner. There were bodies both male and female behind the tellers' cages. Jason figured one of the desks had to be the bank manager's.

He looked at the vault to the left of the tellers' cages. It was open. They must have just opened for the day and the vault would be open for them to get money for the tellers' drawers. Jason walked over to the vault.

There was a barred door that stood between him and the safe deposit boxes. It did have a key lock. If he could find the key, he could get to the boxes.

Jason went back to the lobby and over to the desk where the man's body sat. It was little more than bones and hair. Jason moved him out of the way and he collapsed into a pile of bones inside his clothes.

"Sorry, buddy," Jason said.

He then began to open the drawers. When he didn't find anything, it occurred to him that the key was probably in the guy's pockets. He moved the guy's arm to get inside his suit jacket pocket. He found nothing on the outside, or the inside. Jason hated going through his pants pockets, but that was the most likely place they would be. He put his hand inside the guy's pants pockets and, lo and behold, there was a small ring of keys.

Jason walked over to the barred door. He tried each key until he found one that fit. The barred door swung open. Jason went to the back of the bank to see if he could find a utility room. He found a bathroom with a large trash can. He brought the trash can out to the lobby and propped it against the barred door. The vault door was held open by a stop.

He found number 27. He took the key out of his shirt and tried to open it. It required two keys. He took each key on the ring and tried it. He was able to open the lock with the fifth key. He then used his key to open the box.

He slid the box out of the slot and took it out of the vault. He laid it on the manager's desk and opened it. Inside was a notebook. That was all. Jason took it out of the box and stuffed it into his pocket. He then walked out of the bank and took off his mask.

The air felt good, although now he could smell himself. He was glad he wore his old clothes. He would throw them out. He took the notebook out of his pocket and put it into the backpack before slinging it onto his back. He then rode home to Ricky.

When Jason got home he took off all his clothes before going in the house. He ran to the shower and ran the water over himself for 20 minutes. The smell had gotten into his nose. He tried to brush it out with a toothbrush, but the head of the brush was too big. He knew it would eventually go away, but he really hated that smell.

He dried off and put on some clean *old* clothes. If any smell should linger, he could throw them away, too.

He went to the kitchen and threw some toaster pastries in the toaster. When they popped, he put them on a paper plate and headed for the office. He put the notebook on the desk. He forgot something to drink and ran back to the kitchen to get some orange juice. Now he was ready to read the notebook.

The notebook was filled from cover to cover. Antonio's handwriting was careful and neat. He had wanted the reader to be able to discern what he had to say.

The story began with his finding Margaret DeMorte in Brazil, the Mortevida plant, his job at Wilmer and March, his discovery of George Ranier, and the fact that the doctor who had delivered Jason had been blackmailing his father in order to make Antonio give him the "Fetura" drug, a purple solution that cured cervical insufficiency. There it was again. His father had been working on a *purple* drug.

Jason decided to stop skimming through it and read the notebook straight through. He needed to know what his father was doing that had caused his death and why Jason had survived when everyone else had died. He believed the answer was in this little notebook, a notebook his father had died protecting.

It took Jason three hours to read the notebook. His father had been very thorough in his explanations. He described how Jason's grandmother had died during a miscarriage. He wrote about his love of chemistry and how he had met Jason's mother. He wrote about James Wilmer giving him money to go to Brazil where he met Margaret DeMorte and got his first Mortevida plants.

Antonio also wrote about giving the drug to Chloe to prevent her miscarriage and how the puppies had been purple. Suddenly Jason made the connection. His mother must have taken Fetura. He was the purple baby she and her friend were talking about. He and Ricky had both been saved by this drug. They had also been protected from whatever had killed everyone and everything else.

Antonio wrote in detail how Dr. Tomlinson had given the drug to over 300 women without his knowledge. Jason stopped. If they had given the drug to that many women, then there had to be that many children somewhere in the world. He wasn't alone.

Jason felt excited for the first time in weeks. There were other people in the world. Even though they were only 10 years old, they were living, breathing human beings. Jason just had to figure out how to find them.

There was a folded sheet of paper between the last two pages of the notebook. It was a list. There were 100 names on it, names and addresses of women. Antonio had made a list of the mothers.

At that moment, Jason wished he could kiss his father. He had known who those women were and where they had lived 10 years ago. Now it was just a matter of finding their children. Jason would need to find Tomlinson's office. If he had records, then Jason could find the children. Jason was going to catch some sleep and then head over to Justin's and the big satellite dish.

Chapter 40

Jason took some bread out of the freezer and made a peanut butter and jelly sandwich. He fed Ricky, picked up the sandwich, and went to Justin's house. Ricky trotted along beside him. They entered Justin's house through the back door and went up the back staircase to the third level of the house.

The whole top of the house looked like something out of a spy movie. There were radios and several computer screens. All around the room were built in window seats filled with weapons and ammunition. One held the remaining gas masks. The others had books on using the satellite dish, coordinates, and instructions on tracking infrared human figures. One of the monitors showed the weather, another one the Internet.

Jason had been busy moving bodies for three weeks and hadn't been in the tower since the last time he and Justin had been there together. There was a sign hanging over the entrance to the room that read "Command Central."

Jason turned the main computer on. He switched on the monitors and took a seat. The monitors lit up and the Windows logo appeared. Finally, the home screens loaded and Jason turned on the satellite dish feed.

The second monitor switched to the satellite. There was nothing but fuzz on the screen. Jason switched the direction of the satellite and nothing happened. Now he was getting pissed off.

"Ricky, there must be something in the way up there. I gotta go up and look."

The little dog was sitting on one of the window seats looking out at the ocean. He watched as Jason walked over to the ladder leading to the skylight. There was a weatherproofed skylight / door on the ceiling that Jason unlatched and climbed through to get to the roof. David Carson had often envisioned himself escaping through that door as intruders entered his house. He could climb to safety within seconds, brandishing his AK 47.

Jason stood on the roof walked over to the satellite dish. It was a huge thing, and it had U.S. Air Force stamped on it.

"Geez Mr. Carson, did you steal this thing from the government?"

There was a ladder leading up to the satellite dish to enable repairs. Jason hesitated. He couldn't afford to fall off anything without help being close by. The ladder looked steady enough, but he was really high up, and the dish was at least another six feet above the roof. He figured if he moved slowly he had only to peek over the edge of the dish to see if there was anything covering the receiver.

Jason slowly climbed the ladder. He needed only two steps to get a look over the edge of the dish. There was a large palm frond covering the receiver. The hurricane must have blown it off the giant palm tree David Carson had planted years ago. Jason climbed up one more rung and held onto the ladder tightly.

The wind was blowing harder up here. He climbed up another rung and felt the wind shaking the dish. He wrapped one arm around the ladder. With his other arm he reached for the frond. He managed to grab the edge of it and pulled. It was stuck on something. Jason was afraid if he pulled too hard he would break off the end of the receiver. He had to risk going higher.

Jason went up another two rungs. Now the edge of the dish was even with his waist. He had nothing to hold tight to but the edge of the dish. He bent over and reached as far as he could. The frond was loosening. A big gust of wind blew and Jason had to grab the edge of the dish. The wind calmed down and he went back to gently pulling the frond. A huge chunk came off in his hand. He couldn't tell if that would be enough to clear the lens. He went up one more rung. The edge of the dish was mid-thigh. If the wind blew he would have to dive into the dish.

He bent over, and just as he was about to get the frond off the dish, the wind blew hard, knocking him into the dish. The dish rocked.

Even though it was well anchored, Jason dared not move for fear of toppling the dish. He stayed where he landed until the wind died down. He slowly crawled over to the receiver, pulled the rest of that damn frond off and let it blow away. Now he had to climb over the edge of the dish and down the ladder without losing his footing.

Jason crawled back to the edge of the dish. He carefully got on his knees and took hold of the handles on the inside of the dish. He pulled himself up, swung his long left leg over the edge of the dish and landed it on the outside rung. He took a deep breath of relief. He then was able to get his right leg over and onto the rung. Now all he had to do was climb down without falling.

The wind had stayed light. He took the rungs slowly, one at a time. When his feet hit the roof he almost kissed it. Jason sat down until he caught his breath. He decided he didn't like adventures anymore.

Jason climbed down the ladder into Command Central. Ricky was dozing on his window seat. He resumed his position in front of the monitors and again tried to bring up the satellite. The weather tracking monitor came to life.

Jason could see the Florida coastline. It was clear. He panned towards the ocean and could see various cloud patterns. He then focused on bringing up the satellite he and Justin had used to pan over Europe.

Thank God the satellite Internet worked. Justin's father had paid through the nose for that. It wasn't available in their area, so David had to pay a pretty price to get a "private contractor" to set him up. So far, no one had caught him. Jason logged onto the Internet and up came the Yahoo logo. The page was in French.

Jason turned on the page translator. The news feeds reported that the American Internet was still down and they hadn't been able to contact anyone in the continental United States, Canada or South America. They feared a terrorist attack.

Obviously they had no idea what happened and were reluctant to come to North America to find out until they were sure there were no biological weapons involved or nuclear fallout. There had been communication with Hawaii and Alaska. Those reporters said that neither state could account for the blackout. The article was dated a week ago.

Jason tried to find something newer. He found one dated yesterday that said the French, British, and German governments were sending out a plane to fly over the U.S. to try and discern why they had been unable to contact anyone. The collapse of the United States would devastate the rest of the world. They felt it was time to take initial steps to find some answers. It didn't say where they were sending the planes. Jason wished he knew so he could camp out there and light huge bonfires to get their attention.

Jason had finished his sandwich and felt hungry again. He went downstairs to see what he had stored in the Carsons' freezers. David Carson had installed huge grocery type freezers all along his basements walls. They were filled with all kinds of meats, vegetables, and processed foods. Mr. Carson wasn't exactly the vegan type.

Jason decided to make some real food for a change. He took some chicken out and a bag of zucchini. He then grabbed some scalloped potatoes. He took the food upstairs and fired up the outside propane grill. He washed the chicken and rolled it in seasoning.

He knew it would take longer to cook frozen chicken, so he put the zucchini on a baking sheet with the pan of scalloped potatoes and set the oven timer for 30 minutes. He then took the chicken, placed it on the grill and lowered the lid. When the timer went off, he would put the potatoes and zucchini into the oven. That way everything should be done at the same time. He went back upstairs to check the monitors.

Something on the weather monitor caught his attention. Living most of his life in Florida had made Jason very familiar with that particular cloud formation. A large, not-quite-circular rotation with a hole in the middle was making its way across the ocean heading for the Bahamas. If he was a weatherman, he would say that this tropical depression could turn into a hurricane. It would be given a name, and everyone would go into hurricane prep mode. This one had not completely formed yet, but it was big. Jason decided to keep his eye on it. He then turned his attention to the satellite scanner.

Jason put the codes into the satellite tracking software he and Justin had used before. Jason could see the computer searching for the right satellite dish to connect with. He saw it connect and within a few minutes could see Europe from several hundred feet above land. He zoomed in until he was as close as he could get.

He started to scan by moving his mouse. After panning over forests and farmlands it struck him that he knew there were people alive in Europe, so why not look here at home? Jason searched the website for the codes for Florida and waited for the software to connect him to a satellite floating over the North American continent.

Soon he could see the outline of the Florida coast. He decided to switch on the infrared tracking, which would enable him to see any entity with a warm body. He zoomed in and panned to the west coast of Florida. The software showed him he was over Sarasota so he moved his mouse a little until it said St. Petersburg. He then zoomed in.

The software began showing him street names. He was able to find his street and slowly moved his mouse. He zoomed in further until he could see the top of the Carsons' house and the big satellite dish. Since he was not outside, he couldn't see an infrared version of himself. He scrolled around the beach and neighborhood and found nothing. The buzzer went off, meaning it was time to put the potatoes and zucchini in the oven.

He left the screen on and went to the kitchen. Ten minutes after Jason left Command Central, two little infrared figures appeared in the back yard of the house three doors down. By the time Jason finished his food and returned to Command Central, they were gone.

Chapter 41

Jason took Ricky to the beach with his ball. He threw the ball and Ricky would run and fetch it. After four throws, the little dog took the ball and ran back to the house.

"Ricky you lazy slug, get back here!"

Jason ran back to the house and Ricky was waiting on the porch. Jason noticed the wind had picked up. He remembered the storm heading this way and ran back to Justin's to check the weather satellite. When he got to Command Central, he saw the clouds had tightened their formation. This storm was moving fast.

He decided to close the storm shutters on both houses for now. Maybe he would even go over to the Bennett's and close theirs too. Strange thing about the Bennetts, when he went to take care of their bodies, they were gone, all three of them. Jason supposed they were on a trip somewhere when the tragedy struck so they fell wherever they were.

Jason's mom had been good friends with Jessica Bennett and Jason felt he should protect their property. He would watch the storm and then go over and close their shutters. Right now he had to protect Command Central.

Jason woke up the next day in front of the monitors. He had fallen asleep sometime around 4 a.m. and now he was stiff from being hunched over the keyboard. He stretched his arms out over his head and looked around for Ricky. The terrier had followed him upstairs last night and was once again asleep on his favorite window seat.

"You know, Rick, you are really out of shape." Ricky opened one eye and looked at Jason. He then closed it again. "We're going on a hike today. We'll jog and then we'll eat."

Jason got up and signaled for Ricky to follow. They went back to their house. Jason put on his new sneakers and got out Ricky's lead. The dog might decide not to run at some point and Jason could use the lead to "coax" him. The little bugger was getting fat. Jason forgot that he was not only getting fat, but he was getting really old.

They took off down the block and onto the main street of town. Jason turned right and jogged about two blocks, with Ricky keeping up pretty well. Finally, Ricky just stopped and plopped down. Jason had to stop.

He pulled the lead, but Ricky wouldn't budge. Short of dragging him, Jason had to leave him alone. He took off the lead and continued to run. He knew Ricky would begin to follow him, but at a much slower pace.

He ran to the end of the fourth block and turned around. Ricky was loping along very slowly. Jason decided to take pity on him and head back towards home. When Ricky saw that Jason was coming back, he too turned around and headed for home. When he got to the turn in the road, he stopped. He turned to look at Jason and then back at the street in front of him. He did this several times until Jason was closer to him. Jason walked up to Ricky.

"What's up, buddy? How come you stopped?"

Ricky was growling. Jason looked around the corner and saw a little terrier that looked just like Ricky.

"Where did you come from?" Jason was smiling. The other dog was growling a little too, but neither dog looked like it wanted to fight.

"Baby Girl! Baby Girl, where are you?"

Jason heard a young female voice coming towards them. She came up behind the other dog and she knelt down behind her. She had short wavy blond hair and a pretty face. She hadn't yet seen Jason.

"Why didn't you come when I called?" Then the little girl looked up and saw Ricky. "Oh, my, who are you?" she said. Then she looked behind Ricky and saw Jason. The look of shock on her face made Jason back off.

"I won't hurt you. Look, I have a dog just like yours." The little girl stood up and stepped back. She looked like she was going to run. "I live on that street." Jason pointed around the corner. "My name is Jason. Do you have a name?"

"Of course I have a name." She squinted her eyes and gave Jason a very mad look. "I don't have to tell you though." She had backed up a little more. Jason followed her.

"Okay, you don't have to tell me your name, but what is her name?" Jason pointed at Baby Girl.

"Baby Girl."

The little girl turned around and ran with Baby Girl following behind her. Jason walked slowly to keep from frightening her, but he kept up because his legs were so much longer. He saw them go into the Bennetts' house and slam the door.

"Now that was interesting, Ricky."

Jason kept walking and stopped in front of the Bennetts' house. He decided to leave her alone and went on by. When he got back to his house, he showered and looked at his face. He was actually sporting enough of a beard to shave. He decided to let it grow some more.

Ricky was sitting in the kitchen chair when Jason came back down.

He must be hungry, Jason thought.

He opened a can of food and put half on a paper plate. He put it on the floor and Ricky came down the little stairs and over to his bowl. Suddenly Jason remembered Antonio's list.

Jason thought he had seen something on the list that didn't quite click in his head at the time. He ran back to the office and picked it up. He'd been right. Number 98 was Jessica Bennett. That meant that little Mark Bennett was a purple baby. That also meant *he* was alive. But where did he pick up that pretty little girl?

Now Jason could go over to the house because she wouldn't be there alone and Mark should remember Jason. He would wait till dinnertime to see if they wanted to eat with him. In the meantime, he decided it was time to go into Teresa's bedroom.

*****

Jason climbed the stairs to the second floor. He wasn't looking forward to opening Teresa's door, but he had to see if he could find her diaries. He knew she'd been keeping them for years. He hated invading her privacy, but if she had written anything in them that would help him find Tomlinson's office, he needed to read it.

When he got to the landing he stopped. He looked at her door. He slowly walked over and turned the knob. The door creaked as it swung open. He smelled the faint odor of her perfume mixed with soap and hairspray. She had made her bed that morning.

Her clothes were all hung in the closet and put away in drawers. There was a book by her bed next to her glasses. On the other nightstand was a picture of the three of them, Teresa, Antonio and Jason on his eighth birthday. Jason walked in the room and decided to start by looking in her dresser drawers.

He pulled them out and searched each one. There were no diaries in there. Then he opened the drawers in his father's armoire. The clothes were all gone, but Teresa had stored photo albums and other paperwork in there. Jason took the photo albums out and sat on the floor.

The first one had pictures of his parents' wedding. They looked so young and happy. There were pictures of their honeymoon in Rome. His father was very handsome. They had taken pictures of his grandfather and another old woman with the description "Nona". Photos of Ed and Dorothy were also placed in the album.

The next one had pictures of Ricky and Jason when they were both babies. There were also pictures of Chloe. Jason noticed that there were pictures underneath the ones displayed. He lifted the top photo and pulled out the hidden ones.

The first one was of Ricky and another dog, a female. It looked like his father's hands holding Ricky up to show his belly. It had a kind of purple sheen to it. The female was lying on her back and she too had the same purple belly. Then he looked at the other photo.

It must have been taken shortly after Jason's birth and it showed his mother with Jason in her arms. Jason's face had the same purple sheen to it. Jason slipped the photos back where he'd found them and put the album back in the drawer. He opened the next drawer and he found stacks of diaries with years emblazoned on the covers.

Jason looked through the diaries until he found the one written the year he was born. In it Teresa described their trip to Florida and her decision to let Antonio treat her with the Mortevida drug Fetura. She also described her first trip to see Dr. Tomlinson. She had taped his business card on the inside cover of the diary and Jason pulled it off and stuffed it in his pocket. She described his birth and his purple body.

He skipped ahead to the year his father had died. She described a conversation she'd had with his father regarding Tomlinson's threat to have Antonio deported. She wrote about Jason's birthday and the plans to go to Orlando. That was the end of that diary. He picked up the next one. This one was written after Antonio had been murdered.

Teresa wrote about the house being ransacked and leaving Jason with Ed and Dorothy for a week. She wrote about fortifying the house and her visit with Vinnie Rawlings. She wrote about Tomlinson's disappearance and her suspicions regarding Vinnie. She stored the newspaper articles in the diary along with a copy of the list of women Antonio had written.

228

Jason noticed the sun was setting. It was close to dinnertime. He had been lying underneath the half-open drawer while he was reading. He looked up before he got up and noticed something taped underneath the drawer. It looked like an old manila folder.

He opened the drawer further and was able to rip the file off the drawer. The tab on the file read "George Ranier." Jason thought he had seen that name in Antonio's notebook. Antonio had alluded to the fact that George had created something sinister with the Mortevida plant. Antonio didn't give a more detailed explanation.

Jason opened the file and saw it was some kind of report for Wilmer and March Pharmaceuticals. The report detailed George Ranier's attempts to make the perfect biological weapon out of the plants he had brought to the company from the rainforest. The weapon proved too lethal and was placed in the deep freeze. So, George Ranier had created a weapon out of the plants. But how did this file get here?

Jason had found what might be the answer to the big question – what had caused the tragedy? The more Jason thought about it, the more he began to believe that he and Ricky survived because they had been infused before they were born with an antidote to the poison, a poison that had somehow been unleashed on the world. It was the only thing that made sense. Jason placed the file in the drawer with the diaries. It was time to pay Mark Bennett a visit.

*****

Jason went to the widow's walk with his binoculars to see if the kids were outside. He saw them tending the garden behind Mark's house. Jason had found that garden the day he went to look for the Bennett's. He had watered it regularly, thinking he would enjoy some fresh vegetables. He was glad now that he had.

He went down the stairs two at a time. He whistled for Ricky and opened the sliding glass door. Ricky trotted ahead of him to the side yard to take care of business before joining Jason as he walked down the beach.

Jason and Ricky walked up to the fence surrounding the backyard. He looked over the fence and saw Mark and the little girl weeding between the rows of vegetables.

"You have to keep the weeds out or they strangle the plants," Mark was telling her. Ricky barked and they both looked up.

229

"Hey, Mark, how ya doin'? Can I come in?" Jason was smiling but he noticed the little girl was frowning at him again.

"I can't remember your name, but I know you live over there." Mark pointed in the direction of Jason's house. "And you're friends with Justin."

Jason nodded. Mark waved him in and Jason opened the gate. He let Ricky in first. When Jason was inside, he closed the gate and stood surveying the garden.

"I'm Jason. I watered them for you," he said. Mark looked at the garden too.

"Thanks. I thought they looked too good for me being away so long."

"Your friend wouldn't tell me her name," Jason said, nodding at Mindy.

Mark looked at the little girl.

"Why wouldn't you tell him your name?" Then Mark turned to Jason. "When did you meet her?"

"When Rick and I were on our morning run. We met her and her dog." Jason noticed the female lying by the sliding glass door panting from the heat. "Hey, Baby Girl."

The little dog raised her head. Ricky quickly walked over to her. They appraised each other. A flicker of familiarity passed between the dogs but quickly faded. Ricky walked over to her and she growled half-heartedly. Ricky then licked her neck and face and she let him. They had bonded.

Well, *they* like each well enough, Jason thought, as he recognized the female as the same dog in the picture with the purple belly. She had the same pattern on her face. That would explain her survival during the tragedy. But how did she end up in Florida?

"Can *I* tell him your name?" Mark asked the little girl. She looked down and whispered something Jason couldn't hear. Then Mark said, "Her name is Mindy."

"Okay, Mindy. I always like to know the name of a pretty girl."

"What do you mean by that!" Mark's eyes glared at Jason.

"Nothing buddy, geez, you two don't make it easy, do you. Anyway, I wanted to ask you if you want to have dinner with me. I have lots of food, and I figured it would be nice to have human company for a change. No offense, Ricky."

Mark looked at Mindy. She nodded her head once.

"I guess. Okay," Mark said. "When do you want us to come over?"

"Half an hour. We can eat on the deck behind my house. See ya then." Jason whistled for Ricky and he followed Jason through the gate.

Jason went home and took some hot dogs out of the freezer along with buns. He put some French fries in the oven and put ketchup and mustard on the table. He figured this was his favorite meal when he was their age so it must be theirs too. He forgot Mark's vegan history.

When the food was ready, he looked out on the deck and saw the kids had already come over. They were seated on the picnic benches looking at the ocean. The little female dog was on the bench with Mindy. Jason opened an extra can of dog food and put it on a paper plate. Tonight they would all dine together.

Chapter 42

When they were done eating, Jason asked Mark and Mindy to come over to Justin's house to see what the weather satellite was up to. Mark agreed immediately, excited at the prospect of seeing the inside of crazy Mr. Carson's house. Mindy held back.

"Why don't you like me, Mindy?" Jason asked her.

"I don't know you." Mindy looked at the table as she spoke to Jason.

"Fair enough. Well then, while Mark and I go check out the satellite, will you watch Ricky for me?" Jason tried to give her his best smile. It really bugged him that this kid seemed so afraid of him.

"I can do that." Mindy looked up at Jason. She wasn't looking mean now.

"Good. Come on, Mark."

Jason and Mark got up from the table and walked over to Justin's house. Mark ran ahead to the house while Jason turned to look at Mindy. He waved and she waved back. It was a start.

Mark was waiting for Jason as he walked inside the house.

"Up those stairs to the top floor." Jason pointed to the back stairs. Mark ran up the stairs and Jason followed him. Mark's eyes grew big when he saw Command Central.

"Holy crap!" Mark exclaimed. "This looks like Batman's cave." He ran over to the computer.

"Stop! Don't touch the computer. I'll bring up the screen." Jason walked over to the computer and Mark reluctantly relinquished his seat. He had a face on. "Look, Mark. If you touch something you don't understand, I can't get it fixed. If you have a computer at home, I'll see if I can hook it up to the modem here so you can check out the Internet, okay?"

Mark thought for a moment and then nodded his head. "Okay."

Jason brought up the weather monitor and moved the mouse to show Florida. He then scrolled down to the islands just below Florida and then over to the east. Then he and Mark looked at the screen and both sucked in their breath. The mass of clouds had formed into a huge circular band with a well-defined center.

"Oh, boy," Jason said. "I think we better get the shutters closed. That thing is moving fast. And I also think you guys should move in here for a few days. It's the safest house here. You go down and tell Mindy about the hurricane."

*****

It took some convincing on Mark's part to get Mindy to move into the Carson house, especially if Jason was going to be there too. She finally relented when the weather turned and it was clear a big storm was coming.

The Carson house was raised up about four feet. The basement was actually the lowest floor. It had strong weatherproof shutters and a cement wall that rose up from the ground to help keep the water out from under the house for as long as possible. It also shielded the pilings from the worst of the storm surge. Mindy looked at the house once everything was in place and could see it was the best thing to do.

Jason closed up his house by moving all the frozen, refrigerated, and dog food to Justin's. After he activated the storm shutters, he shut down the power. He then did the same at Mark's house. Mindy and Mark had harvested the vegetables and were bringing them over to the Carson's. They then got their clothes, toothbrushes and pillows and brought them over. The last thing Mark brought in was his laptop computer.

Jason showed Mark and Mindy the second floor of the Carson house. He led Mindy to Caitlyn's room and Mark to Justin's room. Jason would sleep in David and Janice Carson's room. Once they each set up their new quarters, they met in the kitchen to have some lunch before heading up to Command Central.

Mindy was beginning to warm up to Jason. She even smiled at him sometimes. She was given the task of taking care of the dogs for the duration of the storm. Jason would cook and Mark would clean up. Jason threw a couple of frozen pizzas in the oven and pulled out some paper plates. When the pizzas were done, he cut them and placed them in the center of the table.

"Grab what you want," he told the two hungry kids, who proceeded to grab two slices each. The kids ate like starving dogs with a meaty bone. They surprised Jason with their appetites.

"Slow down, there's plenty. If you want, I can throw another one in the oven." At this rate, the kids would eat Jason out of house and home. "So, where were you guys? I went over to Mark's house, but it was empty."

233

Mark and Mindy looked at each other. They weren't sure how to answer Jason's question. They knew where they had been, but they didn't know how to explain Jacob Wilmer's underground city full of kids.

"Come on, it can't be a secret. Mindy, how long were you guys here when we found each other?"

"We came the day before." She kept her eyes on her pizza.

"Okay, but where did you come from?" Jason couldn't figure out why they were having such a hard time telling him. Then Mark decided to come clean.

"I was taken from my house last week. These four guys came and took me to this place in Palm Harbor. It was some kind of....well, it was..."

"It was an underground city," Mindy said. She was looking right into Jason's eyes. "The people were scientists and they couldn't leave the city unless they put on these suits. They gave us food and there were these little houses to sleep in." That was the most she had said in front of Jason, who was momentarily tongue-tied.

"They took me too, out of my Grammy's house. They also took Baby Girl and brought her with me. They had a big field for growing crops and a room for animals, but they all died except the chickens. Calvin drove us here because he thought we should be able to live where we wanted to and I have to find my parents."

"Wow! That's the most I've ever heard you say," Jason said. "Tell me more about this place. Did you see where it was, when Calvin was it, when he drove you here?" Jason didn't really believe the story, but he didn't want to insult Mindy or stop her talking.

"I know where it is. I took a walk outside one day and found the entrance. It's off 19 in Palm Harbor. I remember a sign that said 'Palm Harbor 2' at the end of the dirt road. I didn't go to the highway, but I think I could find it again if I had to."

"Did you live with your Grammy, Mindy?" Jason asked between bites.

"No, I was staying with her while my parents..." Mindy stopped. She pulled the brochure out of her pocket and handed it to Jason.

"Where did they go?" Mark asked.

"That hotel; it's far away. I think they took a plane."

"This is in Las Vegas." Jason was wiping the last of the pizza from his face. He opened the brochure and saw the phone numbers written in big numbers.

"When they come back, they won't be able to find me," Mindy said. She looked as though she might cry. "I want to go home and wait there."

The boys didn't know what to say. They both knew her parents were most likely dead, but she seemed so sad they didn't want to make it worse.

"What if we go there every day to see if they came back?" Mark asked. "And come back here at night?"

"You would go with me?" Mindy said quietly.

"Of course I would, I said I would, didn't I?"

"Hold on a minute. Right now you can't go anywhere, not until the storm is over. But listen to this. When it's over, we can go in my mom's car. We may have to steal gas along the way, but we can all go together. We'll even take the dogs." Jason was looking at Mindy.

"Please, can't we go tonight? It's not that far from here if we go in the car. Please Jason, take me over there tonight."

Now that she liked him, Jason was reluctant to say no. Instead, he took her upstairs to show her the weather map, which now showed the huge hurricane floating over Puerto Rico headed for Key West. The thing was out of control and Jason believed it would be here in a matter of hours.

"Do you really want to risk getting caught outside in that? Mindy, please, don't make me have to say no. I really don't want to be the bad guy, but we can't risk all our lives for something…something that will be there in a few days. I promise you, as soon as this storm passes, we'll go to your house."

Jason had knelt down to be eye-level with Mindy. She had her sad face on and it almost got to him, but not quite. Jason would have to make sure the locks were secure so keep these kids inside for their own good until the storm passed. The dogs would have to go to the basement to do their thing. Jason had brought some sand in for them.

"Okay. I'll wait."

Mindy went over to Ricky's window seat and sat down facing the window. She stared out at the ocean, keeping her back to the boys. Jason went back to the weather map and tried to imagine the size of the hurricane. He decided it was time to close the last shutter, causing Mindy to get up and go to her room.

"Can you hook my computer up to the modem now?" Mark was asking.

"Sure, kid. Give me a minute to close up the house."

Jason walked downstairs to the second level. He could hear Mindy talking to Baby Girl. He stood quietly listening for a few minutes before going to the next floor.

"Just think, Baby Girl, we can go to my house soon. I bet my parents will be there waiting for me. Aren't you excited? Your eyes look excited. Baby Girl, I can't wait to see my mom and dad again."

Jason felt the full weight of the responsibility he had taken on. How could he tell this sweet little girl that her parents were dead no matter how hard she willed them to be alive? He decided to take the coward's way out and go along with whatever Mindy wanted to believe. It would make his life easier in the long run, and would keep Mindy happy.

Jason took the stairs in his usual manner and made sure all the shutters were tight and in place. He checked the concrete wall, and it was also ready. He then closed the shutters on the first story and went up to check the upper floors. When he was sure everything was secure, he rejoined Mark in Command Central.

The barrel of wind and water was wielding its way across Florida, headed to the West Coast and would most likely reach the Tampa Bay area.

He could hear the wind picking up, and the rain had started. He imagined what the streets would look like after the storm had passed. He hoped he could get the car out in a few days because he promised Mindy he would. No matter what, he would get her to her house; even if they had to wade to a dry street and steal a car, Mindy would go home.

Chapter 43

Jason had fallen asleep in front of the monitors again. Mark was also asleep on a window seat, his laptop on the floor next to him. Mindy climbed up the stairs. She peeked into Command Central and saw the boys were asleep. She then tiptoed down the back stairs to the kitchen.

The hurricane shutters were closed on all the windows and the sliding glass doors. She went into the living room and checked the front door. Jason had bolted it shut and Mindy could not budge the lock. Baby Girl had woken up and followed her downstairs.

"You can't go with me this time, Baby Girl," Mindy whispered. The little dog sat down and stared up at her. "I have to go by myself. I don't want you to get hurt." Baby Girl stood and wagged her tail. "No, you have to stay." Baby Girl barked. "Shhh!"

Mindy stopped and listened to see if the boys had heard the bark. She didn't hear anything overhead so she continued to try and open the bolt. She felt it give a little. She walked over and grabbed the dog stairs. She propped them up against the door. She had a better handle on the bolt now and was able to turn it completely around. She got off the stairs and moved them out of the way.

Mindy opened the lock on the doorknob. She opened the door a crack. The wind was blowing and it was starting to rain. She opened it a little more. There were no streetlights and it was pitch black out there. Baby Girl barked again.

"Please shut up," she whispered to Baby Girl. Mindy bent over and pet the little dog. "I have to find them, Baby. I just have to." Then the door slammed shut and Jason was standing over her.

"There is no way in hell I am going to let you out of this house. What is wrong with you?" Jason was furious. He thought they might try to get out, but the reality of it really pissed him off. This kid would be lost in no time between the dark and the storm. "Why would you think of doing something so stupid?"

Tears welled up in Mindy's eyes. She was upset at being yelled at and at being caught.

"I was going to stay on the road. I would be okay."

"Stupid, you're really stupid. There's no way you could stay on the road. The wind would knock your bike right over. You could be hurt and alone, and I wouldn't be able to find you."

Jason was so mad he was shaking. Mindy was scared he might hit her. When he grabbed for her she tried to pull away until she realized he was trying to hug her. She fought him a little, but then let him hug her.

"Mindy, please, I can't stand anyone else dying. Please don't do that again."

Mark had heard the noise and come downstairs. He saw Jason hugging Mindy and picked up Ricky's bowl and threw it at them.

"WHAT'S GOING ON?" Mark was very mad. He didn't like them hugging like that. Mindy was his friend, not Jason's.

Jason looked up, surprised by Mark's outburst.

"Mindy was trying to leave. I stopped her." He took his arms off Mindy. "I think we should all go to bed now."

Jason walked up the stairs, leaving Mark and Mindy in the kitchen. Mindy walked over to Mark.

"I think we should see if he has any chocolate," she said.

Mark turned off his mad face and calmed down. Mindy took the dog stairs and put them next to the cabinets. She climbed onto the counter top and began to look through the cabinets.

In the middle cabinet, she found a box of chocolate bars with "David's" written on it. She grabbed two and threw one to Mark, who caught it first try. Mindy then jumped off the countertop and sat at the table. Mark joined her and they both ate the chocolate.

"Do you like Jason?" he asked her.

Mindy thought for a moment. "He has a nice dog." She said. "I like his dog."

"Yeah, but do you 'like' him?" Mark had an anxious look on his face. He had found a friend, the first one he had ever had, and jealousy was something new to him.

"I think you're my best friend right now. Jason isn't my friend yet, but maybe later."

That seemed to appease Mark. He looked relieved to know he was her best friend. He chose to ignore the fact that she had said "right now."

*****

By morning the wind was howling and the rain fell in sheets hard against the walls and shutters. Jason woke up and heard the kids laughing. They were in Command Central. Jason took the stairs

238

two at a time and peeked in the door. They were sitting in front of Mark's laptop playing a game.

Jason went to the kitchen and pulled some waffles and sausages out of the freezer. Everything was still cold. If the storm lasted much longer, he would have to direct the power to the freezers until the sun came out again. He put the waffles in the toaster and threw the sausage in a pan. He then went to look out the front door to see what was going on outside.

The street was flooded with about six inches of water. Jason knew from living at the beach most of his life that the storm surge following the hurricane would be worse than the hurricane itself. He hoped the Carson house would be high enough to withstand it. If not, he would be stuffing two kids and two dogs in an SUV and heading for the hills.

In the meantime, he would track this thing on the satellite. He just hoped the wind wouldn't knock the satellite over. He went into the garage and checked the gas in the SUV. It had a half tank. He decided to put some food and water in the back just in case they had to leave in a hurry.

When the food was ready, he called the kids to the table. The kids scrambled down the stairs together, almost knocking each other over. "Was I such a pain in the ass?" Jason thought as they raced each other to the table and sat down. They were giggling and out of breath. Jason put the food on the table and the kids grabbed it fast. Jason put his hand on top of the waffles.

"ENOUGH!" he yelled. "Slow down and take one piece at a time."

They both looked at him then at each other and laughed. He sounded just like their mothers. Their laughter incensed Jason more.

"What's so funny, huh? You think it's easy taking care of you guys? I cooked all morning...." Then he realized that he sounded just like *his* mother. He had turned into his mother! He appreciated her more in that moment than he ever had before. Then he smiled. "Yeah, okay, just slow down."

They each slowly took a waffle and a sausage, but they couldn't stop giggling. Maybe it was just the stress relief they needed. It had been a long time since they laughed like that. Suddenly, there was a loud CRACK.

Jason bolted from the table and ran up the stairs. He looked at the anchors for the satellite dish. They were intact. He then went into Command Central and climbed the ladder to look at the dish.

The dish was fine, but the stupid tree Mr. Carson had planted had broken in half and landed on the roof.

Jason climbed down and looked at the screens. They were going in and out intermittently from the rain, but they were all right. The weather monitor showed the storm passing through and heading out to sea. Now Jason would have to watch for the storm surge. When the wind died down, he would open the shutters.

He ran back to the kitchen to finish eating. The kids had left him one sausage. He threw another waffle in the toaster. He gave the kids some orange juice to keep them there so he wouldn't have to eat alone.

"What was your Grammy like, Mindy?" He asked.

"She was nice. I liked her. She was like Mr. Carson. She thought something bad was going to happen so she dug a hole in the shed and put guns and food down there. She had a friend teach me how to shoot. He gave me a little gun that fit my hand."

Mark looked impressed.

"Did you ever shoot anything?" he asked her.

"Just a rat I thought would hurt Baby Girl." Mindy looked down at her plate. She didn't like thinking about the rat.

"Was it a big rat?" Jason asked.

Mindy nodded her head. "Like a cat."

"Whoa, that's a big rat. You had to be very brave." Mindy looked up and smiled at Jason.

"I'd like to blow off a rat's head," Mark was saying. "See the head fly off and the guts fly all over. My mom didn't believe in guns. And if she saw me eat this meat, she would slap me silly."

Mark was laughing again, which made Jason and Mindy laugh too.

"Why was that rat still alive?" Mark asked.

"It must have been in a storm drain or something. It had to have been underground when it happened," Jason said.

"What was *it*, Jason?" Mindy said.

"I don't know," Jason answered.

For a while they were quiet. Then they began telling their stories one at a time; Mark and how he took his parents out to sea, Mindy and how her Grammy left and never came back, Jason and how he cleaned the beach and streets by taking bodies out to sea in the 20-foot boat.

"Is the boat safe out there?" Mindy asked.

"I took it to the other side of the street to the canal, away from the ocean. I tied it behind a neighbor's house."

"I didn't know what happened," Mindy said. "When Grammy didn't come back, I waited a long time. I had to take Baby Girl outside and then I saw the man across the street on the porch, but he never moved or waved back at me. All the other people left because of the hurricane. They had to leave because it was mobile homes.

"Grammy went out to get water and batteries. We were gonna go to my house when she got back. After a couple of days I looked across the street and the man was still there. When I walked outside, the smell was really bad. I stayed inside for a while and only took Baby Girl out sometimes. After a while the smell got better, but the man looked real bad. I just didn't look at him anymore."

"I was afraid at night," Mark said as he looked at Jason. "When I saw somebody was moving the bodies I got scared. I...I didn't know it was you."

"I wonder why we never saw each other?" Jason asked.

"Because I would stay at home. I locked the doors and kept the windows shut."

"Sorry kid. I didn't know you were there. If I had, I would have helped you. I thought I heard a truck one morning, but I had just woken up and thought it was a dream."

They sat quietly around the table. In that hour of conversation, they had found a common bond that would hold them together from now on. They were more than friends; they were brothers and sister in the trenches, akin to soldiers in war. All their inhibitions were gone, their masks stripped away.

Jason took Mindy's hand and Mindy took Mark's as they sat together thinking of how much they had changed in just a few weeks. Then they cleared off the table and headed for Command Central.

Chapter 44

The storm had passed and the water was rising. Jason took out the stick David Carson had made to measure the water height. The water measured just under four feet high. It looked like the worst had passed, and Jason decided to ride it out. If the water rose above the dock, then he would take the kids away.

The sun was shining again. Three days had passed and but for the water, it was a beautiful day in Florida. The kids were getting cabin fever. They were picking fights with each other or running up and down the stairs.

Jason was also getting antsy. They had played every board game in the house and watched every DVD. And the water was getting lower.

"I think it's time to map out Mindy's house," Jason said. With the water receding, he was eager to get them out of the house. When it measured six inches, he would take them out to the main streets and try to find the Lane house.

He tried to log on to Google but the American site was still down. He didn't know if a foreign Google would have the same maps as the American Google. He remembered the satellite had found his street so he went to the tracking software. He was able to pull up St. Petersburg.

"Where do you live?" he asked Mindy.

"It's on 22nd Avenue, but I don't remember the number. We found it before, so we can find it again."

Jason moved the mouse until he found 22nd Avenue.

"When Calvin drove us over there, he turned this way off of 18th Avenue South." Mark pointed at the map in the direction Calvin had taken them.

"Good, that's a start. Get me some paper."

Mindy ran around the room looking for paper.

"Justin had a desk, Mindy. He should have some paper and pens," Jason said, still looking at the screen.

Mindy ran downstairs to Justin's room and began going through the desk drawers. She found a picture of Justin with Jason and brought that back to Command Central along with a notebook and a pen. She handed them to Jason. Jason looked at the photo.

"I didn't know he had this. Wow. I remember that day. We had written a song and were thinking we were gonna be famous and wanted to mark the day." Jason looked at the picture a long time. He slipped it into his pocket.

"You wrote a song?" Mark asked.

"Yeah, we played guitars together. We thought we would have a band. You know, kid stuff." Jason thought of all of his dreams as kid stuff now. After what he had been forced to do, his childhood was well behind him.

"I can play. Maybe we can play together." Mark had an excited look on his face.

"Sure, kid. I think Justin's guitar is in the closet. I have to check out my house anyway so I could bring mine back." Jason wrote down the streets going to Mindy's avenue. He then got up and ran downstairs.

"He's going to get his guitar," Mark said. "I'm gonna look in Justin's room."

The water was receding fast now, and Jason was able to easily wade over to his house. He went inside and noticed the floor had gotten a little wet. The house was pretty high so it may have been rain pushed under the doors. Other than that, the place fared pretty well. He went upstairs to get his guitar. The upstairs looked okay too. Those storm shutters were a godsend.

When he got back to Command Central, Mark was plucking away at Justin's guitar. Mindy was looking a little left out so Jason suggested she sing. She looked embarrassed.

"I can't sing." She suddenly became shy.

"Everybody can sing. We'll play something and you make up a song."

"I'll have to go in the other room." Mindy ran downstairs and sat on the last step. The boys began playing in harmony and Mindy began singing a song with her own made-up words.

"Baby Girl, you're my Baby Girl, and I love you very much, and I love your little belly, you're my Baby Girl." Mindy's voice was high and sweet.

As she sang, Baby Girl came over to her and shook her head from side to side as if to dance to her song. When she was done, the boys clapped and whistled. They were standing at the top of the stairs. This embarrassed Mindy even more. Jason came down the steps. He put his arm around Mindy and praised her voice.

"We'll have to have more sing-alongs. In the meantime, I think we could go take a ride. What do you think?"

Mindy's eyes lit up. "Oh, yes, please, can we go right now?"

"Yup, get the dogs ready."

Ricky had been hibernating during the storm. He wasn't used to so many people or dogs in his house. He had taken to sleeping under Jason's bed. When he heard "Go bye-bye" he ran out from under the bed and down the stairs.

Mindy put their leashes on and took the dogs to the garages. Jason put the notebook in his pocket and Mark brought a bottle of water and a dish for the dogs. They piled in the car while Jason closed the door and opened the garage. He then climbed into the driver's seat and they were off.

The storm had left quite a mess on the streets. It had also washed some of the bones from around the area back onto Jason's clean streets. He would have to deal with that later. The water was going down and by the time they reached the highway, they were on dry land.

There were still cars parked in the road and Jason navigated around them. They made good time and soon were at the same turn they had taken when Calvin was driving. Jason turned and the kids told him it was about four or five blocks down. Pretty soon Mindy's school came into view. Mindy and Mark looked at each other and started to giggle. They would be there soon.

"Stop when you see a white house with green shutters," Mindy shouted.

They all saw it at once. It was hard to miss. Parked in front of it were two school buses, and milling around the school buses were at least 100 children.

PART FOUR

DANI AND JOE LANE

Chapter 45

Somewhere outside Las Vegas, Nevada

Dani Lane woke up. She'd been dreaming about Mindy. She and Mindy were sitting in front of a birthday cake, and she was teasing Mindy.

"You look like a monkey, and you act like one too!"

Mindy was giggling. When Dani opened her eyes, she saw a multi-colored stalagmite a few feet in front of her. She could see Jenny, a sixteen-year-old room attendant, sleeping in the next bed. Joe lay next to Dani on his stomach, snoring.

Dani didn't know how long they'd been sleeping. Her body felt stiff from the cold, and when she got out of bed, she stretched. The cavern was huge and very quiet. She could hear Jenny and Joe breathing.

Dani had been keeping track of the days on a little cavern hotel notepad. So far, there were eight strokes penciled on it. Today she added number nine. She had slept in her underwear. She picked up her shorts and tee-shirt and put them in the bathroom. She then headed for the stockpile.

There was food and water for two thousand people stored in the cavern. Someone thought it would make a great bomb shelter, and Dani was grateful they had. They'd be able to survive for years underground, but Dani hoped they would only be here a few more hours.

The water and food were stored a few feet away from their cavern room. She walked down two stairs to the cavern floor and over to the stockpile. She grabbed two gallon bottles of water and took them to the water tank located behind the bathroom. She filled the water tank. She then repeated the process until she had added 20 gallons in the tank. She could wash her body quickly before the water ran out. The others would do the same if they wanted a shower.

Dani appraised her looks in the bathroom mirror. She had just turned thirty-four and there were little wrinkles appearing around her eyes. She had recently cut her light brown hair so it just touched her shoulders. It was dirty and dull. Her gray eyes, so like Mindy's, were bloodshot from lack of sleep.

The fluorescent bulb added a few years to her face, so she didn't look very good. She quickly brushed her teeth and avoided looking in the mirror again. She stepped in the shower and wet herself down. She turned it off while she washed, then turned it back on to rinse. She quickly rinsed out her underwear and dried herself. She put on her tee-shirt and shorts.

Dani left the bathroom and hung her underwear over some chairs to dry. She put on her socks and shoes. Every morning she walked up the winding ramp that led to the elevator. She would push the elevator button, and then she would wait. So far, nothing had happened, but she hadn't given up hope that one day the elevator would arrive.

That morning as she approached the button, she paused and listened. There was no sound. She pushed it. Jenny told her it would take several minutes for the elevator to reach them from the top. Dani checked her watch. Five minutes had past, and nothing happened. Dani headed back to the "room."

Jenny was awake and stretching in her bed. Joe was still asleep.

"I pushed the button," she said to Jenny, "and nothing happened."

Dani noted how good Jenny looked. Ah, to be sixteen again. Jenny's straight blond hair fell perfectly into place when she shook her head. She had blue eyes, rosy cheeks, and her lips had just enough pucker to be called pouty. She was petite, just over five feet tall, and slender. But Jenny wasn't full of herself at all. She was sweet, smart, and optimistic.

Jenny tried the phone on the table between the beds. She could hear a dial tone, but no one picked up on the other end. She put the receiver back, and got out of bed.

"I still don't understand why nobody picks up. There's supposed to be somebody at that desk all the time," Jenny said. "When I'm on the desk, I have to get somebody to sit there if I have to leave, especially when someone's down here."

Jenny felt so bad for the Lanes. She'd brought them down that first day and she felt responsible for them. She had showed them the "room", an island in the middle of the cavern that had two queen-size beds, a sofa, a small table with chairs, a hope chest, a small refrigerator, a microwave oven atop a small cabinet, and a big screen TV. There was a bathroom with a shower too.

Jenny told them the water tank had been filled and if they needed anything, she would bring it to them. The elevator had taken the last tourists back up to the surface, so Jenny summoned it back down. It never came back.

At first, Jenny hadn't panicked. She kept pushing the button and cursing Wally, the tour guide, for not getting his guests off the elevator fast enough. After 10 minutes, she walked back to the Lanes and asked if she could use the phone. When she picked up the receiver there was a dial tone, but no one answered. Then Jenny panicked, but she kept her fears to herself.

She bid the Lanes a good-afternoon and went back to the elevator. It still hadn't arrived. She leaned up against it, trying to figure out what to do next. She heard the Lanes laughing. She opened the gate and put her hands between the elevator doors, trying to pry them open. They wouldn't budge. She felt tears starting and took a deep breath. She wouldn't cry, not in front of guests. She pulled herself together and went back down the ramp.

When Joe Lane saw Jenny returning yet a second time, he knew something was wrong. He made a lame joke in an effort to keep things light, but Dani could tell the girl was anxious. Dani walked over to Jenny and asked her if she was okay.

"I...I can't get the elevator to return," Jenny said.

"Well, I'm sure it's nothing. You can stay with us until it comes," Dani said.

Dani put her arm around Jenny, and they walked back to the island. Jenny sat on the sofa, while Dani and Joe sat on one of the beds.

"There are games in that chest," Jenny said, "puzzles and old magazines, too. Or, I could show you the caves. I'm not a guide, but I've been through them, and I'm sure I could tell you something about them."

"Okay," Joe said. He looked at Dani, and she nodded.

Jenny always carried a large flashlight whenever she came below surface. As she led Dani and Joe through the cavern, she used it to highlight different formations. For a while, she was able to forget the elevator. After an hour, she could tell the Lanes were getting tired, so she took them back to the room.

"I'm sure the elevator is working by now," she said. She left them, and headed back to the elevator. She pushed the button and waited. It still didn't come down.

Dani found her sitting on the floor next to the elevator. Jenny was crying now. She turned her head away from Dani, and wiped her eyes. Dani knelt down next to her and asked if she was okay. Jenny smiled.

"I'm fine, Mrs. Lane. I just can't seem to get the elevator to come back down. I didn't want to bother you again."

"It's silly for you to sit here. It's cold, and we have the sofa. Come back with me."

They stood up and walked back to the room. Joe was eating a protein bar he found in the refrigerator. He smiled when he saw the two women walking towards him. He was disappointed to see Jenny again. What if they couldn't get rid of her? He had been looking forward to sex in the cavern that night.

"The elevator still hasn't returned. I found her on the ground, and told her to come and sit on the sofa," Dani said. She smiled.

"Yeah, sure. Why don't we try the front desk again?" Joe picked up the receiver, but still no one answered.

That was nine days ago. They were all still wearing the same clothes. Dani alternated washing hers, underwear during the day, tee-shirt and shorts at night. Joe and Jenny hadn't washed theirs. They'd been able to take showers using the gallons of water stored in the cavern, but their clothes were beginning to stink.

Joe woke up and turned over. He stared at the ceiling of the cave and sighed. He got up on one elbow and saw Jenny sitting on the edge of her bed. He looked around for Dani and saw her walking towards them from the direction of the elevator. He could see she wasn't happy.

"No elevator?" he asked.

Dani shook her head. She walked over to the box of ready-to-eat meals and looked inside. She pulled out an instant oatmeal packet. She grabbed a bottle of water, a paper bowl, and a plastic spoon from the cabinet. Then she mixed the oatmeal with water and popped it into the microwave. Thirty seconds later, she took it out of the oven and headed for the small table. Dani didn't look happy. Joe got up and went to the bathroom before joining her at the table.

"So, where's mine?" He said smiling.

"Don't push me, Joe. I'm not in the mood." Dani shoveled oatmeal into her mouth. She wasn't enjoying it.

"I was just kidding," Joe said defensively.

"You're never just kidding, Joe. You want me to make you breakfast, so you make jokes instead of just asking me. And your timing always sucks. You just don't get it, do you?" Dani kept shoving oatmeal in her mouth. When she finished the oatmeal, she got up from the table.

"I miss Mindy. I want to go home. And you two smell so bad. Why don't you wash your clothes?!" Dani yelled. She had held her feelings in too long.

"Yeah, well, I want to go home too. I miss her," Joe said sheepishly. "And I take a shower every day!" Dani turned around and glared at him.

"Listen, you haven't mentioned her once since we've been here. All you talk about is getting back to Vegas."

"That's bullshit. I love Mindy!" Joe got up, and walked off the island.

He headed towards the elevator, and Dani could hear him beating on the doors. The noise rang throughout the cave.

Jenny had sought refuge in the bathroom when they started fighting. She peeked out the door, and saw Dani. She came out and sat on the sofa. She could hear Joe's banging and cringed. The owners wouldn't like that. If Joe made a dent in the elevator, he'd have to pay for it.

When he finished hitting the elevator, Joe came back to the island and again sat down at the table. He hadn't had a cigarette in three days, and the door banging had helped relieve some of the tension. Dani was on the sofa now, watching a DVD she'd found in the cabinet. Jenny was sitting next to her, but not too close. They were both ignoring Joe. Joe walked over to Jenny, and put out his hand.

"Can I have your flashlight?" he asked her.

Jenny pointed to her bed. Joe walked over to it and found the flashlight hidden in the blankets. He grabbed it and headed towards the caves.

When he'd first read about the cavern hotel, he thought it would be an adventure. The ad said it was the quietest place on earth, that it was a totally unique experience, sleeping 150 stories below the earth's surface. It was something new to try, and only minutes from Las Vegas. Dani had been excited about it, too.

Now, after nine days incarceration, Joe just wanted out. He missed his cigarettes and his gambling. He felt suffocated in this huge, quiet place. It was the quiet that was the worst. He couldn't fart without those two hearing it. But worst of all was not being able to take a twenty minute shower. Joe loved his showers. But Dani was wrong about his clothes. They weren't that bad. And besides, he couldn't take them off in front of Jenny now, could he?

Joe walked through the cavern. It really was a beautiful place. As he walked, he thought about how many days it had been since a tour came down here. That would be costing the owners a bundle. No tours and no income from the hotel. Why didn't anybody answer the phone?

In his guts, Joe knew something bad had happened on the surface. He couldn't figure out what, but he believed that someone would have contacted them by now if all was well. His mother would have called the hotel in Vegas, or Dani's mother would have flown out to look for them. Jenny had to have parents, too. No, something bad had happened, and Joe wasn't looking forward to finding out what it was.

As he walked back to the island, he could hear the women talking. The movie must be over, Joe thought. He could see them sitting on the sofa. He climbed the stair up to the room floor, and sat at the table.

"Well, ladies, what are we doing today?" he asked.

"We could play a game," Jenny said.

Joe half-smiled at her. They had played every game in the cabinet. Dani sat and stared at the blank TV.

"You could wash your clothes," she said. She sat quietly for a long time while Joe fumed. Then she turned to him. "What if we never get out?" she asked.

Joe and Jenny looked at each other. No one wanted to think about that.

"We have to get out someday, Dan," Joe said. "We have to."

"They have to come for us soon," Jenny said. She didn't sound very convincing.

"You've been saying that for days, Jenny," Dani said. "What could be keeping them?"

"Jenny, is there another way out of here?" Joe asked.

"No, they made the shaft for the elevator, but that's all."

"Didn't they think this might happen? What kind of idiot builds something with one exit?" Joe was yelling and his voice sounded really loud as it bounced off the walls of the cavern.

"Shut up, Joe. She didn't build it." Dani's voice sounded flat. She felt so depressed.

"At least we have food and water," Jenny said.

252

Joe went to the box of food searching for something to eat. He couldn't find what he wanted, so he picked it up and threw it across the room. Food packets flew everywhere. Dani got up and walked over to him. She began pounding his chest with her fists. He grabbed her arms and held her so she couldn't land any more punches. Jenny got up, and ran off the island.

"Stop it, Dani!" Joe yelled.

"You did this. You brought us here!" Dani was still trying to hit him as she yelled.

"Yeah, I did it, I ruined your life. So what else is new?" Joe pushed her away. She fell backwards and landed on her butt. She began to cry.

"I can't take this anymore. I have to get out of here," Dani said.

They didn't talk for several minutes. Jenny slowly approached them from the direction of the elevator. She'd been pushing the button over and over, willing the elevator to move. It hadn't. She climbed the stair, and looked at Dani on the floor.

"You okay?" she asked her.

"I'm fine," Dani whispered.

Joe sat down at the table, and put his head on his hands. Jenny sat on the sofa, and Dani stayed on the floor. As they each contemplated spending the rest of their lives in the cavern, they heard a small "ding."

Jenny got up, and ran towards the elevator. Joe followed her, with Dani close behind. Jenny got to the elevator door first and found it open. She screamed in delight. Joe saw it too, and whooped. Dani grinned.

Joe spotted something on the floor of the elevator. It was right on the threshold. The object was black and looked like leather. It was kind of round with things sticking out of it. Joe kicked it with his foot, and Dani gasped as she realized what it was.

"It's a hand," she said quietly.

*****

"Oh, my God, where did it come from?" Jenny said.

Joe got into the elevator, and kicked the hand out.

"Come on, let's get our stuff," he said as he walked past Dani. She followed him to the island.

Jenny stood staring at the hand. What had happened on the surface that would cause someone to lose a hand? She didn't want to think about it. She just wanted to go home. She got on the elevator, and kept her eyes on the floor. When Dani and Joe finally came back, they got on the elevator, and Jenny pushed the button.

The elevator slowly started up. It took several minutes to reach the surface. During the ride up, no one talked about the hand. Dani also kept her eyes on the floor. Joe looked up, as if staring at the ceiling would get them there faster. Finally, they felt the elevator slow down and stop.

The door opened automatically, and Dani, Joe, and Jenny stared at the cavern lobby. There were bodies everywhere. There was a body in front of the elevator with one hand missing. The smell was so bad, that Jenny began to vomit. She covered her mouth, and ran out of the elevator. Dani and Joe followed suit.

They exited the building as fast as they could. There were more bodies outside the entrance. Jenny almost tripped over one, and Joe caught her by the arm before she fell. They moved as quickly as they could to get to the parking lot.

Joe tried to remember where he'd parked. Dani ran past him, and he followed. Jenny kept as close to them as she could.

Dani found the car first. She waited for Joe, who had the car keys, to open the doors. Joe pushed the button on the keys to open the doors. Dani and Jenny slid inside; Dani in front, and Jenny in back. Joe ran around the car and got into the driver's seat. Jenny closed her eyes, and wouldn't open them.

Dani kept staring at the bodies, trying to figure out what had happened. Joe put the car in gear and drove out of the parking lot at top speed, running over bodies along the way. Every time he hit one, Dani would cringe, and Jenny would hug herself. When he finally got to the road, he headed for Las Vegas.

Chapter 46

The 34-mile trip to Vegas took an hour. Joe had to keep slowing down to go around cars as they got closer to Vegas. As they entered the city, the lights were still blazing. There were bodies everywhere. They were mostly bones and hair. Dani looked through their backpacks to find something to mask the smell. She ended up taking off her shirt and tying it around her face. Joe did the same.

Joe found their hotel and stopped the car in front of it. Jenny was asleep so Dani and Joe quietly got out of the car, leaving the door open so as not to wake her. There was a body lying in the doorway to the hotel. They walked around it and into the lobby. It was filled with bodies, some sitting, others lying on the floor.

Joe went behind the counter, looking for a pass key to open their room. He found one in the cashier's drawer. He and Dani decided to take the stairs rather than risk being stuck in the elevator. Their room was on the eighth floor. By the time they reached it, they were breathing heavily.

"Let's get this over with fast," Dani said between breaths.

They found the room as they had left it. Dani found her suitcase and put her clothes and toiletries in it. Joe did the same. They worked fast and got what they needed. When they were done, they took one more look around and then headed downstairs.

When they got to the lobby, they could hear Jenny screaming. They ran to the street and saw her standing in the middle of the road.

"WHERE ARE YOU? WHERE ARE YOU?"

Jenny was hysterical. Dani dropped her bag and ran to Jenny. She put her arms around her and held her.

"We just went to get our stuff. You were asleep. I'm so sorry."

Dani rocked Jenny like a baby. Jenny's shaking body began to calm down. Dani guided her back to the car. She and Jenny slid into the back seat. Jenny put her head on Dani's shoulder and cried.

"Ready?" Joe asked. He looked at Dani in the rearview mirror and she nodded. He'd left the car running so he closed his door and drove out of Vegas, rolling over the bodies that littered the streets. He couldn't avoid them. It was the crunching of bones that got to Dani. Her body began to shake and the tears rolled down her face. Joe looked at her in the mirror again.

"It'll be okay. I promise," Joe said. Dani looked at him and nodded slightly. "Where are we going?" he asked.

"Jenny, where are we going?" Dani asked.

"Boulder City," Jenny whispered.

"Which road do I take?" Joe asked.

"Go south," she said.

The drive to Boulder City took half an hour. Joe looked at Dani in the rearview mirror. Jenny was looking out the window. Dani touched her hand.

"Which way, Jenny?" she said.

"Keep going," Jenny replied.

They drove through the center of town for several minutes. Suddenly Jenny began to yell.

"Stop here, please!"

Joe stopped the car and Jenny opened the door and got out. She ran up to a house, climbed the front steps and opened the door. They heard her scream.

Dani got out and ran to the house. As she entered the house, she saw Jenny on her knees on the floor. Her mother was at the kitchen table. Her brother was on the floor in front of the TV. It was hot in the house; the bodies were now bones and hair. Most of their flesh had melted away but for a few bits that clung to the bones. Dani walked over to Jenny and knelt beside her.

"Where is my dad? Where is my dad?" Jenny was screaming.

"He must have been at work. Jenny," Dani said, trying to keep calm.

"No, he dropped me off at work. He should be here!" Jenny was crying hard.

"Whatever happened...this thing that...it must have happened right after we went down into the cavern. He would have been driving home," Dani said. She waited for Jenny to respond, but Jenny just kept crying.

"Listen, you have to get your things. There's nothing you can do for them now. Please, I'll help you."

Dani pulled on Jenny's arm, but Jenny wouldn't move. She just stared at her little brother with tears rolling down her face. He'd been so young. She had fought with him all the time and now she wished she could tell him she was sorry.

Dani got up, opened some windows, and went to the hallway, looking for the bedrooms. She wondered why the air conditioning wasn't working. She found Jenny's room and looked around. She

256

went back to the living room. Jenny had gotten up and was now staring at her mother, holding her hand over her nose. Dani passed her and went into the kitchen.

She found a grocery bag and headed back to Jenny's room. She filled it with clothes and then went into the bathroom. She tried the light switch, but the lights didn't come on. There was enough light from the window to make out the soap and shampoo. She took the liner out of the trash bin and put the toiletries into it. She took the two bags back into the living room.

"Can we bury them?" Jenny's voice was barely above a whisper.

Why, they look fine the way they are, Dani thought. She was glad she hadn't said it out loud. How could she have thought that?

She put her arm around Jenny's shoulders. "If we move them, they'll fall apart," she said quietly.

"Oh, God." Jenny broke down again.

Dani steered her towards the front door. Dani then ran back into the living room and grabbed the two bags she had packed. She closed the door and took Jenny's hand, leading her back to the car. She put Jenny in the back seat with the bags and she got into the front with Joe. She hoped Jenny would fall asleep.

*****

Jenny was quiet in the back seat. She hadn't said much since leaving her house. She was keeping it to herself for now. Every so often she would look out the window, but then a car would appear with a body in it and she had to turn away. Most of the time, she slept.

The car had a GPS built in. Dani played with it for a while until she figured out how to program it. She input her home address and the thing began to talk. As long as Joe followed it, they should be home in a few days.

They were going across long stretches of road in the desert, so there weren't that many abandoned cars. Dani noticed how bad they smelled. The smell of human decay will cling to your clothes. It will also cling to your walls, your car, and anything else in its path.

"We have to find a store that was closed when this thing went down. Somewhere without a dead body in it," Dani said as they drove past a strip mall.

They had encountered plenty of convenience stores and were well fed. There was also plenty of gasoline. Most cars they passed had gas in them and Joe had picked up a siphon at an auto parts store during one of their stops.

Dani kept her eyes peeled for a clothing store. She saw a sign for a consignment shop that was closed on Sundays and Mondays. She told Joe to stop.

"I think it was a Monday, wasn't it, when we came to the cavern?" Dani asked.

"Yeah, it was," Jenny said. She had been in a mood ever since she got a whiff of the clothes Dani had packed. She threw them out the window and now had nothing else to wear. The clothes she had on smelled bad too.

Joe was looking for a motel; somewhere he could take a shower. He saw a billboard showing the Shady Rest Inn coming up in one mile.

"Let's stop there," Joe said.

"Let's stop at the store first," Dani said. "We'll have nothing to change into if we take a shower first." Dani was right. Joe hated it when she was right. He would have figured it out if she had given him another minute.

Joe turned into the consignment shop parking lot. Dani hopped out of the car and ran to the door of the store. She turned around and gave a thumbs up. That meant the door was locked.

Joe got out of the car and looked around for a big rock. He found one in a clearing next to the consignment shop and threw it through the window in the door. An alarm went off. Dani took off her jacket and wrapped it around her arm. She pushed the glass out of the way and was able to reach in and open the door.

The store had the musty smell of used items that looked clean but still bore the markings of their former owners. Joe ran to the back to find the source of the alarm. Dani smiled when she saw the racks of clothes. There was something for everyone.

She hit the ladies rack while Jenny went for the juniors. The alarm stopped, and Joe returned. He was able to find some jeans and tee shirts as well as a good pair of boots. Dani found jeans and tee shirts also, and was thrilled when she found bras still in boxes. Jenny found new underwear, and she and Dani squealed with delight. Jenny also found a pair of jeans that were a little big so she would have to find a belt.

Joe looked through the bins of men's boxers and found some new ones in the bottom. He also grabbed some socks that didn't look too worn. When the girls saw his socks, they began rooting around for some too.

Dani and Jenny then hit the shoe racks and found almost-new sneakers. Jenny finally found a belt, and both she and Dani found new handbags. Then they went behind the counter for plastic bags and filled them up with their treasures.

"Where will we put them? The car has that...smell," Dani said.

"Oh, yeah." Jenny replied.

"We could hang the bags out the windows." Joe suggested. "It's only a mile to the hotel."

Dani's eyebrows went up. She smiled at Joe.

"What, you're surprised I came up with a good idea?" She patted his butt and they left the store. Jenny held her bag out the window while Dani held the others. She asked Joe to drive slowly.

"I'm afraid of losing the boots," she said. They were the heaviest thing in the bags.

Joe pulled into the hotel parking lot. Before they brought the things in, they checked the hotel for bad smells. There were none in the hotel itself, but when Joe went around to the back by the attached house, he smelled decaying flesh.

When he came back, he told them to put the bags down until they checked out the room farthest from the house. He also took the suitcases out of the back and dumped them by the side of the hotel.

Joe kicked the door open. The room was far enough away from the house that it had avoided the awful smell. They each took turns using the bathroom while the others waited outside.

They had to take their clothes off outside and throw them away. Dani held a blanket up while Jenny stripped and Jenny did the same for her. Jenny looked the other way when Joe stripped, but Dani watched him. She still got hot and bothered by the sight of him. Despite their constant bickering, this was one area of their marriage that had always worked.

When they were all dressed and felt really good, they decided to spend the night and walked into town to look around. They'd been driving for three days and were about halfway home. They looked in the store windows of the little town. They hadn't seen anyone, not even any bodies, and the town didn't smell too bad.

Joe began to look for another car, one that didn't smell like death. Jenny walked ahead because she thought she'd seen a library.

She thought a book would help her get through the trip. Dani watched Jenny walk away. She felt so sad for the girl.

"What do you think happened, Joe? Why did they all die?" Dani looked at Joe. He knew she was thinking of Mindy.

"Maybe a biological weapon. Maybe somebody got so pissed off they just…" Joe used his hands to indicate an explosion.

"But everything is still intact. This isn't like a bomb going off." Dani said.

"Then it would be some kind of poison."

Dani put her arms around Joe's waist and pulled him close. They stood there for a long time.

"I wanted to tell you something," Dani said. "I'm very proud of you."

"Why?" Joe asked.

"I know you haven't had a cigarette since the cavern."

"It hasn't been easy," he said.

"Why? I mean, you've had plenty of opportunities to grab a pack. What made you stop?"

Joe thought about the question.

"It just seemed like the right time. I don't know. Not having them for three days, then seeing all those dead people…I wanna live."

"Well, I'm glad you did. I want you to live, too." She kissed Joe passionately, and he responded. Then she took his hand and they continued to look for a car.

Jenny found the library. It looked really small from the outside, but it had books and maybe she could find something to distract her.

When she opened the door she noticed it didn't smell bad in there. She began to think that this town had somehow survived and the people were all in church or something. But why would they leave the door of the library open?

Jenny headed to the bookshelves and found the fiction section. She noticed a kids section to the left. Then she heard someone giggling.

Chapter 47

Jenny walked over to the kids section. She peeked around the corner and saw three little boys playing a board game. They hadn't heard Jenny come in. She kept watching them. She then tiptoed to the front door and quietly exited the library. Dani and Joe were holding hands and looking in a store window. Jenny ran over to them.

"Hey guys. Listen, I found three kids in the library," said Jenny.

"Oh, no!" Dani looked like she would cry.

"No, no," Jenny said, "they're alive." She looked from Dani to Joe.

"Kids, live kids?" Joe sounded skeptical.

"Yeah, live kids. Why would I make something like that up?"

"Let's go," Dani said as she dragged Joe towards the library.

Jenny went in first and tiptoed to the kids section. She saw three boys sitting on the floor. When Joe and Dani came in, the boys looked up and saw Jenny. Then they looked at each other. They got up off the floor and ran over to Jenny, encircled her with their arms and jumped up and down.

"Thank you God, thank you, thank you. A grown up. YAY!" The boys were chanting as they held onto Jenny.

Jenny looked up and saw Dani. Jenny looked like a frightened deer. One of the boys spotted Dani and Joe and ran over to them. He grabbed Dani's legs and hugged her tightly.

"Another grown up," he said. The last one ran over to Joe.

"Whoa, let's just shake hands," Joe said. The boy took Joe's hand and pumped it up and down.

"Mister, we are so glad to see you," the boy said.

"Yeah, we're almost out of food," the boy holding Jenny said.

"Who are you kids?" Dani asked.

"I'm Larry, this is my brother Barry, and that's my brother Gary. We're triplets."

"I can see that. Okay. So, you're running out of food. We saw a store a few blocks from here. Have you been there?" Dani asked.

"We were afraid to go too far. Zombies you know. We figured with a church on the corner they wouldn't come too close," Barry said.

261

Joe pressed his lips together hard. Ever since he'd heard their names he had been stifling a giggle. Dani elbowed him, and he lost it.

"Are you laughing at us? We don't like it when people laugh at us," Larry said.

"No, I wasn't laughing at you." But Joe couldn't stop and he ran outside.

"Forget him, kids. He's had a rough couple of weeks. So you've been here alone for a while, huh?" Dani said.

"We woke up one day and our parents...and everybody else too. Something must have happened in the middle of the night to make them all zombies. We moved here because it doesn't smell bad," Gary said.

Dani's heart went out to the boys. They looked to be about ten years of age. They looked so dirty and uncared for. She thought about the fear they must have felt being all alone, thinking zombies were just down the block.

"Would you like to come with us and have a bath?" She asked them.

"Not really," Gary said.

"Well, I think it would be a good idea, especially if you want to come with us," Said Dani.

"Why, where're you going?" Barry asked.

"Florida. We live there. Jenny's coming with us, too."

"Florida, you mean Disney World?" Gary was beside himself.

"Yeah, Disney World, zombie Disney World," Jenny whispered to Dani.

"Yes, Disney World. But you have to bathe if you want to come with us. The hotel has bathtubs. Gather your things and come with us."

"We don't have anything. We left it all at home," Larry said.

"We can take you there if you want." Dani looked from one boy to the other. They looked at each other.

"No, my parents are zombies now. They will eat us because they don't know any better. We'll get new stuff." Gary and his brothers followed Dani and Jenny to the hotel.

While they each took a shower, Dani walked to the consignment store and picked out some new clothes and underwear for the boys. She got enough so they would have something new to wear for three days before they needed washing. When she got back, they were laying side by side on the queen size bed. Jenny was telling them about the cavern. After a while the boys drifted off to sleep.

Dani and Jenny left the room and tried to break the door open on the room next door. Joe had just given the other one a good kick, but the women just didn't have the strength to do it.

Meanwhile, Joe had found another car parked in a garage of someone's house. It had the keys in it and it didn't smell. It also had GPS installed and a third row in the back to seat extra people. When he drove up, Dani told him they were taking the boys, who were now asleep in their room, and they would have to break into the one next door. Joe obliged them by kicking that door in.

There were two beds in this one, and Jenny immediately lay down and fell asleep. Dani and Joe got into the other one. Dani turned her back and Joe put his arms around her. For the first time in a long while, Dani was beginning to feel close to him again.

*****

The boys came into the room and woke up the grown-ups. They jumped on Joe, Dani and Jenny. Joe nearly threw Gary across the room, but Dani stopped him. Dani told the kids to get dressed in the new clothes she got them right now or they would be left here. The kids, still convinced that zombies roamed the town, obeyed her.

Joe grabbed another shower and Dani looked to see if there was any food available for breakfast. They would have to visit a food store before taking off.

Jenny rolled over and began to fall asleep again. Dani gently shook her and told her she really had to get up. Jenny rolled over onto her back and stretched. The boys came back in in various stages of dress and Jenny sat up. Dani helped the boys straighten their clothes. All in all they hadn't done too badly.

Joe was finally out of the shower and Jenny went into the bathroom. Dani went next door to take care of herself. In an hour they were loaded up and on the road to the grocery store.

Larry, Barry, and Gary wouldn't get out of the car. Dani told them they were at her mercy and would have to eat whatever she picked out. They said that was okay since the store was in zombie central. Joe said he would stay and protect them while she and Jenny went shopping.

The store was locked. Dani looked at Joe. He got out and looked for a big rock. He found a semi-big rock and threw it

263

overhand into one of the picture windows. It shattered into little balls of glass, leaving the window wide open. An alarm went off, and Joe ran to the back of the store to see if he could turn it off. He found the breaker box and stopped the alarm.

Dani and Jenny climbed over the sill and entered the store. Dani opened the sliding doors and grabbed a shopping cart. Fortunately, no one had been in the store before it opened the day of the tragedy. There were no bodies in here.

Dani filled the cart with non-perishable food and bottles of water. Jenny took another cart and did the same on the other side of the store. When they were done, they grabbed a handful of plastic bags to take to the car. It was easier to fill the bags in the back of the car than to carry them out already filled. When the food was safely stowed away, Jenny got in the middle row of seats while Dani got in the front passenger seat. The boys were wrestling in the third row.

"If you boys don't stop, I'll blow my zombie whistle and pull you out of the car, understand?!" Dani yelled. The boys stopped and sat down. They dared not move. They didn't know Dani well enough to know if she was bluffing.

Dani played with the GPS for a while, but this one was different and she was having trouble figuring out how to set it. Joe told her to leave it because he had the direction pointer in the mirror and he would just keep going east.

Dani decided not to pick on Joe and to let him have his way. She believed he was really trying, considering all the responsibility that had been thrust upon them. They would have to be allies in this, or they might just kill each other.

Chapter 48

They had been riding for three hours following the "E" in the mirror. They hadn't passed a town or bathroom for a long time, and the kids were starting to squirm.

"I think we better let them out to pee," Dani said.

Joe pulled over and the kids climbed over Jenny's seat and opened the car door. They ran to the side of the road and pulled their pants down. When they were done, they got back into the car and into the third row. Joe had to go, too, and went to the other side of the road.

"We might as well, Jenny. I have some paper in the back."

The women got out and Dani went to the back of the car and pulled out the toilet paper. They went a little ways away from the car where there was a large bush. They both went behind it and squatted. As they were pulling their pants up, they heard a faint yell coming from behind them.

"HELP!"

Dani turned towards the sound.

"Don't go. Maybe it's a trick." Jenny was holding onto Dani's arm.

"What if it's another kid?"

Dani shook off Jenny's hand and walked in the direction of the sound. She looked ahead and saw a line of trees that you couldn't see from the road. Out of the trees came a little girl running towards her.

"Please help," the girl was saying. Dani began to run towards her. They met and the little girl grabbed Dani's hand. Jenny ran back to the car to get Joe.

"I saw you. I saw you over the hill. I saw the car and I ran. I took the shortcut. I just kept running hoping I could catch you." The girl had to be around 10 years old. She was out of breath. She looked very thin.

"What's your name honey?" Dani asked her.

"Rebecca. Becky. Please, come with me. We need help."

"How many of you are there?" Dani didn't know what to do. She could see the distress the child was in, but what if it was a trap?

"There are twenty of us left. We grew up together. Please, we have no food."

The little girl was pulling Dani's hand. Dani turned to see if Joe could see her. She waved that she was going with the girl. Joe looked mad.

"You kids stay here with Jenny," Joe said and he ran to catch up with Dani. When he caught up to her, he grabbed her arm. "What's going on?"

"She says there are twenty of them. She says they have no food."

"Twenty of what? Maybe they're cannibals and we're tonight's dinner."

"And maybe they're the children of the corn, or maybe zombies." Dani was still following the girl.

"Of course not," Joe said, even though he had thought about that.

They reached the woods and the girl walked right into it. They followed her. Joe was determined to protect Dani. The girl kept walking and soon they could see a clearing in the woods where a small town had been built. The road into the town was probably just down the highway from where they were traveling.

There were several houses and a school. They also had a church and a library. The sign in front of the library indicated there was a post office inside. Someone had planned this town for its privacy.

In the center of the town was a small playground and a gazebo, and playing on the playground were several half-starved kids, all around 10 years old. Dani looked at Joe. She had many questions in her eyes. Why were all the children they'd found the same age?

"Hey, kids," Dani said.

The kids looked at her and tried to smile. They were dirty, just like the triplets.

"Where are your parents?" Dani thought that maybe, by some miracle, the poison had not made it this far from Vegas.

"Our parents didn't wake up. After a couple of days, we buried them," Becky said.

"All by yourselves?" Dani couldn't imagine what these kids had been through.

"We helped each other," a boy said.

"I'm sorry. I guess you're all hungry," Dani said.

In unison, the kids nodded their heads. Dani looked at Joe. There were several bags of groceries in the back of the car. Joe looked at her as if to say, "We can't save everybody" but he turned

266

around and walked back to the car. Dani asked Becky to show her around the town. Becky took her to the library.

"This has the story," Becky said, "of how we were born."

In the middle of the library, there was a small plaque dedicating the town to the Fetura Babies of Dr. Tomlinson. Dani thought that was very strange. The doctor who delivered Mindy was named Tomlinson. Dani had taken Fetura when she was pregnant with Mindy. Becky then took her to the back of the library where there were photos of all the children, from birth to just a month or so ago.

"See, this one's of me." Becky was pointing at a picture of a little purple newborn in the arms of a pretty young woman. "That's my mom." Dani noticed that the women in the pictures were all dressed in very nice clothing. Their hair and makeup were perfect.

As she looked at the pictures of the newborns, Dani remembered the first time she had laid eyes on Mindy. They all looked like she had for the first few days of her life. There was a book on a pedestal similar to a church altar. Dani opened it and read about how the town was founded.

The founding mothers of this town had been patients of Dr. Michael Tomlinson. They had joined together to raise their children in a "safe harbor of love and respect." They had come from different parts of the country with their husbands. These couples had money.

They had met on a website sponsored by Dr. Tomlinson. He had created it so that they could share their experiences with miscarriage and with Fetura, a purple concoction that allowed them to carry their babies to term.

Dani remembered Tomlinson trying to get her to go onto the website. She was working at the time and it just seemed like one more thing to do. She never went on it. Apparently these women had decided to raise their kids in some type of utopia, away from the dangers of the modern world.

Oh well, thought Dani, you had too much money for your own good. You should have lived in a cavern.

Dani began to think about the triplets. She wondered if they too were Fetura babies. If they were, then they had some kind of immunity from whatever had killed everyone else. That also meant Mindy would be immune!

Dani's heart beat faster. She'd been so scared to think about Mindy dying. Now Dani had hope that her little Fetura baby would be waiting back home when she got there.

Joe arrived with the bags. He enlisted Jenny and the triplets to help. The triplets at first refused, believing these kids were zombies luring them in. But Jenny said they were live children and for some reason they believed her. They carried the bags into the middle of the playground and the kids descended on the bags like vultures.

"Wait, wait, I know you're hungry, but we have to divide it up fairly. I'll do it," Dani said.

Dani walked towards them and they parted like the Red Sea. She opened the bags and started handing out toaster pastries and bags of snack chips. There were also cans of tuna and chicken, which required a can opener. Becky ran to her house and got one.

Dani opened can after can while the kids used their fingers to dig out the meat. Soon the feeding frenzy died down and they all sat on the ground. They looked at Dani to find out what they would do next. Dani took Joe's arm and pulled him to the side.

"What are we going to do with them?" She looked at him.

"You're really asking me?" Joe wasn't used to her asking him for advice when it came to something so important. Dani usually had the last word. "Well, I would say we have to get a bigger car."

"For sure, but not a car, we need a bus. A school bus maybe. That road leads to the highway. Maybe there's a real town there with a public school. We have to go and find out."

They asked Jenny to stay with the kids while they drove to town to look for a bus. Jenny asked them to bring her some chocolate if there was a store. She said she needed it after the last two days.

As they were heading back to the car, Joe stopped walking.

"I don't think I can do this Dani. I can't do this." He was shaking his head.

"Do what? You don't have a choice, Joe. You can't leave. These are kids. They need adults, and tag we're it."

"I'm not kidding. I really don't think I can handle this."

"I know you're not kidding, Joe. But what you don't get is that it doesn't matter whether or not you can handle it. You have to do it. I have to do it. You won the lottery again, Joe, only this time the prize is kids. Lots and lots of kids!"

Dani continued to walk to the car. Every nerve in Joe's body was trembling. Though he wouldn't admit it, he was scared to death and this time he couldn't run away.

Dani was in the driver's seat when he got to the car. He slid into the passenger seat and they drove down the highway.

The center of the next town was three miles away. It had the usual convenience store with gas pump, a small doctor's office, a hospital, a Big Mart, etc. Dani kept driving through the town until she spotted a row of yellow buses. They had found the school.

She parked the car and they both got out. They walked up to the first bus. Joe had trained once to drive a school bus, but at the last minute decided he couldn't handle the kids. These buses looked kind of old. Joe pulled on the door and it opened. He climbed up the stairs and looked to see if the key was in the ignition. YES! It was.

"The keys are here, Dani."

Dani smiled. There was one less thing to worry about. She was glad they'd found the buses.

Joe sat in the seat and looked at the gauges. He looked for the yellow knob that signified it had air brakes. It was there. He would have to teach Dani how to use them. He put the bus in neutral. He then pulled out the yellow knob, stepped on the brakes, and turned on the bus. He put the bus in drive and pushed the yellow knob back in. He was ready to go. When it came time to stop, he would reverse the process. It had all come back to him. Dani was impressed.

"You look good up there, hon," she said. Joe smiled.

"Why thank you ma'am." Joe pretended to tip his imaginary cowboy hat. "I guess I have to drive this back. It's got gas in it, so I'll see you there."

Joe closed the doors and drove the bus out of the parking lot. He would have to practice wide turns. He made the turn onto the highway. He was doing pretty well. He wanted to practice a little before putting kids in the bus. He drove up and down the highway a few times, turning and reversing. He then drove to the little road that led to the kids' town.

Dani was there with the car parked in the driveway of one of the houses. He parked on the road. He jumped down from the bus and walked over to Dani and Jenny. Dani must have stopped at the convenience store because everyone was eating chocolate.

"So, what's the plan and where's mine?"

Dani handed him a chocolate bar.

"We want to clean them up. We're checking the houses to see if there's running water all around and then we'll give them baths. We need your help."

Joe took a deep breath. "Yeah, I'll help with the boys. Mindy is too self-conscious in front of me. Boys don't care." He stood up and went to the middle of the playground.

269

"Hey, guys, can I have your attention?" The kids turned to look at Joe. "Can I have all the boys line up over here?" Seven little boys walked over to the imaginary line Joe pointed to. "All right, fellas, it's bath time. I want you to go over to that lady over there and she'll tell you what house to go to for your bath."

The boys complained but they did as they were told. It was nice to have someone in charge. Dani lined them up again and waited for Jenny. Jenny ran out to her and said the house they had parked at had two full baths and running water, but it was cold.

"Guys, we have to give you cold baths. I promise to make it shallow and we'll just use it to rinse you off. Okay?" Dani said.

The boys made faces but followed Jenny into the house with Joe bringing up the rear. Then Dani had the girls line up and follow her into the house next door. She'd found two baths in there, too, and she would get the girls washed up in that one. They should have some clean clothes in their respective houses.

It would be a long evening, but once they were clean, they could sleep and be on the road first thing in the morning. She and Jenny would stop at a store and fill the car with food while Joe waited with the kids in the bus. He would then follow Dani as she followed the "E" in the rearview mirror.

*****

The school bus was quiet. By some quirk of fate, all the kids had fallen asleep, and Joe was enjoying the peace and quiet. The road ahead was empty of cars and bodies. It was a rural highway, with a farm here and there. The lack of distractions gave Joe a chance to reflect on the moment that changed his life, and how you never really know what's around the next bend in the road.

Chapter 49

St. Petersburg, Florida

Gladys Stemple was putting her prescriptions in the car when the latch on her purse opened. The lottery ticket she had placed in it was sitting on her wallet. She had taken it out of her wallet so it would be easier to find when she went to Granger's to check the winning lottery numbers.

Gladys had been buying lottery tickets for years, always using the same numbers. She knew her odds of winning were low, but watching those numbers come up every week gave her a small thrill, which at her age was all she could handle.

Gladys didn't have the Internet and had stopped the paper coming to the house when Fred died. She had fallen asleep in the chair last night and missed the drawing, so now she had to go to Granger's to check them.

Gladys looked down and saw her purse open. She snapped it closed without noticing that the ticket had fallen out. It had been picked up by the wind and was wending its way down to the 7-11 on 16th Street North, where Joe Lane sat with his back against the front of the store.

Joe had decided to sit there until he died. It was better than going home and facing Dani and Mindy without the promised pizza. In the meantime, Gladys Stemple was cursing herself at the lottery counter of the Granger's Supermarket for not buying a new purse.

Joe had been sent out to pick up a pizza. He was supposed to take $20 out of the ATM, go to the pizza place and pick up the pizza Dani had ordered over the phone. She would've paid for it over the phone, but Joe said he could get the soda cheaper at the dollar store so, against her better judgment she gave him her ATM card. She made him promise not to stop at the 7-11. She threatened death if he did. So Joe had promised, as he always did, to go straight to the pizza place after buying soda at the dollar store.

As soon as Joe hit the car, he remembered 7-11 was having a sale on soda. He began to think about the scratch-off lottery tickets. Joe loved the scratch-offs. He loved the feeling he'd get as he scratched off each little box revealing a winner or a loser. More often than not, Joe had losers.

But Joe couldn't stop buying scratch-offs. Even when an investigation proved that most of them were losers since there were always more tickets printed than prizes awarded, Joe would still pay a dollar for a worthless piece of cardboard.

Gamblers get their thrills from the anticipation of the win to come. The pursuit of the prize is their reward, and the odds favor the house every time. Joe had worked himself into a frenzy thinking about those tickets. He couldn't get to the 7-11 fast enough. He put the card in the ATM and entered the numbers. He then drove away leaving the $20 bill hanging out of the machine.

When he got to the 7-11, he parked the car at an angle and ran into the store. He knew he had to get to the pizza store before the pizza got cold. He had to wait behind one person at the counter, and while he stood there, he pulled out his wallet. Then he remembered the money hanging out of the machine.

"Shit," he whispered. He ran back to the car. The bank was three blocks away. Maybe it was still there, but he thought there had been another car behind him so the odds were pretty bad.

"Shit," he said again, out loud this time. "Shit, shit, shit."

Joe walked back to the store and sat down on the pavement. He wished someone would drive by and shoot him. It was better than facing Dani. She was gonna kill him.

It was Mindy's birthday and she wanted a pizza. It had been the last $20 they could spend until Dani got paid on Friday, and this was Wednesday. If it hadn't been Mindy's birthday, they would have waited to get a pizza until the weekend.

Dani had specifically told Joe not to go to the 7-11. But if he had gotten a winner, he reasoned, they may have had $100, or a $1,000 to spend on Mindy.

Joe always imagined Dani's face as he walked into the house with $1,000. He imagined her smiling and hugging him. She might even laugh. Mindy would jump up and down and daddy would be a hero instead of a loser. Now Daddy sat in front of the 7-11 like a panhandler. He couldn't go home without a pizza.

As Joe was contemplating the various ways he could kill himself, a lottery ticket blew by his legs and landed on the pavement next to his feet. Joe looked at the ticket. It was a Florida Lotto ticket. Obviously, someone had lost and thrown it away. But you never knew.

That thing that rose up in every addict began to rise up in Joe. Joe had to pick up that ticket and look, he just had to. A teacher of his liked to say, "Anticipation is greater than realization." Joe never quite understood what she meant by that. If he had, he wouldn't be a gambler, and he probably would have left the ticket on the ground.

Joe reached down and picked up the ticket. He turned it over. No one had signed it. Joe got up off the ground. He walked into the 7-11 and scanned the ticket to see if it was a winner. The machine said "Call Lottery Office." That had never happened to Joe before. He asked the guy behind the counter what that meant.

"Must be a big one, man. You want me to call?"

Joe thought about it.

"No, I'll do it when I get home. Thanks."

Joe left the store and ran back to his car. He sat in the car looking down at the ticket. How big does it have to be to not register on the scanner?

He pulled out his cell phone and dialed the 800 number for the Florida Lottery. He input his numbers and it told him to wait. He was connected to a pleasant-sounding woman who asked for his numbers again.

"Well, sir, I'm happy to tell you that you have won one of our big jackpots."

"Really? I really won?" Joe's blood was rising in his body. He could feel himself twitch. "How much?"

"The prize is $5,000,000 sir."

Joe sat with the phone stuck to his ear. He couldn't move.

"Wha...what did you say?"

"$5,000,000, sir."

Joe was having trouble breathing. "Uh...how...do I get it?"

"You'll have to come to Tallahassee to the Florida Lottery Headquarters. We'll need a valid photo ID and a bank account to wire the money to."

Joe was speechless. She was serious. He had won $5,000,000 dollars. As he sat there, he could hear her giving Joe more instructions. What she was saying wasn't registering. He then heard her say he could go on the Internet and find all the instructions. Joe thanked her and hung up the phone.

His biggest worry was he would lose the ticket like the unfortunate person who had purchased it. He took out his wallet and carefully placed the ticket inside. He then put the wallet in his pocket. Then he recalled that that pocket had a hole in it and took the wallet out again. He felt the inside of the other pocket. It seemed intact so he slipped the wallet in there.

Joe was still in a daze. He, Dani and Mindy were millionaires, millionaires without enough gas to get to Tallahassee and claim their prize.

Joe's mom, Mimi, lent them the money to go to Tallahassee. Normally it was Dani's mom, Linda, who helped them out, but she'd met a man named Hector who swept her off her feet, married her, and moved her to Puerto Rico. Dani kept calling her, but Linda was in Europe on an extended honeymoon and hadn't answered her phone.

When they got to Tallahassee and the money was being transferred into their bank account, they decided the first thing they would do is take a vacation together. They hadn't gone anywhere alone together since Mindy was born. It was Joe's idea to go to Vegas. Dani had protested that Vegas was the last place Joe needed to be.

At that moment, Joe decided to give her 2/3 of the prize and he would keep his 1/3 in a separate bank account. If he lost it all, at least Dani's and Mindy's shares would be safe. He also agreed to go sightseeing and not spend every minute in the casinos.

*****

Joe thought about the kind of man he had been. He thought about his foolishness in thinking it would be okay to gamble away 1.7 million dollars as long as Dani and Mindy had theirs.

Their present situation made money obsolete, and Joe was beginning to have strange thoughts come into his head about how his wife and daughter's lives were worth so much more to him than he had ever imagined. He knew he loved them, he had always known that. But what he hadn't understood was how hard he tried to push his family away.

The time on the bus was just what Joe needed. He tried to understand his motives, and what had made him run away all those times when things got hard. There were little fissures forming in his old thinking patterns. Instead of rationalizing his behavior, he was beginning to see it for what it was - cowardice.

Joe had been a coward unable to face the realities of his life, unable to be truthful in order to avoid the consequences of the truth. This dawning realization was causing Joe so much pain that he tried to turn it off, but he couldn't, and over the next few days, it would manifest into a new Joe, a Joe who was able to empathize with other people's pain; a Joe who could be proud of himself for not running away.

There was something else Joe thought about as he rambled over the highway towards Florida; it seemed every time they stopped for food or to look for gas, they would find another kid. It was as if some divine hand were guiding them.

This happened to Joe all the time, though he had never recognized it as a guiding hand, so to speak. He just thought it was luck. It had happened to his mother and father, too. His mom was always finding something just when they needed it, like $2 Stride Rite shoes for her son's huge feet when he was a toddler, or $2 shirts on a rack at J.C. Penney's just in time for the new school year.

Joe's relationship with the Almighty had never been much to write home about. He had gone to church with his mom but it never made much impression on his character. It was easier for Joe to lie than to deal with the disappointment on his mother's face. It was easier to lie than to hear his father yell at him. Joe learned early that avoidance was easier than responsibility, and once he learned that lesson, he never looked back.

Joe got into trouble a lot when he was in high school. He took a joy ride to Philly one day with some friends, hoping to score marijuana. The car was old and not in great condition. The kid driving the car was inexperienced and when the car failed on the road, he couldn't get it out of the way of a truck barreling down on them.

Joe was in the left-hand passenger seat and when the truck hit. He was thrown to the roof of the car suffering a severe head injury. It took a long time for Joe to come back. He was never really himself again after that, not the kid his parents knew growing up. But his tendency to lie had remained intact. He parlayed this ability into a sales position at an appliance store. If you didn't know Joe, you believed him. He was very persuasive.

When Joe met Dani, he was 20 years old. He liked girls. He liked girls a lot and they liked him. He wanted to be monogamous, but when those 16-year-olds came onto him, what was he supposed to do?

"Stay away from them, Joe." His mother would say. "We're talking statutory rape. These are minors. You're an idiot if you mess with that. I'm not gonna bail you out. Maybe your father will, but I won't."

Mimi knew Joe would never survive without two showers a day, so the threat of jail had real meaning for him. She also knew that her son hated to be confined somewhere he couldn't get out of.

Mimi was hoping Dani would straighten him out. She was a nice girl and Mimi liked her. When she became pregnant, Mimi worried because she knew her son well. She knew he would run away from hard things by gambling or smoking pot, or even actually running away.

When Dani lost the baby, Joe did run away. He took off for Jersey, where he had lived before coming to Florida. Dani went after him and brought him back. She loved him and believed he would change. Most young girls believe that if a guy is loved hard enough, he will eventually "see the light." Dani was no exception.

Dani finished college while Joe dropped out and drifted. He worked sporadically and borrowed money from his father, Fritz, on a weekly basis. They were living with Dani's mom now and things were tense. No matter how much Joe wanted to change, he just kept falling back into his old bad ways.

Dani had a good job and was able to pay their bills, but Joe kept taking the money out and buying scratch-off lottery tickets. He would drain their bank account trying to score a big win so he could go home and throw the money in Dani's face. It never happened, and Dani's checks would bounce. It was as though he wanted to push her away, make her leave him.

Joe would accuse her of sleeping with other men. He fought with Dani's mom and ran out in the middle of the night to drive around aimlessly. He flirted with women who came in to buy appliances and took their numbers.

Dani would go to Mimi to find out why he was like this. Mimi would try to give her some answer, but the bottom line was that Joe was Joe. If he was going to change, it would have to come from within himself.

Dani had troubles of her own. When she was 14, her brother Brandon had died in a motorcycle accident caused by a drunken driver. A settlement was made and Dani had been given a great deal of money. It could never make up for the loss of her brother. Dani mourned him for many years.

She married when she turned 18, but the marriage failed. As it was ending, she met Joe. She fell hopelessly in love with him. The more she loved him, the worse he got. But she persevered. She believed that somewhere in Joe was a good man, a man she could be proud of.

The loss of the baby had a devastating effect on Dani. She had longed for a little girl, a daughter she could bond with. She was very excited about having a baby, even though Joe was so unpredictable. She looked forward to doing all the things with her daughter that Linda had done with her.

Dani had a close relationship with Linda and hoped she would have the same with her daughter. When she lost the baby in her second trimester, the doctor told her she had cervical insufficiency and may never be able to carry a baby to full term. Dani hated him and decided to find a new doctor.

Three years later, when she found herself pregnant again, she was scared to do anything. She was scared to move around, and she was scared to go to work. One of the doctors she worked for suggested a colleague by the name of Tomlinson. He told her Michael Tomlinson had had great success with cases like hers. In fact, they seem to be outright miracles. Women who had lost two or three babies were carrying to full term. He made a phone call and got her into see him.

Tomlinson looked like Santa Claus. She smiled when he walked in the door. He was gracious and shook her hand. He made Dani feel instantly at ease. He assured her she had nothing to worry about. He had a drug called Fetura that would tighten her cervix, allowing her to carry the baby.

Fetura was very expensive. When she returned to the doctor's office, he gave her a bottle of purple solution, which she drank in the office. He then sent her home. Dani used the settlement monies to pay Tomlinson's inflated fees. This guy better produce or she would sue, she thought.

Dr. Tomlinson did produce, and Mindy was born right on time. Dani was ecstatic, and Joe tried his hardest to seem enthusiastic. But he left the hospital and went straight to the 7-11. He bought 20 scratch-off tickets without one winner. Joe couldn't handle responsibility, and a big one had just been dropped in his lap.

He began to have fantasies that Mindy wasn't his. After all, Dani had gone to the doctor's office and then had a baby. How did he know it was his? Joe's inability to accept responsibility had always caused him to create an alternate universe wherein he was the victim of everyone else's plots. Dani was usually the perpetrator of these plots.

Now she had a baby, another human being who would force Joe to go to work every day and change diapers and make sure there was food in the house. This was all her fault; his failures were always her fault. The belief that the whole world was against him, seemed to color all of Joe's decisions.

Now Joe had had another big responsibility dropped into his lap, one he couldn't run away from. He silently prayed that he wouldn't let Dani down this time.

Chapter 50

Joe was listening to the kids as he drove the bus. In this world where money was useless, who was Joe Lane? What kind of man was he?

His excuse for buying the tickets had been to try to turn $1 into $1,000. His excuse for chasing women had been that Dani was always nagging him about money. His excuse for sleeping late and missing work was that he was trying to find junk to sell to make money. All the excuses he used for his bad behavior were no longer valid.

The fissures in his head were now growing into cracks and Joe was going to have to find ways to live with his past since he could no longer turn off the bad feelings. No matter how hard he tried, he knew the truth about himself and he couldn't go back to the way things had been.

Even though things had been bad and he'd been a jerk, at least he was familiar with that kind of life. He knew how to navigate those waters. Now when he lied, he would feel that lie himself. This really sucked, and on top of everything else, these kids were driving him crazy.

"Everybody shut up!" he yelled. The kids just laughed and yelled louder. Suddenly Joe stopped the bus and got out. The kids started to get up thinking they would leave too and he stuck his head back in the bus.

"First kid off the bus gets a kick in the ass, understand?"

He must have looked pretty mean because the kids sat back down. He walked to the edge of the highway. He was taking deep breaths and trying to calm down. Dani saw that he'd stopped and she parked the car. She got out and walked back to where he was standing.

"What's up, honey?" she asked him. He had on his "I'm done" face.

"This is too much. I can't stand the noise anymore. Those kids never shut up." Dani looked at the bus and saw the kids making faces through the glass. She suppressed a smile.

"You know, I can drive that thing. Just show me how to use the brakes."

Dani had never driven anything bigger than an SUV. Since there was no other traffic on the road she might be able to handle it.

Getting it around parked cars was the problem. It was awkward and full to capacity.

"You think you can maneuver it around parked cars? Ride up on the grass with a full load like that without it tipping over?

"Maybe we should try to find an interstate where there's a parking lane. There would be a lot more room and maybe less traffic." Dani was trying to convince him she could do this.

"Where's the map?" Joe asked. They had picked up a map in Arkansas when they were sick of making wrong turns following an arbitrary "E" in the rearview mirror. Dani had never been able to figure out the damn GPS.

"It's in the car. I'll go get it."

The last sign they'd passed said "Nashville 100," so they knew they were nearing Tennessee. They needed to find an interstate that would take them south. They'd been going northeast when they should have been going southeast. Dani came back to Joe with the map and they laid it on the ground and knelt down.

"It looks like if we go to Nashville we can pick up 24 and then 75 to Atlanta. At least we'll be in Georgia." Joe said.

They agreed to follow that route. They would switch driving duties in Nashville. Joe put his arms around Dani's shoulders and pulled her close.

"I'm sorry, Dani," he said.

"For what?"

She looked up at him.

"For being such an asshole."

He looked depressed and defeated. There was something different about the way he said it. Dani had heard him say this before, but this time his eyes looked into hers instead of avoiding them.

"It's okay, Joe." She put her head on his chest and hugged him.

Before Joe got back on the bus, Dani got in and told the kids whoever stayed the quietest during the next 100 miles would get a prize. She had no idea what the prize would be, but kids usually fell for that ploy believing the adult saying it already had something tucked away somewhere. They became excited at the prospect of a prize and a hush fell over the bus. Joe looked at Dani with raised eyebrows. She smiled back at him and wished him luck.

About halfway down the road, the kids started talking again. Their voices kept getting louder until Joe screamed at them to shut up. The moment he stopped yelling, he looked at their faces. They all looked scared and tired. They looked sad and dirty.

Something in their expressions caused a familiar stirring in Joe's heart. As his eyes went from the road to the mirror, he could see Mindy's little face as he yelled at her to pick up her stuff, or stop talking, or to leave him alone. He had never had time for her. When he would chastise her, she would walk away and go find Dani. Dani would do her best to comfort Mindy, but what the kid really wanted was him. The thought struck him like a bolt of lightning. She had wanted...him.

Joe had forgotten that all of these kids had just lost their families. They had also lost their homes. He kept checking the kids in the mirror. With the exception of Larry, Gary, Barry, and Becky, he didn't know any of their names. They were just a mass of humanity, all under four feet tall.

Joe was driving by a mall when an idea struck him. He pulled over and entered the parking lot. Dani looked back and noticed Joe had stopped. She turned around and followed him into the parking lot. Joe climbed out of the bus and told the kids to stay put. Dani got out of the car and came over to him.

"I have an idea. I'll be right back," he told her and ran to the office supply store.

The door was locked and Joe threw a metal trash can from the sidewalk into the window. As with the consignment store, the glass shattered, leaving enough room for Joe to climb in without being cut. After he disabled the alarm, he grabbed a shopping cart and walked the aisles of the store until he came upon the "Hello My Name Is" labels. He grabbed three packs of them.

He also picked up the plastic sheaths with a pin in them. Finally, he grabbed all the magic markers the store had. As he walked towards the doors, he noticed a rack of coloring books, word searches, and puzzle books. He filled the cart with them and grabbed pens and pencils. He pried the door open and pushed the cart through it. He then walked the cart to the bus and motioned for the kids to come out.

Joe handed Dani and Jenny magic markers and gave them to some of the kids.

"Listen up," he said. "I want you all to write your name on a label, stick it on these plastic things, and pin it to your shirts. I want to get to know you, so I have to know your names."

281

Dani was surprised by Joe's sudden interest in the kids after his tirade just an hour before, but she played along because it really was a good idea. It took a while but when they were done, all the kids had name tags. Finally they would know which of the triplets was Barry, Larry, or Gary. Then Joe announced that they had all been really good so he would be handing out the prizes. The kids cheered. He asked Dani and Jenny to help pass out the books, pens, and pencils.

"You did good, Joe," Dani said and she gave him a hug.

"Yeah, you never did anything like that before," Jenny said.

Hearing Dani say he did good lifted Joe's spirits. He loaded the kids back on the bus and told Dani they could still switch in Nashville if she was up to it, but if not he would be okay. She agreed and they got back on the road with a bus load of happy 10-year-olds.

*****

They made good time to Nashville. Dani pulled into the parking lot of a Big Mart followed by Joe in the bus. All of them got out to stretch their legs. Joe hoped no kids would pop out of the Big Mart. That store could hold a lot of kids.

The kids they had found had been hiding out in stores where there was a food supply and no dead bodies. They had so many kids now that finding clean places to sleep and getting them all fed was getting harder and harder.

Joe imagined the Big Mart must be full of bodies because the smell was becoming stronger the longer they stayed there. Dani said she would like to try and drive the bus. It would be a nice change, she said.

Dani took her place behind the wheel of the bus. Joe sat behind her and they took the bus for a few laps around the Big Mart parking lot. She was fine at avoiding the parked cars, but they were all in a neat line so that didn't count. What would count is how she handled the cars in the middle of the road.

He showed her how to use the brakes. After three or four times around, they stopped the bus and the kids came on board. Those that had to relieved themselves on the grass. Jenny was handing out toilet paper to the girls.

"Do you want me to ride with you?" she asked Dani.

"It's up to you, Jenny."

282

Jenny thought about hours in the car with Joe. Even though his attitude had changed dramatically, he could be moody and she didn't feel comfortable around him.

"Yeah, I think the change would be good." She sat in the seat directly behind Dani. The kids who had been sitting there protested.

"Oh, go to the back," she said. She then gave them a mean look. They were a little afraid of Jenny. She was still a teenager and she might just beat them up.

Dani told Joe they would have to find food soon and to keep an eye out for a clean store. A clean store usually didn't have any cars parked in front of it and the doors were locked. After Joe got into the SUV, he pulled out and followed the signs to 75, with Dani right behind him.

If Dani had ever visited Dr. Tomlinson's website, she would have noticed how many women had come from Atlanta to seek his assistance. She would also have known they would soon need another bus.

Chapter 51

Somewhere near Atlanta, Georgia

Dani was driving the bus. Jenny had taken the seat behind her. A little girl came up to Jenny and asked if she could sit with her because the boys kept pulling her hair. Jenny moved over so the girl could sit by the window.

She told Jenny her name was Kelly. They talked about all the things they liked. It turned out they liked the same music and the same clothes.

Jenny told Kelly how much she missed her friends, how she wished she could go on Facebook and Twitter, and how she even missed being in school. Kelly missed her friends and her dance classes. After a while, Kelly leaned against Jenny's arm and fell asleep. Jenny put her arm around Kelly and the little girl snuggled up to her. Jenny had made a good friend.

Dani saw a sign saying Atlanta was just 50 miles away. The sun was setting and she hoped there would be some lights on in the city. Otherwise they would have to spend the night on the bus. When they stopped at a town earlier that day, they had filled the car with food. When they found a place to stop, they would all eat. The kids had been given bags of chips earlier to keep them from being too hungry. They each had a bottle of water too.

Dani longed for a place to take a bath, but they had been having trouble finding clean hotels. The last one had been two days ago. The kids needed baths too.

Joe was really suffering without his two showers a day, but ever since his dramatic change, he no longer complained about it. Dani hoped this change was for real. For years she had been walking on eggs around Joe, never knowing what would set him off. Now he seemed happy, genuinely happy, even around the kids. If he stayed this way, it would be the miracle she had prayed for come true.

That afternoon they'd stopped at every clean store they could find looking for clothing. The kids' clothes were dirty and would need to be changed if they took baths.

Dani and Jenny ran up and down the aisles of the mostly small, privately owned stores grabbing shirts, pants, underwear, and socks. The sizes didn't matter. If they had to, they would tie something around the pants to hold them up. Jenny filled a cart and then threw men's ties and belts on top.

As she drove, Dani asked Jenny to keep talking to her. She was feeling sleepy. Jenny rattled on about her life before the tragedy and her friends at school. Dani liked hearing her talk. She imagined Mindy might be like this someday, and Jenny's mother could rest in peace knowing someone was taking care of Jenny. Maybe someone was taking care of her Mindy, too.

The last miles seem to go on forever. Just before they entered Atlanta, they saw a large hotel that announced it was under renovation. Joe stopped and Dani pulled in behind him.

"I'm gonna check the inside. Maybe they haven't done too much, or maybe they're almost finished," he said about the renovations.

The door was locked and as usual, Joe looked around for something to break in. There were concrete blocks along the side of the building that would do nicely. Joe lifted a block and brought it to the front of the hotel. He wasn't able to lift it over his head so he kind of threw it underhand. It smashed through the glass in the door and Joe was able to turn the lock. He lifted the light switch and the lights came up. He could hear the kids cheering. Much to his surprise, no alarm sounded.

The lobby wasn't too bad. There was dust and now shattered glass balls all over, but it looked like they were almost done fixing it up. He took the stairs to the first floor. He switched on the lights up there and went to the first room. The door was open. They hadn't programmed the locks yet. He turned on the lights and noticed the room looked pretty good. He looked in the bathroom and checked the water. It actually worked.

Joe thought about the electricity and water. The hotel must have had well water and some sort of independent electricity supply. Most of the places they encountered didn't have electricity or water. He sent up a little thank-you to God and went downstairs to get the kids. Dani was standing in the lobby when Joe came down.

"Water and electricity," he said with a smile. "And there are three floors. We should be able to find a place for everybody."

Dani and Joe got the kids inside and brought out the food. The kids sat around the lobby while the food was handed out on paper plates. Joe had managed to find boxes of crackers, jars of peanut butter, jars of jelly, jars of applesauce, and pudding. Anything they could eat without cooking. Tonight they would feast.

285

Dani, Joe, and Jenny formed an assembly line to put peanut butter on crackers and put them on plates. Jenny put the applesauce and pudding out on the counter. The kids lined up and grabbed a plate and a dessert. Once the kids were eating, the adults finished what was left. They would have to find more food in Atlanta in the morning.

When they were done eating, Dani announced that they would all take a short shower before getting into bed. The boys groaned and the girls cheered. The hotel had plenty of soap and shampoo. Dani, Joe, and Jenny timed the kids so everyone could get wet, soaped up, shampooed, and rinsed. Then they put on the clean clothes and got into bed. The kids were exhausted and passed out quickly.

After they got the kids settled in their rooms, Dani and Joe lay down on the sofas in the hotel lobby and fell asleep, while Jenny shared a recliner with Kelly.

*****

The sun in his eyes awakened Joe. He sat up and stretched. Dani was still asleep. He decided to go a little farther down the road to see if he could find some food. There must be a grocery store somewhere, hopefully one without dead bodies in it.

Joe got into the SUV and turned onto the highway. He saw several pancake restaurants and gas stations. They all had cars in front of them. He drove farther down the highway and saw a Granger's Supermarket without any cars. It looked like a brand new store that hadn't opened yet. Joe pulled in.

He was able to pull the doors apart. He thought it was strange that the doors weren't locked. Maybe somebody had come in alone to let the other workers in.

He sniffed the air and didn't smell decay. He took a shiny new cart out of the rack and began to cruise the aisles. The shelves were full on top but the bottoms were nearly empty. There was nothing in the freezers or refrigerated cases. That stuff would have been brought into the store last.

Joe thought he heard something coming from the back of the store. He kept filling the cart as he walked towards the sound. He heard talking. Joe walked all the way to the back and saw the swinging doors that led to the storage areas. He went through the doors and looked around.

286

"Who are you?" a voice asked him.

Joe turned around and saw five kids lying on the floor in sleeping bags. He looked at the shelves and saw more kids. He wasn't sure how many there were.

"I'm Joe. I...how did you guys get here?"

"Julius brought us."

Who the hell is Julius? Joe thought.

"Julius finds kids and brings them here," a girl said.

"Who is Julius?"

"He's an old man. He lives across the street."

Joe walked back to his cart. He pushed it out to the car and looked across the street. He saw a big, old Victorian house with a wide porch. After he put the food in the car, he walked across the street.

He climbed the stairs and knocked on the door. There was no answer. He tried the door and it opened. The house had that decayed flesh odor.

Joe could see a room to the left and a room to the right. In the room to the right was a large overstuffed sofa with a small, old black man lying on it, fast asleep. This must be Julius. How he'd avoided death was a story Joe wanted to hear.

Joe gently shook Julius's shoulder. The old man slowly woke up and looked up at Joe.

"Where'd you come from?" he asked Joe.

"Vegas," Joe replied. He seated himself in a chair across from where Julius was sleeping.

"Vegas. Lordy, you must have been ridin' a long time." Julius turned his body around to face Joe. He then put one leg on the floor so he could use it to move his body around. Then he put the other one down on the floor. He sat up and looked at Joe.

"How'd you know I was here?"

"The kids told me."

Julius nodded his old woolly head.

"Yeah, the kids are a handful. I don't know how many there are, but I just keep findin' em." Julius was scratching his stomach.

"Where do you find them?"

"Ah, here, there and everywhere. I drive around and there they are. Sometimes in front of a house, sometimes in front of a store."

Joe knew what it was like to just drive around and find kids. Joe asked Julius the million dollar question.

"How did you survive, Julius?"

287

The old man sat back on the sofa and slowly began to tell Joe his story.

*****

Shawna Jackson had converted her Atlanta boarding house into a senior group home three years earlier. At the time, she had to install a large, walk-in cooler. In order to save money, Shawna had her brother scour the junkyards to find an abandoned walk-in that they could refurbish. Terrell had found just what she was looking for and installed it in the basement.

He was able to install a new motor and clean out the inside like new. The only problem was the handle on the door. It was old and loose so Terrell tightened it until it held, but it had a tendency to loosen up over time. Shawna would call him to come over and tighten it. Over the next three years she would call on Terrell 14 times. After his last visit, he told Shawna that she had to think about getting a new box.

"I can't tighten the thing anymore," Terrell told her. "I looked for the part in the junkyard and can't find one. You really have to think about gettin' a new one."

Shawna told him she would, but her finances promised something else. There was no way Shawna could get a new walk-in box, and with an inspection coming up, she didn't know what she would do. She decided to let it go another week or so until she could think of something.

Julius Beadle lived in Shawna Jackson's group home. He was a 68-year-old black man whose daughter had placed him with Miss Jackson. Julius didn't think he belonged there. He was well able to care for himself. But he thought it was a nice enough place and Miss Jackson kept it clean. His food was always hot and good.

Julius was not allowed to have the things he loved to eat like fried chicken and gravy. Miss Jackson would give him lots of his favorite vegetables boiled and baked, but Julius longed for sweet potato pie.

When everyone went to bed, Julius would don his coat, gloves, and scarf and sneak down to Miss Jackson's walk-in box to eat a piece of pie. He did this most nights after he heard Miss Jackson's door close. The handle on the walk-in door was a little loose, but Julius would place a box in the way so the door wouldn't close behind him.

The night before the tragedy, Julius had donned his coat, gloves, and scarf as usual. He had felt really cold last time, so this time he also added a hat. He opened his door a crack and saw that Miss Jackson had turned out her light. He tiptoed out of his room and down the stairs. He carried a small flashlight to light his way. He was careful to hold onto the railing so he wouldn't fall and wake up the house.

Julius made it to the bottom and rounded the corner heading for the kitchen. The basement door was off the back of the kitchen. Julius didn't want to turn on the lights here in case someone woke up. He did turn on the basement stairs light though. It was dark and spooky down there.

When Julius got to the bottom, he walked over to the walk-in box. He was in a heightened state of anticipation. He pulled on the handle. The door opened, but the handle came off in his hand. Oh, no! Now Miss Jackson would be mad. She would know it was Julius.

Julius opened the door wide and put the wooden box he always used in front of it to prop it open. The box wasn't pushed back far enough and began to slide. He entered the walk-in and searched for the pie. Julius' hearing was not what it used to be and with the hat pulled over his ear as well, he didn't hear the box shifting and the door closing with a good slam.

Julius' back was to the door so it took him a while to notice it was closed. He found the pie and took out his mini-pocket knife to cut a slice. He had a fork in his pocket so he could eat the pie right out of the pan. He ran his finger around the bottom of the pan, gathering any crumbs left behind. When he was done, he savored the last, sweet taste of it on his tongue and turned to leave the box. Then he noticed the closed door.

There was no way to get the latch open. He pushed and pushed on the knob inside the box. The knob went all the way in, but the door didn't open. He left the knob stuck in the hole. Julius knew they would come in the morning to get food for breakfast, but he would get caught. He didn't know what to do.

Julius woke up and was shivering. He was sitting on a wooden pallet on the floor and he must have fallen asleep. He didn't know what time it was. No one had come for the breakfast food yet. His legs were cold and stiff.

Julius had to relieve himself. Miss Jackson was gonna be real mad if he pissed in the walk-in. He found a half-filled bottle of apple juice and poured it onto the floor. He used the bottle to relieve himself and put it on the floor next to the door in case he needed it again. Hopefully he wouldn't have to do a number two.

Julius slept a lot during his stay in the walk-in. He took boxes off the shelves and emptied them. He ripped them open so he could use them to keep his legs covered.

At some point, the electricity went out and the box warmed up. Julius then took his coat, gloves, scarf, and hat off. He was very worried. It was dark in the walk-in, and his little flashlight wouldn't last very long if he kept it on all the time.

No one had come for a very long time and he was afraid he would die in the box. There was plenty of food so he had been eating, but he also had to defecate and used a pie plate inside a plastic milk bottle crate so he could sit while he answered nature's call.

Julius was getting tired of being stuck. He figured if he was going to die, he would go down fighting. He searched the walk-in for anything he could use to push open the latch.

He tried the pocket knife but it was too short. He found a screwdriver stuck in the back of one of the shelves holding the cans of food. It was below the fan so whoever had fixed the fan last had left it there. It must have been Terrell.

"Thank you, Terrell," Julius said when he found it.

Julius would have to pull the knob out to get the screwdriver into the hole so he could push the latch open. There were no screws around it. Whatever held it in place was inside the door. He would have to break the knob off and stick the screwdriver into the door.

Using his flashlight, he looked around for something heavy. There were large cans of soup on the shelf, and Julius picked one up. It felt heavy to him. He used all his strength to lift it up and bring it down on the knob.

Julius had to do this several times and would pause between each hit to sit down and catch his breath. It was hot in the box. Finally, after striking it 10 times, the knob broke off. Julius then used the screwdriver to push whatever metal was left in the hole outward to get it out of the way. He could now see the basement through the hole. There was light coming from the basement windows. It gave Julius hope.

Now came the hardest part, getting the screwdriver in just the right position to push the latch so the door would open. Julius tried and tried, but he couldn't get the right angle. He was getting so mad that he just started stabbing at the door. He broke through the metal and kept stabbing.

Pretty soon he had a good size gouge in the door. He could see where the latch was secured and was now able to push on it and open the door. When the door swung open and after catching his breath, Julius hurried out as fast as his old arthritic legs could carry him.

He was very tired and took the stairs one at a time, stopping for breath many times over. He finally made it to the top and saw Miss Jackson lying on the floor.

She had obviously been there for a few days. Her face was pulled back and her teeth were exposed. She also had a very distinct odor. Julius shuffled past her to try and find the telephone. He was going to dial 911 for help.

When he finally found the phone, it was dead. He wondered if the other residents had seen Miss Jackson. There were three people living there besides Julius. Even though he didn't feel like it, Julius began the long climb up the stairs to see if they were up there. Julius took the stairs one at a time and paused at each step.

Julius found the other three residents dead in their beds. They, too, had a distinct odor. Julius had to decide what to do. He knew he needed to get them all out of the house or it would be unbearable.

One by one he pulled them out of their beds on their sheets and then pushed them down the stairs. He had to follow the bodies down the stairs, kicking them if they stopped. He then pulled them on their sheets out the back door, kicked them down the stairs, and rolled them into the yard. That's where he left them, wrapped in their bed sheets.

Then Julius picked up Miss Jackson's legs and slowly pulled her out into the yard with the other residents.

Now that he had taken care of the bodies, all Julius wanted was a shower and a good night's sleep. It was daylight, but that didn't matter. He climbed back up the stairs, pausing at each step, went into the bathroom and turned on the shower.

There was no hot water. He had to use a wash cloth to clean himself so he wouldn't have to stand under the cold water. When he was done, he changed his clothes and got into bed. After many hours of sleeping on a pallet in the walk-in, he felt so happy to be in his own bed.

Julius wasn't very fond of the other residents. In fact, he barely knew their names. But he would really miss Miss Jackson's homemade pies.

Chapter 52

During the next couple of weeks, Julius would drive around town in Miss Jackson's car looking for other people. He began spotting kids wandering around town, all kinds of kids. There were Asian kids, black kids, brown kids, and white kids. They all looked to be around the same age.

Julius would ask them if they wanted some help. Some would shy away while others would run to him. Julius decided the best place for them was the new Granger's store across the street from his house. It hadn't been opened yet, it didn't smell bad, and there was plenty of food.

He asked the kids where they lived. He would take them by their houses and have them grab some kind of bedding or sleeping bags if they had them. If their houses smelled, he would find a clean store and the kids would grab something to use for a bed. He showed the kids how to set up a bunk on the grocery store shelving. He liked this arrangement because the store was so close to his house that he could check on the kids every day.

"I'm not sure, but I think there are about eighteen kids in there," Julius said.

"Wow, eighteen! That must be really hard for you, taking care of them I mean." Joe was thinking of how hard it was for him, and he had Dani and Jenny. "Listen, I have to go back to my family. We're taking a bus load of kids to Florida. That's where we live. Do you want to come with us?" Joe couldn't believe he was saying this. But he couldn't leave this poor old man with all these kids to care for.

"And the kids?" Julius asked.

"Yeah, of course, all of you."

"You go and I'll think on it," Julius said.

"We'll stop by Granger's on the way out of town," Joe said.

Joe walked back to the car. The kids had gotten up and were out in the parking lot. They watched Joe as he got in the car and drove away. When he got back to the hotel, he noticed that his kids were up and he asked some of them to help him bring in the food. Dani was sitting on the sofa like she had just woken up.

"You're not gonna believe this, Dani," Joe said.

"Where were you?" She yawned.

"I went into town to find food and I found something else."

293

"What?"

"Eighteen kids and an old man."

Dani was speechless. She sat on the sofa thinking about eighteen more children. Then it registered in her brain that Joe had said "old man."

"An old man, how?"

"I'll tell you over breakfast. Anyway, I asked the old guy if he and the kids wanted to come with us."

Dani's eyebrows shot up. "*You* asked him?"

"Yeah, I surprised myself. He said he would think on it."

"I don't know if I can do it, Joe. Eighteen more kids. We'd have to get more name tags and another bus."

Dani got up and headed for a bathroom. Joe sat looking at the kids as they grabbed something to eat from the pile of toaster pastries and fruit snacks he'd picked up at Granger's. He tried to imagine 18 more of them milling around the hotel lobby. It blew his mind.

When Dani came back, she was cleaned up and looked pretty good. It was amazing what clean hair would do for you. She looked at Joe and sighed.

"You know, we never even counted the kids we have now," she said to Joe.

"Maybe we should. Why don't we take a head count?"

Dani told the kids to go outside and line up. They groaned at having their breakfast interrupted.

"Take your food with you. We just want to count you." Dani said as she followed them out the door.

The kids lined up in the parking lot. Dani told the first girl to count out "one" and then the next "two" and so on. The kids were counting well and when they finished the last little boy shouted "sixty-two".

"Joe, we have sixty-two kids here. I never imagined there were so many."

"They do take up the whole bus," Joe said.

"But with the others it would be...eighty. Eighty kids."

Dani felt overwhelmed. Before she knew the actual number, she'd been able to think that maybe there were forty. Forty seemed like a doable number. But sixty-two! She didn't know how they'd been handling that many kids. Now Joe was talking about adding another eighteen. She didn't think she could do it.

"Julius should know where the school is, so we can get another bus." Joe said. He didn't seem to mind the idea of that many kids. What was wrong with him?

"Joe, I can't do it. It's enough. There has to be someone else. I can't do it."

Dani got up and ran. She went up to the second floor and found an empty room. She closed the door and locked it. She didn't know Jenny was in the bathroom.

Dani sat on the bed and started to cry. Jenny came out and saw her.

"Dani, what's wrong?" she asked.

"Joe found eighteen more kids. I can't do it." She put her face in the pillow.

"Geez, eighteen more kids."

Jenny sat down next to Dani. Dani thought about Jenny. The young woman had been so helpful throughout the entire trip. She never complained and she had even befriended one of the little girls. Dani began to feel guilty about her outburst.

"Dani, we can do it together." Jenny put her hand on Dani's shoulder. Dani felt her hand and turned to her. She held onto Jenny and cried into her shoulder. "We can do it. We'll be all right."

Jenny was remarkably calm. This trip had to have been just as hard for her, but she was ready to take on more kids. Was Dani the only one who saw just how crazy that was?

"What else can we do?" Jenny asked.

Dani sat up and hand-brushed her hair. She looked at Jenny. Jenny smiled, and made a face, causing Dani to laugh.

"I will need to get away and scream every now and then," Dani said. "But you're right, what else can we do? Joe said they had an old man taking care of them. He's all alone. So if he could do it...I guess we can."

Dani and Jenny walked back downstairs and saw that Joe had gotten the kids on the bus. Jenny and Dani packed up the leftover food and carried it outside. Joe said he would drive the bus to give the women a break.

"You'll have to follow me to the Granger's," he said as he climbed into the bus.

Dani and Jenny got into the car and they all turned onto the highway. When they got to Granger's, Julius was standing in the parking lot with the eighteen Atlanta kids. Each kid had their bedding neatly wrapped and ready for travel, and Julius had packed his satchel.

Chapter 53

Wilmer Biosphere, Palm Harbor, Florida

Calvin had to wait until the hurricane passed before heading to St. Petersburg to check on Mark and Mindy. The biosphere had suffered no ill effects from the storm. It had actually benefited from it.

The pasture had been almost completely cleared of all traces of the poor animals that had died there. The storm had been over for two days when Calvin decided to make the trip to St. Pete. He got up early and donned his hazmat suit. He climbed out of the hatchway and walked over to the Mercedes he had decided to keep.

He'd taken quite a bit of heat from the team when they found out he'd taken Mindy and Mark back to Mark's house. Gerald had been absolutely apoplectic. But Calvin said he'd had enough and if the kids wanted to go, then he would help them. He told the team that the kids were still suffering no ill effects from breathing the air and they had everything they needed at home.

Gerald still wanted to study the kids and had Andrew program all the locks. Andrew had given Calvin the code for the back hatchway so Calvin could come and go as he pleased. There was a general mutiny afoot, and the team no longer regarded Gerald as the commander in chief. Gerald continually took his frustrations out on Christie, and she was reaching the end of her patience.

Since Mark and Mindy had left, the kids of the biosphere were asking when they, too, could leave. They all missed the outdoors and were tired of the mall-like atmosphere of the biosphere. Christie kept putting them off, and when one would ask, it would prompt her to go to Gerald to beg him to test the air quality.

"It has to be cleared by now, whatever it was that killed those animals, it must be gone, Gerald."

Whenever the animals were mentioned, Gerald would feel the sting of pain and guilt that always rose up whenever he thought of Martha. Martha had been a sweet, tan little heifer when she was brought into the biosphere with the rest of the cattle and sheep. When Gerald saw Martha, he immediately took a liking to her.

Gerald would visit her daily, spending time brushing her and talking to her by the hour. Calvin would joke with the others that Gerald seemed to be in love with the cow. Gerald did indeed love

297

the cow as he had never loved any animal before. His attachment surprised even him.

The other animals were just patients to Gerald, but Martha, whom he named after his grandmother, was special. She seemed to have affection for Gerald as well. When Gerald would visit her in the animal room, Martha would nudge his hand to make him pet her. Then he would brush her soft tan coat and give her special little treats.

Gerald had been awake the night before the tragedy, working with a pregnant cow who was suffering from uterine torsion. He had been trying to untwist the cow's uterus. He and Calvin had to rock the cow until they were able to flip the uterus. By the time they were done, they were both exhausted. Calvin had eaten his breakfast and gone to bed.

That day the sun came out for the first time in a week and Gerald decided to let the animals outside for some fresh air and grass. He pushed the button that raised the big door leading out to the pasture. He then started waving his hands at the animals, pushing them towards the door and into the fresh air. As Martha walked by he gave her backside an affectionate pat. He watched her walk outside, admiring her graceful exit. Once the animals were all outside, Gerald closed the door because the air conditioning was going full blast.

He went back to his lab and set his alarm for two hours just in case he dozed off. He sat at his computer to enter the notes regarding the pregnant cow from the night before. He put his head down for just a minute and fell fast asleep.

The loud, piercing alarm that woke Gerald meant that some major event had taken place outside the biosphere. At first, no one knew what it meant as they had never heard it before. They had been in the biosphere preparing it for some as yet unnamed calamity, but had never imagined it would really happen. Some of them thought it was Andrew testing the doors and locks.

No one reacted very quickly until someone began shouting that the locks had engaged by themselves and Andrew couldn't get them open. Calvin, aroused from his sleep by the noise, came out of his room and remembered the animals. He ran to the animal room and looked at the screen showing the pasture.

He saw that all the animals were down and not moving. He pushed the button to open the door but a warning sign came up instructing him that until the air quality returned to normal, the doors would stay locked. Gerald began frantically banging on the door.

"You can't open it, Gerry," Calvin was saying, but Gerald wasn't listening. His only thoughts were of his beloved Martha. He looked at the screen, but he couldn't see Martha's soft tan coat.

"Hold on, Martha!" he was shouting as he tried to pry the door open with his hands. Calvin grabbed Gerald's arms and tried to pull him back.

"Gerry, I told you, you can't open the doors!"

Calvin was still holding onto Gerald when Gerald pulled away from him, turned around and punched Calvin in the face. He ran to the stairs and climbed them as fast as he could. The whole time he was running, he was yelling for Martha to hold on. He burst into the field and ran towards the hatchway door. As he ran he passed Christie, she asked him what was wrong.

"Martha's out there. I have to save her."

Christie followed him to the hatchway door. She had heard the alarm but still didn't know the doors were sealed. She watched Gerald push the buttons to open the three entryways and climb the ladder to the hatchway.

Gerald pushed the button for the hatchway, but it wouldn't open. He banged on it and he lost his footing. Gerald fell straight down and hit his head on the floor.

Christie ran to him and found him unconscious. She got on the PA system and asked for help. Andrew and Simon got there first and were able to pick Gerald up and carry him up the stairs and into the Town Square. They laid him on a bench and waited for him to come to.

Calvin came up and told them what had happened to the animals. This was the first time they'd heard of the danger outside. Calvin also told them that Gerald had punched him and asked them all to keep the idiot away from him.

When Gerald woke up, he again began to rant about Martha. Andrew and Simon held him until he calmed down. Christie brought him a Valium, which Andrew and Simon made him take. When it was determined that Gerald would be okay, they left him sitting on the bench alone.

Gerald wandered up to his lab and took out his cellphone. He had a picture of Martha he had taken a few days before. He downloaded it into his computer and made a copy of it for his desk. He also used it as wallpaper for his computer's monitor.

Gerald began to change. He'd never been much of a social animal before, but now he never joined the others, even for meals. He spent all his time in the lab, and one day Christie suggested he learn how to use the satellites to see if he could find any signs of life on the outside. Gerald liked this suggestion. It galvanized him into action and gave him purpose.

Within 24 hours of activating the satellite, he found a little infrared figure in Tarpon Springs. He gathered the others together to decide how to go about saving this little person. Andrew said he would try reprogramming the locks so that he, along with Simon, Pat, and George could go and pick up the child. Wilmer had ordered hazmat suits with the intention of sending someone out to inspect the damage caused by a nuclear blast. The team could now use them to get in a truck and find the little human who was apparently alone.

Andrew worked on the locks until he was able to open them. He left them open because Gerald hadn't been able to find anything living except this one little person. Whatever was out there was deadly enough to drop a cow in seconds. How this little person had survived was the big mystery, but the odds of someone finding the biosphere and breaking in were next to zero.

He and the team would suit up and take a truck to Tarpon Springs with the coordinates Gerald gave them. There they would hopefully find the little infrared figure alive and well. Gerald was anxious to test this person so he told the team to handle the child carefully.

When the team got outside, the only indication of what was to come was the pasture full of dead animals. They saw Martha at the farthest corner of the pasture. They got into one of Wilmer's trucks and started down the dirt road that led to US Highway 19. When they got to the access road, they could see cars parked on the highway.

Some cars had driven right off the road. Some were piled up into each other. They were all filled with at least one dead body. The team hadn't expected this. For some reason, they thought it was just some fluke that had killed the animals.

As they drove up the access road to the entrance of US 19, there were hundreds of cars for miles each way. They would have to drive on the grass to get past the cars if they were going to get to Tarpon Springs. George suggested taking a back road to Tarpon. There would be less traffic to navigate around. So George guided them through the back roads until they came to Alternate 19 and headed north.

There was traffic here too, but now there was more room to maneuver. They were also close to where Gerald told them the little figure could be found. Simon read the directions and Andrew followed them until they were on the right street. They slowed down and patrolled the area with all eyes searching for the little person.

There were cars in driveways with no bodies in them. This meant the houses were full of them. Suddenly Pat spotted a little girl sitting on the porch of a small, pink, stucco house. She was a little Hispanic girl with long brown hair. She was sitting there with her head in her lap. When she heard the truck, she jumped up and ran towards it.

Andrew stopped the truck and they all got out. The little girl ran over and took Andrew's hand.

"*Por favor*, please, I need help! *Por favor! Mis padres estan muertos.*"

She was crying and the tears were streaming down her face. She was a pretty little thing and Andrew squatted down to look her in the eye.

"English please, honey. We don't speak Spanish."

"My parents, they are dead. Please, help me."

She grabbed Andrew's hand as if to lead him into her house.

"We can't go in there, sweetie. We came to take you back with us. We have a place for you to stay, with food and a nice little house just for you."

"But my parents, please, how can I leave them like this?"

"Hey, Andrew, maybe we should, you know, we could dig a hole," Pat was saying.

"I think we could do that for her," George added.

"Did any of you bring a shovel?" Andrew asked.

They all stood shaking their heads.

"We have a shed," the little girl said very quietly.

"What's your name, honey?" Andrew asked her.

"Maria Elena," she answered.

"Well, Maria Elena, we'll take care of your parents. Where would you like them to go?"

She looked very sad. She knew they were going to put them in the ground. This was an awesome decision she had to make, and she wanted to think about it. Finally, after looking all around her, she settled for a spot at the end of the road where there was a park.

She took Andrew's hand and led him down the road. While they walked to the park, Simon, George, and Pat went to Maria Elena's shed and found a good shovel. Pat went down the road with the shovel while Simon and George went inside to find Maria's parents.

The smell in the house was strong. The kid must have been living on the porch. Her parents' bodies were extremely decomposed. George and Simon took a blanket and rolled Maria Elena's mother onto it, causing her bones to rattle. They picked up the ends and carried her out of the house and down the road. They laid her beside the spot Maria Elena had picked out. They then did the same for her father.

When Pat had finished one hole, George took up the shovel and started digging the other one. Andrew and Simon laid her mama in the hole and they all kicked the dirt over the top of her. When both of her parents were buried, Maria Elena said a little prayer in Spanish. Then she said goodbye.

"Adios, papa y mama."

Chapter 54

Every time Gerald found an infrared figure on the map, he would dispatch the team to pick them up. In between, the team would move the cars off the highway and pile the bodies on the side of the road.

They took the cars to parking lots where they could easily extract the gasoline from the cars' tanks. They would also hunt for food and other supplies that the growing population of the biosphere required.

Once Andrew found the stash of food underneath Wilmer's residence, the food forays discontinued and the only time the team left the biosphere was to find office supplies, pharmaceuticals, or clothing for the children.

When Mark Bennett moved into house number 200, Christie had told Gerald is was time to take daily checks of the air quality. If the air was clear, then they would start to search for a place to live topside.

Christie argued that if there were more children out there, they would need more room to house them. Gerald in turn argued that they had everything they needed in the biosphere and that even if the air was good, they should continue to use the facilities.

Gerald of course had alternative motives for keeping the air quality a secret. From the day they brought in Maria Elena, he was determined to discover why she had survived when his Martha hadn't.

Wilmer and March Pharmaceuticals had invented a wonderful machine that was able to take a blood sample and determine what type of disease or bacteria plagued the owner of the blood. The machine could also type the blood, and run a DNA panel. It proved too expensive to manufacture, so Wilmer took the only one produced and installed it in the biosphere. When a child was brought in, a blood sample was taken and run through the machine. So far, the children's blood had been remarkably normal.

Gerald couldn't understand what had kept these children alive, and it was driving him crazy. The downward spiral that began with the death of Martha was deepening into a full-blown mania.

Gerald was tired of Christie's interfering with his plans to extricate cells from the children's bodies. He was sick of her protecting them, as she did with that cretin Mark, an evil boy who'd put them all at risk by leaving the biosphere. Christie had sealed her fate the moment she picked up Martha's picture from his lab and used it to free that miserable boy.

Gerald had decided that Christie was expendable, as was Calvin, the other thorn in his side. He was working on a plan to get rid of them and it was shaping up nicely. He would use the Nembutal he had ordered to euthanize animals should the need arise. Since there were no animals left except those scrawny chickens, he planned to inject Christie and Calvin with the Nembutal and then suit up and drag their bodies outside. They complained of being cooped up, anyway.

It would be easy to explain away the sudden descent into madness that drove them above ground, only to be killed off by the poisonous air. The only thing Gerald had to work out was getting them up the ladder and out the hatchway.

Their bodies would be dead weight and almost impossible for Gerald to hoist up alone. He would figure something out. In the meantime, he decided to lure one of the kids to his lab to try and take a cell sample by cutting into their skin. It would be no more than a scratch.

Chapter 55

Joe and Dani left Atlanta in two buses and headed south on Interstate 75. They'd found a school bus in Atlanta and divided the kids up evenly, with Julius traveling with Joe.

I-75 was a heavily traveled highway. When the poison struck the area, it was during the morning rush hour and some parts of the highway were loaded with cars. Navigating the abandoned vehicles slowed them down considerably. Dani and Joe became expert bus drivers in no time.

It took ten hours but they finally hit Tampa and Interstate 275. They were close to home. Joe felt an adrenaline rush as they crossed the bridge over Old Tampa Bay and saw signs for Largo. His first instinct was to head towards his mother's mobile home.

Dani was following him and she knew where he was headed. The road leading to Mimi's park was full of cars. Joe tried to navigate around them, but the shoulders here were too tight. He stopped the bus and got out. He walked around to Dani's bus and asked her to open the door.

"I'm walking," he said. "I have to see if my mom...or if Mindy is there."

Dani didn't say anything. She wanted to go too, but she had to stay with the kids. Julius was asleep and it was too much to ask of Jenny, so she just nodded. Joe took off on foot in the direction of Mimi's park.

He walked up the small road leading into the park. He had to walk two blocks down to get to Mimi's home. When he turned onto her street, he could see the skeletal remains of her neighbor still sitting on his porch across the street.

Joe approached his mother's home slowly. The place didn't look that different except for the leaves and other debris left there by the last hurricane. He climbed the long metal ramp that led to her front door. The door was open. He could smell that there were no bodies in there.

Joe walked from room to room. The kitchen had bags full of empty cans. There was a pile of dirty dishes in the sink. He walked to the little room Mindy had stayed in. Her book bag was there as well as the pictures of them she'd brought with her. Her pillow was still here too. But where was Mindy?

Next he went into his mother's room. The bed had been slept in, but otherwise it looked the same. Where was his mom, or Baby Girl? There were no clues here as to what had happened to his family.

Joe went to the shed and looked inside. He moved the dirt out of the way and checked the plastic containers. Some of the food was missing, but the guns were still there. After a quick look around, Joe headed back to Dani and the kids.

Dani was disappointed when she saw Joe walking towards them alone. She knew he hadn't found his mother or Mindy. When he got to the bus, he told her that no one was there. Dani breathed a sigh of relief. They decided to head for St. Petersburg.

They took Second Avenue to St. Petersburg. Second Avenue was a side road. Motorists avoided it because there were so many schools located there. Kids were constantly being dropped off or picked up, so anyone trying to get to work on time would stay away from Second Avenue. Joe had been right to come here. The road had few abandoned cars. School had been out when the poison struck.

There was a turn in the road ahead, but Joe could see the roofs of two or three large buildings looming over the trees. As they drew closer, the buildings appeared. They resembled three large churches; brick façades covered with Ivy. He also saw a big, wooden FOR SALE sign in front of a huge wrought iron fence. He slowed the bus and came to a stop.

On the front gate was a sign that read "St. Thomas School for Boys." The place looked like it had been closed for a long time. Joe got out of the bus and walked over to the gate. He looked back at Dani and motioned for her to come over. She told the kids to stay put, got off the bus, and joined him.

"It was a Catholic boy's school," he said.

"St. Thomas. I remember this place. It was closing because they couldn't afford to run it anymore. I remember they had all kinds of fairs and things to raise money. I think I brought Mindy up here once for a carnival. It was pretty big inside," Dani said.

She knew what Joe was thinking. The building looked big enough to house 80 kids. It had classrooms and probably a big dining hall. But did the church leave everything in it when it closed school?

"You want to go in and check it out?" she asked.

"Yeah, let's get the kids off the bus and let them stretch."

306

Joe checked the lock on the gate. It was a standard padlock. He could easily break it if he could find the right-sized rock. As he was looking for one, the kids began to gather at the gate. He asked them to look around for rocks, and a boy with the name tag "Adam T." found one and ran over to Joe holding up a large rock.

"Is this okay, Joe?" he asked.

Joe took the rock and held it. He made a big show of checking the weight of the rock and then said, "Perfect." He took the rock and hammered away at the padlock. After three good whacks, the lock broke, Joe removed it and the chain holding the gates closed.

The kids ran ahead of Joe and Dani. Jenny hadn't been out of the car in so long that she ran too. Julius walked a little ways until he saw a bench and sat down to rest before moving on. Dani and Joe took each other's hands. It was nice to be out of the buses.

The buildings were situated about a mile from the road. They looked to be over 50 years old. The bricks in the walls looked in good condition. These buildings had been designed to look like the buildings in old New England towns. The landscaping had taken a beating from lack of care. The grass was overgrown, as were the weeds.

As Joe had seen from the road, there were three large buildings, at least three stories high. There were several out buildings as well. Joe and Dani approached the first building and checked the door. Joe couldn't kick this one in.

They went around the back and found an entrance leading to the basement. That door had a glass window, which Joe broke to get in.

Joe and Dani walked down the stairs into the basement. It was full of dust and cobwebs. The walls were lined with washing machines and dryers. There was a large breaker box for the electricity and a generator for power failures. There was a sump pump that must have gone off when the basement flooded.

Dani found the stairs leading up and they climbed them quickly. The door at the top opened into the kitchen, which had a huge stove and refrigerator. It had a big double sink and what looked like a fairly new dishwasher. The first room off the kitchen was a large dining room with one big table.

"Maybe this is where the priests ate," Dani was saying. "Maybe this is where they lived."

The rest of the building contained libraries and small classrooms. The top floor contained several bedrooms. Dani was right. These rooms were for adults. There was a main room in the center with a television set and a computer. There were several comfortable chairs.

There was an elevator that ran from the first floor to the top floor. The bedrooms had one bed each with a dresser and a chair. There were two large bathrooms with two shower stalls in each.

Dani and Joe went through all the large buildings to see how they were set up. Joe broke into the basement of each. They found that each building had about 15 rooms on each floor and were set up like dormitories.

Each room had two beds, two dressers, two desks, and two wardrobes. There were common rooms on each floor with a television set.

Close by were giant bathrooms with showers and urinals. There were also stalls with toilets. The bottom floor had a small apartment for a house parent and a kitchen. There were accommodations for 30 kids on each floor.

"Why did they leave all this stuff here?" Dani asked.

"Maybe they thought another school would buy it, or they thought it would sell faster furnished," Joe said.

Joe and Dani looked around the rest of the campus. There was a large communal dining room and kitchen in one building. Another had a basketball court and other athletic equipment. The rest had classrooms.

Joe and Dani then went back to all three buildings to check for running water. The water worked. It must have been well water.

Dani went to the study in the first building, looking for any information she could find about the school. As she walked in the front door, there was a library to her right. She saw two desks in there facing each other.

The first desk was empty. The second desk had a booklet on it called "A Short History of St. Thomas' Boys School." She pulled out the bottom drawer, which still contained files. One was labeled "City of Largo." She took it out and laid it next to the booklet and sat down on the old wooden rolling chair behind the desk.

The file contained letters from the city offering the church money for the property the school sat on. It was dated June 14, 2003. This was the height of the real estate boom and the city was being wooed by a certain big retail chain.

The chain required huge parcels of land. This was the perfect location for such a store. There was nothing else here but the schools, and there were plenty of residents within a five-mile radius to support such a venture. The tax incentives were enormous, but first the city had to acquire the property.

The church refused to sell. Then the city told the school it had to hook up to the city's water or risk being shut down due to a contaminated water supply. Water testing took place that showed the school's water was safe, but the city council took a vote and it was decided that the St. Thomas Boys School would have to comply or be shut down.

The school appealed the city's decision and failed. School officials began efforts to raise money in order to lay the miles of pipe necessary to hook the entire school into the city's water and sewer systems. When it was clear they weren't going to meet their deadline, they closed the school and put it up for sale.

That was a year ago. The real estate boom was over, the economy was in the toilet, and the big chain had found another property in another town.

At some point, the school was forced to raise tuition, prompting parents to find less expensive ways to educate their children. School officials still hoped to sell the school to a university, but it was bleeding money. They voted to close it before a buyer could be found. Those students still attending were transferred to a school in Tampa.

So, the school had well water and the sewerage was not hooked into the city. That meant it had to be cleaned out when it got full. Other than that, the building was in pretty good shape and had running water.

They could bring in bottled water until the supply ran out and then they could decide what to do. For now they had a place to stay with plenty of room and supplies for housing and teaching.

Dani went to find Joe to tell him what she'd learned. The kids were having a ball running around the place. They had been cooped up so long it felt really good just to run. Dani found Joe playing basketball with some of the kids and she told him this was a good place to stay. They had water. All they needed was some way to light the place up at night.

It would be getting dark soon, so Joe and Jenny headed out to the mall to see if they could find supplies to light the inside of the buildings. Dani got the kids inside the buildings and told them to find a room and a roommate. She told them that they would be staying here from now on.

Julius found a nice room in the first building. It was on the first floor behind the kitchen. It had a bed and a recliner. Julius opened the windows to let the late afternoon breezes in. He sat in the recliner and kicked off his shoes. He was asleep in minutes.

Joe and Jenny found a camping store at the mall with a body on the outside holding a key. The poor guy hadn't even gotten the door open. They used the key to open the door and found several oil lanterns and bottles of oil. They also grabbed long stick matches. They also picked up battery operated and solar powered lanterns.

They broke into other stores and found candles and flashlights. These would have to do for now, until they could figure out how to electrify the place. Joe would have to check out the generators they'd found in the basement of each building.

They filled the back of the car with food they found at a Granger's. There were some bodies in there, but it was too late to search for something else. The food was in cans and the smell would not get through that. They also took several cases of bottled water.

When they got back to the school, they brought all the stuff they found into the first building to divide it up. The food was put away and the water stacked. The lanterns were filled with oil, but Dani didn't feel comfortable putting them in the kids' dorms. She gave the kids the battery and solar powered lanterns and flashlights, and kept the oil lanterns with the adults.

After getting everyone settled in for the night, Dani and Joe slept in the house parent's apartment in the second house. She and Joe made a plan to visit their house in St. Petersburg the next day to collect their clothes and see if Mindy had gone there. Dani had wanted to go tonight, but she was just too exhausted. As they drifted off to sleep that night, Dani said a prayer that she would see her Mindy in the morning.

Chapter 56

The Wilmer Biosphere, Palm Harbor, Florida

A few days after Mark and Mindy left the facility, Gerald stood on the landing overlooking the playground, listening to the laughter of the children playing below. When one of them looked up and saw Gerald, he signaled the others and they all looked up.

They stopped what they were doing and just stared quietly at Gerald. They were all a little scared of him, and they definitely didn't trust him. He tried to smile, but it resembled a snake trying to turn up the corners of its mouth.

He walked down the stairs and looked over the children. He spotted a chubby little boy sitting on a bench and he approached him. The boy looked right and left, trying to find an escape route, but it was too late. Gerald was upon him and was asking him his name.

"Austin," he replied.

"Ah, a wonderful city, Austin, I went there once for a conference on cattle. Lovely city." Gerald sat down next to Austin. Austin moved away.

"Now, son, you don't have to be scared. I have a proposition for you. I have a video game in my lab. It is a very special game that I had the team bring back for me. I would like to give it to you in exchange for a sample of your cells. If you're willing to accompany me back to my lab, it will only take a few minutes."

"What game?" Austin asked. Gerald could see he was ready to take the bait. His beady little eyes were squinting at Gerald. Gerald had done his research before coming down here.

"Something called Resident Evil 5."

Austin's eyes lit up. He could feel the excitement rising in his stomach. It was quickly taking over the part of his brain that warned him to stay away from Gerald. He had wanted that game for his next birthday, which of course never came. Maybe this was fate. He was supposed to get this game, and if this wacko wanted some of his cells, he could have them. Austin imagined Gerald taking a swab to his cheek like he had when collecting his DNA.

"Okay," Austin said.

They got up from the bench and, with Gerald leading the way, climbed the stairs to the upper floor and Gerald's lab. When Austin got inside the lab, he began to look at all the scalpels and needles Gerald had placed on a stainless steel tray. He looked on another table and saw a machine with long wires attached to it. He saw test tubes and a microscope. Austin had sat through too many World War II documentaries. He remembered Joseph Mengele very well.

"You're gonna cut me up! You're gonna do experiments on me. No, you won't!" Austin bolted for the door. Gerald got in front of him and stood in his way.

"I am merely going to take a sample of your cells. I promise it won't even hurt."

"You get out of my way, you wacko! HELP! HELP ME, SOMEBODY!"

Austin began kicking Gerald in the shins. Gerald pushed Austin to the floor and jumped on top of him. He held him down and tried to get him to lie still so he could cut into Austin's arm.

Christie heard Austin's screams. She tried to get in the door, but Gerald's legs were blocking it. She could see inside and saw Gerald fighting with a child, but she couldn't see Austin's face. She pushed and pushed until she jammed the door into Gerald's leg. He rolled off Austin and glared up at her.

"All I wanted was a little skin scraping. This little moron wouldn't lie still for one second."

Gerald's hair was in his face and he looked like a madman. Austin jumped up and run out the door.

"Are you crazy?" Christie asked him. "What the hell did you think you were doing? I told you no cutting. There is no reason to cut these kids. We have enough data. Leave it alone, Gerald, or else."

"Or else! Who do you think you are to threaten me? There's nothing you can do to me, Christie."

"I can kick you outside." She looked at Gerald defiantly. She knew being outside was the one thing he feared most.

"You could never get me out there."

"Not by myself." she said.

The implication was clear. The team would gladly help her push Gerald out the hatchway. Gerald knew they all hated him.

He got up off the floor and walked over to his computer. Martha's face stared back at him. He knew he had to wait, but the temptation to strangle Christie right then and there was overwhelming. He tried to calm down by breathing in through his nose and out through his mouth.

"If I ever see you in here with a kid again, I will kill you, Gerald." Christie turned around and walked out the door.

Gerald looked again at Martha's peaceful countenance. Martha had been the only one who really loved him. Christie reminded him of Arlene. She was evil and manipulative. She had managed to turn the team against him.

Gerald got up and walked across the lab. He took a hypodermic needle out of its plastic wrapper and pushed the plunger down. He went to the cabinet where he stored the bottle of Nembutal. He pushed the needle in the bottle and filled the tube. He placed it in the drawer of his desk. The next time that bitch came in here, he thought, he would have a surprise for her.

*****

Calvin turned onto US 19 heading south. He was cruising at high speed so it didn't take him any time at all to get to St. Petersburg. A few more miles and he would be at the 18th Avenue exit.

It was a beautiful summer day. He wished he could take off the damned mask and enjoy the air. Even if it was hot, it was real. The biosphere was so, well, sterile.

Calvin couldn't get sunglasses on underneath the headgear. The glare was very strong this morning and his eyes were playing tricks on him. He thought he saw a flash of yellow up ahead. Something big, like a bus, maybe? But that was impossible, wasn't it?

Calvin pushed the accelerator down. He hadn't been seeing things. There was a bus up ahead, no wait – two buses and what looked like a sedan. He doubted very much that 10-year- old kids were driving them. He tried to catch up but lost them.

Calvin pushed the pedal down further and was going really fast now, over 90 miles an hour. He could still see the buses, but they were turning off the highway. They had exited at 22nd Avenue. He remembered taking his little lady there. He decided to follow the buses.

Calvin was close to the sedan now. The driver wasn't wearing any headgear. He kept close as he didn't want to lose them. He wasn't so familiar with the area that he couldn't get lost. They passed the school Mindy said she'd gone to so he knew they were close to her house. He saw the buses slowing down.

They stopped in front of the little white house with green shutters and parked. Calvin slowed down and pulled over. He watched as the bus doors opened and dozens of children got off the buses. He saw a man and a woman. He also saw what looked like a teenage girl and an old man, and none of them was wearing a hazmat suit.

Chapter 57

Calvin sat watching the people milling around in front of Mindy's house. He slowly exited the Mercedes and walked slowly towards the buses. He could hear the laughter and screams of the excited children. These children had to be just like the ones back in the biosphere. Where had they come from? Was it possible the little lady was right and her parents were alive?

Julius saw the spaceman coming towards him. He decided to wait and see what the spaceman would say. It was never a good idea to get too excited at the beginning of the day. The spaceman walked right up to him.

"Mornin'," he said to Calvin.

"Mornin'," Calvin replied. "Where you all coming from?" Calvin waved his arm to indicate the group of kids.

"Well sir, we were in Atlanta when these folks showed up with a bus. I had eighteen kids I'd found. They asked if we wanted to come to Florida and we said yes. We got another bus and here we are." Julius said. "I have to go find a chair, if you'll excuse me." Julius walked towards Mindy's house.

"CALVIN!"

He heard his name coming from the opposite side of the street. He turned and saw his little lady running towards him. She was followed by Mark and another boy, a tall boy. He couldn't wait to hear that story.

"Little lady, you look real fine," he said as she jumped up into his arms.

"Calvin, where did these buses come from?"

"The old man said they came from Atlanta. Georgia, that is."

"This is my house. Why did they come here?" Mindy stopped. Her face lit up. She ran towards the house just as Dani was coming out the door.

"MOMMY! Mommy, Mommy, Mommy!"

She ran into Dani's arms and hugged her as tightly as she could. "I waited for you. I always said you were alive. I knew it. Oh Mommy, I missed you so much."

Mindy was crying hard now, sobs of pure joy. She looked up into Dani's face. Dani knelt down and she was crying too. "Where were you, Mommy?" Mindy asked.

"Daddy and I were stuck in a cavern." Dani was sobbing now too. Mindy gave her a squinty face. "There was a room inside, like a hotel. Daddy thought it would be exciting to spend a night there. The elevator got stuck, so we couldn't get out for 9 days. When we got out, we saw all the people. They were...."

"Dead," Mindy said.

Dani looked at her little daughter and couldn't imagine what her child had seen in all those weeks she'd been alone. Just the trip down US 19 had been bad enough, and although someone had moved the bodies off the road, they were still visible and unsettling.

Dani hugged and hugged Mindy. Joe came out of the house and saw Mindy. He ran over to her and she fell into his arms. Joe cried so hard at the sight of her. He never felt such love for anyone in his life. She was his little girl.

"You got your hair cut!" he said.

"Pat did it," Mindy said. "He works at Wilmer's."

"I like it," Dani said, and Joe nodded.

Mindy took his hand and Dani's and walked over to Calvin.

"This is Calvin," she said.

"How'd you do?" Calvin said and put out his gloved hand.

"You know dude, I don't think you need that anymore," Joe was saying as he shook the gloved hand. "We've been riding around for a week like this, and we aren't purple babies."

Calvin stepped back from Joe. "Purple babies?" he asked.

"Yeah, the reason these kids all survived. They were purple babies." Joe forgot that not everyone had heard of the purple babies.

"Have you been walking around like that for long?" Dani asked Calvin.

"We put these on when we leave the biosphere," Calvin said and looked at Mindy.

"That's where I met Calvin, Mommy." Mindy was beside herself with happiness. She couldn't stand still. She then caught sight of Mark and Jason standing to the side waiting to be introduced.

"Oh, sorry, Mom, this is Jason and Mark. I've been staying with them at the beach." Dani raised her eyebrows at the sight of the two boys her daughter had been "staying with". Jason walked over and put out his hand.

"Hi. I'm Jason Russo. And for the record, I was a purple baby."

"How? You're so much older than the others."

"I think I was the first. No, wait. Ricky and Baby Girl were the first. I was the second."

Mindy ran over to the car and let the dogs out. They followed her back to her parents.

"That's your mom's dog, Joe," Dani said as she walked over to pet Baby Girl. "And he looks just like her." She said pointing to Ricky.

"Yeah, they're brother and sister." Jason bent down and ruffled Ricky's head.

"No way." Joe said. "We got her in Jersey."

"Yeah, well my folks came here from Jersey. He was born a year before me."

Joe and Dani looked at the dogs. They looked like adult dogs, but not old dogs.

"How old are you, Jason?" Dani asked.

"I just turned eighteen."

"So the dogs are over eighteen years old." Dani kept looking at the dogs. "But these can't be the same dogs. It's not possible. They look too young."

"I think the purple stuff may produce longevity," Jason said. "I have a notebook my father wrote that told the whole story, about how he got the plants to make it and how to use it. He gave it to some doctor named Tomlinson, who screwed him over."

"That was my doctor, Michael Tomlinson." Dani looked at all the kids milling around the buses. "He was busy, wasn't he?"

"He gave it to over 300 women," Jason said as he waited for their reaction.

"300! We only found 80. Where are the other 220?"

"There were 200 at Wilmer's." Mark had spoken for the first time.

"But that leaves 20 unaccounted for. Where could they be?" Joe looked at Dani.

"That's the thing. I couldn't find a total list of names," Jason said. "I have one with 100 names on it. Who knows where Tomlinson's records went after he died?"

Jason saw something out of the corner of his eye that he was having trouble assimilating. He turned and saw the prettiest girl he'd ever seen. He turned back to Dani and Joe, but kept turning to see if she was real.

"Her name is Jenny," Dani was saying. "She lost her family in Nevada. Why don't you go introduce yourself?"

317

Jason smiled and turned to walk over to Jenny. When Jenny saw him, she blushed and looked in another direction. It had been so long since she had talked to a boy, and a good looking boy at that. She found herself suddenly shy. She looked down at her clothes and her hand touched her hair. She then looked up and smiled and they began to talk.

"They'll be fine," Dani told Joe. "They must be relieved to find somebody over 10 and under 30."

"Really, man, you can take the suit off." Joe was talking to Calvin. Calvin was looking at the kids.

"Was the old man right? Did these kids come from Atlanta?" Calvin asked. Dani and Joe nodded their heads.

Calvin had been quiet during the little reunion the Lanes had enjoyed. The mention of purple babies had set him thinking about his children. He knew his wife had sought the help of a doctor in St. Petersburg when she had suffered two miscarriages. If it was the same guy, then there was a real possibility that his kids were alive. If they weren't here, then they had to still be somewhere in Atlanta.

Calvin looked at Joe and Dani. Then he put his hands to his head and pulled the zipper around his neck open. It went almost all the way around his head. He then lifted the headgear off. He unzipped the front of the suit and let it fall to the ground. He felt the hot breeze against his sweaty skin, and it was the most beautiful thing he'd ever felt.

"Man I didn't think anything could feel so good," he said. "I hate that damn suit."

Dani and Joe laughed.

"Yeah, it really sucked." Joe said. They all knew he wasn't talking about the suit.

Over the next few hours, Dani and Joe recounted the story of their trip across the country and how they kept finding children. Jason and Jenny discovered they had a lot in common, and Mindy and Mark talked to the kids about how they had survived and what they'd had to do when their parents died. When they were done, it was getting dark.

Calvin said he wanted to head back to the biosphere to tell them it was safe to come out. He said he would be back in the morning.

"We won't be here," Joe told him. "We have a place we found in Largo, where we'll be spending the night. Why don't you tell us where that biosphere is and we'll meet you there."

Calvin thought of Gerald. He didn't know how old Gerry would take having all these strangers descend on his biosphere.

"Ah, why don't we meet in the Big Mart parking lot in Palm Harbor? It's on 19."

"Sounds good. What time?" Joe had picked up a watch in Atlanta.

"Around 10," Calvin said and waved. He got into the Mercedes and drove away.

Dani, Joe, and Mindy went into their house and packed up all the personal items they could fit into the car. They could always come back another day to finish packing.

"Well kids, has everyone gone to the bathroom?" Dani asked the kids.

They all yelled "YES" and she instructed them to get back on the bus. She turned to Mindy and asked her to join them. Mindy looked at Mark and Jason. She felt like she was doing something wrong by leaving them. She also felt a little guilty for having parents when everybody else didn't.

"It's okay," Mark said. "You go with them. You should." He turned and walked back to Jason's car. Jason and Jenny were standing by Jenny's car.

"I guess I gotta take the kid home," he was saying to her.

"Why don't you meet us at the Big Mart tomorrow?" Jenny's eyes looked hopeful.

"Sure, 10, right?" She nodded her head and Jason smiled. "I'll see you then."

He wanted to kiss her but it might be too soon, and everybody on the bus was watching them. Instead he put his hand on her cheek and then walked back to his car. He waved at her before driving away. She sighed and got into the car. Tomorrow couldn't come soon enough for her.

Chapter 58

Gerald's slow descent into madness had finally manifested itself. He obsessed constantly about Martha and the fact that these children were unnatural. He stayed in his lab, writing in his notebooks, which he kept locked in his quarters. He had stopped looking for live people on the satellites. He never slept and never washed. He was beginning to look like a mad scientist.

Gerald sat hunched over his microscope examining a slide of cells he had collected from one of the children. He had grown tired of listening to Christie's objections and had taken matters into his own hands. The night before, he had decided to collect specimens from 10 of the children while they slept.

He sneaked into their houses after they had gone to sleep, covered their mouths with the chloroform he'd held back from the team's abductions, and cut a section of cells from their upper left thighs. As a veterinarian, he had spayed and neutered animals frequently, so stitching the wounds afterwards was no problem. He may not have been as sanitary as he should have been, but he was in a hurry – and this was science! He did make sure the bleeding had stopped before he left them.

Gerald had decided to take samples from the first 10 children who had been brought to the biosphere. That meant Maria Elena would be first. Since they had been placed in houses in order, it was easy to go from one to the other quickly. He was very careful to pack the slides so they would not move or break.

He had an insulated lunch bag containing a small box with slots in it for the slides. He carried the chloroform and a rag in another bag. He put the sewing needles and sutures in another part of the lunch bag along with a scalpel.

It was after midnight and the adults had finally gone to bed. Gerald took off his shoes and walked in his stockinged feet to the door leading into the city. The metal floor hurt his feet so he had to move quickly.

Gerald descended the stairs, always watching for movement and listening for the sound of voices or footsteps. When he reached the bottom step, he quickly looked to the right and left. When he was sure he was alone, he put his foot on the floor and turned towards the tiny houses.

When he got to number 1, he listened for any noise coming from within. He turned the doorknob and pushed the door open. He looked inside and could see the sleeping form of Maria Elena on her bed. He went inside and, after glancing around the street, he closed the door.

There was a night light burning near Maria Elena's bed. It gave off just enough light for Gerald to do what he needed to do. He took out the chloroform and put some on the rag. He walked over to her bed and stood over her. She was on her side. He would have to turn her over.

He put his hand on her arm and rolled her over on her back. Her eyes moved as he put the rag over her face. She had been deeply asleep and barely registered what was happening. It had been easy knocking her out.

Gerald then retrieved his lunch bag and brought it over to the bed. He rolled the covers back to expose Maria Elena's left thigh. He went into her bathroom and found a towel. He placed it under her left leg. He had forgotten to bring a bottle of alcohol, but Gerald decided he wouldn't have the wound open very long so infection would be minimal. He really didn't care about hurting the girl; he only cared about her cells.

Gerald cut into Maria Elena's flesh. She didn't move. The chloroform had done its job. He quickly took a tiny portion of her flesh and placed it on the glass slide. He covered it with another glass slide and placed it in the slotted box.

Gerald moved quickly. He didn't want a bloody mess to alert his victims as to what had happened. He was hoping the children would be so frightened by the discovery of their involuntary donations that they wouldn't want to tell anyone.

Maria Elena's wound wasn't too deep and as Gerald stitched it up, the blood subsided. He had to work fast. His stitches were fairly neat considering the lack of light and speed with which he worked. Since he'd also forgotten to bring bandages, he left the wound uncovered. Gerald figured the air would help it heal faster.

When he was done, he collected his tools and left Maria Elena's little house and entered number 2. Gerald repeated the process 9 more times. He then returned to his lab to run the slides through his microscope

Gerald was unable to discern anything unusual about the cells. He decided to run them through Wilmer's machine. He opened one of the slides to remove the tissue to prepare it to go into the

321

machine. Since this was something new, Gerald wasn't sure how long the machine would process the sample.

Gerald was very tired and his patience was thin. He paced the lab floor and balled his hands into fists, hitting himself on the sides of his thighs. The faster he walked, the harder he hit himself until his legs throbbed. He forced himself to calm down by slowing his pace until he stopped and returned to his chair. He decided to inventory the items he had hidden away in his lab until the machine stopped.

When Christie had started haranguing Gerald about testing the air quality so the kids could go outside, Gerald had moved all the environmental detectors into his lab. He had brought a locking device with him when he came into the biosphere which he'd intended to put onto a footlocker he kept in his quarters. Soon after he arrived, however, he saw that there may be a need to keep his lab secure and he didn't trust Andrew because the coding of the door locks could be overridden.

He had installed a hook and latch on each side of the door. If he was inside and wanted privacy, he locked himself in. If he had to leave, he used it to secure his lab. The device he used had been created to protect bicycles in New York City. It claimed to be resistant to bolt cutters. Gerald had spent a great deal of money on the lock, but his innate paranoia required absolute security.

Gerald had attached the lock to the lab door when he came back from stealing the children's cells. He had a cabinet next to his computer station. He opened it and took the detectors out. There were three – one to test for radiation, one to detect radon and carbon monoxide, and one to detect poisonous gases.

He turned them on to check the batteries, then he returned them to the cabinet. He then did an inventory of the syringes and other medical supplies. He had moved them in here when George abandoned his lab for the kitchen. As he was replacing the supplies in their cabinet, Gerald heard the machine ding.

The digital panel indicated that a report had been sent to his computer. Gerald walked over to his computer and sat down. He clicked on the desktop icon marked "DNA Reports" and then clicked on "Sample Reports." There were several reports stored there from the blood tests he and Christie had run when the children arrived. At the very bottom was the new report. Gerald opened that report and confirmed his worst fears.

322

The cell samples indicated all the normal biological information. Then, the very last entry indicated that there was an unknown chemical inherent in all the cells. This chemical was unknown to the computer in the machine. This machine was the latest model and would have every chemical known to man. So, where had this chemical come from?

Gerald's crazed mind drew the only conclusion it could; the children were not human. They had to have come here from somewhere else.

As Gerald continued this train of thought, he could see the whole dastardly plot set out before him. Aliens had impregnated human women 11 years ago. Those women gave birth to these horrible children. Now, the aliens had decimated the population of earth and were set to take over, using these children. Why, they were probably plotting right now to kill the adults and leave the biosphere. Of course the poison hadn't hurt them. But it had hurt his Martha!

Gerald began pacing again. This time he used his hands to hit his head. He just didn't know what to do. These idiots he lived with would never believe his story. But the report didn't lie. These children were inundated with some otherworldly chemical that enabled them to live while others died. Gerald had to do something. He had to come up with some way to kill them before they killed him.

Gerald thought of his syringe full of Nembutal. He didn't think he had enough to do them all in, but they were children so he could halve the dosage.

Gerald took out the syringe he'd planned on using to kill Christie and put half of the Nembutal back into the bottle. He could grab them one kid at a time. He could visit them at night when they were asleep.

Yes! That's what he would do. It was always best to do things at night. Kids were sleepy then and had little fight in them. He'd found that out the night before when he took the samples. Not one of those drugged kids had any fight in them.

Gerald sat down and looked at Martha's picture. He smiled at her and said, "They will pay for what they did to you, Martha." He stroked her picture and he thought for just a moment that she'd winked at him.

Chapter 59

When Christie woke up that morning, she noticed more hair on her pillow. She had started noticing her hair loss a few days before. The stress of being a mother to 200 kids was taking a toll on her. For weeks the guys had been out on the road moving bodies and getting supplies. She couldn't complain then. But since Andrew had found the kitchen in the Wilmer basement, the guys had been hanging around playing with the kids and taking it easy. She was getting fed up watching them go to bed while she made sure the kids were all put to bed at night. Something had to be done. They had to start helping her.

She was also upset about Gerald. She had told the men that his erratic behavior had her really worried. She didn't trust him around the kids. They had blown her off, telling her that "old Gerry" was harmless and she shouldn't worry. But they hadn't spent time with him since the tragedy had occurred. They'd been out on the road and now Gerald wasn't even eating with them. They didn't know what he'd become.

Christie thought of going on strike. She thought if she stayed in her quarters today they might notice what this place was like without her presence. Maybe they would like to handle the daily fights, the constant bullying, the girls' begging her for attention. Let the men handle it for a change.

Instead, she decided to go to the field. She would stay there all day and if kids showed up, she would direct them to one of the men. She looked at the clock and noticed it was just after 6. She got up and showered quickly. If she was lucky, she could get through the city unnoticed. Then she could spend the whole day alone.

She left her quarters and had to pass Gerald's lab. She tiptoed past and saw Gerald gazing at Martha's picture. She hurried by and went through the door to the landing and down the stairs. She didn't see anybody so she ran through the city until she reached the door to the field.

She loved to see the crops growing. They had finally begun to grow as she had hoped they would. They would have a wonderful harvest, and with the freezers they had found, they would be able to preserve them and have vegetables to eat while the next seeds were planted and harvested. It was working the way Wilmer had planned.

She walked down the steps leading to the field and made her rounds. The sprinklers were working nicely. She stopped and breathed in the air. The smell of earth and vegetables mixed in the air and gave her the sense of being outside. Oh, if only she could go outside she might be able to shake off this terrible tension.

Christie had lost weight. She was finding it difficult to eat, not only from a lack of appetite, but from constant interruptions caused by kids needing her for this or that. Not today. Today they would have to find Andrew, Simon, Pat, or George. They were more than capable of handling a 10-year-old's problems.

When she was done walking the field, she went to the animal room to find Calvin. She wanted to ask him about Mindy and Mark. She had been hurt when he took the kids away, but she understood now how those kids must have felt. They had to get out. She wanted to ask Calvin to take her with him when he went to visit them.

She went down the stairs into the animal room and walked over to Calvin's quarters. She thought it strange that he lived here and not with the others. He'd told her it was his choice, that he liked the privacy.

Christie knocked on his door and there was no answer. She hated intruding, but she really wanted to talk to him. She turned the knob and it was open. She opened the door and didn't hear anything. She called his name, but he didn't answer.

She went back to the field and walked to the back of the building. She saw the hazmat suit was missing and knew that Calvin had already left to visit the kids. She felt real disappointment.

Christie was getting hungry and decided to find something in the ground that was ready for picking. She sized up some tomatoes and peppers. She decided on the tomatoes. She picked two and took them to the shed to wash them. After they were thoroughly cleaned, she took them into her office.

She didn't have a plate or utensils so she decided to just bite into them. The flavor of fresh food awoke all her senses. The tomato was just right. She savored every bite and then ate the other one. Real, fresh food. It almost made her dizzy.

Just as she was finishing her tomato, she noticed the clock said 9:30. She had been here only three hours, but it felt like a whole day. Even though they drove her nuts, she was actually missing the kids. Maybe she should go upstairs and call a meeting on the PA system. If she could get all of them, kids and men, into one place at one time, they could figure out how to handle their present incarceration without Christie losing all of her hair.

Christie walked up the stairs and out the door. The city was alive with noisy kids playing and talking. Christie walked past the tiny houses and into the town square. She saw many familiar faces, but she also noticed some missing. She saw Katie and Alyssa, but not Maria Elena. That didn't happen very often.

Christie walked on to the cafeteria. Breakfast for the kids was over and the men were all sitting around a table drinking coffee. She came over and joined them.

"Listen, guys, I need your help." She looked from face to face. No response. "I really mean it. I need your help."

"Then just tell us what you want us to do," Andrew said.

"LOOK AROUND! Don't you guys notice anything? These kids need supervision, and I'm the only one who seems to realize it. I need you guys to step up and help me with these kids!"

The guys still didn't respond. Apparently, they found nothing wrong with the way things were.

"You know, I used to think you guys were great. But now I think you're all useless, with the exception of George, who at least cooks." Christie got up and stormed out of the cafeteria.

"Okay, does anybody have some suggestions?" Andrew asked.

"What do you mean?" Pat asked.

"You didn't see her just ream us up one side and down the other?" Andrew was getting where Christie was coming from. He hadn't been much help to her in the last few days either. But she had never asked for help so they thought she'd had it all together.

"Women don't know how to just ask. They always yell at you," Simon was saying.

"Gentlemen, I have been listening to you and I think I can help." George had brought over a plate of cookies. "Christie has been watching over our charges for some time now. Maybe we should give her a vacation of sorts. Let her leave the compound, so to speak."

The men listened to George and you could see their minds working.

"You mean suit her up and give her the keys to the truck?" Pat said.

"Well, maybe, but I think what she really needs is a few days in the Wilmer residence. Alone." George's eyes were twinkling. He had spent a night there, and it had done wonders for his spirits.

326

"You're right, George. That's just the place. It's quiet, it's clean, and the virtual room is a great place to sit. I have to get the sounds turned on," Andrew said. He got up and went to his computer room to hook up the sound to the virtual room.

"George, you talk to her. Tell her what you said." Simon got up and left the table with an old newspaper he had been carrying around.

"Must be going to the can," Pat said. "But he's right, George, you talk to her." Pat got up to leave and George grabbed his sleeve.

"Patrick, we have another birthday party coming up. I need your assistance in the kitchen today."

Pat looked crestfallen. He had hoped to sneak away to his quarters and take a daylong nap. But George held onto his sleeve and wouldn't let go.

"Okay. What do I have to do?" Pat sat back down.

"You just have to sift some flour and get some eggs from the freezer in Wilmer's. You can also grease the bread pans. While you're doing that, I'll begin pulling the cakes out of the freezers."

George got up and went to the kitchen. Pat sat at the table for a few minutes thinking about his bed. He then got up and followed George.

*****

Maria Elena had had a bad dream. She dreamt that someone was hurting her and she couldn't stop them. When she woke up, her left leg hurt and she pulled down her covers to look at it. On the top of her left thigh was a long cut with stitches. She didn't know how it happened and she began to feel sick to her stomach.

When she went to get out of bed, her leg was throbbing. Like all the children of the biosphere, Maria Elena had never been sick. Having pain like this was a new experience. In the past if she had scraped her knee or knocked her elbow, the pain would last only a short time, and the injuries would heal quickly. She didn't know how to respond to this kind of pain.

Maria Elena didn't want to leave her house. For some reason, her injury caused her to feel shame. When Katie and Alyssa came to the door to take her to breakfast, she told them she wasn't hungry and would come out later. Katie didn't like the way she sounded and decided to find Christie.

Maria Elena washed herself and got dressed. Her pants were rubbing against her cut so that every time she moved the pain would resume. She sat on her sofa and tried to watch a movie. She felt so sad and uncomfortable. Something about that dream would not let her rest. It was so real.

*****

Andrew went to Christie's quarters. He passed Gerald's lab and noticed Gerald sleeping in front of his computer. He walked over to Christie's quarters and knocked on the door. She opened it and let him in. She'd been crying.

"We came up with a way to help you. Well, George did anyway," he said. "We want you to spend a few days in the Wilmer residence. It's really nice in there and the virtual room is very relaxing." Andrew was waiting for her to jump in his arms and thank him with kisses. Christie just sat on the bed looking more dejected than ever. "Well, what do you think?"

"It sounds nice, but it doesn't solve the problem. You guys don't get it. I just can't do it anymore."

"Do what? We can't help you unless you tell us." Andrew sat down next to Christie.

"I should think it would be obvious. One woman, 200 children! These kids need attention, somebody chasing after them, reminding them to go to bed, to brush their teeth. I can't do it anymore."

"Well then, we'll yell at them and chase them." Andrew was truly perplexed. This was not such a big deal.

"But will you be there when they cry? Or when they fight and you have to fix it before they start beating each other up? Or will you just wrestle with them?" Christie's face was covered in tears. "I'm a scientist. I finished first in my class. I had a child, but she died before I could even get to know her. I just wasn't prepared for this. This can't be my life." The tears were flowing harder now.

"I didn't plan on moving dead bodies around for three weeks either. Shit happens." Andrew wanted to get up and leave her. All she could do was complain when they'd all been through hell.

"But you moved those dead bodies *together*. I have no one, Andrew. I'm the only woman here. You guys never think of that. I have *no one*."

She had a point. The guys had each other. Even when Pat puked each time they went out, they'd had each other to deal with it.

She'd had the responsibility of all these kids on her shoulders for weeks now.

Calvin had worked the field, but he didn't help with the kids, and when the guys came back from a day of bone duty, they didn't want anything to do with the kids either. He felt like an asshole for never noticing.

"Sorry. I didn't think about it." Andrew looked sincere.

Christie knew how hard it had been for all of them. If they would just take on some of the responsibility, she could relax a little.

"Will you guys just help me get them to bed at night?" she asked.

"We'll do whatever you want. Just tell us. We really don't know." Andrew smiled at her. She smiled back.

"Okay. I will. You can count on it. And I'll take up your offer and go to the residence. I'll go tonight."

She got up off the bed and began to take some things out of her drawers. She bundled them up in a plastic bag and then looked at Andrew.

"Is the door open," she asked, "to the residence?"

"Oh, yeah, I left it open when I ran the sound check on the virtual room. You're all set."

They left her room and she locked the door. They walked past Gerald's lab and he was still asleep. Christie turned to Andrew.

"He's getting stranger. I really don't trust him near the kids." She looked very tired.

"I'll keep an eye on him while you're away." Andrew was walking towards the door. Christie grabbed his arm.

"I didn't tell you, but Gerald tried to take a sample from Austin the other day. He had him pinned down in his lab and was going to do God knows what to him. I stopped him, but he looked like a madman. Please, keep him away from them."

Andrew thought a minute. She really looked scared. Something was going to have to be done about good old Gerry.

"I'll watch them, and I'll get the guys to help."

That seemed to make Christie calm down a bit. They left the lab area and went onto the landing. They could see the kids playing in the playground.

"They must get really bored sometimes, having to be in here all the time," Christie said. She looked at them. "We have to get those detectors out of Gerald's lab. He can't hold us hostage anymore."

329

"Hostage is a strong word." Andrew's eyes were just a little too merry.

"That's exactly what we are, and it's gone on long enough. When I come back, we'll get those detectors."

Christie then passed Andrew and went down the stairs. She started to run until she reached the door to the residence. She opened it and when she closed it, she locked it.

*****

Andrew thought about what Christie had said. He knew she was afraid of Gerald. He went to his quarters and found a baseball bat he had brought to the biosphere as part of his personal effects. He took it to Christie's lab and put it by her computer. He would feel better with it there in case Gerald ever came in to her lab when she was working there alone.

Andrew came down the stairs and saw Simon sitting on one of the benches. He was pretending to watch the kids.

"I saw her and thought I better look like I care," Simon said.

"Yeah, really, but she does have a point. There are a lot of kids here. But that's not our real problem. Good old Gerry assaulted one of the kids the other day trying to get a sample. Christie broke it up, but she says he looked really nuts. We have to keep an eye on him. He may be getting dangerous."

Simon nodded, which meant he was on board and would watch the lab doors while he sat on the bench. Andrew went into the kitchen and found Pat covered in flour and George covered in eggs. They'd had a little spat and were now cleaning up.

He informed them that they were on watch duty and they agreed it was the best course. He also told them Christie had gone on vacation and they all had to get the kids fed and in bed for the next couple of days. They said fine and finished cleaning. As Andrew left the kitchen, he saw Calvin walking towards him.

"Andrew, can I have a word?" Calvin asked him.

"Yeah, just me?"

"Yeah, just you, for now."

They walked back to the animal room and to Calvin's quarters. Calvin poured Andrew a shot of scotch and one for himself, and then for the next couple of hours related the story of Mindy's parents and the purple babies.

Chapter 60

Andrew was thinking about everything Calvin had told him. All evening they'd been trying to come up with a plan to integrate the new group of children and adults into the biosphere.

Now that they could go outside, they wouldn't have to live here. It could be used as a sort of medical facility, or a gathering place. It had air conditioning, and the field was producing food. If they could import some animals, they could have milk and cheese.

Calvin told Andrew about meeting the group tomorrow at the Big Mart. Andrew told him to bring them over, that he would deal with Gerald. He then left Calvin to help Pat round the kids up for bedtime. As he was heading towards the houses, Katie walked up to him and asked him if he would check on Maria Elena.

"Is she sick?" Andrew asked.

"When Alyssa and I went to get her this morning for breakfast, she told us she wasn't hungry. We haven't seen her all day and she won't answer her door."

Katie looked worried, so Andrew took her hand and walked with her to Maria Elena's house. He knocked and there was no answer. He opened the door and he and Katie walked inside.

"Hello." Andrew called. There were no lights on and the room was dark. "Katie, put on the lights."

Katie ran to the wall and flipped the switch. The lights came up and Andrew could see Maria Elena asleep on the bed. He walked over and put his hand on her hand. She was very hot. He felt her forehead and turned to Katie.

"Go and get George as fast as you can," he told her.

Katie ran out the door and Andrew went to the bathroom to get a cold washcloth. He noticed towels on the floor with what appeared to be blood on them. He wet the washcloth and came back to Maria Elena. He placed the cloth on her head and she stirred.

"Donde estoy?" Maria Elena asked.

"Hey, sweetie, how ya feelin'?" Andrew was squatting next to the bed so she could see his eyes.

"Where am I?" She seemed very foggy.

"You're in your bed. You haven't been outside all day."

Andrew took her hand, and it was so warm. He turned the cloth on her forehead over.

"My leg hurts. It's been hurting all day." Maria Elena said tearfully.

Andrew thought of the bloody towels in the bathroom.

"Where on your leg?"

Maria Elena took his hand and put it on her thigh. She winced. He could feel a swelling even through her blanket.

"Can I look at it?" he asked. She nodded and he pulled the blanket down.

Maria Elena had taken off her pants and had only her underwear on. The wound was swollen and red. There was pus mixed with blood oozing out of the wound. Even with the swelling, Andrew could make out the stitches. She hadn't done this on the playground.

Andrew became enraged. He suddenly remembered Christie telling him about Austin and how Gerald had pinned him down on the floor. Had he cut this sweet little girl? He pulled the covers back up.

"George is coming, sweetie. Does it hurt really bad?"

Maria Elena nodded her head. It was all he could do to keep from running to the lab and throwing Gerald down the stairs. Katie came back with George, who asked her to wait by the front door. George walked over to Maria Elena and felt her forehead.

"I need my bag. I'll have to go to the labs." George could see the look on Andrew's face. "You stay here with her. Don't leave her alone."

George went to the labs and saw that all his medical equipment was gone. He knew in an instant that Gerald had taken it. He walked over to Gerald's lab and tried the door. It was locked. He started banging on it and Gerald appeared in the window.

"I need my bag, Gerald, and the medicine." George was being as nice as could be. He wanted Gerald to feel safe enough to open the door.

"I felt it was safer kept in here since you spend so much time in the kitchen." Gerald was smiling at George. His eyes looked strange.

"I thank you for your consideration. I do appreciate it, Gerald. But please, I need my bag. I need to remove a splinter from Pat's finger." George knew that Gerald's feelings about Pat were neutral.

"Very well, I'll get it for you."

Gerald walked to the back of the lab. He pulled the bag out from under one of the cabinets and brought it to the door. When he opened it, George pushed his way into the lab.

"Oh, thank, you Gerald; now I just need to get some antibiotics."

George began to walk to the medicine cabinet. Gerald followed him and watched as he took out the penicillin and a topical antibiotic ointment. He also grabbed gloves, sutures, a mild sedative and needles. Lastly, he took a bottle of alcohol and put the items in his bag. He turned and Gerald was blocking his way.

"Must be some splinter, George."

"It is. He managed to embed it under his fingernail and now the infection may be in his blood. I have to hurry, Gerald. Please allow me to pass."

"Yeah, Gerry, let him pass."

Gerald turned around and saw Simon standing in the hallway with the bicycle lock in his hand.

"It's not nice keeping the medicine from the doctor now, is it?" Simon walked away, taking the lock with him. Gerald chased after him demanding the lock back.

"I don't think so, Gerry. I think we need to get everything out of there that you don't need to do your job. Oh wait, you don't have a job. All the animals are dead, except for some skinny chickens. Have you been by to see them lately, Gerry?"

George took this opportunity to check his bag to make sure he had everything he needed and then to slide past Gerald. He ran back to Maria Elena.

Gerald kept staring at Simon, who stared right back. As Gerald watched, Simon lifted up the bicycle lock with both hands and bent it in half until it snapped. He threw it at Gerald's feet.

"As long as we need what's in there, no more locks."

Simon walked past Gerald and out the door into the City. Gerald stood there cursing himself for not having a syringe in his pocket. He should have put one in his pocket before opening the door for George. George. He had forgotten about George. He wasn't treating any splinter.

Gerald cursed himself again for not taking better precautions when he took the samples. Someone must have an infection. Soon they would know about what he'd done.

Gerald had to think of something fast, before they descended on him. He went back to the lab and filled three more syringes – one

333

each for Andrew, Simon, and George. He would keep them in his pocket so he would be prepared when they came for him.

*****

George came through Maria Elena's door with his bag. He looked at Katie and asked her to go to the Wilmer residence and get Christie.

"Tell her I need her assistance with a patient," he said. Katie ran to get Christie. "Andrew, I think you should go and speak to Simon. Please, before you do anything, speak to Simon. He and Pat are in the cafeteria."

Andrew went out the door and headed for the cafeteria. George went over to Maria Elena and removed her blanket. George prepared a dose of the sedative and gave it to Maria Elena to help her through what he had to do next. He would have to remove the stitches and clean the wound. It would be very painful. At least the sedative would help her sleep afterward.

He waited for Christie to arrive before he started. She came in the door ten minutes after Katie had gone for her. She must have been asleep for her hair was disheveled and she was in her nightgown. She had sent Katie home.

"What happened, George?" She took one of the kitchen chairs and pulled it over to the side of Maria Elena's bed by her head. She sat down and began stroking the little girl's long brown hair.

"I think our friend decided to take some cell samples without our assistance." Christie began to get up, but George put his hand on her arm. "No, no, stay here. I need you. The men are going to take care of this. You must help me with this little one."

Christie fought the urge to run to Gerald's lab. While George washed his hands, she put her arm over Maria's head, sheltering the scared little girl.

When George returned, Christie held Maria in her arms while he removed the stitches and cleaned the wound. The little girl screamed with pain and held on tightly to Christie, but she never tried to get away. She knew they were trying to help her.

George worked fast, not wanting to prolong her agony. When he was done, the wound was clean, the new stitches were neat and sterile, but the swelling would take a day or two to go down. George gave Maria Elena some penicillin and prayed she wasn't allergic.

334

He applied the topical antibiotic to her wound and put a loose bandage over it.

"I would prefer leaving the wound open, but she may thrash around during the night. We can take it off and see tomorrow. Please stay with her. I have to go and see what Andrew is planning."

George left Christie with Maria Elena. Christie got on the bed and rocked her until the little girl finally went to sleep. Christie gently let go of Maria Elena and lay down on the sofa. Soon she, too, was asleep. During the night, Maria Elena would moan, but she didn't wake up. George had done a good job.

Chapter 61

George joined the men in the cafeteria. Their faces were glum as they decided the fate of Gerald Todd.

"I wanted to bust him right there," Simon said. "I should have. He's the most useless man on the planet."

"We have to figure out a way of keeping him somewhere. He can't be allowed to be around the kids." Andrew was so angry he had to hold himself to the chair with his hands. "I really want to kill him."

"Don't go near him," Pat said suddenly. "He's got something planned. I know. I'm a skinny guy and when I get around big guys like you, I have to have a plan. Something sneaky that will give me an edge. And that guy is nuts. I saw him the other day when I was in here havin' breakfast. He walked by and looked at me. He had crazy eyes. And I got to thinkin' about how he was the one that put the animals down when they were sick. That made me think he's got somethin' up there that could put us down. One quick shot in the arm and bingo – all the big guys are down."

They all stared in amazement at Pat. He usually didn't talk much, or contribute anything of particular value. He was funny, and the guys liked him. He did as he was told and usually didn't complain.

But this was a whole other side of Pat. This was the kid who grew up in Brooklyn and had learned how to survive. And what he was saying made a lot of sense. Gerald was definitely acting crazy, and he did have access to drugs. They would have to catch him off guard. But where would they take him?

"Take him to the basement," Pat said.

The basement had one access, the door in the floor of the kitchen at Wilmer's residence. That would be easy to monitor. But what would they do with him? They couldn't just keep him in there.

"We need a more permanent solution," Simon said. His look was mean. He had had enough of old Gerry.

"You're talking about murder, Simon," George said. "We don't have the authority."

"I'm alive; that's my authority, George. The son of a bitch needs to die. That's the only way any of us will be safe."

Simon got up and walked away. He was going to the bench to watch the lab door. Andrew suddenly remembered Calvin.

"Listen, I have to tell you something. Pat, go tell Simon to come back for a minute."

Pat got up and walked to the door of the cafeteria. He waved at Simon to come back. Simon waved back that he wasn't interested in coming back, and Pat came back to the table.

"Oh well, you can tell him when I'm done," Andrew said. "I saw Calvin today. He'd been down to St. Pete to see that little girl, you know, the one with the dog. He said she found her parents. He said they've been riding around for a week without suits."

Andrew stopped and let that sink in. George and Pat realized what he was saying. "That's right, no poison in the air. They had two busloads of kids with them that they picked up along the way from Vegas. They're just like our kids. They're coming here tomorrow morning." Andrew paused for effect. "Guys, we can go *outside.*"

George and Pat broke out in huge grins. Pat jumped up and ran out to Simon. He came back a minute later with Simon in tow.

"We can go outside?" Simon said to Andrew.

"Yup, we can go outside."

Simon walked away as fast as he could. He headed straight for his quarters to pack. He wasn't staying in this loony bin another minute. Pat chased after him and asked him where he was going.

"I'm packing, kid. I gotta get outta here."

"But Simon, there's nothing but dead bodies out there. Why don't you stay until we figure out what to do next? We really need your help with Gerry." Pat was almost running, trying to keep up with him.

"Look kid, I know, but I can't stand this place. My solution is to kill the bastard. End of story. I'm done. If you guys want to deal with him, then be my guest. But I'm leaving."

Pat watched him go to the field. Simon's quarters were behind Christie's office. He also had chosen to be away from the others. Pat followed him to the field. Simon turned around and grabbed Pat by the throat.

"Get away from me now or I'll kill you." Simon said. He stared at Pat. Pat looked into Simon's eyes and then looked away. He'd never been afraid of Simon, but the big man was scaring him now. There was murder in his eyes. When Simon was sure Pat understood, he let him go. Then he walked away.

Pat watched Simon leave, and then he turned and ran back to the cafeteria. When he got there, George and Andrew were just

337

getting up to go to bed. He was still shook up from his confrontation with Simon, but his feelings about Gerald had intensified.

"You guys should stay away from Gerry," Pat said. "I just have a bad feeling."

George and Andrew looked at each other.

"Well, one of us needs to keep watch tonight. The other will sleep on the benches down here," Andrew said.

"I'll keep watch," Pat said. He went to the store and grabbed an energy drink. He brought it back and sat at one of the tables.

Andrew and George each picked a bench and lay down. They dozed a little, but never really got to sleep. Every noise roused them. They were a little afraid of Gerald after Pat had told them about Gerald's ability to put things to sleep.

As Pat was sitting in the cafeteria, Austin walked in.

"Hey, buddy, what are you doing up?" Pat asked him.

"I have this thing on my leg." Austin was wearing a tee shirt and his underwear. He walked over to Pat and showed him his wound.

Pat hadn't seen Maria Elena's wound, but he guessed it looked like this. It wasn't as swollen, but it was nasty. Pat hated doing it, but he woke up George and showed him Austin's leg.

George took Austin back to his house and treated his leg. For all Austin's complaining, he was very brave and hardly yelled as George cleaned his wound and re-stitched it. George was hoping this was the last child he would have to treat. He was very tired and lay down on Austin's sofa. He was soon fast asleep.

Pat somehow managed to stay alert most of the night. He dozed off around 4a.m. Gerald hadn't made an appearance. Pat was hopeful he wouldn't show his face down here. Fortunately, Pat was right.

*****

The morning came and the kids started piling out of their houses. George woke up and checked Austin's leg. It looked good. He then walked over to Maria Elena's house and checked her leg. It, too, looked good. He had her get up and walk. She had a little limp, but that would go away as she healed. She gave George a big hug and thanked him.

Christie stirred when she heard them talking. She got up off the sofa. She asked George how things were out in the City and he said the night had been uneventful. She sighed in relief. "So much for my vacation," she thought. He told her about Austin and she was now sure it had been Gerald.

"He's dangerous, Christie. Let him alone. The men are going to handle him. Please, we need you. Stay away from him."

George had his hands on her shoulders. She knew he was right, but her rage was so great she could barely contain it. She told George she would be fine and he left Maria Elena's house.

Out in the city, George began to notice some of the other children limping slightly. He stopped them one by one and found eight more children with wounds like Austin's and Maria Elena's. By some miracle, their wounds hadn't become infected. He applied the antibiotic ointment and a loose bandage and told them all to take the bandage off tomorrow.

George could now understand Christie's need for revenge. These children had been assaulted in their sleep by a maniac. Thank God Gerald hadn't killed them.

George found Andrew in the cafeteria drinking coffee. Pat was getting the food ready for the kids' breakfast. George sat down with Andrew.

"We have to kill him," George said. Andrew's eyebrows shot up.

"I thought we didn't have the authority, George."

"He's a mad man. No one will be safe as long as he lives."

"George, we can get out now. We'll take him somewhere, like a jail or something. I just don't think I can handle murder on my conscience. I don't think any of us can, with the exception of Simon. He's...different - but not you George, and certainly not Pat." Andrew paused. "We have to think of something else. In the meantime, we watch each other's backs. We post somebody at the lab door to make sure he doesn't get out. We take food up there. We leave it outside the door. That's it for now."

"I still think we should put him in the basement," yelled Pat.

*****

Christie went back to the residence and showered. She changed into new clothes and made her way to the cafeteria. She smiled when she saw that Maria Elena had joined the girls for breakfast. She then sat down with Andrew and George.

339

"Well, guys, what's the plan?" She looked from one to the other.

"Christie, I have to tell you two things," Andrew said. "The first is I put a baseball bat in your lab by your computer just in case you find yourself alone in there with Gerald. The second is....you can go outside." Andrew told her about Calvin and about the new people coming to the biosphere.

"For real, you're not kidding. We can go outside," Christie said.

Andrew just kept nodding his head and grinning at her. She started to laugh and jumped up out of her seat. She ran to the field door and opened it. She ran down the stairs and across the field. When she got to the back, she opened all the doors and climbed the ladder to the hatchway. Calvin had seen her running and met her at the ladder.

"You need the code, Christie. 091379," Calvin said. Christie turned and looked at Calvin.

"It's true, right. I really can go out there."

Calvin nodded. He watched as Christie entered the code and the hatchway opened. She stuck her head out and breathed in the air. She climbed up to the surface and stood on the ground. She could hear the breeze rustle through the trees. Calvin climbed out the hatchway. He was on his way to meet Joe and Dani.

"I'm bringing them back Christie. They want to see the biosphere. Do you think Gerald will cause any trouble?" Calvin hadn't heard about last night. He didn't know about the wounded children or Gerald's madness.

"I hope not. I know Andrew and George have a plan to watch him. He's one guy against us all." Christie paused. "Bring them back. I want to meet them."

Calvin turned and walked towards the vehicles. He looked up and noticed the Mercedes was gone.

"Shit, somebody stole my car. I knew I shoulda' taken the keys."

Calvin didn't know that Simon had left the night before. He thought that more people had come out of the woodwork. But there were so many cars on the roads, why take his baby? He would have to take one of the trucks, but it just wouldn't feel the same.

Chapter 62

Christie looked around the parking area and started walking. She walked to the dirt road that led to U.S. 19. She walked to the entrance of 19 and saw for the first time the devastation that Andrew and the men had dealt with. The bones piled up on the side of the road had been laid there by them, and this was just a small sample of what the rest of the country must be like.

The smell was still slightly putrid, but not too bad. Christie turned around and walked back to the hatchway. It felt so good to be outside, but she wanted to check on the kids' wounds.

As she was just about to enter the hatchway, Christie heard vehicles approaching. She turned and saw Calvin's truck followed by two school buses, an SUV, and a sedan. She watched in amazement as the kids clambered off the buses and the adults emerged from the cars. She could just make out Mindy's blond hair and she could see the dog, only now there were two.

Calvin waved his arm to indicate they would be entering the biosphere through the back and to follow him. Christie came down the ladder and positioned herself to allow the others to enter. The kids started coming down first. Christie directed them to form a line along the field and wait until everyone had come in.

The kids kept staring at the huge field. They couldn't believe it was underground. When Dani came down the ladder, Christie almost kissed her. She was so glad to see another adult woman. Then she saw Jenny come down and she was beside herself. She wasn't alone anymore.

Once everyone was inside, Christie told them to go to the top of the stairs and out the door. Mindy and Mark raced ahead to show the kids where to go. They all ran up the stairs. The adults had to keep reminding them to slow down.

"You have a really great kid there," Christie said to Dani.

"I know, and I missed her so much." Dani was awestruck by the size of the biosphere. She had no idea that this was what Mindy had been talking about. It was just amazing.

"You don't know how glad I am to see you," Christie said, with tears in her eyes.

"I think I do. Jenny is great, but I really needed someone older to talk to."

The women stopped walking and hugged each other. Then they proceeded up the stairs to the second floor. Christie could hear Jason talking to Calvin.

"You have to tell me about them," she said to Jason, pointing at the two dogs.

"They were the first purple babies," he said.

"Purple babies?" Christie looked at Dani.

"That's what all these kids are. They all came from the same place. Their mothers were treated by the same doctor who used this purple solution to prevent miscarriage. I was one of the mothers."

"Is that what kept you alive?" Christie was confused.

"No, no, we were trapped in a cavern." Dani kept walking and left Christie to ponder that answer.

Jason stood by Christie and told her he had files at home that explained everything. Christie told him to bring them the next time he came to the biosphere.

The kids were running towards the center of town, with Mindy and Mark in the lead. Mindy saw her old friends Maria Elena, Katie, and Alyssa and ran to greet them. Mark's mood became dark when he saw her run to them. He stopped running and held back until Jason caught up with him. Jason was with Jenny so he was no fun either.

Mark hated being left alone again. He kept walking slowly. He got to the Town Square and stood to the side watching the kids meet and greet each other. Mindy waved to him to come over, but he just stood there. He looked up the stairs leading to the labs. He wondered if Gerald was still up there mooning over his cow.

Mark slowly climbed the stairs. The kids were too distracted to notice and the adults were lost in conversation. Andrew and George had forgotten they were supposed to be watching Gerald. Pat was cutting birthday cake in the cafeteria and passing it out to everyone.

Mark got to the landing before Christie noticed him. She excused herself and started towards the stairs. She called to Mark, but the kids were too loud and he couldn't hear her.

Jason looked up as he heard Christie calling to Mark. He saw Mark standing on the landing. He was standing right below it, so he ran over to the stairs, and climbed them two at a time. When he got to the top, he grabbed Mark's arm.

"Hey, buddy, where are you going?" Jason asked. Mark turned around and Jason could see he was in one of his moods.

"Nowhere, I'm just bored, I guess." They both leaned against the railing and looked out over the City.

"Interesting view up here, isn't it?" Jason ruffled Mark's hair. "Come on Mark, let's go back down. They've got birthday cake."

Jason watched Mark's face to try to figure out what is really going on. He saw Mark watching Mindy with her three girlfriends.

"She cares about you, too, Mark. She just hasn't seen them for a while. Didn't you make any friends while you were here?"

"No." It was always hard to get Mark to talk when he was in a mood.

"Well, I'm going back down. I'm really wantin' that birthday cake."

Jason waited for a minute when he saw Mark thinking. Mark shrugged his shoulders and turned to follow Jason down the stairs.

Jason walked down the stairs first. Mark began to follow him, but he felt something grab his shirt sleeve. He hadn't seen Gerald's hand come out of the door.

Gerald grabbed Mark. Mark tried to break free, but Gerald was stronger. He pulled Mark through the door and into his lab before Mark could holler for help.

Mark continued to struggle, trying to get away from Gerald. Gerald had a mad man's grip on Mark. He took one hand off of Mark as he tried to take a syringe out of his pocket. Mark felt Gerald's grip loosen and noticed Gerald's attention was on something else. Mark used the opportunity to pull away from Gerald and head for the door. Gerald was right behind him.

He pulled Mark away from the door and threw him across the room. Mark landed on the floor and slid into a cabinet. He looked up at Gerald, afraid to move. Gerald was holding the syringe in his hand and was slowly approaching Mark.

Jason took the stairs two at a time and got to the bottom of the stairs before he turned to make sure Mark had followed him. Christie grabbed Jason's arm.

"WHERE IS MARK?" Christie was yelling above the noise in the town square.

"I THOUGHT HE WAS RIGHT BEHIND ME."

Jason could see the panic stricken look in Christie's eyes. She remembered using Martha's photo to blackmail Gerald into giving up Mark. She was petrified that Gerald may try to extract some twisted revenge on Mark.

"WE HAVE TO FIND HIM," she yelled.

Christie ran up the stairs with Jason right behind her. Christie remembered Andrew telling her about the baseball bat he'd placed in her lab. She sprinted past Gerald's lab. The bat was exactly where Andrew said it would be. Christie picked it up and headed for Gerald's lab. Jason was just about to open the lab door when Christie stopped him.

"He's crazy," she said.

Jason looked into Christie's eyes. He could hear Gerald ranting at Mark. Christie held up the bat.

"I'm going in first. I'll hit him over the head and you grab Mark," she said.

Jason nodded his head. Christie quietly opened the door.

"You risked our lives you selfish boy. You could have killed us all. You are an evil boy who must be dealt with," Gerald yelled.

Mark was pinned against a cabinet. Gerald stood over him, syringe in hand. He was standing between Christie and Mark.

"Martha never hurt anyone. You did this. This whole thing is your fault. My Martha would be here if not for you, you stupid, self-centered boy."

"I didn't even know her. I wasn't here." Mark was crying out, but Gerald wasn't listening. He didn't see Mark, only the accumulation of his failures and his own inability to save Martha.

Christie walked slowly towards Gerald. Mark saw her and she nodded.

"You liar! You went out the hatch that day. You were there. But you survived. You're not human. I know your secret. You're an alien and all your friends are getting ready to destroy us."

Gerald's eyes were wide and his forehead glistened with sweat. Jason was following Christie, but he couldn't see a way to grab Mark. Jason understood what Christie had meant by Gerald being crazy. He thought of running for help but he didn't want to leave Christie alone with Gerald and he wanted to try and save Mark. Christie kept moving closer to Gerald. Gerald continued his rant.

"You are just like my wife. You take and take. You steal from me and call the police. You have me arrested for your crimes, Arlene, your crimes."

Gerald was moving closer holding the syringe just a few feet from Mark. Mark kept looking at Gerald, trying to think of something to say that would snap him out of his crazed rant. Mark saw Christie raising the baseball bat and relaxed a little.

344

"And that stupid lawyer couldn't help. It was his job to stop her. It was his job to make it go away. Neil Cramer. If he were here right now I would spit in his face. Someone beat me to it. Someone killed the son of a bitch before I could."

Christie stopped. She heard Neil's name and couldn't figure out how Gerald had known him. She heard Gerald say he had wanted to kill Neil.

Her mind went in circles as she tried to figure out what Gerald had to do with her wonderful husband. At that moment all she understood was that Gerald was angry that someone had killed Neil before he could. Rage began to rise up in Christie. This horrible man had survived a nationwide tragedy while her wonderful family had suffered a terrible death.

"So here you are, my boy. You came back. Did you bring your little blond friend? She was another troublemaker, wasn't she? Just couldn't mind her own business. Well, after I finish with you, I will lure her up here with her stupid dog and take care of them, too."

Gerald's eyes were wide. He was breathing hard. He was within one foot of Mark. He raised the needle up and as he did, Christie lowered the bat down on his head.

Gerald was stunned by the blow. He wavered a little, trying regain his footing. Blood is streaming down his face. He looked down at Mark and remembered the needle in his hand. Once more he came at Mark. Christie hit him again, harder this time. Gerald fell to the floor. Christie dropped to her knees and brought the bat down on Gerald's head, over and over.

Her daughter's face flashed through her mind. She remembered her husband's kisses while she brought the bat down again and again. Gerald would pay for all the hurt she'd endured, all the pain she'd felt for the children of this place. She hit Gerald's head until there was nothing left but shattered bone and blood.

Mark had been trying to get past Christie. When she stopped hitting Gerald, Mark crawled past her to Jason. They ran to the landing and started calling for help. Andrew heard them and looked up at the landing. He ran up the stairs as fast as he could.

"She lost it," Jason said.

"Who lost it?" Andrew asked.

"Christie. She just couldn't stop hitting him," Mark said.

Chapter 63

Andrew stood at the door to Gerald's lab. Christie was huddled against the wall next to the door, unable to move. He saw the lifeless body of Gerald Todd.

Andrew knelt down next to Christie. She didn't seem aware of him, so he touched her hand. Her body was shaking and she was gasping for breath. Andrew stood and helped her up off the floor. She couldn't take her eyes off of Gerald's body. Andrew put his arm around her and gently guided her out of the lab.

On the way to Christie's quarters, Andrew saw George coming towards the lab. He watched as George looked into Gerald's lab. George's face indicated that he and Andrew needed to talk. Andrew nodded his head as he took Christie into her quarters.

George stood over Gerald and looked down at the bloody mess. The whole lab seemed to be covered in spattered blood. He noticed Jason standing at the lab door.

"What happened?" George asked. He was shocked by the carnage.

"Christie just flipped out when she saw that dude go after Mark. She just kept hitting him."

George turned away from Gerald's body to face Jason.

"Go downstairs, son. Would you please ask Pat to come up here?" Then George remembered Pat's vomiting episodes. "On second thought, don't. Just let him be."

Jason left George standing next to Gerald's body.

"What a mess," George said out loud.

After George assessed the condition of the body and the lab, he began to think of a way he and Andrew could dispose of the body. No one would cry over Gerald's death, so no one would care how they buried him. They could build a pyre and send him to Valhalla, but that would be too good for him. Putting him in an unmarked grave would be more appropriate. Getting him through the hatchway, however, would be hell.

George left the lab and went to the first hospital room. He grabbed a sheet and went back to cover Gerald's body. George wished Simon were here. He was strong, and would have been a great asset right now. George left Gerald and walked over to Christie's quarters. He knocked on the door and Andrew told him to come in.

346

Christie was sitting on the bed. Andrew was trying to get her out of her bloody clothes, but she wasn't helping him and he was having a really hard time. George walked over and sat down next to her. She was covered in human detritus. It was hanging from her hair and her face, as well as her clothing. Andrew had tears in his eyes.

George put his arm around Christie and asked her if he could help her change her clothes. She seemed unaware of George's presence until he said that. She looked up and saw Andrew. She felt so ashamed. George asked Andrew to leave for a few moments.

After Andrew had left, George gently helped Christie out of her clothes and helped her into the shower. After he'd washed off the flesh and bones clinging to her hair and body, he dried her off and helped her into her nightgown. The last thing he did before he tucked her in was to give her a sedative.

Andrew was feeling numb. When he walked into Gerald's lab and saw Christie huddled next to the wall, he could feel her pain. She was so utterly distraught. She didn't deserve this, and it broke his heart. When he brought her to her quarters, she just sat on the bed and wouldn't move. He tried to soothe her with words, but they did no good. It made Andrew feel completely impotent. He was glad when George took over. He was glad to get out of that room.

When George left Christie's room, he saw Andrew standing in front of Gerald's lab looking down at the body.

"What the hell are we gonna do with him?" Andrew asked.

"I was wrapping my mind around that one too. We have to get him outside. Do you think the two of us could get him through that hole?" George was mentally weighing and measuring Gerald.

"Yeah, push and pull. At least he has arms."

George bent over, rolled Gerald over, and picked up the corners of the sheet. Andrew picked up the other corners. They got him out of the lab and through the three chambers by starting and stopping while Andrew punched in the door codes until they reached the hatchway ladder. They had to put him down while Andrew climbed the ladder to input the code that would open the hatchway. When it was open, he came back down the ladder and once again picked up Gerald.

They couldn't get the right grip on him and Andrew couldn't walk up the ladder backwards. They decided to tie the sheet around his chest and then pull him from above.

Andrew pulled while George pushed until they got him above ground. Then Andrew pulled Gerald's body behind the truck farthest from the school buses to hide it until morning when they could bury him. He didn't want their guests seeing Gerald's bloody sheet-draped body as they left the biosphere.

Andrew came down the ladder and saw George trying to clean up the blood they had dragged along the hallway. He grabbed another sheet from the hospital room and wet it down. He and George managed to get most of the blood off the floor. The walls would be a problem for another day. In the meantime, they piled the dirty sheets by the hatchway ladder, cleaned themselves up, and rejoined the party downstairs. Andrew peeked in on Christie before going downstairs; she was sleeping soundly.

*****

Jason and Mark were waiting at the bottom of the stairs when George and Andrew arrived. They looked at the two men and decided not to ask them what they had done with Gerald.

Mark was still shaking from the experience. George put his arm around Mark and led him to the cafeteria. He took him to the back of the kitchen where he kept the good chocolate. He gave Mark a big chunk and told the boy to go sit down at a table and eat every drop.

Jason seemed lost. The adults seemed to forget that he was only eighteen. The things he'd seen in the last four weeks had changed him considerably. But this, this was horrific.

Jason didn't know what to do with his feelings. Jenny came up to him and asked him if he was all right. When she touched his arm, the tears began to roll down his cheek, and his embarrassment was overwhelming. She put her arm around him and led him away from the others.

They found a bench down the street and sat down. He put his head on her shoulder and cried hard. Jenny just kept rubbing his shoulder. His pain was contagious. Soon she, too, felt the tears welling in her eyes. After a while, Jason stopped shaking and crying.

Jason looked at Jenny as she wiped the tears away from his face. He took her face in his hands and kissed her for a long time. They then wrapped their arms around each other and stayed that way until Dani found them and told them it was time to go.

348

Dani asked Andrew where Christie had gone. Andrew said she wasn't feeling well and had gone to bed. Dani asked Andrew to give Christie her best and to tell her she would love to have her come to the school to help start a farm. Andrew said he would relay the message and wished them all goodnight.

Pat took them to the back hatchway and let them out. Calvin drove them back to the Big Mart and promised Mindy he would visit them again soon.

Chapter 64

When Calvin got back to the biosphere, he felt so good. He'd never realized how much he loved being outside until he couldn't be. He wandered back to the Town Square where Andrew, Pat, and George were sitting on a bench. Andrew and George had just told Pat what had happened to Gerald. Now they would have to tell the story again.

"So you guys managed to get his body out the hatch?" Calvin asked.

"Yeah, we kind of hoisted him up with sheets. He's out by one of the trucks. We have to bury him first thing tomorrow because the kids are expecting to go outside. They can never see that."

Andrew was just beginning to feel what had happened. The numbness was fading, and the fact of Gerald's murder was becoming a reality. He hurt so for Christie. What she must have held inside to have it explode that way.

"Thanks for not asking me to help," Pat was saying.

"I thought about it, but then I remembered the vomiting," George said.

"That was real thoughtful of you, George." Pat clapped George on the arm. Then he walked into the cafeteria and started cleaning up the debris left by the party guests.

* * * * *

Christie woke up in the morning and opened her eyes. She could see the photograph of Neil and Haley. For a moment, it was just an ordinary day. Then she suddenly remembered what she had done.

The image of Gerald's body loomed before her eyes. It only made it worse to close them. She got out of bed and felt dizzy.

The sedative George had given her was wearing off, but there was still enough in her system to make her woozy. She walked slowly to the bathroom and looked into the mirror. George had done a good job. There was nothing left in her hair to indicate that she had heinously murdered someone.

In this world, there wasn't a process of justice by which she could atone for her crime. She would just have to live with it.

Gerald was despicable, but he was human. Christie never would've believed herself capable of that kind of rage.

She decided to get dressed even though it was the last thing she wanted to do. Having the kids to care for might do her good, and they were waiting downstairs for her right now.

When she left her quarters, she was surprised to see how clean the hallway was. She had expected to see some debris from the night before. She'd been hesitant to come into the hallway but had made herself do it. She was glad to see that the men had taken care of it.

She averted her eyes when she walked past Gerald's lab. She'd never be able to look in there again. She was going to ask the men if they minded her moving into the Wilmer residence. She couldn't imagine them saying no, but she wanted to ask anyway.

When Christie got to the bottom of the stairs, Maria Elena ran over to her. The girl was looking so much better than the last time Christie had seen her. Maria hugged her and thanked her for all her help.

Christie hugged her back and didn't want to let her go. In another life, she would have adopted Maria Elena. But here in the biosphere, she couldn't do that and hurt all the others who so craved parental attention. She would have to satisfy herself by giving Maria Elena an extra hug now and then.

After they parted, Christie walked into the cafeteria where breakfast had just been served. She got in line and took some food. When she sat down with Andrew and tried to eat, everything tasted like dirt.

"That may be the shot George gave you," Andrew said.

But Christie knew it wasn't the shot. She wondered if she would ever enjoy anything again. How could she after what she had done?

George came out of the kitchen with his apron still on. He sat down with Christie and Andrew and looked Christie in the eye.

"You will make peace with this someday, Christie. It will happen. You're a good person driven to an act of violence. It's not the first time that has ever happened, and it won't be the last. We are animals, you know." George then got up and left them alone.

"Well, that was weird," Andrew said.

"He's just trying to help. Maybe he's right, but I just don't feel like I'll ever get over this."

351

Andrew took her hand. "If you'll let me, I'll help you. You're not alone."

Christie looked at Andrew. He looked so handsome, and she cared so much for him. She had been afraid to care that much for anyone again after losing her family the way she had, and it didn't help that the whole country had died overnight. What was certain in this world anymore? Maybe Andrew was the only certain thing she would ever find.

"I'll let you help me," she whispered.

She didn't smile because she was about to cry again. She didn't want to put him through that so she held back the tears. She tried to eat again and this time she could taste a little bit of the food.

Christie was glad Andrew hadn't walked away after seeing what she'd done, and if he stayed she would be good to him. She wouldn't push him away or make him feel unnecessary. Andrew touched her face.

"You're beautiful, Christie." That did it. She couldn't hold back the tears anymore.

Chapter 65

Joe stood watching the bees. He'd found a hive in a bush some distance from the main compound. He wanted to cultivate them so they could have fresh honey, but he didn't know how. He made a mental note to go to the library on his next trip to town.

Some of the biosphere kids had come to live at the school. By the end of the summer, the insects had also arrived. The insects had been distracted by the rotting flesh available to them on all the roads and residences of Pinellas County, but now they were turning their attention to the residents of St. Thomas.

Dani and Jenny set out to find every citronella candle they could. They also had to find a good flea shampoo to help the suffering canines. All in all, it was getting mighty uncomfortable to be outside.

The buildings had window screens, but the mosquitoes still managed to follow the kids inside whenever the doors opened. Joe went on a hunting expedition to find mosquito netting and came up with nothing. The only thing they could do was cover the kids in citrus oil and hope for the best. This growing problem prompted an urgent need to get the electricity turned on.

The generators required gasoline and lasted only a short time. They needed a permanent solution so they could use the air conditioning. Joe went to the biosphere to see if they had any suggestions. Maybe one of them was an electrician.

Joe climbed through the hatchway down the ladder and into the back room of the biosphere. There was nobody tending the garden. A week ago, the kids had harvested the field and the school had been given half of the crops. Now the field was freshly planted so it looked flat and brown. Joe walked past the field looking for Calvin or Christie.

He made it to the field door without seeing anyone. When he opened the door, he was assaulted by the sounds of out-of-control children. They seemed to be everywhere, throwing things and screaming at the tops of their lungs. Joe walked to the cafeteria, ducking to avoid being hit by flying objects. Andrew and Pat sat at one of the cafeteria tables.

"Hey guys, what the hell is going on?" Joe said as he sat down at the table.

"Christie went to stay with Jason for a week," Pat said. He sounded very tired. "The kids just won't listen to us."

"Have you tried talking to them?" Joe said sarcastically.

"What do you think?" Andrew answered. "They're little heathens. They won't settle down."

"Can we go somewhere quiet and talk?" Joe asked. Andrew got up and led Joe and Pat to the Wilmer residence. When he closed the door, there was a blissful silence.

"We really gotta get these kids under control before Christie gets back, or she'll kill us." Pat bit his lip. The words had escaped his lips before he realized what he was saying. "Sorry."

Andrew gave him a mean look and then led them to the living room. They each took a seat on one of the overstuffed chairs the Wilmers seemed to favor.

"Okay Joe, what can we do for you?" Andrew asked.

"We need electricity. We need air conditioning because the bugs are driving us crazy. It's just too hot to keep the kids in a classroom for more than a couple of hours." Joe looked anxious. He really hoped the guys could help him. "Are there any electricians here?"

"Jasper died the day of the...of the thing," Pat said. "He supervised the installation of the satellite dish and the solar panels."

Joe's eyes lit up. "Solar panels! That would work. Florida is covered in them. We would just have to take them off roofs and install them at the school. Does anybody know how to do that?"

Andrew and Pat stared at Joe with blank faces.

"Sorry dude, I just do pipes," Pat said.

"And I do software," Andrew said.

"Has anybody tried to contact Canada?" Joe asked.

Andrew and Pat looked at each other. No one tried to get on the Internet since Gerald's death. The equipment connected to the satellite was in his lab. There had been a half-hearted effort to clean the walls and objects in the lab, but it had been so covered in blood that they gave up after a while. Now they realized they would have to finish the job so they could use the computers.

"Maybe we could get the kids to help," Pat suggested.

"What are we gonna tell them, it's spaghetti? Besides, Christie would....really be mad at us," Andrew said.

"Christie isn't here," Joe said. They all looked at each other conspiratorially.

"It wouldn't take that long, Andrew. We got most of it up. I'll work with them. We'll pick out the instigators and they can help me." Pat was looking at Andrew, waiting for him to say no.

"It would have to stay a secret. What if one of the kids snitches us out?" Andrew really didn't want Christie finding out about having kids clean up that lab.

"Maybe if we just don't mention it," Pat said hopefully. "That we cleaned the lab, I mean." Then Pat thought of something else. "Can't we just move all that stuff outta there? Does it have to stay in that lab?"

Andrew got up and put his hands on Pat's head. He leaned over and kissed the top of Pat's head.

"That is genius. I must be loopy from all these kids to not have thought of that myself. We can move it to George's lab. He never goes in there anyway. Then we can seal off Gerald's door like it never existed. Pat, you're amazing." Andrew went to hug him and Pat moved out of the chair so quickly he almost fell down.

"No more kissing," Pat said.

"I was just gonna give you a hug." Andrew puckered and chased Pat around the chair. When he stopped, he looked at Joe.

"Can you help us move that stuff today? The sooner we get it done, the better. If I can hook onto the Internet somewhere, I can find instructions on hooking up the solar panels. If we have to do it ourselves, the Internet's our best bet."

"Sure, I can stay for a while."

The men left the residence and found the main street of the City covered in books and paper from the library. That was it, as far as Andrew was concerned. He was locking the kids in their houses until they settled down.

Joe took over and stood on a bench. He told the kids it was clean up time. At first they ignored him, but Joe could yell really loud, and when he did he sounded mean. Joe began yelling. The kids stopped and listened.

"GET THIS MESS CLEANED UP NOW!" he yelled.

The kids ran around picking up papers and books from the floor. They kept a wary eye on Joe. Andrew and Pat helped the kids by directing them where to put the debris. When they were done, Andrew sent them all to their houses and locked the doors for an hour's timeout.

The men went up the stairs and began moving the computers out of Gerald's lab. With the three of them working, it took no time at all.

Once Andrew got the computers hooked up to the satellite modem, they were able to find an English Google page. It was probably from Britain. They searched solar panels and found several videos on solar panel installation on YouTube.

"This may not be as bad as we think. These instructions are pretty straightforward. We can do this, guys." Andrew always loved a new project. "We just have to drive around and find the solar panels. Somebody will have to stay with the kids." Joe and Andrew looked at Pat.

"Hey, listen, I'm wiry. I can climb onto roofs like nobody's business. You need me out there."

Pat was right. They did need him to get the panels down. They would have to wait for Christie to come back from Jason's so they could go out to search for the panels.

"Send somebody over to get me when she gets back. I'll tell Dani we have a plan." Joe shook their hands and started towards the field room.

"Wait," Andrew called after him. "You can go out here." He pointed to the front hatchway.

"I didn't know there was another way. Thanks. That saves me the walk."

*****

When Jason suggested Christie spend some time by the ocean, Dani had encouraged her to go.

"You need some peace and quiet. The ocean is very soothing. Take some time off. The guys will be fine. They're grown-ups, right?" she said.

Dani had told the men that if one of them said anything to stop Christie from going, Dani would bring the rest of the kids to the biosphere for a vacation. The men all wished Christie a happy vacation and made sure she was ready to go when Jason and Mark came to pick her up.

For a week Christie, Mark, and Jason sat and watched the ocean, played board games, and shared their feelings about that awful day. At the end of the week, they all felt a little less burdened by their experience.

On the way back to the biosphere from St. Petersburg, Christie had Jason stop by the school. She wanted to see how they were doing, and she missed Dani. They had become good friends in a short time.

When they arrived at St. Thomas, they were greeted by the sounds of the kids playing on the basketball court. Jason and Mark went to watch the game while Christie went to find Dani. She found her grading papers at one of the desks in the first building parlor.

"You're actually teaching them!"

Dani looked up and smiled when she saw Christie.

"We gotta keep them occupied. They would drive us crazy if they just hung around. It's not so bad. They're all the same age and we split them into two groups. Julius helps and so does Jenny. It works."

"You look happy, Dani."

"I am happy. Joe is so...he's so much better than before. He really did change. I wish his mom could see him. He was such a screw-up before. I really like him, ya know?"

"Yeah, I know. I feel that way about Andrew too. He's a good guy."

The two women smiled. It was good to be with a friend.

"The guys came up with a way for us to have electricity. They're gonna take solar panels from the empty houses and install them here. But they need to leave the biosphere to do it. They were waiting for you to come back. I thought maybe Jenny could help you with the kids."

Christie looked grateful. She didn't mind helping the school, but the thought of being alone again with all those kids was overwhelming. Calvin had gone to Atlanta to search for his children, so she had the field to care for too. He was going to come back, but they didn't know when.

"Please, ask her if she'll come," Christie said.

Dani took a break and walked Christie to the kitchen for a cup of tea. It felt strange to do something so normal after weeks of chaos. Dani and Christie sat at the big table in the dining room, and shared memories of the last few weeks. When the tea was gone, Christie sighed.

"I guess I have to get back to the facility," she said. "You don't how much I've missed having another woman to talk to. It's so good to have you, Dani."

"I do understand. Jenny is great, but she is still so young. We need to do this at least once a week. Next time, I'll come up there."

As they parted at the car, Dani and Christie hugged each other.

"I'll see you next week, Dani," Christie said. She waved as Jason drove away from the school. Dani waved goodbye and returned to her papers.

A week later, the men began to go out in the truck and search for solar panels. They picked up a bunch of rechargeable tools at a home supply store and charged them at the biosphere so that Pat could get the panels removed quickly. When they found a house with panels, Pat would climb up the ladder and dismantle them, then he handed them down to Andrew and Joe.

They would fill the truck, take the panels back to St. Thomas, and go out again to retrieve the boxes and inverters they would need to wire the panels to. By the end of the week, they had enough materials to cover the big buildings. The smaller ones would have to wait.

Now came the hard part. They would have to install them. Pat mounted them on the roofs by putting them on the way he had taken them off. But who would wire them to the boxes and inverters?

"I think I can do it," Joe said, "if somebody guides me through it."

They picked up a laptop from an electronics store. Andrew charged it and then downloaded all the instructions they'd found on installation. As Joe handled the wires, Andrew read the instructions and Pat handed Joe the tools. When they were done, they stepped back and looked at the panels. They looked like the pictures.

"We have to wait a few days while the cells collect energy," Andrew said. "It may be sooner, but to be sure, we should wait until we switch it on. You'll have power for several hours a day and then it may kick off until the cells fill up again. Maybe you'll have to cut the air overnight so you won't lose the lights."

"With fall coming, it should be cooler anyway," Joe said.

They let three days go by before switching on the box and inverter. Dani stood in the kitchen by the light switch and when the guys yelled to her, she flipped the switch. All the kids cheered as the overhead lights came on. They now had electricity.

Chapter 66

Jason arrived at the school one day to visit Jenny and talk to Dani. He told her he wanted to find Tomlinson's medical files. He wanted her to help him find the doctor's office.

"I may still have a file at my old house. I kept all the info in case I wanted to have another baby. We could go down there on Saturday."

Dani could leave on a Saturday without disrupting the school schedule. They agreed that Dani would drive down to Jason's on Saturday and they would find Tomlinson's office.

Mindy asked if she could go with Dani so she could visit Mark. Dani was reluctant to leave them alone until Mindy reminded her that they had been alone for a long time without any trouble. Mindy seemed so much older than her 10 years.

On Saturday morning, they put Baby Girl in the back seat, climbed into the sedan and drove to St. Petersburg. Dani really enjoyed the time alone with her little girl, and Mindy loved having her mom all to herself.

Mark was happy to see Mindy, although he tried not to show it. He put on one of his moods and acted mean. Mindy was used to his moods and decided to play on the beach with Baby Girl. If Mark wanted to join them, he could, but she wasn't going to let him spoil her fun.

After a while, Mark came out and sat on the beach. Mindy threw sticks for Baby Girl to chase. She watched Mark out of the corner of her eye, and then Mindy walked over and sat next to him.

"You get so mean, Mark. Why do you do that?"

"I don't get mean. I just get mad." Mark looked down at the sand. He had a stick in his hand and was drawing lines.

"What are you mad at?" Mindy was now using her finger to write in the sand. She was writing her name.

"I get mad because you like those girls so much." Mark dropped the stick and put his arms around his knees.

"I like you better." Mindy looked at Mark. He turned and looked at her.

"Then why don't you stay here?" He looked into Mindy's eyes. He looked like a little boy.

"Because that's where my parents are." Mindy thought for a minute. "You could come there, ya know." Mindy smiled. "We could be in class together. You could sit behind me."

"But your friends will still be there."

"You have to learn to share, Mark. I would have to share my time between you and them. You would have to find a friend of your own. But we could still be together sometimes. It's more than we are right now."

"Do you really think I could find a friend?" Mark sounded dubious.

"There are over a hundred kids there. You'd have to be a moron not to find a friend there."

Mark looked at the ocean. He would miss the beach too much if he left it.

"I can't go. I love it here."

"Then come back on weekends. I bet Jason would bring you. He loves seeing Jenny."

Mindy was right. Jason did drive up there all the time to see Jenny. He could bring Mark back and forth.

"Do you think your mom would let me?"

"Of course she would." Mindy was grinning from ear to ear. "I'll ask her. So, you'll come?"

Mindy's eyes were excited. Mark had seen that look when she thought she was going to see her parents. He felt happy that she would be excited about having him live at the school. That meant she must like him at least as much as she liked her parents.

"I'll come." He braced himself for the hug to come. Mindy put her arms around his neck and hugged him tightly.

"Yay! I'll ask her when they come back. Let's go find something to eat."

Mindy called Baby Girl and the trio walked back to Jason's house to look for food.

*****

Jason drove Dani to her old house on 22nd Avenue. They parked in front of the little white house with green shutters and got out of the car. Dani went inside and into the back bedroom where she had a filing cabinet.

360

Dani opened the second drawer of the filing cabinet. She found a file marked "Baby." She took it out and laid it on the bed. It was the file she had kept during her pregnancy.

The file contained a business card with the address for Dr. Tomlinson's office on it and a note from his secretary. She took the file with her and left the house. She and Jason then drove to Tomlinson's office.

The office was located near St. Petersburg General Hospital. As they approached it, Dani remembered the first time she came there and drank the purple solution.

"He called it Fetura. He said I should drink it all. It didn't taste bad. So, your father made that stuff, huh?" Dani was watching Jason as he navigated the parked cars in the road.

"Yeah, he tried it on our dog Chloe when she was pregnant and when that was a success, he used it on my mother. She'd already had one miscarriage. I have a whole notebook about it." Jason finally found a place to park and they got out of the car.

The air smelled pretty clear. Dani avoided looking at the occupied cars as she walked to Tomlinson's office.

"There's another doctor's name on the sign. The files may be in storage somewhere," Jason said to Dani.

"When Tomlinson died, someone had to be made guardian of the records. It's worth a look inside anyway, just in case."

Dani walked up the stairs and opened the door. The strong scent of death greeted her. She backed away. She wanted to run, but she stopped herself.

"I should've brought the masks," Jason said.

He took off his tee shirt and wrapped it around his face. He walked inside the office, sidestepped the bones sitting at the reception desk, and found the file cabinets while Dani waited on the porch. There were only two cabinets, with the oldest file dated 2009. Dani's records wouldn't be here. He left the office feeling very discouraged.

When he got outside, he put his shirt back on. It smelled, but not too bad. He and Dani went back to the car and got inside. They sat for a few minutes trying to decide what to do next. Dani pulled out her file and opened it. Towards the back she found her medical file.

"Oh, my God, I had requested a copy when Tomlinson died. I didn't even remember that. The name of the woman I wrote to was

Maisie Gates. The address has a lot number. Could that have been a mobile home park?" She kept reading.

"This is the whole file, Jason. This woman must have been the guardian. But that's weird. I would think they would've been kept somewhere more, well, you know, office-like. I wonder if she still lived there before…"

"There's only one way to find out," he said.

Jason's car had a GPS so he programmed the address and they followed the lady's voice to an older mobile home park in St. Petersburg. The first house was number one, the next two, and so forth. The road curved around until you were back out on the street. Maisie's lot number was 57.

The park looked abandoned. There were no cars, so it was an easy ride through the park. They found lot 57 and parked the car.

The mobile home was an older single-wide with a ramp leading up to the front door. It was across the street from the community Laundromat. Maisie's home was remarkably neat. She must have taken good care of it. There was a walker perched on the top of the ramp.

"She may be in there," Dani said.

Jason turned the knob. It was unlocked. He opened the door and took a whiff. There was no smell other than the musty smell coming from the ground underneath the home.

The door opened into the kitchen. It was clean, with a few dishes in the dish drainer. Dani walked into the next room and called to Jason. When Jason came in, he followed Dani's eyes to the corner of the room. In the corner, on an old, beat- up recliner, sat a living, breathing Maisie Gates.

Chapter 67

Maisie frowned at Dani and Jason.

"Bet you didn't expect to find me," she said. "I heard your car pulling up so I was ready for ya." Maisie was a tiny, older African-American woman who spoke with a strong Southern drawl. "Who do you all think you are just walkin' in my house?"

Dani walked over to the chair next to Maisie.

"You're right, we didn't expect to find you," she said. "I apologize for just walking in."

Jason sat on the sofa pushed up against the opposite wall.

"Hmm, well, make yourself to home why don't you," Maisie said, looking down her nose at Jason. Jason stood up. "No, no, just sit. So, why'd you all come here?"

Dani began to ask her about Dr. Tomlinson. Maisie got a strange look in her eye. She wasn't sure she wanted to talk about Dr. Tomlinson. But she waited until Dani was finished before she spoke.

"Why are you all so interested in Dr. Tomlinson?" she asked them. "I worked for him a long time. You do look familiar to me. Were you ever one of his patients?" She was taking a good look at Dani.

"Yes, I was a patient about 11 years ago. That's why we came looking for you. You're the records guardian, aren't you?" Dani asked.

"Well, I do have some records. But not too many left. When the doctor died, most of the women asked for their records. I sent out almost all I had."

"Do you remember how many there were?" Jason was sitting forward on the sofa.

"Let me see. I remember thinkin' there were a lot of babies born with that purple..." She stopped herself.

"We know about the purple solution, Maisie. You can talk about it." Dani wanted Maisie to keep talking. Maisie pursed her lips and thought a minute.

"Alrighty. Well, I know there were about 300 children born. I can't remember how many records I sent out. You," she pointed to Jason, "come with me."

Maisie raised herself up off the recliner, grabbed her cane, and painfully made her way to the back of the home. Jason followed her into what must have been her bedroom. She took him to the closet and pointed to the top shelf.

"Bring down that box." She pointed to an old banker's box with the cane.

Jason lifted it off the shelf and followed Maisie back to the living room. He put it on the coffee table and took off the lid. The box was about a quarter filled with files. It also contained letters and other paperwork from the doctor's office. Maisie must have stuffed whatever she could in the box along with the files.

"There was another box, but those files got sent out and I threw the box away. I'm tryin' to remember…," she said. "I had to keep track of the files I sent out or the government would have been on me, for sure. Let me think. I have a drawer in my room with some papers in it. I might have put it in there."

"May I look?" Jason asked Maisie.

She waved her hand to indicate he could and Jason rose from the sofa and went back to the bedroom. He opened several drawers until he found one full of papers. He took the drawer out and carried it to the living room.

Jason placed the drawer on the coffee table next to the box. As he looked through it, Dani looked through the banker's box. She found 25 files.

Dani asked Maisie for something to write with and Maisie pointed her cane towards the kitchen. Dani found a pen and some paper and began writing down the names and addresses of the women in the files. Jason found Maisie's handwritten list of women she'd sent files to.

"I made that copy 'cause I had to send the original to the government," she said. She'd made an exact copy including names and addresses. Dani added those names to the ones on her list. When she was done, she added them up.

"There were 312 women given Fetura," Dani said.

She looked at Jason. So far they'd found 280 children. If Calvin was right and his kids had been purple babies, then that would make 282. That left thirty children unaccounted for.

"Some of the children were from Europe, Canada, and Mexico. Those children may still have families. But it looks like we have all the ones from the states with us," Dani said.

Jason was looking through a ledger. He found a page with Antonio's name on it. It was a record of the deliveries Antonio had made to Tomlinson.

"My father only gave Tomlinson 100 tubes of the stuff. Tomlinson told my dad he'd given it to over 300 women, and we know he did. How did he treat all those women?"

Maisie had been listening to their conversation.

"Who's your father?" she asked.

"Antonio Russo. He made Fetura."

Maisie smiled. "Antonio Russo, bless my heart. I remember Antonio. He was such a sweetheart. He would come into the office and flirt with me. I just loved that man."

"You knew my father?" Jason's focus shifted to Maisie.

"Oh, yeah. He would bring these little tubes of Fetura to the office. I would take them in for the doctor and mark 'em in that ledger. But then he stopped comin' in and would send 'em to us in the mail. They were powder. You had to add water to 'em." Maisie looked like she was thinking about something. "I know the doctor was dividin' 'em up, making four doses out of one tube."

"Leaving 22 tubes unaccounted for. Where are the other tubes?" Jason said.

For several minutes, Dani and Jason went through the files again, searching for an answer to the missing test tubes filled with Fetura. Then Dani got an idea.

"I know this is gonna sound like a strange question Maisie," she asked, "but how come you're alive?"

"I don't rightly know. They evacuated the park for the hurricane and nobody came back. I had to take my walker around to find food in the other homes. I guess I just ate right."

"But that's not possible. Everyone died. How is it that you didn't?" Jason knew where Dani was going with her question.

Maisie got up. She motioned for them to follow her. She took them into the kitchen and opened a cabinet. Inside was a row of ten tubes filled with a fine purple powder.

"I took them when Michael died. I wanted to protect him."

Jason and Dani stared at the tubes. There were still twelve missing.

"Some are missing," Jason said.

"You might as well sit down," Maisie said. "I'll tell you the story."

*****

365

Maisie Gates was a young widow when she went to work for Michael Tomlinson. He had just opened his own practice and Maisie was the second person he hired. He looked very young and one day Maisie suggested that he grow a beard. It would make him look older, she said. So Michael Tomlinson grew a beard.

Michael had become a doctor despite his family's penchant for law enforcement. His father had been the sheriff for years and had expected his son to follow in his footsteps. But Michael had no heart for the law. He was a man of science and he followed his passion to become a physician, although he wasn't past using his legal ties to thwart the occasional traffic ticket.

Maisie remembered Michael as a nice man. The women who went to him came because their doctors hadn't been very attentive and Michael's patients would rave about his kindness and consideration.

After three years, Michael had a thriving practice. He treated Maisie well by giving her annual raises and covering her health insurance. Her job there allowed her to buy a one-bedroom mobile home in a park not far from Michael's office. Her life was good and she loved her job.

About two years before Michael began treating women with Fetura, he was diagnosed with colon cancer. He underwent all the traditional therapies in order to combat his cancer. He would go into remission for a while, but it always returned.

Michael's bills were exorbitant and he was finding it difficult to pay them and his business expenses. He was in danger of losing his house and everything he had worked so hard for. His body was fighting the great fight, but he knew he was nearing the end of his choices in treatment. As long as he could, he would continue to treat patients and deliver babies.

Michael treated a woman named Teresa Russo. Her husband was a biologist. Teresa had cervical insufficiency and she'd come to Michael because she'd heard he'd performed miracles on women with this condition.

Teresa saw Michael throughout her entire pregnancy and he never saw any evidence of cervical insufficiency. She delivered a healthy baby boy. The only remarkable thing about this baby was his color. He was a light shade of purple. His placenta had been purple too.

Michael was incredibly curious as to how this had happened, but he was reluctant to ask. Teresa's husband seemed to change the subject whenever it came up, so Michael let it go and saw Teresa once a year for her annual visits.

Michael's doctors told him they'd reached the end of their options for treatment and he would do well to get his affairs in order. He was in pain most of the time, but he kept pushing himself. He wanted to leave this world with a clean slate. He had to find some way to make money and to make it fast.

The last time Michael saw Teresa for her annual visit, he suddenly began to think about the purple placenta. He believed that Teresa had been taking something that had virtually cured her condition. He decided to talk to Antonio Russo and find out what he had done to make his wife well, for Michael believed the biologist was responsible.

Michael would use any means possible to get Antonio to talk to him. He would even blackmail him if necessary. Michael needed money desperately. He came up with a plan to put before Antonio.

Michael could use the drug, or whatever it was, to help women carry their pregnancies to full term. For this, he would charge them $10,000 just for the treatment. His services would still be billed to their insurance carriers.

Michael Tomlinson sat in his office after calling Antonio Russo and wept. What he was doing was the antithesis of how he'd lived his life. All he wanted to do was pay his debts and keep his practice open a little while longer. He also thought of taking this drug himself to see if it could somehow stop the cancer. Why did it all feel so wrong?

*****

Michael met with Antonio and took him to the yacht club. He used all his powers of persuasion to push Antonio into giving him the drug. Michael could see the disgust on Antonio's face. No one had ever looked at him like that. Antonio excused himself and left the table. When Antonio didn't come back, Michael sat there thinking he should drop this fantasy and apologize to Antonio.

When Michael left the club, he could see Antonio sitting in his car in the parking lot. Michael's guilt was overwhelming. As he approached his car, a pain shot through his body so intense that he almost fell over. His body was reminding him why he had come here. He got into his car, and then he saw Antonio approaching in his side-view mirror.

Antonio agreed to help him. Michael continued the charade and made it sound like they were doing something noble. He said it would be like a trial to get Antonio his FDA approval. Even though Antonio had told him to stick to 100 women only, Michael figured he could change Antonio's mind once he saw how well it worked and how happy the women were with their babies. Michael was amazed at the whole "we'll sell it as a supplement" thing that had come out of his mouth.

He drove away from the yacht club and back to his office. He took out the files of the women he knew had a history of cervical insufficiency and prepared new files for them. He kept these files in a separate cabinet with a key only he and Maisie had access to. He told Maisie to come into his office and he handed her a list.

Michael told to her that these women would be getting a special drug that was not approved by the FDA. They would be selling it as a supplement and this information was to be held in strictest confidence.

Maisie had no reason to doubt Michael's honesty and she readily agreed to keep anything that was said between them private. He told her that the next time any one of these women was due for an appointment, to let him know a week in advance so he could prepare the supplements for them. He then called Antonio to find out when he would be bringing in the first batch of Fetura. Everything was in place, and soon Michael Tomlinson was back in the black.

The women were all thriving and the babies were being born. Michael would arrange for a private room at the hospital where the babies were delivered and kept for three days. Usually by that time the purple sheen had worn off.

Most of the women had enough money to pay for the extra time in the hospital if their insurance companies balked. They wanted to stay there anyway until the babies were a more normal color. Michael would hire private nurses to assist in the deliveries. In this way, Michael was able to keep his practices a secret.

Michael's pain was growing worse as the cancer ate away at his intestines. It had spread to his other organs. One day, in desperation he took out one of the tubes of spores and mixed it with water. He drank it down as fast as he could. The effect was almost instantaneous.

Michael's pain stopped and he began to feel energy coursing through his veins. He felt like a teenager again. The effect usually lasted a few weeks and Michael would have to treat again. He went to his doctors and they were amazed by his test results. His cancer was getting better.

Michael knew he would have to continue the treatments until the cancer disappeared. He would need more tubes of Fetura than he had anticipated. He would have to find some way to convince Antonio that their original agreement of 100 women would have to be renegotiated.

To make ends meet, Michael had been dividing the tubes into smaller portions and so far had treated over 300 women. The drug worked just as well whether they got a full dose or a fifth. But he was afraid of running out now that he had to take it, so he called Antonio and arranged a meeting.

Antonio refused to even consider giving him more Fetura. He was concerned about his patent, and about being deported. Michael played on this fear by telling Antonio that he'd been selling the drug as FDA approved. This was a lie of course. He also told Antonio that he'd treated over 500 women, another lie. But Antonio was turning pale and Michael knew he had him.

Michael told Antonio to send him 100 more tubes of the spores. Antonio agreed, but Michael never received the tubes. The next thing he knew, Antonio was dead and there would be no more Fetura delivered to Michael.

He had to stop taking new patients looking for the miracle supplement. He had enough to treat himself at least 100 more times if he used one-fifth of the tube. But what if that wasn't enough to cure the cancer completely?

One day he walked into an examining room and saw a young, bleached blond with too much make-up on. Before he could say more than three words, she jumped off the examining table and handed him a slip of paper. She said Antonio had sent her. She then ran out the door and got to her car before Michael could catch her.

When Michael called the number, she'd answered and told him she had the plants and was willing to give them to him for a price. He arranged to meet her and went to his bank to withdraw the money. If it were true, he could make the drug himself. It couldn't be that hard. He may even be able to get the formula from Antonio's wife – for a price.

Chapter 68

"That's all I know," Maisie said. "He told me he was meetin' somebody that evening and to lock up the office when I left. I never saw him again."

"How do you know all this?" Dani asked her.

"Michael wrote stuff in his journal. He kept it locked up in his desk. I went over there the next day to open up like I always did. The police had left a message for someone to call when they got into the office. I called and they told me they had found Michael's car.

"I kinda panicked and went to the cabinet where he kept the drug. I took them out and put them in my car. Then I went to his desk and tried the key. It opened it and I found the journal. I took that too. When they found his body, they made me guardian of the files so people could get their records." Maisie paused. "I thought he was a good man. He always did right by me. He must have been in awful pain to do those things."

"Then why did he have my father killed?" Jason was looking at Maisie. His eyes were hard.

"Son, he never did nothing like that. He would have put that in the journal. Why kill the goose that laid the golden egg?"

"She's right, Jason. He needed your father. He wouldn't have killed him." Dani looked over at Jason. He was still angry.

"Then who did? Who killed him? Who had a motive?" Jason was trying to hold back his anger.

"Maybe it was just a botched robbery," Dani said.

"They didn't take his wallet. They left everything. This was no robbery, Dani. This was murder."

"Could have been the drug company," Maisie said. Jason and Dani both turned to look at her. "They kept harrassin' Michael for the drug."

"What drug company?" Dani asked.

"One of the big ones. Starts with a W." Maisie was thinking hard.

"Wilmer?" Jason asked.

"Yup, that's the one. They kept sending Michael letters telling him to cease and desist. I remember that 'cause they came all the time. Michael just ignored them. I filed them away."

"You wouldn't have a copy of one, would you, Maisie?" Dani asked.

"Maybe in there." Maisie pointed to the box and drawer.

Dani and Jason scrambled to search through the papers again. Jason could find nothing from Wilmer and March Pharmaceuticals. Finally, Dani pulled a sheet of paper out of the banker's box with the Wilmer and March letterhead.

It was dated the year Antonio had been killed. It said that Wilmer and March was aware of Michael's illegal use of their product and that he was to cease and desist or face a lawsuit to recover damages.

"What are they talking about, *their* product?" Jason said.

He remembered reading his father's notebook. Antonio had been afraid to file for the patent in case Wilmer and March caught on and took the plants from him, but his lawyer had been able to file for Antonio and he got his patent. Jason remembered the file he had found tucked under his father's dresser drawer.

"They found out," he said.

"Who found out what?" Dani asked him.

"Wilmer's. They found out about the plants. They knew about my dad's drug."

Dani and Jason sat and looked at each other. They then looked at Maisie. It was time to leave, but they just couldn't leave her here alone.

"Why don't you come with us, Maisie," Dani said to her.

"I'm fine. I have enough food, and the purple stuff is workin' fine."

"You're taking it?" Dani asked.

"I have diabetes. When the medicine didn't work anymore, I started taking little bits every couple of months. I just got better and better." Maisie smiled. "You don't have to worry about me."

So that explained how she'd stayed alive during the tragedy.

"But don't you get lonely? You'll run out of food eventually. We have a big place with plenty of room. Why don't you think about joining us? We can always use another adult. You could help us teach." Dani was trying to look excited.

"I'll think on it. You come round tomorrow, and I'll give you my decision."

Dani and Jason left Maisie's home and headed back to the beach. Jason was quiet and Dani was thinking. If Wilmer's had arranged for Antonio's murder, what had they hoped to gain? Surely

371

one doctor in Florida couldn't make that much of a dent in their profits. Or was it revenge for Antonio stealing their property, even though they hadn't used it in over 40 years?

"I'm sorry, Jason. I'm afraid we have more questions. At least we know there aren't any more children out there alone somewhere. Maybe I'll bring Mindy with me to meet Maisie tomorrow. I hope she decides to come with us."

Jason didn't respond. He was too lost in all that Maisie had told them. The man he'd hated all his life, the man he believed had killed his father may actually be innocent. Somehow he had to find out. He decided to go back to the school with Dani and spend the night. He wanted to talk to Andrew at the biosphere.

Chapter 69

Jason appeared at his door while Andrew was working on the computer. He asked Andrew if he could help him search for something in Wilmer's mainframe.

"I don't know if the corporate mainframe is working. I've had no reason to go into it, and if the electricity is off, we can forget it." Andrew was looking at the monitor and didn't see Jason's face. He turned to look at him and saw that the kid was really mad at something. "What are you looking for, Jay?"

"I always thought Tomlinson killed my father. Now I think it may have been someone else."

"Who's Tomlinson?" Andrew had been out of the loop about the purple babies. He knew about the kids, but he didn't know how they got that way.

"My dad found this stuff that prevented miscarriages. Tomlinson was the doctor who used it. But then my dad stopped giving it to him, so my mom thought he was the one who murdered my father."

"Your dad was murdered?" Andrew was half-listening to Jason while he typed.

"Yes, Andrew, he was murdered." Jason smiled sadly at Andrew. "And if Tomlinson didn't do it, I want to find out who did."

"What makes you think hacking into Wilmer's will help you find out?" Andrew was typing fast. He was trying to see if Wilmer's corporate was online.

"I think they hired someone to kill my father."

Andrew stopped typing. He turned his chair and looked at Jason.

"Jason, you're not gonna find that kind of information in their corporate files."

"Then where will we find that kind of information?" Jason kept his gaze steady.

Andrew sat thinking. Those kinds of deals went down in private. The parties didn't keep written records. What you would need is a witness, and since almost everybody in the country was dead, including Jacob Wilmer, the odds of finding a witness were pretty much nil.

"Isn't there a special place here Wilmer built for himself? Maybe he kept something there."

"The door's open," Andrew said as he got up off the chair and followed Jason out the lab door. They went down the stairs, and a bunch of kids ran over to ask Andrew to play with them.

"Not right now, guys, I have some work to do."

The kids protested but he and Jason kept walking. They got to the residence door and Andrew knocked.

"Christie's been staying here. I don't want to scare her by just walking in," Andrew said. They listened but no one answered, so Andrew and Jason entered the residence.

It was so much nicer in there, like someone's home. They looked around to see if there were any obvious places Wilmer might have stored paperwork. The living room was pretty straightforward – sofa, chairs, tables, etc. Andrew led Jason through the hallway that led past the theater, the virtual room, and the kitchen.

"All the bedrooms are in the back. There's a library and a study back there, too."

Wilmer had built the residence to resemble his New Jersey home. There were more rooms in the back than in the front, like someone had just kept adding on with no thought as to how the home would look in the end. When he and Jason walked to the end of the hallway, they were standing before three doors.

"The library is that way," Andrew said, pointing at the first door. Jason searched the library while Andrew went into the second door, the study.

Wilmer had planned on being the last man standing and had taken the best of Western Civilization with him, sparing no expense. The living quarters were full of rare original art pieces, and the library contained several first editions. There were glass cases containing books you couldn't touch due to their age. The books on the shelves were alphabetized and surprisingly clean. The biosphere's filtration system kept the dust away.

Jason was glancing at the books rather absentmindedly when he stopped dead in his tracks. He walked backwards looking at the books again. He was right. He had seen it. There on the middle shelf was a book titled "Mortevida."

Jason pulled on the book and the library wall opened up to reveal a secret room. The room contained stacks of gold bars and empty glass cases waiting to be filled. Why had Wilmer used the name Mortevida to open this room?

Jason walked the length of the room, but he couldn't find anything unusual. He ran his fingers along the walls. He found a door set into the wall without a doorknob. Jason could just make out the outline.

Jason felt around the wall looking for some kind of button to open the door. His hand moved over a section of the wall and it lit up, revealing a number pad. Jason ran out of the room and into the study. He found Andrew going through the contents of the desk.

"Come on, Andrew, I found something and I need you." Jason ran back to the library with Andrew following close behind.

"Holy crap," Andrew said when he saw the secret room.

"Come over here and watch." Jason slid his hand across the wall and the number pad lit up again. "I need the code."

"I didn't do that one. It must have been programmed by somebody else." Andrew looked at the number pad. "If it's a safe, we'll never get it open without the code. There are no gaps in the door for a crowbar to pull it open and I'm no safecracker. He must have something pretty special in there."

"What do you think he would use for a code?" Jason wasn't going to give up that easily.

"How did you get in here?" Andrew asked.

Jason showed Andrew the book he had pulled down.

"What made you pull on that one?"

"It was the name of the plants my dad brought back from Brazil. They were named after the lady who discovered them. Her name was DeMorte. She had given the plants to a guy in 1953 named George...."

Jason brought up the number pad and entered the name Ranier. The door swung open. "That son of a bitch Wilmer thumbing his nose at you again, George," Jason said out loud. He looked into the wall safe and saw what Wilmer had been hiding from the world.

*****

In the stainless-steel-lined safe, there were 20 glass shelves. On each shelf were rows and rows of glass tubes. And in each tube were the lovely purple Fetura spores.

The tubes were sealed. They looked quite old to Jason. Then it hit him. These were not Fetura spores. These were Mortevida spores.

375

Jacob Wilmer had kept them for himself all these years. He'd brought them here because he knew if he ever got sick, these spores would save his life. Not his chemical pharmaceuticals, but these little purple spores scraped from the edge of a poisonous plant from the rainforest. Wilmer had known all along what he had, and there was no way he was going to market it.

Jason turned to Andrew.

"Those are the purple spores that made me invincible," said Jason. "He kept them for himself, the greedy bastard. If he'd produced them in the first place, my dad would never have tried to do it himself. He would have lived, at least for a few more years."

"But that doesn't answer your question, does it?"

Andrew picked up one of the tubes. On the side were numbers that looked like dates. Most of them were created in 1955.

"All the lives he could have saved." Andrew looked very sad and tired.

Jason saw something in the back of the cabinet. It looked like a small notebook. He took several rows of tubes out carefully, one by one, and laid them on the floor. He was just able to reach in and grab the notebook without knocking anything over. He and Andrew went back to the study and sat on the couch.

Jason flipped through the notebook. It had belonged to Jacob Wilmer. It contained abstract thoughts and doodles, with Jacob's brother James being the victim of Jacob's hangman drawings. Jason flipped a few more pages and then Andrew grabbed the notebook out of Jason's hand. He was looking at a page with a date written on it and the words "Orlando. Send Simon."

"That's a day before my birthday," Jason said. "My eighth birthday. That's when..." He stopped talking.

Suddenly everything came together in Jason's head. Maisie had told him that Tomlinson was incapable of killing Antonio. She was so sure of Tomlinson's innocence, that it had rattled Jason's faith in what he'd believed to be true all his life. But now, looking at the note written in Jacob's hand, it became clear that Wilmer had sent Simon to Orlando to kill his father.

"Geez, I never would have thought that Simon...I didn't even know he worked for my father before we came down here. He never said a word," Andrew said.

"He killed my dad. Wilmer killed my dad." Jason kept shaking his head.

"Why would he kill your dad?" Andrew asked, and then returned his attention to the notebook. He flipped through a few more pages but found nothing else of interest in it. "Really, why would Wilmer kill your dad?"

"You really don't know anything, do you?" Jason said shaking his head.

For the next two hours, Jason recounted the story of his family, George Ranier, Tomlinson, Maisie, the dogs, and the children living in the biosphere and St. Thomas. When Jason finished, Andrew was sitting on the edge of the couch, rocking back and forth.

"But Jason, if Matthew Wilmer passed on making the drug, why would Jacob kill Antonio? It just doesn't make sense."

"Maybe because the greedy son of a bitch decided to make it after all once old Matthew died. My dad was helping people. Maybe word was getting around. Maybe another company was getting ready to buy it from him and Tomlinson. I bet that would have pissed off Wilmer."

Andrew stopped rocking and sat back on the couch. He sighed deeply. He held the notebook in his hand. He flipped through it one more time, and then stood up.

"Come on Jay, I've gotta show you something." Andrew walked out the door and Jason quickly followed him.

*****

Andrew led Jason to Jacob's bedroom. He walked through the bathroom to a door that Jason hadn't seen before. Andrew opened the door and beckoned Jason to come inside. Jason was just about to enter when he looked up and stopped dead in his tracks.

It was a woman's frilly bedroom. From top to bottom, it was filled with small boxes of varying shapes and sizes. There were two paths in the carpet; one leading to the bed from the doorway and one leading from the bed to the bathroom.

The walls were covered with rows and rows of shelves. And on the shelves were 12" fashion dolls perched on stands. There were hundreds of them. They were all naked and they all had one defining feature – their hair was permed into wild, curly halos.

Some of the dolls had corkscrew curls, other waves, and others had frizzy tresses. Jason just kept staring at the dolls. He'd never seen so many. The boxes were also filled with dolls, but they were new and hadn't been taken out and curled yet. Jason turned to Andrew with wide eyes.

"How did you know about this?" he asked Andrew.

"Because I set them up. They were my mother's."

Chapter 70

Jason turned around and walked back to the library. Andrew closed the bedroom door and joined him. They replaced the spores and closed the safe door. They closed up the library and then the study. As they were walking through the living room, Jason began to talk.

"They don't know who you are, do they?" Jason asked Andrew.

"Nah, they don't. It wasn't on purpose, it was just easier, you know. My dad wasn't that popular and they would've treated me differently if they knew." Andrew paused to collect his thoughts. "I came down here from Jersey and worked in Tampa setting up the servers and connecting everything. My dad wasn't thrilled that I wasn't that interested in running the family business, but he let me run the IT department. I worked for him since I graduated from college. I wanted to transfer down here, but my mother....." Every time Andrew thought of his mother, he would get a catch in his throat.

"She...wasn't well. She had good days and bad days. The dolls...kept her happy. It got to a point where my dad had to make a decision about hiding her somewhere, to save her from embarrassment. She had lots of friends and they were always calling, asking her to come to this event or that luncheon. We didn't know what to do and then one day I got the idea to build this place, a place where she would be safe. He made up a story about a nuclear holocaust and how he would have to take her underground. This whole place was for her."

Andrew and Jason were sitting in the comfortable overstuffed chairs in the living room. They were just like the ones in Andrew's New Jersey home.

"As long as I was nearby, her good days went on longer. Sometimes, when I feel really bad, I come in here and think about her being in her bedroom. It makes it a little easier. Before I left Jersey, she gave me...." Andrew's eyes grew wide. "She gave me a box to bring down here. I never got around to emptying it. It's in the basement."

Andrew got up and ran to the kitchen. He pulled open the floor door and went down the steps. When he couldn't find any room in her bedroom, he'd brought the box down here. Andrew spied the big, cardboard box pushed into the back of the basement.

He had transported the box in the back of his car from Jersey to Florida. His mother, Emily, hadn't wanted Jacob to know what was in it, so Andrew had assumed it was more dolls. Jason was behind him when he got to the box. Andrew opened it.

"Are we taking it upstairs?" Jason asked.

"Yeah, the light's better up there."

Andrew picked up the box and carried it to the stairs. Jason went up first. Andrew lifted the box and handed it to Jason, who carried it to the dining area where there was a big empty table.

Andrew opened the box and poured the contents out. Jason sat at one end of the table and Andrew at the other. They began to sort through all the pictures and bits of paper that the box contained.

Andrew's mother had written thousands of tiny notes. They were all just thrown into the box with no rhyme or reason. It would take days to sort through them. Jason began looking at the pictures. He found one of a purple baby.

"Who's this?" he asked Andrew and held it up.

"I have no clue. Does it have a name on the back?"

Jason turned it over and read, "Andrew, 1972." Jason's eyes lit up. "You're just like me, Andrew. You would have lived anyway."

Andrew grabbed the picture out of Jason's hand. The baby in the picture was tiny. It was definitely a newborn. You could only see the infant's head. The rest was wrapped in a blanket, but the face of the infant was purple. Andrew thought of the tubes in Jacob's safe. He'd always counted himself so lucky he'd been inside the biosphere. The fact that it didn't matter pissed him off. Why hadn't she told him?

"He must have given that stuff to my mother." Andrew had never seen this picture before. His mother must have hidden it for years.

Jason continued to look through the pictures. He was looking on the backs of them now and found one of James Wilmer. He was standing in front of what looked like a vineyard. He had his arm around a young man and looked exceedingly happy. The back of the photo indicated that the young man was named Alfredo.

"Was your uncle gay?" Jason asked.

"I don't know. We never talked about him."

"Well, your mother sure did." Jason held up an album filled with pictures of James and his life in Italy. There were letters and a label from his wine. In all the pictures, James looked so happy. He was pictured with other young men, but Alfredo seemed to be in the most pictures.

"He must have sent them to her," Andrew said. "I never knew they corresponded."

Jason kept digging through the papers while Andrew got to know his uncle through the photos and letters in the album. James was a prolific writer who loved to describe Italy in detail. As Andrew went through the letters, he saw something and looked at Jason.

"What was your father's name again?" he asked Jason.

"Antonio Russo," Jason replied.

"He's mentioned in my uncle's letters. He gave him money to go to Brazil."

"I remember reading that in my dad's notebook." Jason and Andrew looked at each other. "Do you think that's how your dad found out about him?"

"Keep looking. Maybe she says something somewhere," Andrew said and continued to read the letters.

In the back of the album was a letter from an attorney in Italy. It had been written in English. It was sent to Emily with a copy of James' will.

In his will, James had left his apartment in Florence to Andrew, and his vineyard to Emily with a codicil stating that Alfredo could live there until his death. There was no mention of Jacob. Andrew was also to inherit James' fortune. James had died in 2001 and Andrew had never been told. His anger was beginning to boil over.

"No one ever told me anything. Not a damn thing. Why didn't she tell me?"

"Dude, moms are different," was all Jason would say.

"Yeah, and mine was crazy to boot. You find anything else in there?" Andrew asked, pointing to the pile on the table.

"Your mom must have named every doll." Jason was patiently going through a stack of index cards. "They all had birthdays, too."

"I'm sorry, Jason." Jason looked up. "For what he did," Andrew said.

"We still don't know for absolutely sure he did it. But thanks."

They spent another hour going through the papers. Christie came in and found them there. Andrew smiled at her. He asked Jason to leave so he could speak with Christie.

Andrew asked Christie to sit down. He recounted the story of his life to her and apologized for never coming clean with her about his true identity. When he was done, he got up from the table.

"Where are you going?" she asked him.

"I'm leaving. I thought you might want to think about things."

Andrew backed away from the table and Christie jumped up from her seat. She threw her arms around his neck and pulled him close.

"All that time looking at the ocean, all I could think about was how much I missed you. I need you, Andrew. I won't make it without you. You're my rock, and I'll never let you go." She looked into Andrew's eyes and began to cry. "Do you really think I give a damn who your father was?"

Andrew could feel the tears coming and tried his best to hold them back. The only person who'd ever said she needed him was his mother. Hearing Christie say it was like a dream come true.

The tears were now rolling down his cheeks, too, and they both began to laugh. Christie always felt guilty when she laughed, like somehow she should never enjoy another thing after what she had done to Gerald. Andrew saw the look on her face, the look she'd worn for days after she'd killed Gerald. He took her face in his hands and looked into her eyes.

"It's gonna be okay, Christie. I love you."

He kissed her so gently that she melted even further into his arms. She hadn't felt this safe since Neil died.

"I do have to tell you something, though. Something I just found out," he said. "My mother took that purple stuff before I was born." He watched for her reaction.

"Well, that just means you'll probably outlive me, so it's okay."

They stood in the dining room holding each other for a long time. Then Christie took Andrew's hand and led him to the little bedroom off the kitchen she'd been sleeping in and closed the door.

PART FIVE

JACOB WILMER

But the Children Survived

Chapter 71

1960

Matthew Wilmer never coddled his boys. Every summer they attended a summer camp in upstate New York where his boys could mingle with less affluent children. There was a camp on each side of the river; a girl's camp and a boy's camp. During the day, the camps shared facilities allowing the girls and boys to socialize.

It was Jacob Wilmer's fourteenth year and he was plagued by a hormonal onslaught that was making his life a living hell. He'd begged his father to let him stay home that year, to work in the warehouse, but John Wilmer told his son that he was still too young and wouldn't be covered by the insurance. So Jacob and his twelve-year-old brother James were packed into the family's limousine and driven to camp one balmy morning in June.

Jacob hated going to camp. The rustic cabins were communal, and the bunk beds were hard. There was no privacy, and his brother James was always with him. Before they got to camp, Jacob had squeezed James arm hard and told him to stay away from him.

James knew better than to argue with his brother. Jacob had a mean streak, and James was often the object of Jacob's fury. When they got to their assigned cabin, James took the bunk farthest away from Jacob's.

Jacob tried to keep to himself as much as possible. The river was a quarter of a mile from the campsite. Jacob would go there before they blew reveille so he could have some time alone. He would glance at the girl's camp across the river. Thinking of all those budding breasts and bathing suits caused Jacob no end of grief.

When the girls rowed across the river for shared activities, Jacob would plunge himself into the cold water to avoid embarrassment. He had no control over himself, so the cold water was the only way to deal with his automatic erections.

There were huge rocks that stretched across the river, forming a ridge that went all the way to the other side. Some of the rocks were submerged while others rose up high, a temptation few young boys could resist. Every year, one of the younger ones would fall between the rocks. Fortunately, they were small enough to slip through and come out under the rocks. They could then wade back to the river bank with nothing but their egos bruised.

The counselors warned against climbing those rocks. They were covered in moss and slippery as hell, and a bigger child could easily be wedged between the rocks underwater, unable to get up or out. There was a drowning 20 years ago; precautions had been taken and new rules applied. However, small boys seldom obeyed the rules when there were rocks to climb, and some still tried walking across the river.

One morning Jacob came to the river just before dawn. He saw a girl standing on the first rock. The early morning sun reflected off the water, causing her auburn hair to shine like red-gold flames surrounding her head. Jacob stood mesmerized by the image.

He tried to think of something to say, but his brain had turned to mush. She was kicking her leg out in front of her as though she were dancing on the rocks. She hadn't noticed Jacob yet. As he approached her, she turned to get off the rock and Jacob could see her face.

It was the most beautiful face he had ever seen. His body reacted immediately. The girl stood between him and the cool water. She smiled at him. He turned around, desperately trying to hide his growing arousal. The girl walked over to him.

"I'm out of your way now," she said.

Jacob closed his eyes and wished he were dead. He began to walk sideways, trying to avoid turning around. When he thought he was past her, he turned toward the water and ran in. The mountain water was really cold, and soon he was able to walk back onto the sand.

The girl looked at him with a sly expression. Jacob noticed her eyes. They were bright green. He'd never seen anyone with eyes that color. She was sitting on the beach with her arms around her knees.

"Hello," she said.

"Hi," Jacob replied.

"You're out here early," the girl said.

"I like to be alone," he said, still trying to hide his embarrassment.

"My name is Ellie," the girl said.

Jacob looked down at her. She patted the place next to her and Jacob sat down.

"Your lips are trembling and blue. That water's cold," she said.

"Yeah, it usually is." Jacob wished he could think of something smart to say.

"I've seen you here before," Ellie said. "You're a Wilmer, aren't you?"

"Yes, Jacob Wilmer," he replied.

"My dad works for your dad. His name is George Ranier."

Jacob knew George Ranier. When the man came to town, he would be invited to the Wilmer dinner parties, and he usually ended up drunk and passed out on the living room sofa. He couldn't believe this lovely girl was Ranier's daughter.

"Do you live in New Mexico?" Jacob asked Ellie.

"No, we live in New Jersey with my aunt and uncle."

Jacob was happy she lived close to him. That meant he might see her again when camp was over. He was already falling in love with her.

"It looks like the others are arriving," Ellie said. "Maybe I'll see you tomorrow."

She stood up and walked away toward a group of girls gathering near the sailboats. Jacob watched her, noting everything about her body. He would definitely be here tomorrow before reveille.

Jacob and Ellie met every day at sunrise. They would talk about what they wanted to do and where they would go to college. Ellie was sixteen and planned to go to New York to work for a television station. She wanted to be a TV reporter. She was going to major in journalism in college, and was getting excited about graduating from high school next year.

Jacob told her he would be working for his father someday and taking over the company when he was old enough. After a few meetings, Ellie let Jacob hold her hand.

"How old are you, Jake?" she asked him one morning while they were sitting on the beach. No one had ever called him Jake before and he liked it.

"Fourteen," he said.

"You look older than fourteen," she said. "I thought you were seventeen."

Jacob's heart beat faster. She thought he looked older!

"I guess it doesn't matter," she said. "At least while we're here. Nobody knows we see each other anyway."

Jacob wasn't sure what she meant by that. He loved Ellie, and he believed she loved him too, although they hadn't kissed yet.

387

"You're too young for me, Jake," she said. "But I like you, so while we're here, we can see each other."

Oh, Jacob thought, that's what she meant.

He felt a little tug at his heart. Suddenly he felt sad. Maybe if he kissed her now, she would change her mind and know that he was old enough for her. He put his arm around her and tried to plant a kiss on her lips. She moved a little, and he ended up kissing half her lips and her cheek. Ellie burst out laughing.

"I'm sorry, Jake," she said, still laughing. "I wasn't expecting that."

Jacob started to get up, and Ellie grabbed his arm. She pulled him back down to his knees, put her arms around his neck, and kissed him on the lips. The kiss lasted a long time. Jacob really needed to get to the water. Ellie pulled away from him and looked into his eyes.

"That's how you kiss a girl, Jake," she said.

*****

During one of their meetings, Ellie began to talk about her plans for the future. Jacob loved to hear her talk about all the things she wanted to do.

"I'll travel as a reporter. I'll go to exotic places, and meet all kinds of people. It's going to be an adventure, Jake!"

Her enthusiasm was contagious. Jacob could see himself traveling with her to all those foreign places.

"Can I go with you?" he asked her.

"When you graduate from college," she said smiling. "You'll be old enough then."

Ellie was a risk-taker. She wanted to walk across the rocks to the other side of the river. Jacob would get nervous when she jumped from the first rock to the second one, but she wouldn't listen to him when he asked her to get down.

"Scaredy cat! There's nothing to be afraid of. The rocks are flat on top," she would say.

She would walk over the first rock and jump to the second. Jacob would always get a catch in his throat when she would leap into the air.

"There's moss on them," he'd yell. She'd just laugh at him. "Please don't go any farther, Ellie."

He would feel panic rising in his chest. The rocks were high, and someone had died walking over them. Eventually she would take pity on Jacob and turn around. When she was back on dry land, she would tweak his nose and take his hand. It made him feel like a child when she did that, but he was so happy she was off the rocks that he'd always forgive her.

The summer passed quickly that year. James rarely saw his brother. He would wake up to find Jacob's bed empty, and wonder where his brother went every morning. One night before he went to sleep, James decided to get up before Jacob and wait outside the cabin so he could follow him. In order to wake up early enough, James drank several glasses of water. It worked like a charm.

Around five a.m., James woke up with a full bladder and jumped out of bed. He changed into his jeans and tee-shirt before heading outside. He relieved himself by a tree, and stood against the side of the cabin waiting for Jacob to come out.

James waited for about half an hour. He could hear Jacob getting out of bed and putting his clothes on. James peeked around the corner and saw Jacob leave the cabin, heading towards the river. He let Jacob get far enough ahead of him so he could follow undetected.

When James reached the river, he found a place behind some trees where he could hide and still see Jacob. He knelt down and watched his brother greet a tall redhead. She was pretty, but too old for James. He wasn't that interested in girls, anyway.

He could only see the back of Jacob's body, but his body language told James that Jacob was feeling shy. James tried to think of some way to use this against his brother. But how could he pay back Jacob without getting beaten up?

As James watched, Jacob and the girl sat on the beach and talked. The girl laughed a lot, and when Jacob turned his head, James could see him smiling. Jacob didn't look mean. James wished he knew what the girl was saying so he could say the same thing to Jacob. Maybe then he wouldn't be so mean to James.

The girl put her head on Jacob's shoulder, and then she kissed him. James eyes grew wide. His brother had a girlfriend! Someone actually liked Jacob!

The girl stood up and walked towards the rocks. Jacob ran after her, and took her arm. She turned towards Jacob, and pushed his arm away. She was yelling at Jacob, but James couldn't hear what she was saying. She kept walking to the rocks and when she got there, she climbed up on the first one.

Jacob stood there balling his hands into fists and hitting himself. James could tell Jacob was getting mad, but he wondered why. The girl seemed okay up on the rock. She was old enough to do what she wanted to.

People began to appear on the beach. A counselor came over to Jacob and yelled at the girl. She got down off the rock and walked up the beach, away from Jacob and the counselor. After they talked for a few minutes, Jacob walked up the beach towards the campsite, passing within a few feet of where James was hiding. James waited a few minutes before joining his brother in the canteen for breakfast.

James saw Jacob sitting by himself at the end of one of the long tables in the canteen. He avoided looking at him. James sat at a table with some of his cabin mates. He knew he could never ask Jacob about the girl. He wanted to find out her name though, so if he saw her today, he would ask her. He'd have to be sure Jacob didn't see him talking to her. Otherwise, Jacob would beat him up.

*****

Two weeks before the end of the season, Jacob met Ellie by the river. The sun was full up, and she was already on the rock. Jacob was sick of arguing with her, so he waded into the river and began to swim. He thought if he were in the water, he could save her if she fell, or maybe she would jump off the rock and join him.

Ellie was feeling particularly daring that day as she jumped onto the third big rock. She slipped just a little and caught herself. Jacob swam closer to the rocks.

"Ellie, stop!" he yelled.

She waved her hand at him and inched closer to the fourth rock. The gap between the third and fourth rock was larger than the others. This was the gap that took the life of the camper 20 years ago. Ellie knew the story. She checked her footing, and she was sure she had a firm grip.

The distance between the rocks was about the same as the long jump she'd easily made during her track finals earlier that year, but she wouldn't have a running start here. Still, Ellie's ego wouldn't let her back down. She wanted to make it across.

"I know what you're thinking, Ellie," Jacob yelled, "but it's too far. Don't do it!"

Ellie pretended not to hear him. She looked at the rock ahead of her and measured the distance with her eyes. She just knew she could make it. She stepped back and propelled herself off the rock, making it to the next rock. The moss was slippery though and she lost her footing, falling feet first into the crevice.

James, who'd been watching behind the trees, ran to find a counselor. Jacob was screaming Ellie's name. She didn't yell back. He went under the rocks where he could see her legs kicking. He tried to crawl under them to grab her legs, but she was wedged in tightly. Jacob had to surface to grab some air, and when he went back down to her, her legs weren't moving.

Several counselors came running. One waded into the river. He pulled Jacob out of his way and went under the water. He could see Ellie's legs wedged underneath, but he couldn't pull her out.

Another counselor climbed on the rocks and jumped over them until he was on the third rock looking down at Ellie. He could see her eyes staring back at him. He hung over as far as he could, but he couldn't reach her without falling in himself.

Ellie had drowned within minutes of falling in. It took a man hanging from a helicopter flying overhead while another pushed her from underneath to finally pull her body out of the crevice.

*****

Jacob stayed in his cabin the rest of that week and the next. James would check on him, but Jacob wouldn't look at him. When they went home, Jacob went to his room and stayed there until school started.

When school began, he would come home and go to his room, coming out only for meals. It took a year for Jacob to finally come to terms with Ellie's death, but he never really got over it.

Ellie was the first girl he'd ever cared for, the only person he'd allow to call him Jake, and the first person he'd ever allowed himself to love with his whole heart. He swore he would never make that mistake again.

391

Chapter 72

Rutgers College, New Brunswick, New Jersey

In 1964, Jacob Wilmer saw Emily O'Connell sitting on the other side of the university's gymnasium. The Homecoming dance was in full swing, and Emily was surrounded by several young men. She smiled, tilted her head back and laughed at something one of the boys said. Her long, auburn hair softly caressed her shoulders.

Jacob's heart began to ache for another auburn-haired beauty he'd lost years before. Emily even looked like Ellie. Jacob slowly made his way across the gym.

Emily saw Jacob coming towards her. She'd set her cap for the Wilmer heir at the beginning of her freshman year at Douglass College. She'd made it her business to know his course schedule. She would always manage to show up just as he was leaving his classes, if her scheduled allowed it. Till now, however, Jacob hadn't noticed her. But tonight, her hair loose and her shoulders bare, she reminded him of his long ago first love.

Jacob stood in front of Emily and asked her to dance. She thought she might decline, thinking he would be more interested if she were unavailable. But Emily wanted to dance with Jacob, so she threw caution to the wind and accepted. As they moved around the floor, Jacob noticed Emily's eyes. They were green, emerald green.

Jacob found Emily's charms appealing. They dated throughout their four years in college, and married a week after graduation. While Emily never aroused a great passion in Jacob, she served him well by always looking beautiful on his arm. In time, his feelings for her grew.

Jacob loved Emily as one loves a dear friend. She gave him a son, an heir to the Wilmer fortune, and fulfilled her societal responsibilities at luncheons and charitable functions throughout Monmouth County, New Jersey. For Jacob Wilmer, life was good.

*****

Rumson, New Jersey, 1980

Andrew Wilmer watched as his mother feverishly worked the rollers into the doll's hair. She chattered away, trying to draw him into her world. Andrew had no interest in the dolls whatsoever, but he loved to see his mother so happy. He loved her more than anyone in the world. He rarely saw his cold and distant father.

Every morning Emily would bring him down the cellar stairs and over to the little chair she'd provided just for him. After he was seated, she would turn on the hot plate. Their maid, Ethel, always left a pot of water on the hot plate. After she turned it on, Emily would pick out a doll.

Tomorrow he would turn eight and Andrew had told his mother he no longer wanted to come with her to the cellar. He had friends now, and he wanted to join the Pee Wee Football team. Emily had pouted, but she understood. This would be their last day together in her fashion doll beauty parlor.

Andrew's favorite moment came when his mother would lower the doll's head into the pot of boiled water. He wished just once it would melt into a plastic blob. Maybe if it did, she would finally stop doing this.

When Emily had turned out the last doll, she held it up and smiled.

"Isn't she lovely, Andrew?" she asked.

Andrew nodded. She put the doll on a stand, and found an empty spot in the cellar to display her. Then she turned to Andrew with tears in her eyes.

"I will miss our time together," she said. Andrew was a kind-hearted boy. He got up from his chair and put his arms around his mother. She was just a head taller than he.

"Mom, it's gonna be alright," he said. Emily nodded, and then they walked up the cellar stairs to the kitchen.

Andrew did join the Pee Wee Football team. On Saturdays, their butler John would drive him to the games and watch on the sidelines. He even managed a cheer now and then. When the game was over, he would drive Andrew home.

Andrew would run through the front door and down the cellar steps to Emily. He would tell her about the game and she would feign interest. Seeing the excitement on her son's face touched Emily's heart.

As Andrew got older, he would visit his friends after games and spend less and less time at home. Emily missed seeing him, and spent more and more time alone in the cellar. Her doll collection grew to enormous proportions, but Ethel and John were the only ones who knew.

*****

Rumson, New Jersey, 2001

Jacob Wilmer had received a report from Simon, his "investigator," saying that his brother James had been writing to Emily ever since he'd left the United States. Jacob hadn't been aware of their correspondence. He despised his brother for turning his back on his family and his country. James had been living in Italy for years. Before her death, he had written to their mother, but never visited.

Jacob wasn't aware of any relationship between Emily and James. He felt as though his wife had betrayed him and he couldn't shake the feeling. The one person he cared for besides his son Andrew was his wife Emily. He just couldn't understand why she'd kept this from him.

Jacob called Ethel into his study. Ethel had been Emily's maid for over thirty years. She was a soft-spoken African-American woman who always felt ill at ease in front of Jacob. Being called to see him in his study was extremely nerve-racking for her. He had rarely spoken to her, and she couldn't imagine what she had done to prompt this summons. When she knocked on the study door, Jacob told her to come in. She opened the door and kept her eyes on the ground.

"Come in, Ethel. I have to ask you something. Please, close the door," Jacob said. He watched Ethel slowly approach the desk, keeping her eyes on the floor. "Everything is fine, Ethel, you haven't done anything wrong."

Ethel was taken aback by Jacob's soft, reassuring voice. He was usually ranting at the servants. She looked up at him and tried to smile.

"Ethel, I just wanted to ask you where Mrs. Wilmer is today." Jacob fixed his snakelike eyes on Ethel.

"She's at a luncheon, sir," Ethel said softly.

"How long will she be gone?" he asked.

"She said she'd be back around four o'clock." Ethel hoped that was all he wanted to know. She was trying hard not to shake in front of him.

"Very well, thank you, Ethel. You may go."

Jacob always had trouble smiling. It was a reluctant effort he reserved for Emily and Andrew. He was trying to smile now, but only one end of his mouth went up. The other side seemed set in stone. Ethel turned and left the room, closing the door behind her.

Jacob waited a few minutes and then exited the study. He climbed the stairs to the second floor and looked around to see if anyone was watching before he entered Emily's bedroom. He closed the door behind him and locked it, just in case.

He began searching the room by going through Emily's dressing table drawers and then her dresser. He searched her nightstands, her desk, and her hope chest. Finally, he found a hat box on the top shelf of her closet and took it down. He opened it and found what he was looking for.

The box contained pictures of James with a man identified on the back as Alfredo. They were standing in front of a vineyard. There were letters Emily had tied with a ribbon. Jacob sat at her desk, slipped the ribbon off and began to read.

The letters were a chronicle of James' life since he'd left the family in the 1970s. The first letters were about James' decision to leave the family and his reasons for doing so. Jacob read them in disgust. He hadn't known his brother was a homosexual. He was sure his parents never knew either.

It's just as well he'd buried himself in the Italian countryside, thought Jacob.

There was a letter written in the late 1980s regarding a young student named Russo whom James had sponsored. He'd sent Antonio to Brazil to meet a woman named Margaret DeMorte. Jacob stopped reading. The name DeMorte triggered memories of his father's obsession with biotechnological weaponry.

Jacob had had a hell of a time with his father when the government turned down Wilmer's prototype. Matthew Wilmer had retired after that and was never quite the same. That weapon had been his dream, and that woman's plants had almost made it possible. Why would James be sending this Russo to see her? And why was Russo's name so familiar?

Jacob had always questioned James' motives. He believed James was determined to bring down the Wilmer family. He continued to read, hoping James would elaborate on his gift to Russo.

James had become a professor at the University of Florence, where he taught English Literature. He and Alfredo lived on a vineyard he purchased sometime in the early 80s which was just starting to produce a decent wine. He'd sent a label to Emily. Then, just when Jacob had given up on seeing Russo's name again, it appeared in a letter James had sent eight years ago.

Antonio's father lived in Florence and was acquainted with James. James bought his bread at Guido's bakery and would often ask after Antonio. It seemed Antonio had discovered a supplement that would prevent miscarriage in certain women. He'd created it using the plants he'd gotten from Margaret DeMorte. Guido had told James this because he'd been thanking James yet again for helping his boy.

Jacob knew exactly what James was referring to, the purple potion of Helmut March. He'd used it himself when Emily was pregnant with Andrew. She'd had a miscarriage with their first baby.

Jacob's father had had a safe full of the purple potion at his beach house in Mantoloking. His father had it sent from New Mexico right after Helmut March's promotion to partner. When Jacob told him about Emily's situation, Matthew Wilmer had given Jacob a tube of the spores and told him how to use it.

Jacob took some himself just to test it. He'd been having a little trouble in the bedroom and the purple potion enabled him to plant the seed necessary to create Andrew. He'd given Emily the rest of it when they found out she was indeed pregnant. His father had told him to arrange a home birth and without asking why, he did. When Andrew emerged with skin the color of a lavender sky, he understood why.

Emily was besotted with Andrew and didn't seem to mind his color, but Jacob was very disturbed. He was relieved when, three days later, the color faded away. But he never forgot his son's little purple face.

There was a picture of Andrew with the purple face in the hat box. He didn't know Emily had photographed him that way. It was a Polaroid that one of the servants must have taken. He put it in his suit pocket. Then, thinking Emily might miss it, he put it back.

When Matthew Wilmer died, they'd closed up the beach house. Jacob had the purple spores transferred to his house. He'd built a special temperature-controlled safe to store them in. He mixed a dose of the purple potion whenever he visited his mistress in Manhattan.

Jacob thought about Russo using the same potion to actually treat women. Russo called it a supplement. But where was Russo? James' letter didn't mention where he was living. Was he treating women in Italy?

Jacob decided to have Simon look into his whereabouts and find out just how much money he was making on this purple "supplement." He'd always thought his father had misjudged the usefulness of Helmut's potion. Matthew Wilmer had always maintained that it would nullify his other patented drugs. Matthew was making too much money on those drugs and didn't want to harm his bottom line. The purple potion, he said, was just too damn good. Now Russo was selling the stuff, Wilmer's purple potion, and Jacob didn't like anybody stepping on his toes.

There was a copy of James' will in the box. The will specified that Andrew was to inherit James' Florence apartment and his money. Emily was to have the vineyard but must allow Alfredo to live there for the rest of his life, and Alfredo would keep any monies made from the sale of the wine the vineyard produced. When James sent the will, he'd enclosed a picture of himself and Alfredo. There was also a letter. The letter was dated some months before James' death.

When he finished reading, Jacob carefully placed the items back into the hat box and replaced it on the top shelf of Emily's closet. He looked at his watch. Three o'clock. He opened the door and looked around. He didn't see anyone lurking about so he went down the stairs and into his study unnoticed. When he got to his desk, he picked up the phone and telephoned Simon.

Chapter 73

Simon found Russo fairly quickly. He called in some favors from an old pal of his who worked as a private detective. The guy found Russo working for Wilmer and March Pharmaceuticals.

Simon laughed to himself when he realized that the man had been an employee of Jacob's all along. That made his sales of the purple potion even more interesting. The little *goomba* had big balls to be selling the boss's own product right under his nose. How did he think he was gonna get away with it?

Simon asked a lawyer who'd gotten him out of a spot of trouble recently to find out if Russo had ever applied for a patent on the Mortevida. The lawyer told him Russo had and had been given one. He had named the plant the Dono di Russo.

Simon then asked if Wilmer's had ever applied for a patent and the lawyer came up empty. The old man had never patented the plant. What an idiot. What had he planned to do if the government had contracted the weapon? He would have had a real mess on his hands then. Without proof of ownership, Uncle Sam would have snatched it right out of old Matthew's hands.

When Simon told Jacob this, Jacob was livid. His respect for his father plummeted. How could he make such an error in judgment? He had nothing to use against Russo. Simon then told him that Russo was an employee of Wilmer and March. Jacob decided Russo would have to be fired. He was making a fool out of Jacob and nobody got away with that.

"That may cause problems," Simon said.

"How?" Jacob asked.

"He could go public, you know, saying things like Wilmer's could have had it but they blew it. Make the whole company look bad, like your judgment sucks. The board wouldn't like that, Jake."

Jacob hated it when Simon called him Jake. Only one person had been allowed to call him that. Simon knew how much he hated it and got a kick out of pissing Jacob off.

Jacob thought about what Simon was saying. Since he'd taken over the company, he'd been struggling to keep full control. He was getting older now, and Andrew had no interest in taking over. Andrew only wanted to work with his damn computers. This could work against Jacob in a big way. Russo could gain publicity for his purple potion and make millions.

"Maybe we could blow the FDA whistle on him. If he 'd put the stuff through trials, we would have heard about it."

"He and some doctor are selling it as a supplement. No FDA required." Simon sat looking at Jacob. Simon was a hard read. He never gave anything away. Jacob hated that about him.

"Where is he right now?"

"Tampa," Simon answered.

"Keep digging and see what else you can find."

Simon flew to Tampa and followed Russo around for a few days, reporting his comings and goings. He told Jacob about the doctor Russo was doing business with, some guy named Tomlinson, and how it seemed they'd had a falling out.

Simon had hired a woman to make an appointment with the doctor. He told her to try to find out how many women he'd treated with the purple potion. She found out Tomlinson had treated over 300 women. She also found out that the treatment cost $10,000 and that the doctor called the purple potion Fetura.

Simon used his detective buddy again to check into Russo's bank accounts and credit cards. The guy found out Russo was going to be staying at a resort in Orlando in a few days.

When Jacob did the math, he was beside himself with rage. That little nobody had hauled in over $300,000 of Jacob's money. Simon asked Jacob if he wanted Russo taken care of.

Jacob understood what Simon was asking, but he needed more time to think. He'd never ordered a hit on anyone. He couldn't take it lightly. As he sat at his desk, he took out a little notebook he wrote in to clear his head. Sometimes he drew in it, sometimes he would jot down ideas for new drugs, etc.

He opened it to a blank page and wrote the date of the first day Russo would be in Orlando. Under it he wrote, "Orlando. Send Simon." He knew what he was writing. Seeing it in black and white made him feel both powerful and nauseated. Simon was right though. Russo could ruin Matthew Wilmer's reputation and by doing so ruin Jacob's, too. He was too old to rebuild it. His brother James had done this. Jacob could see that now.

James had always been a thorn in his side. There was no reason for him to be born. Jacob should have been enough. Jacob hated James more now than when he was alive. He balled up his fists and banged the table repeatedly. His body shook violently from his desire to physically murder James with his bare hands. But James was dead. He had even taken that away from Jacob.

Jacob forced himself to breathe. He had to calm down. So, James had tried to get Jacob by giving Russo the plants. Well, Jacob would have the last laugh.

He picked up the phone and called Simon. He told him to go through Russo's house and get any plants that might be there. He also told him to look for any scientific research associated with the Dono di Russo. He didn't want Russo's family to keep the formula for Fetura. Simon said he would call when he'd taken care of things.

Simon booked a room in the Russos' resort. He followed them for a day. He sat behind them when they ate at a restaurant and overheard their plans for the next day. They were going to the water park.

The next day, Simon watched Antonio and his son come down the water slides. He waited for Russo to go to a bathroom, or some other location where he would be alone. After a while, he saw Russo's wife send him to the lockers.

As Russo was opening a locker, Simon came up behind him with a knife in his hand. He grabbed Russo and thrust the knife straight up through his ribs and into his heart. Then he let Russo go and walked on as though nothing had happened.

He had checked out of his room before going to the water park, so Simon drove straight to St. Petersburg. He broke into the Russo house and searched for the plants and the formula. He found neither. He caught a plane from Tampa to New Jersey after calling Jacob with the report.

Jacob hung up the phone and sat motionless behind his desk. He was responsible for the death of another human being and he didn't know quite how to handle it. He'd never been in a war, or had to defend himself. But even though he hated doing it, it gave him an instant feeling of relief. Russo would never hurt Wilmer and March.

Chapter 74

Emily Wilmer's mother had been a resident of the Blaine Residence in upstate New York for many years. She had been mentally ill for most of her adult life and had died while still a patient at Blaine's.

Emily had begun to show signs of the same mental illness when Andrew was a young boy. Andrew was the only one who could calm her down or keep her focused. As he grew older and made a life for himself, Emily had many bad days.

Jacob had taken her to Palm Beach to hide her from her constantly inquiring friends. He'd bought a home on the beach, and it seemed to help Emily. But there was one aspect of her illness that Jacob had a hard time dealing with.

Emily was a hoarder. Her illness took the form of hoarding one particular item - twelve-inch fashion dolls. At first she bought collector dolls that were issued once or twice a year. As her passion for them grew, so did her collection. In 2003, her son introduced her to the Internet, and she was able to order them online and have them delivered to her house.

Jacob had been unaware of his wife's fascination with the dolls until they began staying at Palm Beach for months at a time. Emily had to replicate her collection for Palm Beach.

In New Jersey, Jacob hadn't entered Emily's bedroom since 2001. He had no idea what it looked like now. When he accidentally opened the door of her Palm Beach bedroom looking for her, he was taken aback by what he saw.

From the floor to the ceiling, still in boxes, were stacks of dolls. The only empty spot in the room was the path from the bed to the bathroom and to the bedroom door. Jacob was afraid to confront her for fear of making her sick. She'd been doing so well at Palm Beach. He decided to just ignore her room as long as the dolls stayed in there. Emily seemed to need her secret, and Jacob needed her to be sane.

When they came back to New Jersey, he peeked into her bedroom and it looked just like the one in Palm Beach. He asked Ethel to come to his study again, and this time he asked her about the dolls.

He asked if she'd known about them and she said yes. He asked her how long her bedroom had been that way, and Ethel looked down at the floor.

"It's okay, Ethel. You're not in trouble."

"I know, sir, I just don't know how to tell you." Ethel looked up at Jacob. "I guess she started putting them in the bedroom when the basement got full."

Jacob's eyebrows rose. "The basement?"

"Yes, sir. She filled it up and had to put them somewhere else."

Jacob rose from his chair and walked to the kitchen with Ethel following close behind. As Jacob descended the steps into the basement, he couldn't believe the sight he beheld. From one end of his 4000-square-foot basement to the other were fashion dolls, lined up on stands, with wild big curls on their heads. In one corner, stacked to the ceiling, was a pile of dolls with hideous frizzed hair.

"When they don't come out good, she throws them over there." Ethel pointed to the pile. "And over there is where she does the perms."

She pointed to a small part of the basement where there was a comfortable chair with a small table. Ethel led Jacob over to the small opening. She showed him the little rollers Emily used to wrap the dolls' hair. She showed him the wrapping papers and styling gel. She then showed him the hot plate she boiled the water on.

"My God, it's a miracle she didn't burn the house down. How long has she been doing this?" Jacob was still in a state of shock.

"Since Andrew was little. She does it when she gets upset or sad. She sits here rolling up the hair, and she looks so happy. Sometimes I have to go out for the gel and papers. She runs out quick."

"Where is Mrs. Wilmer?" Jacob asked.

"She's at a charity auction today. She was good this morning. But sir, she's having fewer and fewer good days." Ethel was very concerned about Emily's mental state. "There was another delivery today, sir. There's no room in her bedroom. Where should we put them?"

"Have John take the boxes to the garage. We'll have to decide what to do with them later." Jacob looked at Ethel. She had a look of deep sympathy in her eyes. "Thank you for...helping Mrs. Wilmer, Ethel. I'm sure you understand that this...this news must never leave this house."

"It never has before, sir. I love Mrs. Wilmer and I would never hurt her. But if you take the boxes out it'll...she'll get bad," Ethel said.

Where had he been all the years Ethel had protected Emily?

"Where does she get all these dolls?"

"She orders them on the Internet," Ethel replied.

"How does she know about the Internet?"

"Andrew showed her. He thought it would cheer her up to look at stuff on there. She took to it real fast." Ethel was smiling at the thought of Emily on the Internet.

"But where is the computer?" Jacob couldn't understand how all this had been going on right under his nose.

"It's next to her bed, on the other side where you couldn't see. It's a laptop computer." Ethel was so tickled by Jacob's confusion that she had to keep herself from laughing out loud.

"Where is Andrew?" Jacob asked.

"He hasn't come home yet."

"When he does, send him in to see me."

"Yes, sir."

They reached the top of the steps and Jacob went to his study and sat behind his desk. He was completely flummoxed. For the first time in his life, he didn't know what to do.

Chapter 75

When Andrew came home, Jacob called him into the study. He told him to shut down the Internet in his house. He next told Andrew that he'd been trying to come up with some way of dealing with Emily's declining mental state. He told Andrew about the dolls and Andrew said he already knew.

He told Jacob that he'd been watching his mother curl the dolls' hair since he was a little boy. Jacob was floored that his son had never confided in him. Andrew said Jacob would've just gotten mad, and it did make his mother happy. Jacob asked Andrew what he thought they should do with his mother.

"You can't send her to Blaine's. She would go ballistic. We need somewhere safe." Andrew had been reading about biospheres on the Internet. He told his father that they could build something like that on the empty piece of property they had in Palm Harbor, Florida.

Jacob had forgotten about that property. He'd bought it on a whim, thinking it might be worth something one day. It was a huge piece of land surrounded by woods. It would be the perfect place to hide a facility like that. Andrew could computerize the place. Then Jacob said, "Why not make it a real biosphere and have a farm and animals?" They would tell Emily they were going down there to avoid a nuclear holocaust.

"She'd never agree to leave her family up here," Andrew said. Emily had a large extended family in New Jersey and New York. Jacob despised them all, but she enjoyed her family, and the thought of leaving them in a nuclear wasteland would guarantee her never going underground.

"We could build little houses, one for each of her useless relatives. We could invite them down to visit. We would need a dining hall of some sort. We could also have a library and a wing for scientific research. This could really be interesting, Andrew. It would work."

Andrew felt good that he had been able to please Jacob. It didn't happen very often.

Jacob hired Martin Prevost to design the biosphere. When the biosphere construction was completed, Andrew moved into it with a handful of electricians and plumbers. He set up the computers to run the satellite dish and all the locks and entrances in the facility.

When Christie Cramer arrived, Andrew remembered her from the New Jersey laboratories. He'd had a little crush on her, but she only had eyes for her fertilizer. When she was transferred to Florida, Andrew had thought of following her, but his mother's condition forbade it. Now, he might have a chance to get to know her.

Andrew set up the virtual room for his mother. He also set up her bedroom with the wall to wall dolls she'd requested he take with him in his car when he drove to Florida. She asked him to make sure he put them in her room.

The walls were full when he still had one large box to empty. He decided to leave it until she came down. He stored the box in the basement. The basement was huge and he had no idea what his father planned to put in there.

When the furniture arrived, Andrew set it up just like it was at home.

Jacob didn't tell Andrew everything he planned to do with the biosphere. The truth was, Jacob had been told he had cancer. He had started treating himself with the purple potion, and had divided what he had between Florida and New Jersey.

Jacob had Simon bring the spores down and supervise the installation of the wall safe to store them. Jacob had forgotten he stored his little notebook in the safe, a notebook full of ideas and doodles. When Simon packed the tubes up for transport, he threw the notebook in the box as well.

Jacob also had Simon supervise the installation of the supermarket-sized freezers in the basement and had them filled with food. He asked Simon not to tell Andrew. He didn't want Andrew to know that he planned to seal them all in the biosphere until he or Emily died.

Jacob knew Andrew would object to being held prisoner, but it was the only way Emily would be able to cope with her incarceration. Jacob believed that one day, Andrew would see the logic behind Jacob's actions and forgive him, maybe even thank him.

Jacob hired Christie Cramer and Gerald Todd because he knew they were in a vulnerable state and would most likely agree to his offer of research in the biosphere. He supplied them with everything they needed to make it look official.

He also employed a doctor recommended by a colleague. The doctor had been involved in a Medicare scandal and lost his license. He would be grateful for any employment, and Jacob needed a physician in case his cancer took a turn for the worst and he needed pain medication. He would have his New Jersey physician call his prescriptions down ahead of time and have Simon pick them up at the pharmacy.

Jacob then asked Simon to move into the biosphere and pose as a plumber supervising a young guy named Pat Luca, who'd been brought over from Tampa to live and work in the facility. Jacob told him he wanted Simon to be his eyes and ears until he could move in himself.

Calvin was a mechanic in Atlanta when Jacob Wilmer hired him. It was to be a temporary job, and Calvin needed the money. He had a friend working at the Tampa facility who recommended him to Jacob. He was to keep the trucks in tip top shape and help Christie with the field.

The last person he brought in was Jasper, an electrician from his Cranberry facility. Jasper supervised the installation of the wiring of the facility and the satellite dish that Jacob had acquired through a "friend" in Washington, D.C.

When he and Emily actually entered the biosphere, they would take any of their staff who wanted to go. They could also hire servants from the area. Ethel and John were getting older, so they agreed to accompany them to Florida and a warmer climate.

Simon reported that everything was in place. Jacob had given notice to the board to elect a new CEO as he was stepping down for reasons of health.

The week before Jacob and Emily were due to arrive, Andrew heard the alarm and ran to investigate what had set it off, only to find the hatchway leading out had been sealed shut. He had programmed the automatic shutdown in case of a nuclear disaster or poisonous attack as per his father's instructions. He thought the guy was getting a little nutty in his old age, but did it anyway. He was just as shocked as everyone else when the damned thing worked.

Epilogue

Andrew looked at himself in the mirror. The tuxedo was a little big, but it would do nicely. Christie had picked it up when she took the girls to find their dresses. It was black with satin lapels and a black tie. Andrew thought he looked pretty sharp.

He left Jason's bedroom and walked down the stairs to the first floor. The kitchen was empty. Most of the guests were out on the beach, waiting for the wedding to begin.

Andrew walked out onto the deck. He could see Pat and George, but didn't see his best man. Pat saw him and waved, and Andrew walked over to join them.

"Anybody seen Jason?" he asked.

"I think he's with Jenny," George replied. "You've picked a splendid day for a wedding, Andrew."

"Yeah, it couldn't be any nicer," Pat said.

"So, when are you leaving?" Andrew was looking at Pat's boat, anchored to the dock next door to Jason's house.

"Tomorrow morning. Jay says I can stay here tonight," Pat said.

"Well, I hope you find a woman, Pat." Andrew smiled.

"There have to be live women in Puerto Rico," Pat said. "I mean the stuff can't go over salt water, right?"

"That's what they tell us," George said. "I'm thinking of taking a trip to Martha's Vineyard myself. It's been years since I've been there. I have friends there, you know." George looked out at the ocean. "At least I have hope that they're still with us."

"I'll miss you guys," Andrew said. The three had been through a lot together.

"Well, I haven't decided definitely yet, Andrew. And I would come back," George said.

"What about you, Pat? You gonna bring your bride up here to meet us?" Andrew asked.

"Of course I would. You guys are my family now."

Mindy and Maria Elena ran past the men. They were dressed in their bridesmaid's dresses and looked like little princesses. Mindy wore a pastel pink sleeveless satin dress with a full skirt that almost reached her ankles. Maria Elena's dress was lavender with puffy sleeves and ruffles that went around and around her skirt. Baby Girl and Ricky were chasing them and barking.

"Hey, slow down," Andrew yelled. "Christie wants you to stay clean until the ceremony."

The girls slowed down and looked at Andrew. They giggled, and slowly walked to the large group of girls gathered around the buffet table.

"They're gonna get dirty," Andrew said. "Christie won't like it."

"Patrick, I believe it's time to start the music," George said, and Pat nodded as he walked to the deck.

Pat was in charge of the music. He'd found an electronics store close to the biosphere and picked out a massive sound system for use at the wedding. He'd given it to Jason in exchange for the boat. Jason had been giving him sailing lessons for several weeks now, and Pat felt confident he could handle the boat. He'd been cooped up too long, and he looked forward to being alone for a while.

Pat put the CD in the player and the music began. It was the Pachelbel Canon in D. Mindy and Maria Elena ran up to the deck, turned around, and then slowly walked towards the archway that had been placed near the water for the ceremony. The guests had gathered for the ceremony, and made a path for the girls. Baby Girl and Ricky followed them.

Jenny walked out onto the deck. She was wearing a sweet yellow strapless dress with a full skirt covered in crystals. She walked down the steps and over to the archway. Jason was standing next to Andrew wearing a tuxedo. Jenny thought he looked very handsome.

Then Christie appeared at the doorway. She had chosen a simple, straight ivory gown that hung loosely on her slender frame. She looked beautiful. Julius was waiting to escort her to her groom. She took his arm, and walked across the sand to join Andrew at the archway.

George had been chosen to officiate. He was taking his post very seriously. George wasn't a religious man, so he chose to read "An Apache Song."

"Now you will feel no rain,
for each of you will be a shelter to the other.
Now you will feel no cold,
for each of you will be warmth to the other.
Now there is no loneliness for you,
now there is no more loneliness.

408

Now you are two bodies,
but there is only one life before you.
Go now to your dwelling place,
to enter into your days together.
And may your days be good,
and long upon the earth."

The couple exchanged rings. Then with tears in his eyes, Andrew kissed his bride. Christie could barely contain her happiness. She jumped up and threw her arms around his neck, clinging to him with all her strength. Everyone cheered.

Katie rolled her eyes as Alyssa cried. Alyssa looked over at Austin, who had grown a foot taller and looked so cute.

Dani and Joe came up to the happy couple and hugged them. Dani was six months pregnant. The biosphere kids ran up to them and almost knocked them over. It took a while to get them to settle down, but when George brought out the wedding cake, they all ran to the buffet table leaving Andrew and Christie alone.

"I love you Christie. I always have and I always will." Andrew held her hand.

"I love you, too, Andrew."

Christie was teary and couldn't speak. She'd thought her life was over when Neil and Haley died. To be given this second chance was just too much for her. Andrew put his arms around her and held her while she cried into his shoulder.

Maria Elena walked slowly up to Andrew and Christie. Christie noticed her standing close by and put her arm out. Maria Elena put her arms around Christie and Andrew, and they put theirs around her. She was now living with them in the Wilmer residence. They were officially a family.

Mindy noticed Calvin standing by the side of Jason's house and ran over to him, giving him a big hug.

"Calvin, when did you get back?" she asked.

"Little lady, I'd like you to meet my children, Joshua and Aaliyah. "

The boy and girl were behind Calvin. They slowly walked around him and stared at Mindy. They'd been alone at their house when Calvin found them. They were hungry and scared. They'd buried their mother in the backyard, and their resentment towards Calvin was palpable. He'd left them alone and their mama had died.

Calvin had tried to talk with them as he drove them to Florida, but they were resistant. It would take time, lots of time, for them to come around. Calvin was learning to be patient.

Mindy took their hands and pulled them towards the buffet table.

"George made a cake. You've gotta see it," she said as she pulled them along.

The other kids came up to them. Soon Joshua and Aaliyah found some of the Atlanta kids and opened up. They even smiled. Calvin felt hopeful for the first time since leaving Atlanta that his children would be alright.

Julius and Maisie came over to greet Calvin. Julius asked about Atlanta, and Maisie commented on how beautiful his children were.

As the party broke up, the kids said their farewells to Pat. They all hugged him and told him to come back soon. Dani and Joe wished him a safe trip and Mindy said goodbye. Baby Girl followed them to the school buses.

Andrew and Christie were spending the night at the Carson's house. They hugged Pat and wished him well.

Julius and Maisie held hands as they walked to the school buses. They had taken to each other immediately and were now inseparable. They helped each other up the steps of the bus and sat in the first seat behind the driver. Julius liked to give Joe directions as he drove.

George was tired. Joe and Dani had taken the kids to the school for the night so George could help clean up Jason's beach. He had a bottle of wine he'd put aside for this evening, and he and Pat sat on the deck and drank a toast to pleasant journeys.

Jason drove Jenny back to St. Thomas and kissed her goodnight. He was going to be nineteen in a few weeks, and he was going to give Jenny a ring. They both knew how short life could be, and Jason didn't want to wait any longer. He knew he loved her and believed she felt the same way. As he kissed her goodnight, he was sure of it.

*****

People were starting to return to the United States. Planes were flying American citizens home for free, and the servicemen and women were returning in droves to reclaim their homeland. No one was prepared for what they found when they came home. The

410

landscape was covered with bones from sea to shining sea. It would take years to clean up from the disaster.

The people from the biosphere were connecting with the returnees little by little. With more adults available, the kids were finding homes and leaving the biosphere and St. Thomas.

As the school emptied, Joe and Dani were thinking of getting a house for their growing family. They could still run the school as a day school with Julius and Maisie's assistance.

Christie kept the field well-tended and hoped to get pregnant soon. Andrew spent his days searching for people on the satellite.

Jason had gone to Vinnie's greenhouse to find the Dono di Russo plants. They were all withered and dead, but he scraped up the purple spores and took them back to the biosphere, just in case.

Pat found a lovely woman in Puerto Rico with long brown hair. He kept it trimmed, and she kept him happy.

George found his old friends on Martha's Vineyard and invited them to the biosphere for a holiday.

Dani gave birth to a little boy and called him Joey. He had blond hair and gray eyes, just like his big sister.

Alyssa and Katie stayed with Mindy and became her sisters.

Ricky and Baby Girl had a 20th birthday, and everyone came to the biosphere for the party.

And in New Jersey, Jacob Wilmer sat in his overstuffed chair, sharing a cup of tea with the skeleton of his lovely wife, Emily.

About the Author

Amy Jambor hails from the state of New Jersey, but has lived in Florida for almost fourteen years. She is a mother, a grandmother, a writer, and a wife. Married to the love of her life for thirty-seven years, she knows that true love exists and longs to share her dreams and fantasies with the world. Writing is something she has always loved and plans on doing for a long time to come. She invites you to join her in a world of illusion and make believe where anything can happen.

http://aljambor.com/
https://twitter.com/ALJambor
https://www.facebook.com/ALJambor
https://www.pinterest.com/amyjambor/

www.ingramcontent.com/pod-product-compliance
Lightning Source LLC
Chambersburg PA
CBHW071146250626
47159CB00001B/9